Raves for the Previous Valdemar Anthologies:

D0034038

NOVELS BY MERCEDES LACKEY
available from DAW Books

And don't miss:
THE VALDEMAR COMPANION
Edited by John Helfers and Denise Little

Moving Targets

and Other Tales of Valdemar

Edited by

Mercedes Lackey

DAW BOOKS, INC.

DONALD A. WOLLHEIM, FOUNDER

375 Hudson Street, New York, NY 10014

ELIZABETH R. WOLLHEIM
SHEILA E. GILBERT
PUBLISHERS

http://www.dawbooks.com

First Printing, December 2008
1 2 3 4 5 6 7 8 9

DAW TRADEMARK REGISTERED
U.S. PAT. AND TM. OFF. AND FOREIGN COUNTRIES
—MARCA REGISTRADA
HECHO EN U.S.A.

PRINTED IN THE U.S.A.

ACKNOWLEDGMENTS

"Moving Targets," copyright © 2008 by Mercedes Lackey and Larry Dixon

"An Unexpected Guest," copyright © 2008 by Nancy Asire

"The Power of Three," copyright © 2008 by Brenda Cooper

"What Fire Is," copyright © 2008 by Janni Lee Simner

"Dreams of Mountain Clover," copyright © 2008 by Mickey Zucker Reichert

"The Cheat," copyright © 2008 by Richard Lee Byers

"A Dream Deferred," copyright © 2008 by Kristin Schwengel

"The Sworddancer," copyright © 2008 by Michael Z. Williamson

"Broken Bones," copyright © 2008 by Stephanie Shaver

"Live On," copyright © 2008 by Tanya Huff

"Passage at Arms," copyright © 2008 by Rosemary Edghill

"Heart, Home and Hearth," copyright © 2008 by Sarah Hoyt and Kate Paulk

"Haven's Own," copyright © 2008 by Fiona Patton

"Widdershins," copyright © 2008 by Judith Tarr

Contents

Moving Targets
by *Mercedes Lackey and Larry Dixon*

Mercedes Lackey is a full-time writer and has published numerous novels, including the best-selling Heralds of Valdemar series. She is also a professional lyricist and a licensed wild bird rehabilitator.

Larry Dixon is the husband of Mercedes Lackey, and a successful artist as well as science fiction writer. He and Mercedes live in Oklahoma.

Herald Elyn refrained from tearing her hair out. It wasn't as if she wasn't used to these four. They'd been assigned to her in a bunch when they'd all first been Chosen. They'd gotten into trouble in and around Haven as a group, and now, four years later, it would have been reasonable to assume that this foursome was beyond being able to surprise her.

It would be reasonable to assume that. Reasonable, but, unfortunately, wrong.

Elyn stared at the wagon, hoping it was a hallucination. It wasn't.

It was a traders-caravan built to the specifications of a rich man with vague notions of "the romance of the open road." So it was big, big enough that it took two stout horses to pull it. Expensive leaf springs sandwiched between wishbone axles peeked from behind carved, bent-wood coachwork. It was luxuriously appointed within. And without.

It was yellow. Bright yellow. And there were flowers

1

painted on it, scrolling around the windows and door. The roof was red.

Elyn groaned silently. Heralds were supposed to try to be inconspicuous. Hard enough when you were wearing a white uniform that screamed: "I'm the Herald! Shoot me first!" But with this? They'd look like a lot of traveling actors. Or clowns. Would people even believe they *were* Heralds and not just entertainers dressed up as Heralds?

"We could have it repainted," said Trainee Laurel helpfully, gleefully gesturing at the wagon and then standing with one hand on her hip. "In fact, we probably should. White, with a blue roof. And with the crest of Valdemar on the side. The people would love that!"

Elyn had to admit that she was probably right about that last part. Laurel was a pretty thing with abundant red hair, kind hearted, with a formidable Gift that was from some place in the Empathy family. She could make anyone like her and want to do what *she* wanted. Fortunately, she had a strong code of ethics. Unfortunately, she tended to think the best of *everyone*. They'd quickly learned not to allow her any say in judgments after she pleaded in favor of a violent murderer, who had been caught literally red-handed, by saying that his mother didn't think he'd do that kind of thing.

Repaint it white. As if that will make us less of a moving target? At least no enemy would ever take this wagon seriously. "We don't have time," Elyn said, truthfully. "It would have to be sanded down to the bare wood. Otherwise, everything else will bleed right through."

"Blue. Dark blue. *Solid* dark blue, no decorations. I already have the paint, and I rounded up the workmen," Trainee Alma said as she trotted up with two of the palace carpenters in tow, each of them carrying two buckets of dark blue paint. "I calculated it very carefully. One coat will do it. Night Blue cut one-to-

three with Sky Blue has a drying index of six candlemarks, with a twelve-candlemark cure, and has an
unprimed saturation well within limits. There will be
plenty of time for it to dry before we leave tomorrow."
She waved a clipboard of papers and punctuated her
statement with a firm nod that proclaimed that questioning her figures was inadvisable under pain of explanation. Boyish, bookish Alma had been an Artificer-in-
training before she had been Chosen; she made up for
Laurel's lack of practicality and then some. Strong-
willed, rock-steady, and blindingly intelligent, she was
always searching for the most ordinary explanation for
the extraordinary. She also had no discernable Gift.
Elyn sometimes wondered if that was because Alma
herself had not yet mathematically proven she had one.

"Aww. Do we have to paint it?" Trainee Arville
asked plaintively. "I think it's nice." He was the tallest
young man Elyn had ever seen, but you would never
know it, because he was always slouching. He always
looked a little unkempt. Not dirty, but untidy. Except
when in his Whites, he could only be found in faded
earth-tone field-laborer clothes, none of which seemed
to be his size even if they were. Elyn knew he didn't
do it out of carelessness or because he was slovenly.
It was as if everything he put on immediately had a
mind of its own, and that mind was half-asleep.

His Gift was as powerful as Laurel's and as odd. It
was a rare Gift and extremely difficult to train for.
Luck. He could trip and fall and come up not only
unhurt, but clutching something useful, important, or
occasionally even valuable. He was almost never hit
during fighting practice, not because he was good but
because his opponents always made inexplicable mistakes. Small children and animals adored him.

"Yes, Arville, we do," Alma said firmly. "Otherwise
no one will take us seriously."

The fourth member of the quartet shrugged. "I
doubt Father would care if we painted it pink,"

Trainee Rod pointed out. Laurel opened her mouth to speak, but when Elyn shot Laurel a look that said *don't even think it*, she decided against it. Rod continued. "I doubt he even knows what color it is now. He probably just threw money at a bunch of coachmakers and said, 'Build me the best traveling van anyone has ever seen.' What matters is that the horses he sent along are terrific." Trainee Rod . . . or rather, Rod's father . . . was wealthy enough that he could do things like that. Rod should have been spoiled rotten. He wasn't. Rod's father should have been livid that he was Chosen, but he wasn't. Guildmaster Fredrich of the Goldsmith Guild was so proud of his son that he nearly burst every time he looked at the young man. Then again, that handsome boy, blond and blue-eyed, certainly had a face and body that seemed created to wear a Herald's Uniform.

And Rod certainly did not have the head to be a Goldsmith, much less a Master, and even less a Guildmaster. His younger brother had seemingly inherited all the real cunning in the family, as Rod had inherited the looks, so when the Big White Talking Horse showed up, it was actually a relief all around.

Not that he was stupid; he just wasn't nearly intelligent enough to succeed in the business as his father had; he was certainly no match for his brother or Alma when it came to feats of outright logic, and he only had a casual consumer's understanding of market forces. But he was clever about mechanical things. Most importantly for a Herald, he was absolutely determined to do the right thing and doggedly persistent about seeing that it got done.

As more than one senior Herald had remarked to Elyn, together the four made one *perfect* Herald. But then again, how many "perfect" Heralds were there?

Most of us just bumble along trying to do the best we can.

She knew perfectly well why the four of them had

been assigned to her. Her patience was legendary, and these four needed legendary patience.

"All right Alma, that solution will probably work. Please go ahead and repaint the wagon, gentlemen," she continued, addressing the workmen. Then she turned to the four ill-assorted soon-to-be-Heralds. "And you lot, get packed, get your new Whites, and get some sleep. We have a long way to go, and I doubt very much that any of you has ever had any experience in driving a wagon."

They all shrugged sheepishly. She snorted. "Something Rod's father did *not* think about. Fortunately, I *have*. And before this is over, each of you will be an expert in everything from harnessing to fixing a broken wheel singlehandedly in the pouring rain."

From the shocked looks on their faces, she could tell that all they had considered was that they were going to have a nice, comfortable, warm place to sleep on this circuit, rather than having to camp in the open or find themselves crammed five into a Waystation made for two at most. It had never occurred to them that a wagon and its team were objects that required care and repair, which was one reason why Heralds seldom used them. Usually, when Heralds needed a wagon, they hired one on, driver and all.

The only reason she was even considering using this rolling house was because this circuit was all in farming country. Flat, level land for the most part, plenty of forage for the horses, and good roads. It was something of a choice circuit to get if you liked things to be mostly uneventful. She'd gotten it on this trip precisely because she had *four,* rather than one or two, to nursemaid through their first year in Whites.

And hopefully, by the time they got to the section of the circuit that bordered on the Pelagir Hills, it would be late enough in autumn that any trouble from there would be tucking itself up to hibernate for the winter.

And if it isn't inclined to hibernate . . . She squared her shoulders and headed for the suite of rooms she shared with them. *Well, that is when we find out what these four are made of—and if I did my job.*

Elyn pulled at her earlobe a little and stared at the wagon. For once, Alma had miscalculated, it seemed— or else the pigment in that paint wasn't what she had thought. A single coat of blue paint had indeed been applied evenly and thoroughly over the entire wagon yesterday, with the end result being that the wagon now was blue . . . more or less. Not so much a Heraldic blue as a shade resembling water, or a bird's egg, or the sky under certain conditions. And the vines and flowers had bled through too. It was less garish than it had been, but the effect was still . . .

"Oh how pretty!" Laurel enthused. "I was afraid it was going to be dull!"

Alma passed both of them with her bags; she rolled her eyes but said nothing as she stowed her things in the storage boxes built into the side.

Elyn had taught them well enough that they got their gear put away and were in the wagon before a single candlemark had passed. Not without some minor bickering, but there was always minor bickering any time adolescents did anything. Elyn was used to that. The question looming largest in her mind, however, was who to single out to learn how to drive first.

She pondered that as she guided the horses down the road reserved for trade, which was a good bit wider than the one Heralds usually took out of Haven. She was glad they had gotten underway so early. She really did not want anyone to see her driving this . . . thing.

The Companions trotted alongside freely, with their stirrups hooked up onto the pommels of their saddles. No point in leaving them bare. The tack would take up too much space, and compared to the usual weight

of a rider, the saddle was nothing. She saw to her
amusement that Alma alone of all of them had done
exactly what *she* had; Alma's Companion, like Elyn's,
carried bulging saddlebags. After all, why not? Without the weight of a rider—

:You turn us into packmules.: Mayar sounded more
amused than annoyed.

*:If you have become a "mule," my dear, you should
ask to see the farrier about your little problem before
your ladyfriends complain. There may be special
treatments.:*

*:Do get your mind out of the gutter, will you? I have
to read it.:*

Elyn snorted and gathered up the reins for the two-
horse hitch. A wagon like this did not strictly need
two horses, but having two would enable them to
move along at a reasonable pace.

Once they were clear of Haven itself, she knocked
on the little door behind her with her elbow. Alma
opened it.

"Rod!" she called through into the interior of the
wagon, "Get out here. Time to learn how to drive."
The wagon and horses were his father's gifts, after all,
so he might as well be the first one to learn the job.
Alma cleared out and Rod's sunny expression replaced hers.

As he squeezed through the little door and maneu-
vered himself onto the little sheltered spring-dampered
bench where the driver sat, Elyn reflected that whoever had bought these horses definitely did know his
horseflesh. They weren't matched, but they were both
solid and compact little draft horses of the sort known
as Zigans. The right side was a bay gelding with a
white nose, the left a chestnut mare with a white blaze.
Both had one white foot, with heavily feathered fetlocks. Both had stocky bodies, about a hand taller
than the average riding horse, and both were about
six years old. Their manes and tails were shaggy and

long, and their coats were too rough to ever be glossy, but they were mild tempered and willing, and disinclined to be spooked by anything they'd seen so far.

"This is how you hold the reins," Elyn said, putting them into Rod's hands. "Don't haul on them, but don't let them go slack, either, or the horses will amble to nothing and stop." She gave him a few more instructions, then sat back and watched him drive. He wasn't bad and wasn't nervous, so she said nothing, just let him give the beasts the minimal attention they needed for the relatively uncrowded road. Behind her, through the still open door, she could hear the others chattering away.

This might not be so bad, after all.

Just kill me now, Elyn groaned silently. Beside her, in the minimal shelter provided by the wagon's canvas awning, five Companions endured a cold downpour with varying attitudes from acceptance to disgust, bracketed by the two steaming draft horses, coats so dark they looked black in the uncertain light. Elyn had finished putting on the last of their feedbags— doing the chore herself because her four charges were currently struggling to pitch a larger shelter for them. Their second-to-last stop on the Circuit yielded them a gift of grain from the locals. That pushed the wagon's weight capacity to brimming, and now the six bunks inside bore six dozen feedsacks, leaving almost no room for people to sleep inside. Arville had cheerfully accepted the gift, saying it was important for people to accept gifts gracefully because it made the giver feel so good and encouraged them to be generous. Besides, they had tents! And the mattresses from the bunks! The rest readily agreed, including the Companions. Elyn endured. They couldn't just unload the grain and sleep inside, because it would attract vermin. Or get soaked. Or both. Elyn insisted, though, that one bunk nearest the driver's bench be kept clear in case of emergency. Being the senior Herald, she slept in it. And now, here they were.

The rain wasn't why she was groaning. Oh, no. These sort of conditions were to be expected when traveling in the autumn. No, no, no. She was groaning because of *why* they were out here in the literal middle of nowhere.

Four moons into a planned circuit of twelve, they had been met by a series of increasingly frantic—and thus, increasingly incoherent—messages from a tiny hamlet on the edge of the Pelagir Hills about spirits "stalking" the place.

Now, in the first place, this little village—Bastion's Stone, it was called—wasn't even *in* Valdemar. So far as Elyn was concerned, they could go hire themselves a priestly exorcist or petition whoever (or *what*ever, there was no telling out there) they paid their taxes to—they had no claim on help from Heralds. In the second place, dispelling ghosts, assuming these were ghosts, assuming such things even existed, was not what Heralds did. In the third place, this was right off their circuit, and answering the call would take them away from people who actually had a right to expect Heralds and their help.

But the four youngsters were all over the idea, to the point that, when Elyn pointed all those things out and flatly vetoed the excursion, *they* sent back to Haven and the Heralds of the Council for permission to deviate from the circuit and to answer a call outside the Border.

And much to Elyn's disgust and their elation, the answer that came back was, "Yes."

Of course, this was ever so much more exciting than the endless round of petty disputes they had been called on to settle and the sad little band of pathetic "bandits" they'd chased down. Thus far, the circuit had been so entirely uneventful that the most they'd had to worry about had been the weather and the wild animals.

But that's what it's supposed to be like, Elyn thought resentfully. *Most of the time, anyway. Property disputes, and ugly domestic quarrels, and minor criminals. And that's important. We can be the impartial outside voice that settles things so that they stay settled. We are the ones who go away, so people don't have to be angry with the neighbor that made the decision that they don't like. We ride in on our pure white Companions, in our pure white uniforms, and people know that they can trust us to be impartial, because we haven't taken a bribe, we aren't friends with anyone, and we owe no one there anything. And if we didn't do that, there would be no justice. That ought to be exciting enough for anyone. We can't all be Herald Vanyels.*

But of course, everyone wanted to be Herald Vanyel. Well, all but the part about dying horribly. Everyone wanted the happy noble bits, not the agony, or drudgework, or the dying. But the glorious heroic stuff? Sign them up!

"We've got the shelter done, Elyn!" Rod called from the other side of the wagon. "We had to sort of improvise, though!"

Kill me now, she thought again, steeling herself. Rod and his "improvisations" were going to drive her not-so-quietly mad. Oh, they generally *worked,* but they looked so precarious she could never see how and never quite trust them.

Ducking her head against the rain, which was coming down harder now, she made her way around the end of the wagon to where the four were supposed to have pitched the canvas half-tent.

Well, it wasn't a half-tent anymore, and it hadn't been pitched. Instead, it was a sort of improvised slanted roof, tied up to various tree branches. To keep the branches from tossing in the wind, *they* had been anchored with the ropes and stakes that should have been used to pitch the tent. And instead of a straight-forward flat or slanted surface, the canvas had been tied into a sort of sloping, flattish V-shape, so that all the rain that fell on it ran into a channel in the center and that in turn poured into the canvas water-trough they carried to serve the horses and Companions.

"We already filled our water barrel," Rod said, beaming with pride. "Rigging it like this gives twice the rain shelter too! If it gets any colder, we can put a fire at this end and the slanting roof will carry the smoke away instead of trapping it."

"Good work," she said, torn between relief that he hadn't tried anything more complicated and a kind of surprised pride that he'd come up with something so useful.

The Companions ambled up and tucked themselves in under the ample shelter with clear relief. Alma turned up in another moment, leading the draft horses, then hobbled them. They hadn't bothered to actually tether the horses this entire trip. It wasn't as if the Companions would let them wander off or get into trouble.

Laurel collected the now-empty feedbags and stowed them in the proper compartment. And now Elyn could go back under the awning to fire up the little cook-stove, since it was her turn to cook.

"Where's Arville?" she asked, suddenly realizing the fourth member of the inseparables was missing—and she was about to cook, which up until this moment had meant he was going to be at her elbow, waiting, with a look on his face like a starving puppy.

"He said he heard something out in the—"

"Look what I found!" Arville cried happily, bounding up to them, arms and legs flapping with happiness like a demented scarecrow. "Look what I found out in the forest!"

The thing bounding at his side was like no animal

that Elyn had ever seen before. The head was something like a wolf's, but the body was lean and had a
curved back like the pictures of hunting cats she'd
seen. When the shaggy, soaked fur dried, it would
probably be a dark gray.

And it came up to Arville's waist. It was *huge.*

If it hadn't been wearing exactly the same puppy-
eager expression that Arville was, she'd have been
terrified of it. It wagged its tail merrily.

And then it talked. Or tried to. Its voice, if it could
be called that, was a mix of bark and howl limited by
the chops and cut occasionally to form words. And it
tried enthusiastically to be understood.

"Reyra!" it said. "Rye Ryu! Ryer Ryeree!"

It skidded to a halt on the wet grass and plopped
its haunches down, staring up at her expectantly, its
bushy tail pounding on the grass and sending up a
spray of drops each time it thumped.

She blinked at it.

"He said his name's Ryu, and he's a *kyree,*" Arville
supplied hopefully.

"Of course he is." She looked at the thing carefully.
Well, it talked. So it probably wasn't going to unex-
pectedly turn savage and tear out their throats. And
it wagged its tail, which was something that hadn't
been covered in her Fear-the-Monster classes. "And
what does Ryu want?" she asked, hoping that the answer was *not* going to be "dinner." They didn't have
enough meat to satisfy something that large.

"Rum ree ru!" Ryu said, his tail thumping soggily.
That didn't need any translation.

"He's kind of—uh—Chosen me," Arville said, looking guilty. "Pelas says it's all right with him."

*Chosen him—some weird beastie out of the Pelagirs,
and it's Chosen him.* She wanted to thump her head
against the side of the wagon. Why couldn't *anything*
these four did be straightforward? She *wanted* to tell
both of them that this was absolutely out of the ques-

tion, that the big, soggy gray thing could just turn itself back around and lope into the forest where it had come from. But two sets of big brown begging eyes were boring holes in her soul, in exactly the clichéd way they were supposed to in silly stories. And Arville's Companion was all right with this . . .

"He'll have to catch his own food!" she said sharply.

"Rall rye!"

"And he *doesn't* sleep in the wagon! It's cramped enough in there as it is, and he smells like wet dog. I don't care if there's a spare bunk when the grain is gone, he doesn't get it. And he definitely doesn't get my bunk."

"Rall rye!" This didn't seem to bother the thing at all. "Rye ree runner!"

"He'll sleep under the wagon, he says," Arville said happily. "When we get to the village, I'll buy him a blanket to sleep on. Won't I, boy?"

The tail thumped soggily. Elyn gave up.

The creature managed to not get too much in the way, dutifully went out and presumably hunted himself some dinner, and settled in under the wagon to sleep as if he had done so all his life. It was all Elyn could do to persuade Arville *not* to settle in next to him. And that gave her some pause when she climbed into her own bunk for the night. The bond that had sprung up between the young man and what *looked* like some kind of savage beast seemed harmless enough—but it also was disturbingly strong and clearly magical in nature.

So what if it wasn't harmless?

:*It's harmless,*: Mayar said instantly in her mind. :*Really. The* kyree *are known to us. Yes, it's a magical beast, like the Hawkbrother bondbirds. In fact, the Hawkbrothers know all about* kyree.: She sensed something like a chuckle from Mayar. :*Ryu is younger than he looks, a mere stripling. He's been lonely. His sort are supposed to go out and find someone to attach themselves to. It's a little like what we do, except that . . . well, never mind. Think of him as a congenital helper, and he's been looking for the right someone to help for almost a year now.:*

Elyn could only shake her head. Well if Mayar saw no problems, and Arville's own Companion had no objections, who was she to interfere?

She only hoped she would have no cause to regret the decision.

And then, just as she was drifting off, she felt the wagon . . . vibrating.

At first she couldn't imagine what it was. Thunder? Earthquake? Landslide? But if it was anything dangerous the Companions would be screaming their heads off.

The she realized what it was. It came from below. Ryu was snoring.

Kill me now . . .

Oh, what a surprise. The most impressive thing about Bastion's Stone was a stone. A great big stone that the cluster of little houses huddled against, like baby chicks up against their mother. It was too small to have a market. It was too small to have an inn— one of the locals who was apparently the only one capable of brewing drinkable beer sold it out of his house, and you either drank it in the yard or took it home to drink with your neighbors. So far as Elyn could tell, the only reason for the village existing in the first place was so that all the villagers could share farming equipment and the team of oxen required to pull it. And, of course, because they had a really big stone.

:It's like a Heartstone, without the heart,: Mayar commented.

Elyn sat down with the entire population of the village in the only structure big enough to hold them all, the communal threshing barn, and listened to what they had to tell her. Her four charges she told (a bit sternly) to stand and listen and not comment or ask questions themselves. She could tell that Alma was almost writhing with impatience at being muzzled, but that was too bad. At this point, these people didn't need to have questions fired at them from five different people. One person had to be the voice of authority, and that person had better be her. Only when she was done would she give them leave to go question people on an individual basis, when it was clear that they were answering to her and not the other way around. Having multiple "authorities" only made for trouble.

As for the villagers, they all seemed to defer to the blacksmith, which was curious. Perhaps it was because he was the strongest, or just because, being in a trade that had "trade secrets," he seemed the most important to them.

But when facing someone wearing a uniform and an air of unquestioned authority, he became almost comically deferential. Regrettably, with that deference came being tongue-tied.

"Just start at the beginning," she coaxed, "when you all first noticed something wrong, no matter how trivial it seems."

He mumbled something. It was a little hard to understand his accent; although what he spoke was similar to Valdemaran, the way the words were pronounced wasn't always the same. She thought it sounded like, "I can't remember."

"Sure ye can, Benderk!" one of the others urged, studiously not looking at her. "Ye were the first t'say! 'Twere the Shadows."

"Sounds like a wee laddie's boggles," Benderk mumbled. At least, that was what she thought he mumbled.

"Tell her, Benderk! Tell her 'bout them Shadows up at Stony Rill! How they was on'y there at twilight, lurkin' like, but then they was them there rustlin's and whisperin's on'y no one was there, an that was by broad day! An' then it weren't jest whisperin's but noises t'make the blood cawld, gibberin's and gurglin's an' a mad laugh 'at made th' dogs run away! Tell her!" The speaker was the fellow that sold the local ale; he had brought a barrel of it, and now he plied Benderk with a mug and a refill, and Benderk evidently found courage therein, for he finally raised his eyes to Elyn's and pretty much repeated what the ale-seller had said.

"We mun know these parts, Lady," he added. "We mun know every beast an' bird in forest. Nothin' never made no noise like that. Nor cast Shadows like the ones at night, neither. Nor man, nor beast we ever seen cast shadows like that. Half again as tall an' broad as me, an' I be no scrawny 'prentice. On'y hunched over, like." He rounded his shoulders and tucked his head down between them by way of illustration. "An' we never saw the Things, on'y Shadows, an' fer all their bigness, left no tracks we could find. So we left Stony Rill alone, an' that seemed t'satisfy it. Reckoned we leave them alone, they leaves us alone." He shrugged, shamefaced. "We bain't fighters, Lady, and this be edge of Pelagir Hills. Uncanny things come out of there, but bain't mean no harm, so—"

She nodded. "A sensible way to deal with things," she said soothingly. "I take it there was nothing much any of you needed up at this Stony Rill?"

He shook his head. "Kids liked t'play there i' summer, but didn' take but hearin' that laugh once for 'em t'find 'nother spot of cool water t'paddle in. We're not lackin' i' water."

Well that was the truth. They must have crossed thirty streams of varying width, depth, and strength to get here.

"But obviously something else happened?" she prompted.

The man nodded, and the others shuddered. "They're comin' into village, of nights."

"You've seen them with your own eyes?" Somehow Elyn doubted they had. And sure enough, one and all, they shook their heads emphatically.

"But we *hear* them!" The words came out in a whisper. "Between th' houses, howlin' and gibberin', and in the mornin', not a sign of 'em. Not a footprint, nor hoofprint or pawprint. Th' dogs an' cats, they all hide when they hears it. An' afore we started lockin' 'em up at night, we lost some beasts to 'em. Heard 'em cry out, and in mornin', was gone, an' no trace of what took 'em."

There wasn't much else that Elyn could get that was useful out of them. "You'll hear 'em fer y'self" seemed to be the only answer.

Despite the fact that the youngsters were burning even more to question the villagers, Elyn let the villagers go back to their homes. For one thing, the closer it got to sunset, the more nervous the villagers became, and she didn't want to have to cope with a load of hysterical people wanting only to get behind their locked and barricaded doors. For another, she was curious to see if "they," whatever "they" were, actually did turn up tonight. Their absence might well tell as much or more than their presence. There was no reason why something supernatural would hesitate to manifest with the Heralds here. But if "they" were not supernatural, then whatever or whoever it was that was doing this might well be cautious about showing itself—or themselves—right now.

Once everyone was cleared away, Elyn set about making sure that the wagon, the horses, and the Companions were all set up for a stay of some duration. The villagers had kindly moved in bedding straw and fodder; horses were not exactly housebroken, so before they could all get themselves involved in a long discussion of what might be going on, Elyn got the Trainees to work arranging things inside the threshing barn. She put Rod to maneuvering the wagon against one wall and assigned Arville to making a stabling area for the horses against the opposite wall. Once the wagon was in place, Rod tied up the horses in their corner.

"We may be here a while," Elyn pointed out. "And there's enough room in here that anyone who would rather sleep outside the wagon certainly can. It might be a bit colder, but it won't be as stuffy, and we can always sct up the stove to keep a limited area warm at night."

But Alma clearly wanted to talk about "haunting," and she had already made up her mind about it; Elyn could see it in the set of her jaw and the furrowed brows. "We need to work out some way to trap these people," she said.

"The villagers?" Elyn said, raising an eyebrow.

"No, of course not! Whoever is running this deception on them!" Alma said crossly.

"And you're so certain it's a deception?" Elyn countered. "I'm not convinced one way or another. If it's a deception, what's the motive? And if it's not, then what are these things? Their behavior matches some of the descriptions of the creatures controlled by the Karsite priesthood."

"The d-d-demons?" Arville stammered.

Ryu's ears went straight up and his eyes widened. "R-r-remons?" he echoed.

"But only some of those descriptions, Herald Elyn," Rod said deferentially. "Not all of them. And we are an awfully long way from the Karsite border. I can't see any good reason for them being here, if that is what they are. And it could just be some new creature from the Pelagirs. Some things from there are friendly."

Ryu thumped his tail, tongue lolling.

Elyn shrugged. "I am not convinced either way. What I *am* convinced of is that we need to proceed with great caution. The last thing we want to do is make things worse."

Alma opened her mouth to protest, but she never got so far as uttering a word. As if something had been listening outside, there came one of the strangest and most hair-raising noises that Elyn had ever heard in her life.

Not loud enough to be called a howl but far too loud for a moan, it seemed to reach to some instinct deep inside Elyn and evoke a chill terror. It had a similar effect on the others, too. Arville yelped and dove under the wagon, joined there by Ryu; Laurel screamed. Rod and Alma both went white to match their uniforms, but they headed for the door of the barn with looks of determination on their faces.

"No! Leave the door alone!" Elyn ordered. Arville and the *kyree* hugged each other and shuddered. The noises multiplied, and Laurel looked around for a weapon, then clutched at her little dagger as if it were going to be adequate to defend herself with. Her sword and war gear were still in storage in the wagon, along with everyone else's, and only Elyn wore a sword at the moment, since during the interview it'd been a sign of rank.

Alma and Rod had their hands on the door already and prepared to fling it open, only to find it had been shut tight, barred from the outside.

The noises were joined by maniacal laughter as Alma and Rod hammered on the door and tried to break it down, then tried the door opposite with the same results. There were no windows or hatches in the upper part of the building, or they probably would have tried to go out that way. The two draft horses were thoroughly unnerved by now, straining at their tethers, tossing their heads, and rolling their eyes. Arville finally climbed out from under the wagon, shaking, to go and try to calm them down. Elyn joined him; eventually they had to resort to pulling bags over their heads; the horses stopped trying to bolt, but they stood transfixed, shaking as hard as Arville.

The Companions were as unnerved as their Chosen.

:We can't tell what it is,: Mayar said to Elyn, as the other four Companions arrayed themselves facing the two doors, preparing to fight anything that burst through. *:We've never heard anything that sounded like that before.:*

"Let's break the door down!" Rod shouted over the noise. "Let's make a ram!"

But it was Alma who stopped him before he could wrench the wagon-tongue off the front or try to pull down one of the interior supports. "I don't think we can," she said. "And it's not *our* building to break down."

"It's just noises," Elyn pointed out, fighting her own instincts to run, or fight, or both. "No one is calling for help, and nothing is trying to break in here. Alma's correct, we haven't the right to wreck this place just to confront what's out there. Besides, breaking the door down will be noisy, and by the time we got out, whatever is making those sounds will probably be gone."

"It's j-j-just trying to scare us," Laurel said, though her teeth were chattering.

"It's doing a g-g-good job!" Arville replied.

And then, just as suddenly as the noise had begun, it stopped.

They waited a moment, and then another, before Rod and Alma rushed for the door.

It was still barred.

Alma kicked it in frustration, bruising her toe. She looked as if she would have liked to swear, but a glance at Elyn seemed to quell that idea.

They waited, but the noises didn't resume, although the door remained barred from the outside. The moments crept by, then a candlemark; it felt like more, but they *had* a marked candle out and burning when the meeting started, and that was all it was. Finally

Elyn spoke, making them all jump. "It's entirely possible that the villagers locked us in themselves."

Rod scratched his head. "We didn't try the door after they left," he admitted, "But why?"

"Remons!" said Ryu, impatiently, as if they were all feeble-minded. Arville nodded.

"But we're supposed to be the ones getting rid of whatever it is!" Alma protested. "It makes no sense for them to lock us in!"

"It also makes no sense for a demon or a ghost or anything else like them to be stopped by mere walls," Rod added.

"It may make no sense, but according to everything I've read, the Karsite demons clearly are stopped by walls." Elyn could only shake her head at all the contradictory evidence. "Perhaps there is some magical boundary set about the buildings here."

Her nerves were slowly settling; the horses were quiet again, enough so that she and Arville pulled the bags off their heads. But they were so soaked with sweat—as were the Companions—that they needed a thorough rubdown and blanketing, lest they get a chill. After that, failing anything else to do, since it seemed futile to keep trying the door, they went to lie on their bunks or bedrolls after blowing out the various lanterns and candles, leaving only the two night-lamps mounted on the front of the wagon burning with their wicks turned down. Elyn set the younger Heralds on short watches, and she was acutely aware of the stiff silence in the building, the sort of silence that meant everyone was staring up at the ceiling or the bottom of a bunk, listening with every fiber, waiting for a resumption of the horrible noises.

But nothing happened. And after what seemed like an eternity of staring into the darkness, she must have fallen asleep, because she woke with a start to hear the doors opening.

The doors!

She very nearly broke her neck scrambling out of her bunk and stumbling out the door at the rear of the wagon. The first thing she saw was Alma throwing open the doors on a gray dawn, frowning heavily. There was no one outside.

"I lay awake all night, listening, and finally I decided to get up and try the door," the young Herald said, scowling. "There was no one there. And the door wasn't barred anymore."

Elyn turned her attention to the kyree, who, with his presumably keener senses, would have heard what Alma didn't. "And did you hear anything?" she asked.

The kyree shook his head. Elyn chewed her lip thoughtfully. By this time the others were clambering out of the wagon, rubbing their eyes sleepily. "That doesn't necessarily mean anything," she pointed out. "Someone intimately familiar with this place could easily slip up to the doors and unbar them."

"Maybe they could slip up to the doors, but slide the bar out without a noise?" Laurel asked doubtfully.

"Let's find out," replied Rod, and Alma nodded. "Look here," he continued, examining it. "If you slide it, yes, it makes a noise." He demonstrated; the bar was one that slid into four cast-metal carriers, rather than dropping down into them. "But if you lift it a little—"

This time the bar made not a whisper of noise as he moved it.

"That doesn't rule out ghosts or demons," Laurel protested.

"Maybe not, but my money is on common men." Rod's chin was set stubbornly, which did not at all surprise Elyn. Rod hated supernatural explanations and usually managed to avoid them entirely.

"Nevertheless, logic dictates that we go about this assuming that either could be true." Elyn turned to the four Companions. "You lot are better suited to

look for the supernatural than we are, so I suggest
you pursue that, while we investigate human interfer-
ence. Now, let's get some breakfast going and discuss
where to start."

Since it had begun, as far as they could all tell, up
at the little stream called Stony Rill, that was where
the five of them headed. This time Rod and Alma
were determined not to be caught off-guard. Well, so
was Elyn, but she wasn't making it as obvious as they
were. If they got any more square-jawed with determination, she would be able to split logs with their chins.
There were times when that was tempting.

Arville and Ryu slunk along like a pair of reluctant
cats, heads swiveling this way and that with every
sound in the woods. Laurel was the only one that
looked normal, though that was superficial; Elyn knew
her well enough to know that she was walking on eggs,
so to speak, and the least little thing would set her off.

Elyn frankly did not know what to expect. They
reached the spot where the villagers had told her that
the "Shadows" were to be seen, and saw exactly nothing. She and Alma searched the area around the little
pool that the Rill formed before it spilled over and
went on its way, looking for swampy areas, odd plants,
vents in the ground, any sign of anything that could
account for hallucinations, and found nothing.

Alma even pulled off her boots, rolled up her trews,
and went wading in the pool, peering into the water.
Elyn wasn't sure what she was looking for, although
she did spent quite a long time at it, and gathered up
some rocks and a sack of sand. Finally, she clambered
out, got dry, and pulled her boots back on. "I think
we should go upstream," she said. "Maybe there's
something there. Swamp gas or something that only
drifts this way when the wind is right."

Rod nodded. "That seems like a good idea to me."

Elyn gave Alma a close look. She had a notion that

while Alma wasn't saying anything, the young Herald thought she might have discovered something intriguing. But Alma wasn't one to say anything until she was sure of herself. Annoying, but the girl was stubborn, and until she was ready, there would be no prying it out of her.

With a stifled sigh, Elyn motioned onward, and the five of them, with their Companions and the *kyree* threading through the underbrush on either side of the stream, made their way along the banks of Stony Rill. A few times more, Alma paused as something seemed to catch her eye, stooped, and picked up what looked like some gravel from the streambed. But still she said nothing.

Meanwhile there still didn't seem to be anything that could have been mistaken for these "Shadows," and no wildlife making odd noises that could have been taken for maniacal laughter.

Elyn was busy trying to keep an eye out for plants and fungi she knew were poisonous and gave hallucinations, when Rod suddenly said, "Is that a boundary marker? No one said anything about anyone living up here—"

"That'd be because that worthless lot down at the Stone'd like to fergit I be still alive," said a harsh voice.

It startled all of them. Ryu and Arville yelped in an almost identical pitch. The Companions all threw up their heads and snorted. Laurel squeaked, and Elyn jumped back just a little. Rod's back stiffened, and Alma clutched the bag of rocks and sand she was holding as if she were prepared to use it as a weapon.

From between two trees, out of a shadow Elyn certainly had not suspected was holding a person, stepped a man. Balding, gray haired, but powerfully built and clearly still fit, he had a bow with an arrow nocked to it, and although he was not yet aiming it at them, it was very obvious that he had no compunction about shooting them.

"Did that pack of scum send ye up here?" he spat. "I got no use fer them. I don' need their help, and I don' want their company. Did they send ye here because I run off their brats? I got my rights! They was tramplin' all over my property! Thievin' brats, stealin' fruit, honey, an' 'shrooms, poachin' my game, aye, I ran 'em off! I'll do it again too, at th' end of a pitchfork!"

"No one sent us here to disturb you, sir," Elyn said soothingly. "We're investigating some rather strange goings-on, and although the villagers did send for us, they don't know we intended to come up here."

"Ye want strange goings-on, ye look no futher than them brats o' theirs!" he spat. "I don' put no mischief past 'em!"

Rod and Elyn exchanged a look. *:We didn't consider that it might have been the children,:* Mayar said thoughtfully. *:That sort of thing* is *known among younglings first coming into a Gift.:*

:Yes,: she thought back. *:And in those with no Gift at all.:* It would not be the first time that bored youngsters terrorized a community by manufacturing "supernatural" goings-on.

"Well, we won't bother you any further sir," Elyn said.

"An' ye won't be settin' foot on my land neither!" he snapped. "Gerroff wi' ye! An' tell that lot down at th' Stone that they kin keep their devilment t'thesselves!"

There didn't seem to be anything much more to say, so Elyn turned around and began picking her way back down the stream. Ryu and Arville were only too happy to do the same, quickly overtaking and passing her. Laurel shivered as she glanced back at the old man, still standing guard at his boundary marker. Rod just shook his head.

But Alma looked very thoughtful.

"I don't know why we didn't consider the youngsters," Rod said, as soon as they were out of earshot of the old man. "That should have been the first place we looked."

"But don't you think that if it was the younglings, that nasty old grump would have been the *first* target they went after?" Alma countered. "Instead, it was the youngsters themselves that were scared out of their favorite swimming place. That doesn't make any sense."

"Maybe it's just one or two loners who were getting even for being left out of things," Elyn suggested, as Alma stooped again, scooping something out of the stream bed.

"I dunno about you, but that stuff last night didn't sound like a couple of kids!" Arville protested.

"Remons!" Ryu seconded. "Rosses!"

"Roses?" Rod exclaimed, looking askance.

"He means g-g-ghosts," Arville stammered. "It s-s-sure sounded like that to me!"

Elyn pulled thoughtfully at her earlobe. "Still . . . I think we should concentrate on the villagers next. Especially the youngsters. Getting the entire village in an uproar—we've studied and heard of that sort of thing before."

Rod nodded, with a satisfied look on his face. "Even if we can't find out something directly, I bet I can find a way to catch the troublemakers," he said.

"I don't think it was kids," Arville retorted weakly, scratching his head. "How could kids be making those . . . howls?"

"I wouldn't be so sure it was youngsters either," Alma said, with an enigmatic look. "I don't think it was demons—but I don't think it was youngsters."

They argued about it all the way back to the village—where they finally shut up, belatedly realizing that whether Rod, Arville, or Alma was right, it wouldn't be very productive for them to be talking about it in front of the very people they were going to be investigating.

Elyn meanwhile separated herself from the rest and, with Mayar, went in search of the likeliest person to know everybody's business, the village midwife.

She spent a good couple of candlemarks with that worthy, using the incident the night before as the opening wedge for conversation. "Well," Granny Merton said, judiciously, "I'd be lying if I didn' tell ye that fair curdles me blood o'nights. An' it's been a nuisance too. The wimmin as is close t'their time, they've taken t' demandin' I bide w' them every night. Cause if babe should decide t'come at night, ye ken, how'm I d'be fetched wi' *that* howlin' aroond th' doors? 'Tis on'y been two, thus far, but a 'ooman my age likes th' feel of her own bed benights!" She patted the thick stone walls of her tiny cottage complacently. "No demon be gettin' through these walls, no, an' I brung too many inter th' world, and seen too many out of it too, to be afeared of ghosts."

Gradually Elyn let the conversation drift, until it ended up as such conversations always did, with the Granny's assessment of every soul in the village.

And that was where Elyn's speculations and investigations ran aground. Because there were only five youngsters about the right age to be the one—or ones—behind the "haunting," and none of them fit the pattern of the sort of child that did this sort of thing. Their personalities were all open; they were neither show-offs nor shy and withdrawn, they were not picked on or bullied, they were all five very close friends, and in general were happy youngsters. Or they had been until the "hauntings" began. Now they were just as terrified as the rest of the village.

And insofar as their *ability* to sneak out and perpetrate the hauntings as a group—that was impossible, because all five of them spent their nights huddled together in one or another of their respective houses, in the main room, with the rest of whichever family they were spending the night with. Out here, a house was just a place to sleep and eat between chores and no one thought much of private rooms or single beds. There were witnesses to every moment of their time when whatever it was howled outside the walls.

This was pretty much what all of the village youngsters were doing; the parents had discovered that if they could be with friends, they withstood it all better. So the children got rounded up after supper, divided up by age groups, and bedded down in a huddle.

Nevertheless, she asked Mayar to go snooping about and see if he could detect any incipient stirrings of a Gift. The Companions in general were much better at that sort of thing than she was.

"Who's the old man that lives up above the pond at Stony Rill?" she asked, as if it were an afterthought. "Shouldn't he be brought down here for safety?"

Granny snorted. "Old man Hardaker? He has no friends down here. Stingiest old rooster that was ever born. Squeezes every groat till it squeaks, goes into a fury if a crow steals so much as a grain of his, counts everything, living or dead, on his land as 'is own property. Fights the squirrels for the nuts, 'e does. They say 'e killed his wife with overwork, treated her like a slave; that I can't speak for, it was afore my time. Sure he got no children on 'er, so I suppose he reckoned t'get work out of 'er instead. If I was a haunt, I'd stay clear of 'im. Give half a chance, he'd find a way t'bind a spirit and make it work for him, and count himself lucky that 'e wouldna have to feed and clothe it!"

Elyn smiled wryly. "He didn't seem to be aware that there was anything amiss here in the village."

Granny made a face. "Never believe it. 'E knows. 'E knows, and if 'e's being haunted too, 'e'll never let on. Gives nothin' away, that one, not even a thought. But 'e can't do wi'out us. We're the only village near enough t'buy what 'e grows, an' the only craftsmen near enough for him t'get what 'e needs. 'E'd never leave his land t'take 'is goods t' market, an' never trust one of 'is 'ands t' do it for 'im." She cackled a little. "No doubt, that makes 'im even more sour, the ald sack!"

Well, so much for the old man. If he, too, was suffering from the haunts, he was probably blaming it on the village and would not give them the satisfaction of knowing he was afraid. Nor would he ever ask for help. And even if he did, it was unlikely anyone here would give it to him.

Elyn poked about the village a bit more and found that Granny's opinion of the old man was universal. No one liked him. Everyone had a story about his penny-pinching and attempts to cheat them. Everyone also admitted that they did their level best to cheat him back. It was a point of honor among the young men to try to steal fruit from his orchard or poach his fish or game. There was no way of telling who had begun the acrimony, but at this point there was going to be no putting an end to it.

She managed to meet the suspect striplings and couldn't make up her mind whether or not they would be capable of the sheer amount of work and ingenuity that the "haunting" would take. They weren't stupid, but they also didn't show the level of intelligence of, say, Rod, much less Alma—and that was what such a task would take, if it was a purely mischief-making endeavor and not the unconscious breaking out of some sort of Gift.

They also all seemed as genuinely terrified as their parents. Elyn was fairly good at telling when she was being lied to even without the use of the Truth Spell, and she didn't get that impression now.

But when she met up with the rest back at the threshing barn, she discovered that Rod had already made up his mind about one thing.

"We can't just huddle in here like a lot of scared children," he said firmly. "And I don't for a moment think that these are demons or ghosts. I think it's people. In fact, I think it's some of the villagers. Maybe some of the younger ones."

"But, Rod!" Laurel exclaimed indignantly. "I *told* you that story they told me, and you still don't think it's disturbed spirits?"

"Wait, wait, what story?" Elyn demanded.

Laurel looked both excited and apprehensive as she turned toward their mentor. "Some of the older boys told me that around early apple harvest time, they went up to the old man's orchard to steal fruit, like always. They heard the sound of someone digging! At night! And then they didn't think anything more about it, except that the next day, Stony Rill was as red as blood! And it was that night that the hauntings began! They think the old man was looking for treasure and dug up a burial mound! And now the spirits are angry!"

"All the more reason to think it's them," Rod snorted, as Alma got an extremely thoughtful look on her face. "What a ridiculous story!"

"It's *not* ridiculous!" Laurel stamped her foot and crossed her arms angrily over her chest. "You just don't like it because they didn't tell you!"

"I don't like it because it's not logical." Rod's chin looked even more granite-like than usual. "If it was spirits that were disturbed because the old man was digging their bodies up, why haunt the village? What did the villagers do to them? Why not haunt the old man?"

"Well, maybe they are! And they just spread out! Or maybe they are trying to get the villagers to do something about the old man!" Her eyes flashed with anger. "Just because you don't believe in ghosts—"

Behind them, a couple of the Companions whickered as if laughing.

"Then they've got to be stupider in death than they are in life," Rod countered. "Because you'd think it would be a *lot* easier to just appear in front of people and say politely, 'That old man is robbing our graves, and we'd hate to have to make *you* miserable because of what *he* is doing, but if you don't make him leave us alone, we'll just have to make all of you as unhappy as we are.' Instead, they're getting nothing done except to make people terrified at night!"

Arville's head swiveled back and forth between them, as if he were watching a game. Ryu just lay flat on the ground with his ears over his paws.

"Oh!" Laurel said, driven to speechlessness with anger. *"Oh!"*

"Anyway, you just stay here in the barn and tell Elyn what you think of me," Rod said ungallantly. "I'll be outside with Arville and Ryu and the Companions laying a trap. Because it's not ghosts, it's people, and I am going to catch them!"

"Wait, what?" Arville replied, looking panicked.

"If you don't need me," Alma said carefully. "I do have something I need to check in here."

:Mayar?: Elyn thought.

:He asked us, and it's a good plan. Certainly better than Laurel's idea of holding a séance to find out what the spirits want. If it's people, we will catch them. If it is demons, well, you will find us stampeding into the barn fast enough. And if it is spirits, we can try Laurel's idea.: Mayar seemed quite satisfied with whatever it was that Rod had decided.

Well, she was supposed to be getting them to think and plan for themselves, wasn't she? And they had certainly plunged into this, not only with enthusiasm, but with some forethought.

"Go ahead and set your trap, Rod," she said firmly, cutting short any protests. "Alma, Laurel, we three will try to make enough sounds in here to make it seem as if all of us are in here." She glanced out the open door. "If you're going to get things set up, Rod, you'd better do so now, and then you'll be in hiding well before sunset. I want all of you that are going to be setting up the trap to go in and out several times so that if anyone is watching us, they'll likely lose count. Get water or wood, anything you think is a good excuse. Laurel, you and I will take care of the camp chores and make a lot of noise about it while Alma does her investigation."

Laurel looked ready to burst with indignation, but she didn't protest. Alma dove into the storage compartments and assembled a mortar and pestle, a couple of buckets of water, some dishes, and some other apparatus, and set to breaking up something in the mortar and pestle that made enough noise to cover just about anything.

Looking very unhappy, Arville and Ryu made several trips in and out of the doors carrying water and small amounts of wood, some odds and ends, before finally going out and not coming back again. The Companions made a more convincing job of it, bringing in quite a good deal of firewood before vanishing one by one. Elyn shut the door after them, lit all the lanterns, and, with Laurel's sulky help, began making noisy supper preparations. At this point, Alma was doing something inscrutable with the dishes and the water; whatever it was, it was making some sound too, so Elyn left her to it.

She stretched out the preparations as long as she could; it wasn't easy to tell in here whether the sun had set or not. Since it was a threshing building, it was as sealed against vermin as could be managed. The food was ready in what seemed to her to be far too short a time, but there was no point in wasting it. She and Laurel ate; Alma came and fetched herself a bowl of the thick soup Elyn had made, then went back to her buckets. Halfway through the meal, she had stopped messing about with the buckets and was pounding again, this time using the pestle as a hammer against a stone, pounding something she had wrapped in a bit of cloth.

She unfolded the cloth, peered at what was in there, and then did something with it. "Aha!" Elyn heard her say.

And that was when everything exploded outside.

The long, moaning howl began. Elyn heard Ryu yelp, Arville burst out with a terrified exclamation of "G-ghosts!" and Rod shout, *"Got you!"*

And *that* was the signal for what sounded like a battle royal.

She ran for the doors, but they were both bolted again. She and Alma and Laurel pounded on them fruitlessly for a while, while outside she could hear not only Rod shouting, but the sounds of fighting, of *other* men shouting, of Arville and Ryu howling, of angry whinnies and hoofbeats.

:Get back!: Mayar "shouted" in her mind.

She cleared Laurel and Alma away from the doors; there was a furious kick and a crash and the door burst open.

Through the now-open doors poured a tangled heap of people and nets, some free and fighting and some not, followed by all five Companions, relentlessly driving them all inside. Arville and Ryu were the most tangled up, but there were some strangers in there too, all of them masked and draped in tattered rags that smelled like mold and rotting wood.

Masked they might have been, but they were fighters; Elyn slashed Ryu and Arville free with her sword while Alma and Laurel joined in the fight. By now all the noise had brought the villagers out of their homes and up to the barn; several of the bravest grabbed pieces of firewood and waded into the affray while the Companions circled the outside of the mob and kept anyone from escaping—

—including one masked miscreant, who, alone among

all of them, was not armed and not fighting. Mayar
was the one who caught him by the scruff of the neck
in his teeth as he tried to get away, and kept him
dangling off the ground while the rest of the gang was
subdued and trussed up.

With them was an assortment of noisemakers that
had produced all the unearthly howls. There were
bull-roarers, a set of several predator-calls strapped
together so they could all be sounded at the same
time, and a contraption with a rough piece of twine
that could be pulled through something like a drum-
head of rawhide, producing a truly uncanny moan.

"I told you it was just people!" Rod shouted in
triumph, when the last of them—the fellow dangling
from Mayar's teeth—was firmly bound and set with
the rest.

By now all of the village—most tellingly, *all* of the
youngsters, including the ones that Rod had suspected—
had crowded into the barn. "Well it might not have
been spirits," Laurel sniffed, examining first her improvised club, which she then cast aside, and then her
nails. "But it *wasn't* who you thought it was."

And hanging in the air was the unspoken *so there!*

"Let's find out who it is, then," Elyn said evenly,
before they could start fighting again. She pulled the
mask off the one nearest her, revealing a fellow with
a lot of bruises, a black eye, and a surly expression.
She looked at the villagers. "Anyone you know?"

Baffled, they all shook their heads. She continued
to pull off masks, to similar bafflement, until she came
to the last. *Then* came the gasps.

"Old man Hardaker!" shouted someone. The old
man snarled, but said nothing. "Why would you do
this to us?"

"I think I know," Alma said in a hard voice, and
came forward with that bit of cloth. "Look."

She opened it up, and a small piece of something
yellow and shining glimmered in the lamplight.

They all stared. "Great Havens," Elyn finally said. "Is that gold?"

The villagers gasped as Alma nodded. "You know how Herald Bevins always says 'Find the motive and you find the criminal?' I went looking for a motive. When we were up at Stony Rill I thought I saw a little bit of gold-sand, so I started gathering up what I thought were likely bits of sand and rock. I panned this out of what I crushed up." She grinned in triumph. "When Rod told me the story the boys had told him, I was pretty sure I was right, anyway. The old man here was digging for treasure, all right, but it wasn't in a burial mound. And when Stony Rill turned red, it was just because he'd been washing the gold-rock. Right, old man?"

Hardaker spat in her direction.

"I made sure it was real gold by pounding it into a flake and testing it against a touchstone. It's real, all right." Alma beamed at the villagers. "You folks have a nice little gold mine here. And before we leave, we'll draw you up a charter so you can all share alike in the work and the profits."

Oh, well done! Elyn thought with pride. *Get them to agree to a charter now, so that there are no quarrels about it after we're long gone. Good thinking, Alma!*

"It's on my land!" Hardaker spat. "Ye've got no rights! And it weren't me! 'Twas them! 'Twas all their ideer!"

"Oh, really?" Rod drawled.

And that was when one of the strangers finally caved in. "You demmed old bastard!" he snarled. "Sell us out, ye think?" He struggled a bit with his bonds, then gave up. "We heerd about ye Heralds. Ye're hard but fair. Lemme tell ye what this old coot had up 'is sleeve. 'E found the gold, aye, an' mined out 'nuff t' pay us with, but wouldn' tell us where it was. Just told us to scare these turnip-heads out. An' if'n he couldn't scare 'em out, we was t'get rid of 'em—however." There was a flicker of uncertainty in the man's face then. "We nivver really reckon'd on hurtin' no one, we figgered these clodhoppers would scare out right easy. But . . . well, *he* was gettin' impatient, an' talkin' 'bout gettin' some'un else in here t'get rougher . . ."

Now Hardaker looked both furious and alarmed. "Was just talk! Meant t'give ye layabouts reason t'do what I paid ye fer!"

"That will be enough, old man," Elyn said impassively. "What we've heard is enough for us." She looked about at the villagers. "Do you consent to giving us the same rights of judgment as we would have in Valdemar?"

They looked at one another and then back at Elyn. "Put it in that there charter," said Benderk, finally. "I' fact . . ." He scratched his head. "Reckon it'd be better all around if—c'n ye make us part of Valdemar?"

Elyn blinked. "Well," she said cautiously, "yes. You folk aren't actually part of any other kingdom. But the Crown would take a percentage from the gold from your mine—five percent, if I recall correctly—in exchange for things like a Guard detachment to keep it and you safe, and for twice yearly visits from Heralds, and—"

"And we mostly trade with Valdemar an' the Crown'd take more than that fer trade taxes," Benderk said shrewdly. "Aye, that'll work." He looked at Alma. "Draw up yer charter, missy. We'll all sign it. What's t'be done with this lot?"

He toed Hardaker.

"As subjects of Valdemar, I can declare his land and goods confiscated and turned over to you. He and these men will be taken to the nearest Guardpost—"

:*I have already passed the news up the line. Guards will be on the way in the morning. We need only stay here long enough to keep this lot locked up until they arrive.:*

"—and men are on the way," she continued smoothly, thanking the Havens for the swift mental communication between Companions. "Meanwhile, we will see to everything, including guarding these men for you." She looked sternly down at Hardaker. "You, I am afraid, are going to be subjected to the Truth Spell to find out exactly how far your intentions toward these people were going to go. And we will find out exactly how many wrongs were originally on *both* sides."

Some of the villagers had the grace to look embarrassed and a little guilty. But not so much so that Elyn feared anything terribly ugly was going to come out of the investigation.

"Nevertheless, I do not think it excuses the intent to drive people out of their homes," she concluded. *"That* was an entirely immoral plan. Clever but immoral."

"And I would have gotten away with it, too, if it hadn't been for you meddling Heralds!" the old man spat.

Elyn could only shake her head. "Let's find a good place to lock this lot up," she only said. "I want *him* confined away from the rest for his own safety." She nodded at Rod. "Take charge of that, will you?"

"Gladly." Rod prodded them to their feet with a toe. " Get going, you."

"And well done, all of you." She finally allowed herself to smile.

And then felt a nudging at her shoulder blade, and turned to look into Ryu's big brown eyes.

"Ru-rer row?" the *kyree* asked plaintively.

"Supper!" Arville said, his expression identical to Ryu's. "We're *starving!*"

Oh, kill me now, Elyn sighed.

An Unexpected Guest
by *Nancy Asire*

Nancy Asire is the author of four novels: *Twilight's Kingdoms, Tears of Time, To Fall Like Stars,* and *Wizard Spawn. Wizard Spawn* was edited by C.J. Cherryh and became part of the *Sword of Knowledge* series. She also has written short stories for the series anthologies *Heroes in Hell* and *Merovingen Nights,* a short story for Mercedes Lackey's *Flights of Fantasy,* as well as tales for the Valdemar anthologies *Sun in Glory* and *Crossroads.* She has lived in Africa and traveled the world, but now resides in Missouri with her cats and two vintage Corvairs.

Sosha paused at the side of the road, drew the back of her hand across her brow to wipe away midday sweat. Her horse snorted and shook its head, tail swishing at flies. The summer day promised more heat and, from the closeness of the afternoon, hinted at an evening thunderstorm. She looked to her left at the fields that stretched off to the distance but could no longer see those her late husband had worked, which his family had possessed for generations. With Zaltos dead these five years, and only his aged parents living, it had fallen to her to keep the farm from being sold. The Goddess had refused—unreasonably, as far as Sosha was concerned—to grant Zaltos children to secure the future of his land. And so, with no one in the family but Mama Datasa, Papa Lorndo, and herself, they had made the difficult decision to rent the farmland to another family.

She grimaced, remembering the arguments that had followed her husband's death from a terrible accident. From the very beginning, his parents had berated her . . . as if she could become pregnant simply by wishing it. To their minds, their beloved son and only child could hardly have been at fault. Zaltos had time and again assured her he thought otherwise. Brimming with simple faith, he believed the Goddess would answer their prayers in her own time. Time, Sosha thought . . . time that had not been granted to Zaltos. Or to her.

She squared her shoulders and lifted the reins, the village of Sweetwater not that far away. Her own parents had perished in a winter fever three years past and had left her with a modest house on the edge of the village. It was to this house she had brought Zaltos's parents after it became glaringly apparent they would have to rent out their land or lose it. So now she lived in the village, her dead husband's cantankerous parents her only company. She had a garden where she raised greens, an equally unimposing barn, and a small henhouse that sheltered a fair-sized flock of chickens. Today, she was returning from collecting rent that Ghanos paid her every month, money she would use to purchase bread, grain, meat, and milk for the household.

A low groan startled her out of her thoughts. She halted her horse and listened. There it was again. She caught her breath and looked around, seeing nothing but the high grass by the roadside. A shiver ran down her spine. She was all too familiar with that sound: it could only be made by a human . . . a human in pain. Sosha reined her horse off the road, half afraid of what she would find. She could hardly continue on. The tenets of the Sun Lord forbade humankind to ignore anyone in need.

As she pushed into the tall grass, her horse suddenly shied, and she grabbed at the saddle to keep from falling. Nearly beneath her horse's hooves she saw an injured man. God and Goddess! Dried blood covered the side of his head, and he lay sprawled on his stomach, one arm flung to his left side and the other reaching for—her eyes widened. Half hidden in the grass, a sword dully reflected the sunlight.

Sosha shivered again, only this time glancing around in near panic. A sword! No one in Sweetwater carried swords. Knives they had in plenty, but the only swords folk in these parts ever saw hung at the sides of men who guarded traders from bandits or weapons carried by the occasional noble who happened to be passing through this area of Karse.

She licked her lips, unsure for a moment what to do. Once again, she remembered the teachings she had received since childhood. She could not ignore this man's plight. He was obviously in need of aid, more aid than she could provide. Somehow, she had to get him to the priest Beckor, who also served as village healer.

Whispering a brief prayer to Vkandis Sunlord, she slipped from her saddle and slowly approached the man. Her skin tingled in apprehension; she was poised to retreat at the slightest hint of danger. Danger? She snorted inwardly. This fellow didn't look as if he could harm anyone in his present condition. She stood only a few steps away, her mind racing. How was she to carry him to the village? He was a large man, broad shouldered. She could hardly lift him atop her horse, and he might not be able to walk. Swallowing her fear, she stooped, reached out, and gently touched his shoulder.

He started at the touch, lurched to one elbow, his face turned in her direction. One very blue eye stared at her; the other was hidden by crusted blood. She jumped back at his sudden movement, gasping in surprise, but he made no move toward her, merely bowing his head and shaking it slowly as if to clear his thoughts.

"Be you hurt bad?" she asked, proud her voice only trembled slightly.

He shook his head again and then quickly reached out to where his sword lay. She backed away, now caught up in fear of what might happen next. His hand found the hilt of his sword, his fingers tracing down to the cross guards. Seemingly satisfied his weapon had not disappeared, he looked up at her again.

"Where?" His voice was not what she suspected. It was deep, calm, and only slightly edged with a thinness she attributed to pain. "Who are you?"

"Name's Sosha. I'll try to get you help, but we be a ways from the village. Can you stand? Got a horse here, if you can ride."

He slowly rolled onto one side, drew up his knees, and tried to stand. She heard him cursing softly, obviously unsettled at his weakness.

"Lord of Light," he murmured, "I can't see out of my left eye."

"Healer will take care of that," Sosha observed, hoping she was right.

He grunted something under his breath.

"You lost a lot of blood," she observed, still poised to run. The side of his green tunic was stained with it. She couldn't tell if it was from his head wound, or whether he had another cut somewhere else. "You need a healer. Sooner the better."

"You're right about that," he muttered, lifting a hand and gingerly touching the cut on his forehead. He stared down at his fingers, which had come away sticky with blood. Suddenly, he glanced around, as if looking for something or someone. "Have you seen any strangers recently?"

She thought back. "Only been on the road a short while myself. Seen no one. Farmer passed a while back on a wagon, but nothing else."

"Two men," he said, still unsteady on his feet. He

felt his side, grimaced, and looked up and down the
road. "Two very large and angry men."

"Ain't seen anyone like that. Now, you be in need
of help. Sweetwater be a short ride from here. Think
you can make it to my horse?"

"Sweetwater? That's the name of your village?"

"That be it." A sense of frustration filled her. "You
coming or not? Going to keep bleeding here by the
side of the road?"

He managed to look slightly embarrassed. "Sorry.
You're only trying to help. I think I can ride. But
what about you?"

"You ain't in a race," she said. "I'll walk beside."

He reached down and picked up his sword, tottering
for a moment as if on the verge of falling. Sheathing
the weapon with an unsteady hand, he once again
touched his forehead, flinching in pain.

Trusting he had no thoughts of harming her, she
turned to her horse and led the animal close. The man
slowly followed, still a bit unstable on his feet. Her
horse backed up, the scent of blood disturbing it, but
she had the reins firmly in hand.

"Stirrups too short for your long legs," Sosha said.
"Want me to let them out?"

He shook his head, winced at the motion. "I'll be
all right." He grasped the saddle and slowly pulled
himself astride.

She shrugged, turned, and led the horse back to the
road. The sun beat down on her head, and she could
taste the salty sweat on her upper lip. After he seemed
to be settled firmly in the saddle, they started toward
the village at a slow walk.

He kept silent as they went, and she echoed his
silence. Once, glancing over her shoulder to be certain
he still sat upright, she caught him looking back at the
road and then around, as if uncertain of his safety.
She gnawed on her lower lip. Who was he? Where
had he come from? And who were the two very large

and angry men he had mentioned? She had seen no horse nearby and doubted he had walked this far out into the countryside from Vkandis only knew where.

One fact was certain: he did not hail from this area. He spoke in a cultured accent, and his clothing was far too fine to be owned by any of the villagers she knew. His boots were made of soft leather, the scabbard and his sword belt decorated in what might be silver. Even so, he did not seem to be of noble blood. Perhaps a retainer of some highborn house.

She sighed quietly. He held to his silence, and she was hesitant to pose any questions. Those could be raised by Beckor, for she had decided this man needed help that only the priest could provide.

Noon prayers to the Sunlord finished, Beckor stood next to his chapel at the center of Sweetwater. The village dozed now under the summer sun. The smithy was quiet; a low murmur of voices drifted out from the tavern. It was a peaceful time; the midday meal had passed, leaving a short period of rest before afternoon labor resumed. Not a soul stirred. He contemplated weeding his small garden but discarded the notion. Sunlight poured down out of a cloudless sky, the air beginning to thicken as if before a storm. Weeding could wait, at least until the day grew cooler.

Movement down the road that ran directly through the village caught his attention. Shading his eyes, he stared in surprise. What in the God's green earth was Sosha doing with a stranger riding her horse? A sudden burst of light filled his vision, and he started at what he saw: Sosha, a man on her horse, and a large golden cat padding alongside. He blinked, and the cat disappeared as if it had never existed. Beckor hurried toward Sosha, trying without success to make out the man's identity. Her face lit up, and she increased her pace.

"God's greeting to you," Beckor said, taking the

reins from her. He looked up at the man, who now slumped forward in the saddle. The fellow stared down out of one eye, the other swollen and covered with dried blood. "Come with me. We need to get you out of this heat."

"Oh, sun-ray," Sosha said, her face flushed and beaded with sweat. "Found him by a field south of here. Can you help him?"

"I'll try." Beckor led the horse around to the side yard. He stopped by the door to his room at the back of the chapel. "Sunlord bless you," he said to the man. "Are you able to walk?"

The man nodded and, moving deliberately, slowly dismounted. He caught himself, his knees threatening to buckle.

"God above," Beckor breathed, reaching out to brush the black hair away from the man's left eye. "Who did this to you?"

The man remained silent. Beckor put an arm around the fellow's shoulder and led him to a shady spot beneath a tree. "Sosha, get some water. And there are clean rags and a jar of poultice in the top drawer of the chest in my room."

She nodded and hurried off. Beckor helped the man sit, straightened, and glanced up at the sky. Who this man was, what he was doing so far from his usual haunts . . . all those questions could be answered at a later time. Now, the most important task ahead was to treat his wound. Vkandis would provide guidance beyond that.

Sosha sat in the afternoon shade, staring at the stranger, who had finished a small meal she had provided from Beckor's store. The blood cleaned from his face, medicine liberally applied, and a strip of clean cloth tied around his forehead, he looked in far better shape than when she had first seen him. The cut over his left eye proved not as deep as she had feared, but head wounds always bled heavily. His eye and the side of his face were swollen but, after careful inspection, Beckor had announced clear vision would return in a few days. The blood down his side had originated from his head wound, though deep purple bruises showed he had suffered more than one hard blow.

There was something about this man. She could hardly keep from gazing at him. He still kept silent, having said no more than ten words since arriving in Sweetwater. And yet, she felt oddly comfortable around him now, with Beckor close by.

The priest sat in the grass as the man drained the last of the water from his cup. Sosha waited patiently for Beckor to ask the questions that filled her mind.

"You have Sosha here to thank for bringing you to me," the priest said. "Now, I think it's time you tell us about yourself. Your name would be helpful."

The man looked from Beckor to Sosha and back. "Torgon. My name's Torgon. I'm from Sunhame. If I tell you more, I could be placing you at risk."

Sunhame? Sosha straightened at that piece of information. Sunhame lay over four days' walk from Sweetwater. What was he doing this far from home? And what risk did he pose?

"That tells me little," Beckor said, "aside from your name. Why would you be placing us at risk? Who have you angered enough to ride you down this far away from Sunhame?"

Torgon's mouth tightened.

"It's ours to decide whether we'll take a risk by helping you." Beckor cocked his head and held his gaze steady. Sosha looked from the priest to the man named Torgon, her heart doing an absurd quick beat. Beckor reached out and touched the man's knee. "Tell us. Perhaps we can help."

Torgon barked a short laugh. "Against the two who

ambushed me? Unless you have some bully boys or men-at-arms hidden in this village, you'll find yourself in more trouble than you could guess."

Insulted, Sosha drew her head back. "We be not defenseless here," she said. "Lot of our menfolk be big and sometimes mighty mean."

Beckor laughed quietly. "She's right about that. Get a few of them in their cups, and you'll behold a sight or two. Who are these men?"

Torgon spread his hands apart, as if giving in. "All right. The risk is yours. I am, or was, a retainer to Lord Jhasko. He's a merchant with a heart cold as winter who bought his way to a title. I also served as his bodyguard and messenger." He glanced around as if he feared other ears could hear. "I doubt there's a shady deal made under the Sunlord's eye he hasn't taken to a level that only the lowest of men would contemplate. I was privy to his secrets, don't you see. And the last secret I had knowledge of was the worst. Jhasko's greed for gold had corrupted him past the point I could tolerate. And, trust me, I'd tolerated a good lot before. This time, he wanted me to murder his chief rival."

Sosha lifted a hand and covered her mouth. Murder? Sunlord protect them all! There might be rare outbursts of violence in Sweetwater, but those usually resulted from too much ale or downright jealousy. She couldn't remember the last time anyone had ended up badly hurt. And, as far as she knew, no one in recent memory had ever contemplated cold-blooded murder.

"Rest assured," Torgon said, "I may have cooperated in some less-than-honorable deeds at Jhasko's orders in the past, but murder . . ." His face hardened. "I refused. It wasn't the response Jhasko expected. He ordered me a second time, and again I refused."

Something cold unwrapped itself from Sosha's heart. This man was no murderer. She bent her head, stared at her hands crossed in her lap, then looked up. "Be you serious? He asked you to kill someone just because they angered him?"

Torgon snorted. "Angered him? It was less and more than that. His chief rival threatened to take business away from Jhasko. And that could not be tolerated. Jhasko had tried different schemes to undermine this rival, but they hadn't worked. As far as he could see, the only remedy was to remove the rival and bring down the competing house."

"Ain't right!" Sosha murmured. "Vkandis Sunlord don't take kindly to murder."

"And?" Beckor prompted.

"And he dismissed me from his service. Told me to be gone from Sunhame before dawn of the following day." Torgon drew a deep breath. "I'd not only lost my livelihood but doomed myself. I knew too much. I'd participated in deeds that could have imprisoned me for years. My only thought was to gather what belongings I could take and leave Sunhame as quickly as possible. Of course," he added, "Jhasko couldn't let it go at that. He'd have me chased down and killed. He feared I'd tell those in power what he'd done in the past."

Sosha glanced at Beckor and saw a change of expression cross his face. "Then those men you told of—"

"Assassins," Torgon said, glancing her way. "Professional killers. They followed me out of Sunhame. I thought I had enough of a lead on them, that I'd disguised my trail well enough. Obviously, I was wrong. They caught up to me by a field and left me as you, Sosha, found me." He grinned slightly. "However, one of them now goes with a sword stroke to his right leg, though unfortunately not enough to cripple him."

Sosha looked up at the sky, darkening now with approaching clouds. "Where be these men now?"

"Vkandis only knows. With luck, they'll believe they killed me. I think what saved my life was six or seven men coming down the road. They looked like farmers or hired hands. Even two assassins wouldn't want to chance their luck against that many burly fellows armed with the God only knows what."

A cold shiver ran down Sosha's spine. "Be they still 'round here?"

Torgon shrugged. "Likely," he admitted.

Sosha looked to Beckor, hoping he would relieve her fears with a few words of comfort.

"Now I see," the priest said softly, dashing those hopes, "why you warned us of the risk we take in helping you." He straightened, set his shoulders, and smiled briefly. "Well, what's done is done. There are places we can hide you until the danger passes."

"They'll go looking for my body," Torgon objected. "If they want to be hired by Jhasko again, they can't return to Sunhame without some proof they killed me."

Beckor nodded. "Then we'll give them proof you died."

"But that be lying!" Sosha exclaimed.

"There are worse things than lying in the Sunlord's sight. Murder and attempted murder offend him far more than a lie spoken to protect another person from death."

The following morning, Zaltos's parents still asleep and her attendance at the rising sun celebration over, Sosha gathered up grain for her chickens. The sun rose in a sky rinsed clear by nighttime rain. She opened the door to the henhouse and slipped inside, greeted by happy clucking and rustling of feathers. Scattering the feed, she picked up her wooden pail, shut the door, and eased inside the barn. Her horse lifted its head and nickered softly from its stall.

"Torgon?" she called softly. "Be you awake?"

"I am," came his voice from the shadows. He crawled out from a pile of straw, strands of it clinging to his hair. The swelling had gone down from his face and he moved less stiffly.

"Brought you some breakfast." She pulled a large sausage and a piece of herb-bread wrapped in cloth from the bottom of the pail. "Hope you don't mind a few kernels of grain. Had to feed the chickens."

He unwrapped the bread and sausage. "That's good," he mumbled, his mouth full.

She watched him eat, her mind wandering to the night before. Beckor had hidden Torgon in his room, out of sight from anyone who might come looking. After sharing the evening meal with Zaltos's parents, Sosha returned to the chapel to find Torgon clad in different clothes. Gone were his boots, his blood-stained tunic, as well as his breeches. Beckor was off somewhere, so she waited with Torgon for him to return. They said little to each other, she still somewhat shy in his presence and he wrapped in what must be his memories of violence.

When Beckor reappeared, he refused to say what he had done to give proof Torgon was dead. If she didn't know, ignorance would provide protection from questioning. Then, under the cover of night, she led Torgon to her house and left him in the barn. Unsheathing his sword, he placed it close at hand and settled down half-hidden by the pile of straw.

Now, as she stood beside him, she felt a creeping unease. Last night, she had trusted Beckor and whatever it was he had planned, but that was then. Today was now, and she feared the two assassins might come to Sweetwater searching for their prey.

"Just ain't right," she said, looking up into Torgon's face. "Nobody should kill nobody for no reason."

"I certainly won't argue with you," he replied. He touched his forehead, wincing slightly. "Some things are even too dark for a lout like me."

"Don't think you be a lout," she protested. "Now keep quiet in here. Sorry for such a boring place."

"Boring's good when the alternative is facing frustrated assassins." His eyes met hers. "You need to take care. Go about your business as if it was a day like any other. And don't hover around the barn. I'll be all right. If anyone passes by, forget you ever saw me."

The sun hung low on the western horizon when two men rode into Sweetwater, to all appearances travelers headed in the direction of Sunhame. Beckor watched them from the front door of the chapel. Big men both, clad in leather and fully armed. Oddly enough, they led a riderless horse. Then, from his vantage point, he could see one of them had his right thigh wrapped in a torn rag. *Sunlord protect!* he thought. *It's the assassins who tried to kill Torgon!* Beckor studiously avoided looking in their direction. They halted by the tavern, dismounted, and went inside—simple wayfarers looking for a place to spend the night before continuing their journey.

Beckor murmured a prayer to Vkandis Sunlord. The game had begun, and he hoped he had prepared a proper ending to it. Something strange had been set in motion when Sosha had found Torgon wounded by the side of the road. And he couldn't discount the dream that had come shortly before sunrise. He had seen Sosha standing next to Torgon, and between them, tail curled around front paws, sat a large golden cat. Golden? For a brief moment, the cat had grown in size, to be transformed into a Firecat! Words that were not words filled Beckor's mind: *Keep these two together.*

Dusk approached, and he entered the chapel to prepare for the sunset service. He clad himself in his vestments, slipped the heavy gold chain of a sun-priest around his neck, and returned to the altar, waiting for the villagers to assemble. One by one, they filed through the open doors and took their accustomed places. He sought and found Sosha, met her eyes and nodded. But arriving last of all, the two assassins entered the chapel, quiet and respectful as any resident of Sweetwater would be.

Beckor tensed at the sight but turned toward the altar, the words of the sunset service coming easily to his lips. Inwardly, he voiced another prayer for the God to grant the villagers safety and to protect the man and woman his dream had revealed as being somehow of great importance.

Sosha arrived at the service later than she would have liked, as Zaltos' father had taken to bed with a slight fever. After dosing him with willow-bark tea, she left him to the care of his wife and hurried toward the chapel. Torgon had eaten his fill earlier, not stirring from the barn all day. He seemed a different person, clad now in a homespun shirt, patched pants, and scuffed but serviceable boots. Only his eyes were the same, startling blue against the tan of his face. She had been unable to keep her mind from him all day. Through all her chores—gathering eggs, feeding and watering her horse, and pulling weeds from the garden—she kept thinking of him.

And now, from her vantage point at the rear of the chapel, she saw two burly men take their places among the villagers. Strangers happened by infrequently but were generally welcome to stay the night at the tavern. One of the two men shifted position, revealing his wrapped leg. Her heart gave a lurch. *Oh, Sunlord! It be those men who tried to kill Torgon!* She barely controlled the urge to dash out of the chapel to warn him. *You silly thing! That be just what they would want! Be you stupid or what? Stay calm, girl . . . don't even look at them!*

She fixed her eyes on Beckor's back as he faced the altar, trusting in him and the Sunlord to make things right.

                    *   *   *

"Sun-ray, a few words with you?"

Beckor nodded, facing one of the two strangers who had lingered after the sunset service and the lighting of the Night Candle. Sosha had left immediately after the benediction, so he assumed she was out of harm's way. And now, what happened lay firmly in the Sunlord's hands.

"I see you've been injured," he said, pitching his voice to obvious concern. His hands trembled slightly and he hoped the stranger did not notice. "Do you need my aid?"

"No," the man responded. "Well, maybe. My friend and I . . . we're looking for someone. A fellow traveler. Ruffians in the fields beyond your village attacked us. We're hoping you might have seen him or heard word of his whereabouts."

Beckor met the fellow's eyes, noting that they missed very little. "What does this man look like?"

"Tall, dark-haired, blue-eyed. He was armed with a sword and wore a green tunic."

"Sunlord bless," Beckor said, bowing his head. "Someone found a man fitting your description yesterday." The man stiffened slightly, leaning a bit forward. "He's dead."

"Dead? You're certain?"

Beckor nodded his head. "I should be. I'm the local healer as well as sun-priest. I buried him yesterday."

The intensity of the stranger's gaze sharpened. "Dead in the fields?"

Beckor's stomach clenched. "No," he said. "Dead not that long thereafter."

"You buried him where?"

"In the field where all our people are buried. The Sunlord demands honor be paid to those who have joined him."

"Ah. Perhaps we might go and pay our respects. He was a friend."

Though the words spoken evidenced concern one traveler might have for another, a coldness lurked beneath. At that moment, Beckor felt the chill of death not far away. Sun-priest or not, what happened next could easily turn violent. He had no doubt these men were ruthless enough that nothing would stop them from finding Torgon, or at least discovering evidence they had completed their task.

Sosha slipped through the barn door, her heart racing. "Torgon? Be you here?"

A rustle from the straw. "I'm here."

"Get you up into the rafters if you can," she said, glancing over her shoulder. "Those men you told us about . . . they be here!"

Torgon stood, muttering curses under his breath. He bent and picked up his sword.

"Vkandis protect! You be in no condition to fight. Hide in the hayloft, man! If they come here, it be dark enough they won't see you."

He wavered, caught between fight and flight. Finally, he sheathed his sword and eyed the ladder he would have to climb. "You're right. For the God's sake, Sosha, be careful! Those two will stop at very little—"

The sound of voices raised in anger silenced him. Sosha turned to the door. "Oh, Sunlord! Get up that ladder! Now!"

She slipped out of the barn, not waiting to see if Torgon complied. Standing by the henhouse, she could see Papa Lorndo at the back door to her house. Confronting him was one of the men she had seen in the chapel. Swallowing convulsively, she slowly walked across the yard.

"Nobody be here but me, my wife, and my dead son's wife," Papa Lorndo said, propping himself against the doorjamb. "Don't know who you lookin' for, but you won't find nobody 'round here but us."

"That's not what the smithy said. Said he saw your daughter-in-law bring a man into town. That's the man we're looking for."

For a moment, Sosha thought her legs would crumple. "I surely did," she said in a small voice. The stranger whirled around and faced her. "Near dead when I found him."

The man's eyes narrowed. "And where is he now?"

"Don't know," she replied, begging Vkandis's forgiveness for the lie. "Took him to our priest."

"Then that's where we're going," he growled, grabbing her arm. "Get moving!"

"Take your hands off her!" Papa Lorndo sputtered. "You can't—"

"Keep your mouth shut!" the man snapped. "Be glad I'm in a good mood!"

He propelled Sosha around the house and down the road toward the chapel. In the early twilight, she could see the harshness of his face, the glint of his eyes. *Sunlord . . . Sunlord! Protect me now!*

His worst fears surfaced when Beckor saw the other stranger coming toward the chapel, one burly hand wrapped around Sosha's upper arm. The poor woman looked both terrified and utterly determined. The moment was now. It all came down to the plan he had put in place the night before.

"What do you think you're doing?" he exclaimed, putting all the outrage he could into his voice. "You don't treat young women like that!"

The man released Sosha, who rubbed at her arm, her eyes pleading for Beckor's help. "What did this priest tell you?" he asked his companion.

"That Torgon's dead. Died yesterday. Says he buried him."

"Huh. Smithy didn't say whether he was dead or alive when she brought him into the village." He glared at Beckor. "We need to know if he's dead or not."

"Why?" Beckor demanded. "Are you kin?"

"No. Friends. We'll have to answer to his family. We need to see his body."

Beckor shook his head. "Small honor you give to me and those who have died. You'd have me disturb his grave?"

The man with the wounded leg stepped closer to Beckor. "Take us there."

The command dripped ice. Beckor shrugged, took Sosha's hand. "Everything will be all right," he said. Then, glancing at the two assassins: "Follow me, if you're still determined to violate the dead."

"Need a shovel," the taller of the two said. "You got one, priest?"

"Around back. We have to go that way to the field where he's buried."

Sosha's heart pounded so loudly she knew Beckor and the two men could hear it. How was Beckor going to prove an empty grave contained a man who was very much alive and, if he had listened to her, hiding in the hayloft of her barn? She voiced another silent prayer to Vkandis and followed Beckor as he led the way to the field of burial.

"There," Beckor said, pointing to the edge of a cleared field. "That's where I buried him."

The taller of the two men stared at the newly turned earth. He rolled his shoulders and began to dig. Sosha watched, fascinated and terrorized, unable to turn away, even if she had wanted to. As the digging continued, time seemed to slow down. Finally, the shovel hit something and the man began to work around it.

"What did you find?" the other stranger asked.

"Damn . . . think it's a boot."

"Let me see." The wounded assassin pushed forward. "Looks like his."

The taller man moved up toward the middle of the grave and began to dig again. Sosha glanced at

Beckor, but the priest stood calmly, his face expressionless.

Once again, the assassin's shovel found something. He scraped at what he had unearthed. "Green tunic. Got blood on it. Must be his." He started to dig around what he'd discovered. "Gah!" he exclaimed, his eyes narrowed. "The stench!"

Both men drew back from the grave, their faces screwed up in disgust.

"What did you expect?" Beckor asked. "Bodies rot. Especially in this heat."

The two strangers stared at the priest. Sosha couldn't help but stare, too.

"Now," Beckor said, "do you mind if we cover him again? The Sunlord will be none too pleased with this night's outcome."

The taller of the two men dropped the shovel. "We'll leave that to you."

Something moved behind the wounded man's eyes. Sosha couldn't tell if it was embarrassment or relief. "We'll tell his family," the man said, sounding somewhat deflated. "Sorry to have caused trouble."

"We heard there have been bandits in this area," Beckor said, pointedly not accepting the apology. "That's why we're on guard when we work in the fields."

The other assassin nodded, taking his cue from his companion, the bluster drained from his voice. "It was a large number of them. The three of us couldn't fight them off. Thank you again. We'll be leaving now."

"Tonight?"

To Sosha, the priest sounded as concerned as someone would be at the prospect of travelers riding out in pitch darkness.

"We were supposed to be at Faroaks yesterday, but we kept hunting for our companion. It's not that distant. Even bandits sleep. Now that we know Torgon's dead, we can continue on."

The wounded man nudged his companion. "And we have to make sure his family is notified. They'll be grief stricken."

"Oh . . . that's true. Don't worry about us, sun-ray. And, girlie," he said, glancing at Sosha, "sorry I scared you."

She lifted her chin and stared back at him, struggling to keep her face expressionless. The two assassins nodded farewell, turned, and left the field. Only when she could no longer see them in the gathering darkness did she allow tears to roll down her cheeks.

"Now, now . . . you'll be all right." Beckor put an arm around her shoulders. "They'll be gone soon." He lowered his voice. "Where's Torgon?"

"Up in the hayloft," she replied, matching his hushed words. "I warned him." A shift in the evening breeze made her gag. "Lord of Light! What be in that grave?"

"Besides Torgon's boots, tunic and breeches?" A small smile tugged at Beckor's face. "Rotted vegetables, meat that's gone bad . . . anything vile I could find to fill them with. You see, Sosha, ofttimes we see what we expect to see, even when it's something else."

Relief descended like a flood. She wiped at her tears and, ignoring propriety, hugged the priest.

His smile broadened. "Let's cover this up and then I'll walk you home."

After the two assassins had ridden out of Sweetwater, Beckor joined Sosha in her barn. Holding a shielded lamp in his hands, he watched Torgon slowly climb down the ladder, favoring his left side in his descent.

"For what you've done for me, sun-ray," Torgon said, after Beckor had explained all that had happened, "I can't thank you enough." He turned to Sosha. "And you . . . you were very brave. My undying thanks to you also."

Beckor noticed how their eyes met and held. He remembered his dream. Keep these two together, the Firecat had said.

Somehow he knew his plan, played out to perfection this evening, was but one step in a journey Torgon and Sosha would make together. And in the darkness of the barn, he could have sworn he saw a large golden cat smiling.

Author's note: Read "The Cat Who Came to Dinner" in the anthology *Sun in Glory and Other Tales of Valdemar*, edited by Mercedes Lackey, which tells the story of Torgon and Sosha's son Reulan and his own experience with a much more talkative Firecat.

The Power of Three
by *Brenda Cooper*

Brenda Cooper's novels include *The Silver Ship and the Sea, Reading The Wind*, and, with Larry Niven, *Building Harlequin's Moon*. Brenda's short fiction includes multiple fantasy stories set in the mythical High Hills, an alternate Laguna Beach, CA, and harder science fiction that has appeared in *Analog Science Fiction, Isaac Asimov's Science Fiction Magazine, Strange Horizons*, and *Nature Magazine*. Brenda's very honored to be included in these anthologies, as she's whiled away many pleasant hours in Valdemar and shared the Valdemar books with countless others. What a treat!

Bard Breda focused on the fight in front of her. In the center of the outside practice rink attached to the salle, two young women wearing worn practice armor sparred with dented practice staffs. Two matching faces wore rivulets of sweat down their foreheads and cheeks, and more sweat glued matching fire-red hair to the slender napes of two necks. For every blow Rhiannon struck, Dionne parried and sent another, which Rhiannon parried. Neither had any advantage over the other, not in quickness, speed, or strength.

Morning sunshine illuminated the two fighters and the two watchers alike. The first of the season's swallows labored around them, chattering over stray bits of straw for their nests. The twins' staffs made loud thunks as they struck each other fairly and well, over and over.

Breda cleared her throat to gain attention from Gavin, her counterpart from the Healer's Collegium. "Do you see why I brought you here? They're mirrors of each other. Can't stand to be apart for longer than a class period, and we've let them live that way. We even let them share a room when they first got here, and somehow no one thought to separate them. Other Bardic students don't room with Healers."

Gavin smiled. "Because you all make too much noise." The Master Healer shook his head. "They seem healthy enough."

"Here, where it's safe. But just last week the Arms-master told me that together they can beat any other pair from their year-groups, even the healers, and yet neither of them can best another single fighter."

Rhiannon and Dionne stopped together and, as if on cue, took great gulps of air.

"They even have the same cuts and bruises," Breda pointed out. Both girls sported purpling bruises on their forearms from failing to block with their staffs, and each had matching scabbed-over bramble cuts on their calves.

Gavin grunted. "When they came to the Collegium, their mother said that if one of them fell, to just wait and call the Healer after they'd both fallen. That's not unusual for twins. We've seen it before."

"Both falling maybe. But sympathy bruises when only one of them falls?"

Gavin arched an eyebrow at her.

Breda fell silent, watching the girls spar. Surely it wasn't healthy for each to be so dependent on the other? If one of them died, she was pretty sure the other one would die at almost the same time. When they left Haven to pursue their special Gifts, it would be rare good luck for them both to live to old age. At least in these times.

"Rhiannon sings well by herself," Gavin said. "Her solos at student concerts make me cry or laugh. A merchant I bought herbs from last week talked about her and was happy when I said some of her herbs might be used by Rhiannon's sister."

Breda sighed. "You've only seen her when Dionne's in the audience. You haven't heard her stumble over chords in class."

His face had a stubborn set. "There's always been Bards who need someone to sing to."

Breda nodded. "I know Dionne is one of your best Healers this year. But how is she when Rhiannon is off on a field trip?"

His silence was enough answer. In the salle, the two started bashing each other equally, so it looked like one girl fighting herself in a mirror. Breda continued, "Healers and Bards are more than their Gifts. It's all right that they're stronger together, but don't you think it's time they learned to live without each other, too?"

"What do you suggest?"

"Send them to separate places. Make them live on their own for a whole year. I've talked with the Bardic Council, and we don't feel we can give Rhiannon her Scarlets until we know she can survive without Dionne."

"Seems cruel. I've never seen two people so connected, even lifebonded couples." Gavin watched the two girls move in unison, balance a mirror of each other, staffs up, staffs down. He waited a few long moments before speaking.

Did old men lose all their backbone? "And?"

"I guess it couldn't hurt." He blinked as if maybe he'd gotten something in his eye. "But she'll hate it. I won't want to tell her."

Breda grunted. "Their safety's more important than their happiness."

"I know. But I still think there's something here we aren't seeing."

What could that be? As Gavin walked away, Breda

felt her own age in the slow, measured steps he took. Maybe she should have told him she'd lost sleep over this very conversation last night. A Healer should be able to spot a clearly unstable emotional situation. So was he just getting old? Or was she?

Dionne bit her tongue for distraction as Rhiannon clambered aboard an old roan mare assigned by the Bardic Collegium, her gittern in a leather case over her shoulder, a leather pack full of clothes and picks and paper for composing tied to the back of the saddle. A strong arm steadied her briefly. She mumbled, "Thank you," but didn't look at Mari, the journeyman Healer she'd be spending her year of living alone with. She didn't want Mari to see her weak. Or more accurately, since Mari had Empathy, Dionne didn't want to provide an opening to get probed through. Instead, she shouldered her own pack full of Healer's herbs and apprentice Greens, turning back for one last sight of Rhiannon, only to find her well and truly gone.

Rhiannon was off to join Bard Lleryn to ride the southern border circuit near Rethwellan. They'd been tasked to help Bard Stefan with his quest to convince the still-healing kingdom that Heralds were as capable as Herald-Mages—now all gone—had once been. Rhiannon and Lleryn weren't likely to actually see Stefan; a full quarter of the younger bards were part of the vast project.

Dionne and Mari would ride northeast, toward Iftel, but only about halfway to the border. Even as a child, she'd never been more than a few miles from her twin. Already they were that far apart, and the gulf felt like a hole in her very self. As soon as Mari laid a fire by their first night's campsite, Dionne collapsed and cried. Mari sat beside her, rubbing her back in great big slow circles, whispering that it would be all right.

But it wouldn't. Not until the whole year passed. And that might take forever.

The next morning, and the morning after that, and every morning for another three weeks, Dionne woke from dreams of Rhiannon. In the crack between night and day when the summer sun was just starting to warm her cheeks, she'd see her twin's face behind her closed eyes, as clear as if Rhiannon were right beside her. She'd know how Rhiannon's day had been. Dionne would know if Rhiannon had been rained on, if she was weary, if she'd practiced her scales enough or started a new song. She also knew that Rhiannon missed her.

Or maybe she was making it all up.

How was she supposed to tell?

The days were no better. Every step took her further from Rhiannon. She tried to be effective for the villagers who needed her. Sometimes she did all right, but nothing like what she knew her best work to be. Mari had needed to help her with every major Healing. Dionne could manage on her own if someone just needed to talk or to have a few herbs from her stores— the simpler things that village wisewomen knew. But the Gift that had earned her the second-highest ranking of her class had become almost inaccessible.

Gavin and Breda were both respected teachers. But what if they were wrong?

After a particularly hard day when Dionne had actually made an old woman's headache worse, Mari built them a fire in a small grove of trees just between villages. The big raven-haired journeywoman twisted her large hands in her lap and looked at the fire for a while before saying simply, "I can't stand it anymore. Your pain. Your power is all leaking down whatever thread you have with your sister, and I can feel it draining away from you. I'm going to take you back to Haven soon if you can't figure this out."

And Dionne would never get her Greens.

"I am trying. Really I am."

"Try harder."

Mari's slightly condescending tone made Dionne's fists clench, but she tried to keep her voice even. "I'm just as tired of failing as you are of me failing. What if Rhiannon and I are just meant to be together?"

"Don't you want families of your own someday?"

Dionne shook her head. "We never have. It's always been us, and that's always been what we need."

"I guess I don't understand."

"I know." Mari was an Empath, and surely Dionne's pain gave her pain. But knowing that just made Dionne hurt more. She threw a stick onto the fire, sending sparks scrambling for the sky.

Halfway across Valdemar, Rhiannon's fingers ran scales in front of a different and slowly dying fire. They were camped in a small copse of trees very near the border and had kept the fire low to avoid unwanted attention. The scales kept her hands supple and warm in spite of the cool night and provided a steady beat to keep her wandering thoughts from going too far. Tomorrow, they were supposed to finally meet up with one of the border Heralds, a man named Deckert. Maybe that would jolt her out of her malaise.

So far on this trip, she'd barely sounded better than a local minstrel at any of the taverns or village squares they'd sung in, and for the last two nights she'd done no better than play a good backup to Lleryn's soaring soprano.

But even if she couldn't sing, surely she could interview a Herald and gather information. Even though she'd tried again and again, her will for singing and performing seemed to have stayed behind with her sister. But the ability to create music was her strongest gift, and surely it hadn't deserted her, too.

At least Lleryn had already crawled into their shared tent, so she didn't see the tears tracing down Rhiannon's cheeks as she sang a new lament she'd penned for far-away Dionne. The night, and her voice, and even the delicate instrument in her lap felt heavy. As she finished the song, even the stars bore down more closely, adding to her melancholy.

"You're very sad." The male voice coming from behind her made her jump. She clutched her instrument to her chest and turned to face the intruder. She saw an old man in Whites, and behind him, a bit like a ghostly image in the darkness beyond the campfire, the outline of his Companion.

She flicked the tears from her face. "Herald Deckert?"

He smiled. "Deck."

"We didn't expect you until tomorrow." She thrust a hand out. "I'm Rhiannon." She stepped aside. "Care to sit by the fire? Shall I wake Lleryn?"

"Don't bother anyone. But warming my old bones would be nice."

"Of course." This was one of the people she was supposed to be singing about, the saviors of Valdemar. She felt awkward. At least the fire had fallen low enough that the old man wouldn't see her blush. "How has the border been?"

He added two dry branches to the fire, so it brightened merrily and warmed her. "The border has been . . . busy. But not as sad as your song. Care to talk about it?"

She shook her head. She'd sound like a spoiled child saying she couldn't bear to leave her sister.

"Well," he said, "I hope whatever the hurt is doesn't trouble a pretty Bard like you for long."

He was old enough his words were simply sweet. As he sat with his hands out in front of him, warming them, the firelight illuminated a nasty scar crisscrossing his left cheek. A hero. He turned back to her. "Did you write that song? Does it have a name?"

She nodded. "I call it the Lament for Twins."

"It is . . . affecting."

He looked sad. Hopefully it wasn't her fault for singing the lament where he could hear it. "What about your Companion? Won't he or she want to get warm, too?" she asked.

"You're camped on the very border. Ashual will be happy enough to stand guard and keep us safe."

The tent flap rustled, and Lleryn untied the strings holding it closed. The young Bard popped her head out. Lleryn was shorter than Rhiannon by a head, but broader, with whipcord muscles and slightly mussed dark hair and dark eyes. "I see we have a visitor."

Deck blinked and said nothing. Rhiannon filled the silence. "This is Herald Deckert, come a night early."

Lleryn nodded, squinting at the Herald. "Welcome." She gestured to Rhiannon. "Can you give me a hand for a moment?"

"Sure." What could she need more than to come say hello to the man they'd just ridden for days to find? She picked up her gittern rather than leave it where the heat of the newly fed fire might warp its sound, and handed it in to Lleryn.

Lleryn took the instrument and immediately extended a hand. As soon as Rhiannon ducked into the tent, Lleryn squeezed her arm and whispered, "Not Herald Deck," while at the same time thrusting a knife hilt into Rhiannon's other hand.

Rhiannon squelched the sharp breath she wanted to take.

Lleryn whispered, "Did you see his Companion?"

Had she? "I saw something white. He said his Companion's name is Ashual."

"That's a name from an old song."

"So what?"

"So if he's a Herald, I'm the Queen of Valdemar. I've met Deckert, and this isn't him. The scar's on the wrong side of his face."

Rhiannon found she was still resisting the idea. "He seems nice. Why would he pretend?"

Lleryn shook her head. "We'd better find out." She opened the door with her right hand, her knife loose in her left hand behind her. She looked back and whispered, "Be careful."

As soon as Lleryn stepped out, she was jerked sideways with a grunt. Lleryn's knife hand came up quickly, only to be caught by the wrist, gripped by the Herald's hand.

Not a Herald then. He couldn't be. Rhiannon bit her lip, then plunged out to help her mentor, bringing her own knife hand up toward the older man's chest. It impacted but slid away sideways. He grunted, feeling the force of her blow, but he didn't release Lleryn. Rhiannon's knife slipped off his chest. She side-stepped, swinging around to the back of him and trying to slash him behind the knees.

Once more the blade slid off.

She tried again, aiming lower, for the back of his heel. She missed entirely.

"Mage!" Lleryn hissed, and Rhiannon looked around for a second pursuer before realizing Lleryn must mean the false Deckert. Was he somehow shielded from a physical blow? Even without Dionne, she wasn't this bad a fighter.

Lleryn leaned her whole body into him, her teeth flashing at his arm where he had her wrist pinned. Except she kept missing—her teeth gnashing open air instead of closing on soft flesh. Even Lleryn's balance looked off, as if she might topple sideways any moment.

Was that it? Did she need to strike a little off?

Rhiannon slashed at him again, missing by more than she thought. Her vision seemed to be sliding a little left of where the mage and the Bard struggled. As if whenever she wanted to focus directly on him, something stopped her. She struck in a place that looked like empty air and felt her knife draw shallowly through his skin near the shoulder.

He grunted.

Rhiannon's vision shifted and the ground came up and slapped her across the side. She coughed and hacked as the world spun around her. Lleryn and the mage were spinning as well, moving a full dizzying turn until Lleryn landed beside her with a grunt, her eyes wide and frightened.

Rough hands wove ropes around Rhiannon's wrists and tied her right foot to Lleryn's left foot. Her stomach stopped screaming dizzy and her head and vision cleared only after both of them were well and truly trussed.

A man Rhiannon would have sworn she'd never seen before stood over them. Tall and raven haired, with wild blue eyes and no scars at all, he might have been attractive if he hadn't just tied her up. Sweat dripped down his temples, and his breath came hard.

"Are you—"

Lleryn interrupted. "It must have been a glamour."

Rhiannon took a deep breath. Something was wrong with this picture. "I thought people couldn't do magic inside Valdemar."

He laughed bitterly. "The watchy things hurt. Which is why we're going over the border right now." He leaned over and offered his hand to Rhiannon. She stayed still, refusing to help him capture her. Maybe he wouldn't be able to get them both up. Maybe he wouldn't be able to stand being here for long. Maybe a real Herald would come along and help them.

"Take my hand." His voice was deep and commanding, as though he was used to being listened to. "Now."

She kicked at him, her foot going wide.

"Why do you want us?" Lleryn demanded.

"Take my hand!" He grabbed Rhiannon's unwilling hand and squeezed hard. Really hard. Something popped inside her hand, and she prayed nothing was broken.

Maybe he'd hurt her so much she wouldn't be able to play anymore. And Dionne. What would happen to Dionne if Rhiannon got killed? Miserably, she nodded. "If you stand back, we'll try to stand up." She glanced at Lleryn, who gave a short, pained nod.

The mage backed up. He looked drained, but she wasn't willing to bet they could get away, especially tied.

At least they'd kept some semblance of control, made him listen to a little. Small satisfaction, but something. Getting up tied together was harder than she'd thought, and they fell all over each other twice. Lleryn growled at the mage once, and Rhiannon growled at him the second time, and he let them struggle through it. He still looked pretty uncomfortable, maybe because of the reported difficulty with using magic since Vanyel's death. Not that she was a mage, but there were enough songs about it.

Rethwellan was close. No more than a few minutes' walk. That was why they'd kept their fire low. She glared at her captor. "Why do you want us?"

"My keep could use a Bard or two."

"You can't imprison a Bard!" Lleryn exclaimed.

"I already did."

Dionne's head spun. Only this time she was sure it wasn't just over another bad day. In fact, it hadn't been that bad—two of the people in the village had needed herbs, and dispensing that kind of help was easy. Mari had stopped trying to sweet-talk, encourage, or force her cooperation. She sat placidly across from Dionne with the firelight brightening her cheeks as she measured herbs into handwoven net tea bags a mother had given her for calming a colicky baby.

They were in a pretty safe rest between two villages, with a pen the horses stamped quietly in, and two other sets of travelers near enough to see each other's cookfires, if not near enough to hear each other.

All in all, it was a calm evening. But still, the fire spun around her, and she gasped and twitched, and suddenly her balance turned so awkward she leaned and then fell off the sturdy log she was sitting on.

Mari leapt up, looking around for an attacker, the herbs in her lap scattering to the ground. She cursed lightly under her breath on her way to kneel beside Dionne. "What hurt you?"

"I don't know." Dionne closed her eyes, searching inside. As a healer, she should know if she'd eaten something poisonous or taken ill. But it didn't seem like that.

And then she *knew*.

"Rhiannon!" she murmured. "Rhiannon!" Her heart beat faster, fear pounding through her veins. Her stomach lurched so hard she nearly threw up her dinner. A bruise blossomed on her cheek.

"What's happening?" Mari demanded.

"I have to go to her!" Now she was half-screaming and half-sobbing. Her vision still seemed wrong, slightly off, but she struggled to push herself up.

Mari extended a hand, helping Dionne to stand up. "Are you sure she's really in trouble?"

Dionne nodded, gasping and struggling for balance. "I have to . . . go." She started toward their shared traveling gear, grabbing her pack and stuffing clothes in it hurriedly.

"Are you crazy?" Mari asked. "She must be all the way across Valdemar. You need someone to help you!"

"So help me."

"How?" Mari asked.

"Let me go."

Mari shook her head, biting her lip and stamping her feet. "I can feel how much you need to."

Of course she could. She was an Empath. Dionne tried to strengthen her need even more, sharpen it.

She reached forward and took Mari's hands, something she'd been avoiding as much as possible. She searched Mari's dark eyes. "I have to go."

Mari grunted. "I'm responsible for you. Gavin told me not to let you come back before time."

Dionne fought back a sob. "Gavin doesn't know Rhiannon's hurt."

Mari blew out a long breath. "I'll take you back to the Collegium, and they can decide from there."

Good enough. Haven was almost on the way. "Can we go now?"

"In the dark?"

"The moon's full."

Rhiannon and Lleryn were both allowed to ride, their hands tied to the pommels of their saddles. The horses were tied together, the reins all ending up in the mage's hands. His horse's heavy gait and broad, ugly face would have shown him for mixed farm and warhorse immediately had Rhiannon seen him during the day, instead of just his white outline in the smoke from the fire.

Almost as soon as they passed the border, their captor began to look better, the moonlight illuminating penetrating eyes and a strangely smiling face that made Rhiannon shiver. His control over their mounts became more sure, the horses nearly sleepwalkers moving at his command. At one point, he turned to them and said, "I'm really sorry. I don't mean you any harm, but you belong in my dream." He looked directly at Rhiannon. "The sad beauty of your song infected me, and I needed to take you. Surely you understand that?"

No. He liked sadness? All while he was wearing that funny grin that disturbed her? Maybe he was a little crazy or a little hurt, but that didn't mean he should be after innocent Bards. She didn't give him the satisfaction of an answer, but instead she looked straight ahead and appeared as unconcerned as possible given the situation.

Just as the first morning sun began to paint the hills with light, they turned up into a narrow, wooded ravine. "I bet this is the way to his keep," Lleryn said.

"Shhh . . ." He silenced them, leading them up a winding trail. Birds began to greet the day, the sound grating on Rhiannon's nerves. What did he really want? He hadn't even taken her gittern or let them take much of their stuff. Although maybe that was to get over the border well before light. Hard to tell, except that he definitely hadn't seemed comfortable in Valdemar.

The keep itself loomed up out of the rock—part carved into cliff, part tall wooden walls that seemed built for defense. In fact, it all looked amazingly well-built, and somewhat fresh and new. Either he'd had a small army to help him, or it was magic-built. But if it was magic-built, the amount of power made her shiver. She watched it grow bigger and bigger as they came closer, colder and more daunting. At one point, Rhiannon was close enough to lean over and speak quietly to Lleryn. "I don't care about our mission. This is going to be tough without a Herald-Mage."

Lleryn grunted, and while her face looked as disconsolate as Rhiannon felt, she said, "It will be all right. Maybe this'll be a good song some day."

Rhiannon blinked back tears and once more pictured Dionne's worried face. She couldn't die here. It was impossible to imagine leaving Dionne alone. "Maybe it will."

Dionne had been through the story twice under the skeptical eyes of Gavin, Breda, and three other teachers when an older man in Whites interrupted and tossed a dented and worn gittern to Breda. "I found this."

Even from a distance, Dionne knew it was Rhiannon's. "How?" she demanded, not caring that she wasn't supposed to speak unless spoken to.

No one reprimanded her.

"I was supposed to meet them. I waited an extra day where Lleryn told me to and then went looking. I found their gear, but not their horses. Bandits wouldn't have left so much behind." He was just beginning to bend with age, and a wide scar ran down his right cheek. His lips were pursed in worry. "I came here since we had some dispatches to send back anyway, and I wanted this reported. It's not the first strange kidnapping along that border—quite a few local farmers have disappeared. I'd like to take some help, if Haven has any to give."

"Thank you." Dionne stood up and looked around. After the last few tough years, Valdemar was short of more than just Herald-Mages. While she'd also have to convince others, these teachers would be the first barrier to cross. "I want to go. I can help find Rhiannon, and that will find the rest of these people."

No one moved or spoke for the space of three breaths. Then Gavin said, "Go on. You won't be any use without her anyway."

A day later, Deckert, Rhiannon, and a second Herald named Cienda, young enough that she still wore her first set of Whites, headed out of Haven. The small group had obtained permission to cross the border for a period of no more than one week and a distance no greater than a day's ride, and specifically to find two missing Bards.

The Healer's Collegium had broken a general rule and allowed Dionne to take one of her father's horses, a three-year-old dun mare named Sugar, with long legs and a long black mane and tail. As beautiful as Sugar was, Dionne felt poorly mounted beside the Companions.

That night and the next she woke sweating from

dreams of Rhiannon, frightened and bitterly unhappy. She could see and feel her sister deep inside, and a few specifics of her surroundings came through as well. Stone walls, and a view from a window of a vast forest. Each morning she told the Heralds every detail she could remember from her dreaming, and they shook their heads. "Sounds like anyplace along the Rethwellan Border," Deckert said.

"At least it doesn't seem like the Pelagirs," Cienda pointed out. "The forest sounds healthy."

"Yes." Dionne closed her eyes. "It is. They're at the end of a long draw between deep hills that are covered in trees."

"Can't be far from where the people have been disappearing," Deckert said. "But we'll have to be very careful since it's on the wrong side of the border."

Dionne swallowed hard, ignoring her own doubts. "I can find her. I know I can."

Either the keep was smaller on the inside than it had looked on the outside, or the mage only allowed Rhiannon and Lleryn access to a small part of it. There was a minstrel, a Healer, and a handful of cooks and farmers and housekeepers. The girls seldom saw them and weren't sure what kept them here. With the exception of the Healer, who wore very faded and patched Greens, it was impossible to tell if the people they saw were Valdemaran or Rethwellan. It was also impossible to tell if they were captive or free, or held in some sort of magical spell. Rhiannon was certain most of it was a spell, and Lleryn argued it could be some of all the above—slaves and workers, locals and people like them, who had been kidnapped.

They'd learned the mage called himself Lompaux of the Greylorn. He had told Rhiannon that the second day, when he'd brought her a new and very lovely gittern and demanded she play the Lament for Twins for him.

He had her sing it for him every night, and every night she grew sadder, and the song escaped her lips with more power. He seemed a willing listener, the kind of audience she had been taught came too easily to song and sometimes had to be brought from sorrow to happiness at the end of a set. At the end of about a week's stay (she'd lost track of the actual number of days), she watched him walk out of the room after a session where he'd asked her to sing for him. It dawned on her that they were developing a bond. In fact, he didn't seem entirely evil. It felt more like he was just trapped in a circle of sadness and a set of decisions he'd made long ago, probably before he was even grown.

Without Dionne, she didn't know how to sing happy songs with the full power of her Gift. But could she touch him anyway? She knew sadness, now that she spent her days locked in the cold keep without her sister. Maybe she could strengthen her bond to him by creating songs to show him the traps he'd set for himself.

Excited, she stood up to go find Lleryn and see what she thought of the idea. The Bard was sitting in the corner of the next room, practicing air-scales over and over, her fingers tapping silently at the air in their rather large prison. After Rhiannon finished explaining, Lleryn chewed on her lip for a long time before saying, "Sure, try it. Just be careful not to let the bond become two-way."

Rhiannon grinned. "It won't. I'll keep my image of Dionne between him and me."

The next morning, they crossed the border, taking the widest trading road that Herald Deckert knew of. He stopped at the first fork in the road, putting up a hand to stop the group. "We have to be careful now," he said. "Having permission from the Rethwellan ambassador won't keep us from getting shot first and the questions asked later. Rethwellan is anti-mage at the moment, though, so if they don't shoot us first, they may not mind our mission." He looked down at his Companion, Kadey. "And the Companions prefer that we just aren't seen. They'll try to help us with that."

Dionne nodded.

The whole group stood still for a bit, and just as she was wondering why they didn't get started, Deckert's gentle voice interrupted her thoughts. "You're the one who's got to find her."

Of course. Dionne closed her eyes. "Stay on the main road. I'll know where to turn."

And she did, again and again, until she led the group all the way to their first view of the imposing keep. She pulled Sugar to a halt, and the two Companions stopped, and everyone just looked. Rhiannon was there—she could feel her from here. She didn't think her twin knew she was close. They didn't have Mindspeech, but they did have something like Empathy, something her mother had always called the oneness of twins. Dionne closed her eyes briefly, closing away the keep, and thought what she wanted Rhiannon to know. *I'm out here. I'm going to get you out of there. It will be all right. Get ready!*

Her eyes snapped open. She was pretty sure Rhiannon had gotten the message, or the sense of the message. But what could either of them actually do?

The Heralds had been staring for some time, and of course they'd undoubtedly been using true mindspeech between themselves and their Companions. She waited, impatient, and less and less hopeful as time went on. She'd done her part, but the next move was up to Deckert and Ciena. And the Companions, of course.

After what seemed like a very long time, Deckert looked over at her. "Most of what you see is an illusion. There is a true Keep there, and twenty or so people. But it's older than what you see, and a quarter that size."

"How do you know?"

He reached down to pat his Companion. "Kadey was able to show me."

"Can he show me?" she asked.

Deckert fell silent for a moment. "It isn't necessary." He sighed and glanced at her. "You're a Healer, and your sister is a Bard. Between the two of you, you know Companions generally only give the least aid possible—the amount we need to do our jobs."

She nodded.

He seemed to shift his focus to Ciena more than Dionne. "And sometimes not even that. For some reason, they want the twins reunited enough to help me see the glamour. I've come to accept that Companions are—in their own way—magical beings. But they keep their own counsel, and Kadey has seldom solved my problems for me."

Both Ciena and Dionne nodded. Ciena was at most a few years older than Dionne, but she seemed so much more poised and controlled that it surprised Dionne to see her given a lesson. Older Healers almost always looked after the younger ones. Of course it was the same with Heralds.

Dionne looked at the Keep, willing herself to see it smaller. It didn't help. "What do we do now?"

For answer, Deckert and Kadey moved forward. Dionne followed, and Ciena, on her Companion Tani, brought up the rear. They were almost halfway to the keep when Dionne suddenly felt dizzy and grabbed the pommel of Sugar's saddle with both hands. Luckily, the tall mare was well enough graced to stop when Ciena, behind them, called out, "Whoa."

Deckert and Kadey stopped, too. Deckert turned in his saddle to look back. "Are you okay?"

Dionne closed her eyes and hung on, taking big, shuddering gulps of warm air. "I . . . I think we should rest. Maybe it's a message from Rhiannon, or maybe she's sick. But anyway, I think . . . think I need to stop."

"Could it be the mage?" Ciena asked.

"I don't know." Deckert dismounted and helped Dionne climb down from Sugar. She leaned hard on the old Herald as he helped her sit on a warm stone by the path.

She felt grateful for his strong hand and dismayed by her dizziness. Still, now that she had stopped, she knew it was exactly the right thing. Her breathing slowed and evened, and her balance returned enough that sitting felt normal even though she wasn't quite ready to stand.

The Heralds didn't question her, but sat quietly. Watchful.

The glowing alto of Rhiannon's voice came to her, wafting down through the forest. The local birdsong stopped.

She glanced at Deckert. "Hide, please, and watch."

To her surprise, Deckert and Kadey faded one way and Ciena and Tani went another way, both so quiet it underscored yet again that the Companions weren't horses.

Just hearing Rhiannon's voice lifted Dionne's hopes, although the song itself had her name in it, and Rhiannon's, a call to her. The song sent waves of sadness through the woods with more power than she'd ever heard from her twin.

Rhiannon rode around the corner, appearing like a vision through the trees, followed by a young man with a confused look on his face and tears falling down his cheeks. He stopped when he saw Dionne, staring fixedly.

She stood.

The song drew to a close, and Rhiannon mouthed, "Heal him," over the back of his head.

Dionne nodded so her sister knew she'd heard. Heal him of sorrow? She'd certainly failed the whole time she was with Mari, but now Rhiannon was here. Strength crept into her muscles, her heartbeat, her stance.

When she saw someone as a patient, she often noticed small things. He stood a little to the left, leaning. His dark eyes and pale skin gave him a sallow look. "Come here," she said simply.

"She won't need to sing the lament if you're here," he said.

An odd response. She licked her lips, watching him. Was he happy about that, or sad?

Rhiannon began the song again.

Dionne stepped toward him.

He backed away, one step for her two.

She held out her hand.

He stood for a long moment, his head cocked, listening as Rhiannon's voice swelled all around them.

Dionne took another step toward him, surrounded by Rhiannon's song, which held him in place. She took his hand. Power filled him, dark, but roiling and misty, as if his very own purpose fought against the man he had become. She touched his energy lightly, trying to understand him.

He flinched.

She looked at him, daring him to pull away.

He didn't.

She glanced at Rhiannon, who winked. That was enough to let go, to trust the situation. They would live or they would not. At least they were together. She took a great, deep breath and closed her eyes, swaying. She grounded, pulling on the strength of the earth and the forest. She let the energy build up around her and in her, and then she sent him some.

He seemed starved. Energy drained from her faster than she expected, driving her dizzy. His pain overwhelmed her, filling her. Perhaps she had done the wrong thing, trusted too much. Maybe she would die here after all.

Rhiannon began a new song, one she had written for Dionne when they were both nine, the year before they started their training. It spoke of healing and joy and helping, and as Dionne poured her energy freely into him, he suddenly began to shake, finally dissolving into tears. He knelt on the ground in front of Dionne. "Now I know why that song called me so much."

Deckert and Ciena had come up on either side of the threesome, and her sister's captor withdrew his hand from Dionne's and said, "I am sorry. I will go with you."

Dionne blinked. Could they trust that?

Inside her head bloomed a single word. *:Yes.:*

So that was what a Companion sounded like. Beautiful.

The Heralds led the man who had surrendered to them away, Deckert speaking softly to him while Ciena bound him securely.

"How did that happen?" Dionne asked.

Again, the voice. *:Your sister's voice has worked on him for almost a week. Rhiannon taught him what he had become, and your Healing showed he needn't stay that way.:*

Dionne glanced at the keep, which now looked no more imposing than some of the Valdemar border keeps, a large, square building with a lookout turret on each corner, few windows, and a stout wooden doorway. There would be buildings and storage rooms inside, and whoever else the mage had kidnapped.

She started toward it, Rhiannon at her side. Along the way, Rhiannon continued the song of joy.

"What will happen to him?" Dionne asked.

Deck smiled. "We'll let him go far away from you two. Valdemar is uncomfortable for mages now, and he is truly changed. Someone so young should have a second chance."

Dionne smiled agreement, and Rhiannon said, "Yes, he should."

Bard Breda and Master Healer Gavin both wore solemn faces as they listened to the twins' story for the second time. They were in a small classroom they'd commandeered for the purpose, Rhiannon and Dionne sitting in student chairs while the two teachers sat at the front. At the end of their story, the girls sat with their hands folded in their laps. Breda was not particularly fooled; they were not as meek as they were pretending to be. In fact, she was pretty sure they'd get up and walk away from their callings if she told them they would have to finish out their years apart.

The girls twitched and fidgeted lightly, a foot here, a little finger there. Clearly, they thought it at least possible that Breda and Gavin would force them to separate again.

Breda had decided Gavin deserved to pronounce their judgment. He looked very solemn and serious as he said, "We guess you want to stay together?"

The twins nodded vigorously.

"You think your bond is something more than we thought, something worth nurturing and feeding."

They nodded again.

"All right."

The two girls screeched jubilantly and held each other, and then seemed to recall they were almost adults and settled back into their seats, still smiling.

Breda leaned over and whispered in Gavin's ear. "I'm glad you were right. May we always learn from our students."

He leaned over and whispered back. "If we hadn't

separated them, we would never have known how strong that bond is."

It was Breda's turn to speak. "You two sound like magpies. We're not done, yet."

Two faces surrounded by red hair looked back at her, pretending innocence.

She leaned down and pulled a box out from under her chair. She took out two new uniforms: one scarlet and one bright green.

The twins held their tongues and reached demurely for the symbols of their new status with reverent hands. Good. Maybe their adventure had helped them understand the new realities of a Valdemar without Herald-Mages. They would have to be part of the solution, as would all of the Bards and Healers and Heralds together.

Three classes of Valdemar, working together. The Power of Three. She could already hear the refrain of a song building in her head.

What Fire Is
by *Janni Lee Simner*

Janni Lee Simner has published nearly three dozen short stories, including appearances in *Gothic! Ten Original Dark Tales*, *Realms of Fantasy* magazine, the first Valdemar anthology, *Sword of Ice*, and the third, *Crossroads*. Her latest novel, *Bones of Fairie*, will be published in early 2009. Visit her Web site at www.simner.com.

All my life, fire has danced through my dreams.

Orange and red, yellow and white—I hold flames in my hands. They caress my skin and melt on my tongue, sweet as sugar on festival days.

But only in dreams. I am a farmer's son. I am no fool.

I know well enough what fire is like.

When I was small, I told my parents about my dreams. I thought they'd be pleased. We worshiped the Sun, after all, saying prayers morning and night to the round stone disk above our hearth. (The merchant's daughter, Cara, said her family had a gold pendant, but I didn't believe her; no one had that much gold.)

Yet as I spoke, my father's face grew hard as the frozen winter fields. "Don't talk of such things, Tamar. Try to dream happier dreams."

It was a happy dream, I thought, but before I could

say so, my mother looked at me, and the fear in her eyes turned the memory of bright flames to cold ash.

"Yes," I told them both. "Yes, I will try."

We cannot hold fire. We cannot taste it. But we can use it.

Fire cooks our food, heats our rooms, lights our homes. After a cold winter night, fire welcomes us to morning.

With fire the day—and the day's work—begins.

When I was older, I called fire into the waking world.

One gray winter dawn the year I turned nine, I crouched in the loft where I slept, longing for the warmth I'd held in my dreams. My palms grew hot, and a tiny orange flame sprang to life in my cupped hands.

From below my father called me down to milk the goats. The flame disappeared in a wisp of smoke, leaving behind only a small red welt.

This time I told neither of my parents what I'd seen. I told myself they were afraid I'd burn myself. They didn't understand that I was older now and knew how to be careful.

I didn't call the flame back again that day. I longed to, though, even when the welt blistered, even when the blister broke and wept.

The day begins with fire. And fire begins with Vkandis, our God.

Every year the Sun's bright rays light the wood our village priest, Conor, piles on the sacred altar. Every year we carry some of that holy fire home to light our own hearths.

As the flames burn in our hearths, they reach upward, yearning, always yearning, to return to the Sunlord once more.

*   *   *

Three days after I first called fire, Cara walked up to me in our village church. "Don't be stupid," she said.

I made sure no one was looking, then stuck my tongue out at her. It was a worship day, and we were supposed to be on our best behavior, but I knew well enough it was girls who were stupid.

"I mean it," Cara said. She was nine, too, but she rarely spoke to me. My mother said that was because she was rich and we weren't.

I didn't care what the reason was. I stuck out my tongue again, then ran off to sit with my parents near the back of the church. Soon Conor entered the sanctuary in his brown homespun robes, and the service began.

Conor's sermon that day was about witchpowers, and I fought not to yawn, because of course I'd heard it all before: how in faithless realms to the north demon-kin welcomed unholy witchpowers into their lives and rode ice-white demons sent from the coldest depths of Hell. Not here, though—here people with witchpowers were cleansed by holy fires that destroyed the powers, yet left the soul intact. As for demons, only trained priests called on them, and only as needed to protect our people.

As Conor went on and on, my gaze strayed from the altar fire to my own hands. I remembered the fire that had burned in them, and I wondered if I could call it back again.

I looked back to the altar. From her seat at the front of the sanctuary—because her family could afford to tithe more than mine—Cara glanced at me. I saw fear in her gaze—the same fear I'd seen in my mother's eyes when I told my dreams. Cara turned swiftly away, but not before I wondered whether I really was stupid.

For until that moment I hadn't realized that something as pure as flame—and hadn't Conor just talked of cleansing fire?—might be a witchpower, too.

*   *   *

For a fortnight I wondered whether I should tell Conor. The priest said we must always report witch-powers, in others and in ourselves, for the sake of our immortal souls.

One spring evening I stood alone in the fields my family farmed. Winter's ice had melted at last—soon it would be time to plant turnips and carrots and beans—but I barely noticed the mud coating my shoes. I watched as the setting sun turned the clouds to molten fire.

I cupped my hands together and imagined a tiny orange flame. My palms grew warm; the flame appeared, looking like a bright sliver of evening cloud. It danced over my palms, taking away the evening chill.

I blew softly, and the flame went out. Could such warmth truly come from an unholy power?

Conor would know. I should ask him.

"Don't be stupid," someone said, as if reading the thought.

I whirled to see Cara trudging through the fields. I'd been so focused on my flame—on my thoughts—that I hadn't heard her coming. Her shoes and the hem of her embroidered dress were stained with mud, and sweat made her dark brown hair escape its braid to curl around her face. I'd never seen Cara dirty before.

"I'm not stupid," I said, even as my heart began to pound. Had Cara seen that flame? Would she tell Conor?

"You need to be more careful," Cara said. "It won't save you in the end, but it'll at least buy you a little more time."

I scowled, even as I realized she had no intention of telling. What if Conor was right, and I was putting my soul in danger by keeping this power secret?

Cara kicked a stone, splattering mud on us both.

"Don't you *dare* tell. Promise you'll be careful, Tamar."

"You're asking me—" I spoke slowly, even as I wondered why Cara had come here at all, "—to keep a secret from one of Vkandis' priests."

Cara nodded soberly. "Even a priest can be wrong."

That was heresy, and we both knew it. If I repeated her words to Conor, Cara might be the one who burned, though my mother said there hadn't been a burning in our village for a long time, not since before Conor had come here.

Either way, I knew well enough I wouldn't repeat anything. Yet still I said, defiantly, "I'm not afraid of fire."

"I am," Cara said. "So promise. By Vkandis' light."

You couldn't break an oath made by the God, or else you wouldn't only burn in this world—you'd freeze in the next. "You have to promise you won't tell either," I said. What was the use in my keeping secrets if Cara only turned me over to Conor herself?

"I *never* tell," Cara said. "How do you think I've lived this long?"

I had no idea what she was talking about. "Promise anyway," I said.

Cara bowed her head, like in church. "I promise I won't tell about your power or mine, not so long as I live."

"What do you mean, your power?"

Cara laughed, a bitter sound. "Didn't I just promise not to tell?"

I hadn't meant not to tell *me*. I let that go. "And I promise I'll be careful, all right?"

Cara nodded sharply. "By Vkandis' light," she said.

"By Vkandis' light," I agreed. Then, because Cara had just sworn an unbreakable oath, I carefully scanned the fields—no one else was anywhere in sight—cupped my hands in front of me, and called the small flame back again.

Cara looked into the light, and her expression turned incredibly sad. "Of course they're not witch-powers," she whispered. "Of course we're not cursed. But they won't know that, not for hundreds of years."

By the fire's light we tell stories. We pray. We dance. On a cool night, the flicker of flames is like laughter, welcome and warm.

Yet if we don't add wood, if we forget to bank the coals, even the strongest fire burns out by morning.

We were careful, Cara and I. I didn't call that small flame to my hands again, not even alone in the gray light of dawn, and Cara never, not once, spoke of what she saw. We hardly spoke to each other either, just like before.

Once a year, Conor gathered all the village children together. He looked at each of us in turn, searching for witchpowers. Yet his gaze was always kind, and it never lingered for long before he declared he saw nothing in any of us save for Vkandis' own light. For three more years after Cara and I swore our oaths, no one was taken for the fires.

The fourth year was different. That year a red-robed priest visited our village. Conor called us together as always, but then the red robe himself began looking us over, one by one.

I told myself everything would be all right—only then I glanced at Cara. Her lips were pressed tightly together, and her face was icy pale. All at once I realized what Cara's power was; I realized, too, just how much trouble we both were in.

The red robe's eyes held no kindness, just a long searching gaze I was sure could see down into our very souls. When he touched Cara on the shoulder, she didn't even look surprised. She just shut her eyes a moment, then followed Conor to the waiting carriage as the red robe continued examining us. He tapped my shoulder next, just as Cara must have known he would.

I felt a spark of anger. I could fight the priest. I could kick, scream, maybe even call flame—but Cara's words echoed through my head. *Promise you'll be careful.* I'd sworn a sacred oath, and attacking a red-robed priest wouldn't be careful at all. It would be, as Cara said, stupid. Stupid enough that the priest might just burn me right there.

I forced my anger down, dousing it as surely as I'd once doused the flame I'd called into my hands. *It's not a witchpower,* I thought defiantly, but I spoke not a word as Conor led me away. I caught a glimpse of my parents, both of them fighting not to cry. I heard Conor whisper, so low none but me could hear, "I'm sorry, Tamar." Then I entered the carriage. Conor shut the door behind me, leaving me alone in the dark.

No, not alone. I heard Cara sobbing softly. As my eyes adjusted, she looked up at me, her eyes bright with tears. "I'm sorry," she whispered. "I'm trying to be brave. Only—"

"Only you knew what was going to happen." Her power was invisible, yet no less forbidden than mine. She could see the future.

Cara nodded, not denying it, but not speaking the nature of her power aloud, even now. "It's not so bad. We still have some time, I know." Yet the bleak look she gave me made the carriage seem suddenly cold.

I had nothing to say to that, so instead I drew her close, not caring that she was a girl. She let me, not caring that she was a merchant's daughter and I was a farmer's son.

"I wish we could have lived in some other time," Cara said. "There will be miracles in other times. But not for us."

Later I learned they often drug the children they

take away, but Cara and I were so quiet, the priest saw no need. We didn't say anything more as the carriage began to move, taking us away from our homes and all we knew. We just held each other in the dark, cut off as we were from the Sun's bright rays.

The surest sign of last year's fire is this year's bright green field. If flames scour the land one season, new growth sprouts the next.
There are seeds that cannot grow without fire.

Twice during our journey the carriage stopped and another child joined us.

The first was a girl, drugged and bound, who thrashed and moaned as if from bad dreams. Yet once, for just a moment, she opened her eyes and looked up at us. My own eyes were used to the dark by then. I saw how still Cara grew as she returned the girl's gaze.

"It's not your fault," Cara told her. "Truly it isn't."

I didn't know what Cara meant, but the girl did. She sighed, closed her eyes, and slid into quieter sleep. The priest didn't drug her again.

The second child was a boy, bound only, trembling from head to toe. "It's all right," Cara told him. "They won't hurt you. You'll be a priest one day. Only try not to speak up in geography class. Nothing good will come of it if you do."

The boy nodded, and his trembling eased. Beside me, Cara sat up a little straighter, all sign of tears gone. As the carriage began to move once more, she whispered, "I know now, Tamar."

"Know what?"

Cara's smile was sad but real. "What I need to do."

It was some time before I knew what Cara meant.

In the meantime we arrived in Sunhame—that great city, said to be designed by Vkandis himself, which I never dreamed I'd see—and were taken to the Children's Cloister. There I realized one more thing Cara must have already known: that no one meant to burn us, not yet. They meant to train us—to be priests if our studies went well, or else to be servants to priests if those studies went poorly.

We still have some time. I remembered Cara's words, yet still I felt a small spark of hope. Maybe we had more time than Cara thought.

To my surprise, I enjoyed my studies, even though I'd never been much of a student at the village school. I enjoyed improving my reading and writing. I enjoyed studying Vkandis' writ. I enjoyed learning my own history and reading glorious accounts of times my people had turned invaders away, or else invaded and claimed some land of their own.

I learned, too, all the things that priests did. Red-robed priests might take children from their families and black-robed priests might light fires in which children burned, but priests of all colors also defended our borders, looked after the sick, and tended to families who lacked food or clothing. They brought Vkandis' wisdom to the smallest villages, just as Conor had. And sometimes they spoke with the Sunlord directly, in order to gain wisdom and carry out His will.

Alone in my small room after evening prayers, I listened for Vkandis' voice, too, but I never heard it. If I felt any anger at that, I forced it down, just as I'd forced my anger down when the red robe took me away. Instead, I prayed harder, and I kept listening.

I longed, during those lonely evenings, to call flame to my hands, but I forced that longing away as well. Only in dreams did I set my power free, where none but Vkandis could see.

No matter that the God never spoke to me; He also never betrayed me to the priests with whom He did speak. I took some hope from that, too.

Maybe, if I studied hard enough and prayed well enough, the Sunlord would decide to spare Cara and me after all.

We can put a fire out by smothering it or by mixing it with water.
Yet it only takes one missed coal to keep a fire alive. Fire will wait, invisible and silent, for tinder or anything else that can catch.

I didn't see much of Cara at the Cloister. Girls were taught apart from boys, and there were fewer of them, just as there were fewer female priests. We shared the same dining room, though, and passed each other in the halls between classes.

Once in those halls I saw Cara lean close to a girl who walked beside her and whisper a few words. I thought nothing of it.

Then another time, I saw her nudge a girl's foot beneath the dining room table, just as that girl was about to speak.

A third time I heard a soft knock on the door across the hall from mine, late at night. When I opened my own door, I saw Cara speaking to the boy who peered out of his room, though girls and boys were forbidden in one another's quarters.

I don't know what Cara told them. I don't know who else she spoke to. I only know that for all of my first year at the Cloister, there were no burnings. The priests remarked on how unusual that was. They thanked Vkandis for blessing us so.

Yet I knew we weren't only blessed by the Sunlord. We were also blessed by Cara, who had figured out indeed what she needed to do.

As the first year gave way to a second, though, I grew uneasy. *Be careful,* I thought, whenever I passed Cara in the halls.

But she hadn't sworn an oath to be careful. Only I had done that.

Fire starts small. A spark, the scrape of flint on steel, a candle's flame. Any of these can burn the world.

Any can be extinguished by a gust of wind or a human breath.

Halfway through our second year, the youngest children began whispering about a bright spirit who looked after them. When I heard that, I broke the rules myself to sneak up to Cara's room.

She opened the door before I knocked and drew me inside. "I know what I'm doing," she said. "I never tell them how I know what I know. I've broken no oaths."

I opened my mouth and closed it again. She'd already answered all I meant to say.

Cara brushed a strand of dark hair from her face. Her unbound hair fell past the shoulders of her gray nightgown, making her look like a spirit indeed. She was beautiful, I realized, and wondered why I'd never noticed before. I reached for her, then drew away. Visiting one another's rooms wasn't the only thing forbidden to male and female students.

Cara drew me close instead and brushed her lips gently against my hair. "I've always had so little time, Tamar. So I do what I can, while I can, in Vkandis' name."

Her words sent ice down to my bones. I drew back a little. "The priests don't know it's in Vkandis' name. If they knew, they'd say demons guided you, not the Sunlord."

"The priests are fools," Cara said. "Or maybe they're just afraid. Do you know I pray every night, just like we're supposed to? I pray to the God my courage won't fail me in the end."

I didn't want her to say that. I wanted her to say that of course Vkandis wouldn't let us burn, that he would spare us both in the end. "If Vkandis gave us these powers, if we can use them to do his will—why would he *let* us burn for them?"

"I don't know. But I think I'll get to ask Him very soon." The quiet acceptance in her voice made me shiver.

I wasn't ready to accept anything. "You could run away," I said. I knew better, though. Guards watched the Cloister by day, demons by night. "If you can see things, don't just use that to protect everyone else. Protect yourself! I'll help you, any way I can, I swear it by—"

Cara shook her head. "No more oaths. Not now." I started to protest, but she sighed softly and took my hands. "You don't understand. When I see things—I never see myself."

"Then you don't know what's going to happen," I said stubbornly.

Cara shut her eyes, as if my words pained her. "It's not myself I see at the end, Tamar. It's you. Only you." She opened her eyes again. "The matron will be by soon. You should go to bed."

I rested my face against her shoulder, just for a moment. The heat that rose in me had nothing to do with my power.

Yet I was good, by then, at dousing heat. I drew away once more, even as I thought about how, if not for the priests, things would have been different between us.

Then again, if not for the priests, perhaps Cara and I never would have spoken at all.

"I'll be as careful as I can, for as long as I can," Cara said. "I can promise you that." But though I begged her, she would not make it an oath.

Protect her, I prayed to Vkandis as I returned to my room. Yet I was a student still. My God did not answer me.

*   *   *

Fire burns, but there's no need to say that.
Everybody knows that.

Two weeks later, Cara was betrayed by one of the
students she tried to help—a girl in love with one of
the novices, whom Cara had warned not to speak her
feelings aloud. The girl was so angry Cara knew those
feelings at all that she ran right to the priests, though
Cara warned against that, too.

When the black-robed priests came for her in the
dining hall, I wanted to fight them. Only the oath I'd
made in Vkandis' name long ago stopped me.

I wanted Cara to fight them, but of course she
didn't; she just let the priests lead her away.

For three days she was locked away so that she
could pray and prepare her soul for the fires. During
those days, the priests said, she'd be allowed neither
food nor water, in order to focus her prayers.

For three days I prayed, too—prayed to Vkandis
for Cara's life. The God was silent as always, but I
told myself that didn't mean He couldn't hear. I prayed
that He *would* hear. Vkandis was a God who answered prayers, after all. I'd learned that in every one
of my classes, and from Conor back in my village, too.

Yet after three days I was led with the other students into a barren gray courtyard. A single stone pillar rose out of the ground at its center, and dry wood
was piled high around it. Looking at that wood, I felt
suddenly ill.

A red-robed priest led us in prayer. My lips moved
to the ritual words, but I scarcely heard them. I heard
only my own silent pleas. *God of Light, please, spare
her. She's done so much in your name.*

Too soon, a hush fell over the courtyard, and a
black-robed priest led Cara out. Dressed in undyed
white, she looked like a spirit indeed, though I knew
white was meant to be the color of Hell's worst

demons. Her feet were bare, her hair bound above her head, her hands tied behind her back. Her lips moved in silent prayer.

Vkandis was a God of miracles. I'd learned that in my classes, too. *Sunlord, please.*

Cara uttered no sound as the priests tied her to the pillar, not even when another black robe crossed the courtyard, holding a burning torch. He brought the torch to the wood.

Vkandis, no!

The wood didn't catch. I caught my breath. *Yes, Sunlord. Thank you, Sunlord.*

The priest's hands moved, a subtle gesture. Wood roared into flame. The flames licked at Cara's feet, and she *screamed.*

She kept screaming as she spasmed against her bonds. Her robe caught fire; gray smoke billowed around her. Her eyes rolled back in her head.

Heat rose in me, the heat I'd spent years learning to hide. Anger rode close behind. I could send that heat into the black robe's torch, commanding the flames to consume him. What use was being careful now?

But killing the priest wouldn't save Cara. Nothing would save her, not even Vkandis' own power.

So I sent my power into the pyre instead, turning orange flames to a brilliant white fire.

That fire consumed Cara in an instant, putting an end to pain and leaving behind nothing but ashes and silence.

I am no God. It was all I could do for her.

I stopped praying to Vkandis. I spoke the required phrases at public services, but those were words, nothing more. My heart was cold as a dead hearth at midwinter, before it is relit from the sacred fires. I had nothing in me left with which to pray.

Cara's cries haunted my dreams, the same dreams

where flames had once danced. No God worth worshiping would allow this. Whatever the Sunlord cared for, it wasn't us.

When a black-robed priest came for me a week later, I was only surprised it took him so long. Surely the priests had ways of knowing that it was me who made Cara's pyre burn so bright. Couldn't they see into our very souls?

Yet the priest didn't lead me to a locked cell to prepare for the fires. He led me to his own rooms and made me take a seat there. His name was Andaran, I remembered—he was the priest who'd lit Cara's pyre.

"Your performance at the burning was—impressive," Andaran said. "There were no hand motions to give you away."

I suddenly remembered that Andaran's hand had moved, right before the wood had burst into flame. He'd *made* that wood catch, I realized with a sick feeling.

His next words made me feel sicker still. "You are ready for the next stage of your training as a priest. At the next burning you will stand beside me as my assistant. After that, I will teach you all the subtleties of calling Vkandis' fire."

It wasn't Vkandis's fire. It was ours. Only ours. Or maybe it was a witchpower after all, if it was granted to priests who used it to kill.

Maybe Cara and I had both been wrong all along.

We think we can control fire. We see it chained in our hearths, and we think we've bound it to our will.

But when a brushfire roars through the fields, we flee. Or else we dig firebreaks, but fire can jump any obstacle. A burst of wind, a flash of lightning, a season without rain—any one of these can wrest a fire out from our control.

No one ever knows for certain what fire will do.

*   *   *

The next burning was only a week later, and the accused was the same girl who'd reported Cara to the priests. She'd been tainted by Cara's unholy words, they told us.

This girl didn't go quietly. She kicked, she screamed, she cursed us all as they tied her to the stone. Yet she hadn't been drugged. She wouldn't be cleansed unless she felt the flames, the priests said.

I stood by Andaran's side, wishing I could run. Yet even if I got past the priests and the guards, where would I go? To the north, where demons rode beneath the open sky and creatures worse than human priests called horrors out of the night? There was nowhere to run and no one to pray to. I waited for Andaran to light the fire.

Instead he turned and handed me the torch. I was so startled I took it.

Andaran's lips curled into a thin smile, and I knew this was a test. "Light the pyre," he said.

Sweat trickled down my face as I stared into the torch's flames. *Careful*, a voice—Cara's voice— whispered. *Be careful, Tamar.*

The hairs on the back of my neck stood up. I told myself it was only the memory of her voice, but my hands trembled as they held the wood. There might be time, yet, to keep my oath—not to Vkandis, who had never listened to me, but to Cara, for whom the oath was made.

Be careful. But careful of what—my own life? Or of what I did with it? If Vkandis would not act, that left only me and my own human choices.

For a heartbeat I hesitated, because I was human and I was scared, because I remembered Cara's screams. But then I stepped back from the pyre, drew the torch to my chest, and called upon its fire.

White-hot flames exploded around me—only me. No one could force me to make others burn. My clothes and skin and hair all caught, yet hot as the fire was, there was time enough for pain.

Through that pain, I saw a vision: a man made of white fire and crowned in white flame. He reached for me, and I knew that when I took his hand, the pain would end.

I didn't take it. Instead I cried out to Vkandis, Lord of Sun, of Light, of Fire: "What took you so long?"

And my God spoke to me at last. "Have you not read your writ, Tamar? I cannot interfere with the free will of my people, not until the fate of the very world is at stake."

Why should it take a whole world to move Him? Cara had died. Wasn't that enough? "Aren't our lives enough?" I knew that if Vkandis withdrew his hand, I would burn forever, but still I cried out, "What kind of God are you?"

"Indeed," Vkandis said, and his smile was terribly sad. "So what are you going to do about it? What choice will you make now?"

It is hard to see clearly by a fire's light. Shapes distort and blur; shadows reach out of the night. The sun lights the world much more clearly.

But it is not always day. And fire is the only means we have to see in the dark.

One day, Cara says, the entire world really will be at stake, and then the Sunlord will act. But that won't be for hundreds of years.

I did not take Vkandis's hand. Yet still he took the pain away, though not the fire. He respected my choice, if nothing else.

Not all priests are killers. Priests also heal the sick, and comfort the poor, and overlook signs of power in their village children to try to protect them. Sometimes these priests have visions that speak through a cloud of flame. When they do, sometimes I am the flame. I am the light by which true priests see.

Sometimes, too, I am the fire that is slow to catch, the moment's hesitation that gives a priest the time to find his courage, to say, *No, I will not do this, though it means my life.*

But maybe you are not a priest. Maybe you only hear a whispered voice offering advice, or else urging you to do what you already know is right.

That would be Cara then, warning you to be careful with the choices you make.

I still do not understand why Vkandis waits. I still have not forgiven Him, although He is my God. Perhaps he does not need my forgiveness.

But I am no God. I am a farmer's son. I will do what I can, when I can, until the very world is at stake.

Dreams of
Mountain Clover
by Mickey Zucker Reichert

Mickey Zucker Reichert is a pediatrician, parent to multitudes (at least it seems like that many), bird wrangler, goat roper, dog trainer, cat herder, horse rider, and fish feeder who has learned (the hard way) not to let macaws remove contact lenses. Also the author of twenty-two novels (including the Renshai, Nightfall, Barakhai, and Bifrost series), one illustrated novella, and fifty-plus short stories. Mickey's age is a mathematically guarded secret: the square root of 8649 minus the hypotenuse of an isosceles right triangle with a side length of 33.941126.

The stench of sickness hung over Herald Charlin's otherwise immaculate room, despite Mola's best attempts at cleaning. It emerged from each of the Herald's struggling breaths, from her every clammy pore; and nothing the healers did seemed to make any difference. Mola hovered over her mistress, watching for any signs of awakening, keeping the room bright with light, fragrant with flowers, and replacing damp blankets and sheets.

No matter what Mola tried, the old Herald's condition remained unchanged, an interminable sleep on the grim border between life and death. Aside from the rattling, uneven breathing, Charlin did not seem uncomfortable. She lay in a relatively peaceful slumber, eyes gently closed, limbs still, expression serene amid the deeply etched wrinkles. Mola kept her elder's thin, gray hair neatly combed, and blankets covered the withering limbs.

Sietra, the youngest of the Healers, slipped into the room carrying a bowl of something steaming in one hand, a cup in the other. About fourteen, she moved with a practiced grace Mola wished she could emulate. Slender, but large-boned, Mola felt like a bumbling fool in the company of the Gifted. Her thin, stick-straight hair was a common mouse brown. Her hazel eyes lacked the striking strength of the sharp blues, grays, and greens or the gentle soulfulness of Charlin's brown ones. Freckles marred Mola's round face, her nose pudgy and small, her eyes narrow and closely set. She seemed grossly out of place in a world of handsome courtiers and beautiful ladies, of talented Heralds and Healers.

The sight of the food raised new hope in Mola. "Did my lady ask for these?" Mola could not imagine such a thing. She rarely left the ancient Herald's side, and nearly a week had passed since Charlin had spoken a word. "Is she able to eat and drink?"

Sietra smiled and placed cup and bowl on the end table. "No, Mola. These are for you. When's the last time you've taken in anything?"

Mola felt her cheeks grow warm, and she smiled at the healer's thoughtfulness. "It's been a while," she admitted. "I haven't really worried—"

"—about yourself?" Sietra finished. "You should. It doesn't do Herald Charlin any good to have her handmaiden starve to death."

Handmaiden. It was as good a descriptor as any other, Mola supposed. Describing her relationship to the Herald did not come easy. Mola's grandmother had served as Charlin's nanny before Elborik, her Companion, had Chosen her. They had had an extremely close relationship, more like mother and child; and Charlin had kept Mola's grandmother with her through her training and beyond. Mola's mother had stepped into the position next, until her untimely death only a few weeks before Mola turned eleven. For Mola, Herald Charlin had seemed as much a mother as a mistress. They had become so close, so accustomed to one another, that Mola often imagined she could hear a whisper of the Mindspeech that flew between the Herald and Elborik. When Mola tended the Companions, in field or stable, she sometimes thought she could just make out a dull rumble of conversation.

Now, Charlin lay dying. She had survived so many missions, so many valiant tours, that Mola had come to think of her Herald as ageless and immortal. Always before, Charlin had bounced back from illnesses, shrugged off injuries; and Mola could not picture her life without the woman who had shaped and raised and loved her for the last eighteen years. Charlin could not truly be slipping away. Something, or someone, had to save her. It always did.

"Thank you," Mola said. "It's so very kind of you to think of me when you have important work to do." The aroma of the stew filled the room, covering the stench of illness the way the flowers had not; and Mola suddenly realized she was famished. But, before she could eat, Mola needed to discuss with someone the dream that had plagued her last few nights. Sietra seemed a likely and benign place to start. "Could you spare me another moment, Sietra?"

The Healer perched daintily on the edge of a chair. "Of course, but I'd rather see you eat."

Dutifully, Mola seized the spoon she had just noticed through the steam rising from the bowl and stuck it into her mouth. The flavor of vegetables and gravy spiraled through her, inciting a saliva riot that nearly drove her to devour the entire bowl in an instant. Instead, she forced herself to push it aside. She needed to talk.

"How is it?" Sietra asked.

"What?"

"The stew. What do you think of it?"

"Delicious," Mola admitted, sucking back drool that nearly leaked from her mouth. "And I promise I'll eat every bite. But, first, I want to tell you about something."

Sietra nodded encouragingly, long blonde braids hopping with the motion.

"I've been having . . . a recurring dream." Mola studied Sietra for some kind of reaction but received nothing but quiet patience. "In it, I see a mountain just south of here, still in Velvar, not a particularly high or difficult one. On it grow some unusual clovers, and a voice in the dream tells me they can strengthen—" Mola made a short gesture toward Charlin, uncertain how much the Herald could still hear and understand.

Sietra continued to look askance at Mola, clearly expecting more.

"That's about it," Mola said. "But it seems so real, more real than any dream I've ever had before. And . . . I've had it every night since . . . my lady . . . lapsed."

As Sietra still said nothing, Mola asked directly, "What do you think?"

"I think," Sietra said with obvious caution, "that you love and miss your lady."

That being self-evident, Mola continued to press, "Do you think it's possible there is such a . . . a healing clover?"

Sietra went even more quiet, but she seemed to be giving the matter significant thought, so Mola waited. Finally, Sietra spoke her piece, "Mola, have you ever had prophetic dreams before?"

Mola lowered her head. "Of course not. I have no magic of any kind. I'm only . . . what I am."

"You mean a devoted, sweet, kind, and generous person? With courage and hope and intelligence? Because I'd hardly use the word 'only' when explaining that."

The warmth in Mola's cheeks increased to a bonfire. "That's . . . that's so very nice of you to say. I'm not Gifted, though. Not in the sense of a Herald or a Healer or a Bard or anything. But this dream. It's telling me—"

"—to *do* something." Sietra shrugged. "Then, perhaps, you should do it."

"Me?" Mola laughed, the sound odd to her ears. She could not recall the last time she had managed such a thing. "Slopping through swamps? Climbing mountains? That's a job for Heralds, not handmaidens."

Sietra's slender shoulders rose and fell. "You'll have a hard time convincing a Herald to go on a fool's mission on no better pretext than a servant's recurring dream. Even if the servant is as wonderful as you."

It was exactly what Mola had figured, the very reason she had not yet told her dream to anyone else. "I have to try."

Sietra rose. "I understand. And I wish you the best of luck." She headed for the door. "Please eat, Mola."

"I will," Mola promised, immediately turning her attention to the stew. She could not have resisted it if she had tried, and she fairly drank it, without bothering to chew.

Mola washed and curried Elborik until her coat shined, though the old Companion never bothered to open her eyes. She lay in the pasture, fetlocks grass-stained and ragged, chestnuts marring the perfect, snowy lines of her legs. Mola had rubbed and oiled her hooves until they gleamed like metallic silver. The mane and tail lay spread in beautiful waves, combed to silky perfection. Even so, brushing could not hide the moth-eaten patches of fur, the ashen eyelashes, and the slumping frame incapable of standing. The Companion was dying slowly, along with her Herald.

Spotting Corry playing with his own Companion, Rexla, in the field, Mola gathered her supplies and dumped them into her pack. She embraced Elborik's neck and kissed her soft nose and furry muzzle. Then, tossing her tack bag over one shoulder, Mola walked toward Corry.

Sun rays turned the blades of grass into sparkling jewels, and the cloudless warmth made a negative mood nearly impossible. As she headed toward Corry and Rexla, Mola found herself smiling for the first time in many days. The all-consuming darkness lifted from her soul, as well as her eyes, as she watched the playful dance of man and animal. Heralds worked hard, and she did not begrudge them their moments of play, even with her own heart so heavily burdened.

Seeing her coming, Corry waved in greeting, and Rexla trotted to her, snuffling her pockets for the sugar and carrots she usually carried. The stallion's blue eyes sparkled in the sunlight, mischievous and joyful, two states she had not experienced in what seemed like months.

Mola shoved the Companion's face away, then found herself immediately drawing him back for a warm hug and a nose kiss.

"Hey," Corry shouted, running toward them. "Save some of that affection for me."

Mola studied her feet. Corry was thirty years old, a Collegium-trained Herald, and far above her station. Yet, he always treated her with great kindness. She found him nearly irresistibly attractive and wondered why he had never bonded with anyone other than his Companion. True, he had a generous, hawk-like nose that had been broken once or twice, and his sandy hair fell in greasy clumps, always into his eyes; but she saw those as endearing characteristics rather than flaws.

When he arrived, Corry threw his arms around

Rexla and began plastering the Companion with kisses. The stallion stomped his feet and tossed back his head, mane flying.

"Ooops, sorry," Corry said in mock apology. "Wrong one." With dexterous ease, he switched from his mount to Mola, hugging her with the same warmth and exuberance.

It was all Mola could do to keep her balance as Corry planted a welcoming kiss directly on her lips.

Mola found herself incapable of breathing. Though chapped, his lips felt spongy, delightful. She wanted nothing more than to suck his tongue into her mouth, to wind herself around him, to become lost in his embrace. But she was only a servant, and he was so much more.

"Sleep with me," Corry said.

Mola disengaged and slapped him. "Stop teasing me, you lizard. I'm in no mood for games."

Corry rubbed his face, becoming appropriately somber. "I understand. I shouldn't joke around while Charlin . . ."

Reminded of the cause of her anxiety, Mola felt tears forming in eyes too sore to hold any more.

Cursing himself under his breath, Corry took Mola into his arms again, this time more gently. "I'm sorry, Mo. So sorry. But Charlin is so very old, and the Healers can't do anything more."

Alerted by the change in mood, or by some mind-magic from Corry, Rexla returned to grazing. Corry led Mola to a grassy hill, where he pushed her down, then sat beside her. "Mola, life goes on. They're not going to send you away just because your—"

Mola stiffened. She had not even considered that possibility. "You mean they might send me away?"

Corry cringed, obviously realizing he had worsened, rather than soothed, her distress. Again. "No, no. Of course not. There are plenty of jobs, and no one would consider such a thing."

You just did. Mola did not speak the words aloud. Corry felt bad enough without her aggravating his guilt and discomfort. "Corry, do you think it's possible that the healers missed something? That there's an herb or plant or magic out there somewhere that might save Herald Charlin?"

Corry studied her in silence for a moment.

Mola stared back. "Corry, don't try to figure out what I want to hear. Just speak the truth."

Corry cleared his throat. "Well. Mola." So far, he had done nothing but delay. "I'm an open-minded man. I'm taught to believe *anything* is possible. Such a thing might exist."

Mola hung on every word.

Corry stopped talking.

Mola dodged his gaze. "Would you be willing to look?"

"Mola . . ." Corry started.

Mola could tell by his tone that he was going to say something she did not want to hear. "I mean, if you had reason to believe such a thing existed. And someone told you where to find it."

Corry squeezed his eyes shut. "Mola, our Healers are some of the best and as well-trained as Healers come. I trust them."

"But if you had reason to believe," Mola insisted.

Corry turned and took both of her hands in his. "Mola, if a trusted, magical source told me where to find a cure for Charlin, I'd ride to the ends of the world for it. But, Mola, there is no cure for old age. Some few mages have managed to greatly extend their lives; but, ultimately, time catches up even to them."

Mola could deal in hypotheticals no longer. "I've been having this dream. Every night for four nights now. There's a healing clover growing on the mountainside. That one there." She pointed southward toward the nearest of the few scattered peaks in the distance. "It's barely a few hours' travel by Companion. Couldn't you, at least, check for me?"

Corry's lids glided shut again, and he gritted his teeth. "I'm sorry, Mola. I have a mission that starts just after midday meal, and I'm not sure how long it will take."

The tears dripped from Mola's eyes, down her cheeks.

"Mola, please. If it's that important, I can get a horse for you." Corry opened his eyes, saw the tears, and cringed.

Mola freed her hand to wipe them away fiercely. "I can't climb mountains. I'm not Gifted. I'm not even trained to use a simple weapon. How could I possibly go on such a trip alone?"

A light flashed through Corry's eyes, then disappeared. "Mola, there's a reason these dreams are coming to you, not to me. Whether that reason is only your concern for your mistress, or if it is something more, it's still your challenge and you must face it however you choose." He unfastened a knife and its sheath, from his belt. "Keep this for me while I'm gone, and use it as you see fit. If you wish, I'll have a horse ready for you at the stable, as well as a pouch of provisions." Glancing toward the rising sun, he sighed. "I have to go now. What you do is up to you, and no one could fault you for dismissing a dream . . . or for following it."

Corry leapt to his feet, saluted a good-bye, and headed to ready Rexla.

A damp breeze stirred Mola's hair, and she reveled in the motion of the sturdy little chestnut mare Corry had chosen for her. She patted the knife at her belt, then the sack of provisions tied securely behind the saddle. Her mission should not take long. With any luck, she would return by bedtime.

As the few scattered mountains drew tantalizingly near, the footing became less certain. The mare snorted frequently, and its pace slowed to a crawl. It lifted its hooves unnaturally high to clear the mud that sucked at its fetlocks. Finally, it stopped completely, twisting its head toward home and nickering uneasily at the swampy ground.

Mola dismounted. "It's all right, girl. You don't have to go any farther." She untied her pack from the saddle, rolling up the twine and placing it in her pocket. Barely a cloud marred the sky, and the afternoon sun warmed the air pleasantly. It would take less than half an hour to reach the cliffs on foot, even slogging through the swamp at its base. "Wait here for me." She did not know if the horse would understand or obey. The Heralds did not have to worry about such things; their Companions grasped everything they said, whether aloud or in Mindspeech.

Mola considered tying the reins to a branch of one of the scraggly trees at the edge of the swamp, but discarded the thought. If something happened to her, the horse would starve. And, if it spooked, it might break its neck or leg. It seemed better to risk the hike home than the horse's life. Sighing, she removed the headstall and tied it to the saddle. To her relief, the horse did not run but settled into quiet grazing.

Mola took a forward step, the muck sucking noisily at her boots. She frowned, studying the trees again until she found a suitable, sturdy branch. Using a combination of the knife's blade and her own strength, she broke free a thick limb a bit longer than a tall man. Using that, she poked ahead of herself, gauging the thickness of water and mud before plunging forward.

The stick did its job, warning Mola of sinkholes and helping maintain balance as she wandered deeper into the swamp. The water rose above her feet, then her calves, and, finally, above the top of her boots. Brack-

ish water soaked her feet, reeking of plant material
and dead things. Mola crinkled her nose and continued walking, her attention fixed always ahead, always
on the mountain.

Mola ran the details of the dream through her mind
as she walked. It always started the same, a strange
and masculine voice narrating the scenes: "Come,
Mola, come. You can find it." It guided her through
the swamp to the foot of the mountain, then up a
craggy path to a ledge, where a five-leafed variety of
pink clover grew. "Pick them, as much as you can
carry. They will make the Herald strong."

The tone never changed, nor the words. The scene
that unraveled in the dream looked eerily similar to
what lay precisely before her now: the sunlit swamp,
the close gray stone of the mountain. Mola could not
help smiling. Filled with sudden excitement, she took
a few skipping steps through the muck.

They saved her. The surprise attack meant to end
her life became a missed strike. An enormous shape
hurtled past Mola, slamming her with a broad shoulder and knocking her into the filth. Huge, reptilian
jaws closed on a rock instead of a woman.

Swamp drake. Mola screamed and tried to run. But
the water hampered her movements, and the mud
slowed her to an awkward stumble. *Don't panic.* Mola
tried to avert her eyes. She knew from the tales of
the Heralds that drakes had hypnotic abilities, that
catching its glance directly would result in her death.
I need a weapon. Survival instinct and common sense
would not allow her to leap bodily upon the thing. *A*
long *weapon.*

Mola dared not stare at the drake, but she kept the
edge of her vision and her ears upon it. For the moment, it was more worried about shoving the stone
from its mouth than catching her, but she had no illu-
sions. The moment it freed its jaws, it would come
after her again.

Mola juggled the twine from her pocket, and Corry's knife. As quickly as she could, she tied the hilt onto the branch, creating a crude spear.

By the time Mola finished, the swamp drake charged her again. Though lumbering and slow, it had the great advantage of bulk. Massive and deadly, it opened its jaws wide, displaying rows of dagger-like teeth. It had lost the ambush but had not yet given up on its prey.

Mola screamed again. Shutting her eyes tightly, she shoved the spear toward the creature's wide-open mouth. The impact of its attack hurled her to the ground, still clutching the branch in desperate, white-knuckled fingers. The drake's massive body flopped on top of her, grinding her into the muck and water. She managed to choke down a breath of mostly air before becoming pinned, underwater, beneath it.

No! No! For the second time in a matter of moments, Mola fought panic. The swamp drake had gone still, apparently dead; its own momentum driving the spear deep. Smashed into the muck beneath the water, Mola struggled to wriggle loose. The drake's body did not budge.

Mola opened her eyes, only to have them stung closed by silt and blood. The world around her had turned scarlet, soft, and utterly wet. Her head started to ache, and her lungs spasmed in her chest. She had only one last chance to free herself before she drowned, murdered by the very corpse she had created. *Charlin needs me. I'm not going to die here!*

Driven by new purpose, Mola writhed and shoved, braced and pushed to no avail. She felt her muscles weakening, the agony in her lungs growing unbearable. Seeking bearings, she buried her hand into the muck. *Soft.* She tossed aside a handful, churning up the water into wild bubbles. Heading down when air was up defied survival instinct, but Mola forced herself to dig. Seizing and kneading, grinding down the muck beneath her, she created just enough extra space to squeeze out.

Mola could not wait until she fully reached the surface before gasping in a lungful of air and mud, blood and water. The combination choked her. She coughed violently, wheezing in air at the end of each paroxysm. She vomited forcefully, repeatedly. *Gotta move. Might be more of these things.* Eyes watering, lashes filled with silt, she grabbed the end of the branch, trying to wrench it free of the sunken corpse. It resisted.

Mola's head felt ready to explode, and she continued to cough as she worked, twisting and pulling until blood boiled into the water and the branch finally slid free. The knife remained attached, to her relief. As she ran as quickly as the swamp allowed, she realized the provision bag still thumped against her shoulder. She had forgotten about it in the struggle and could not help wondering if slipping it off might have allowed her to free herself faster and easier. *A Herald would have thought of that.*

Mola had never seen a mountain up close before, and it surprised her. She had expected a tower of pure rock. The Heralds' tales always involved vertical crags with dodgy handholds and boulders crashing down upon them. Instead, she found a gentle, upward slope as grassy as a pasture and interspersed with trees. Mola climbed mindlessly, swiftly, her only thought to leave the swamp far behind. At length, exhaustion seized her; and she dropped to the ground to rest.

The grass felt warm and comforting beneath her, cushioning the many aches that descended upon her as fear and excitement ebbed. Mola felt bruised and achy in every part, but no one pain stood out from the others. Overtaxed muscles, pulls, and tears seemed the worst of it. Though covered in sticky drake blood, she did not appear to have shed any of her own. She stank of drying innards and swamp slime.

Mola opened the supplies Corry had had packed for her, thrilled to find clean, dry clothing as well as food. It seemed foolish to change now, when she had to wallow back through the swamp, but she needed the comfort. Quickly, she stripped down and replaced her grimy clothes. The soft, clean fabric felt wonderful, buoying her mood as well, and confidence swelled through her like second wind. *I survived a swamp drake!* The thought filled her with pride. *I survived an attack—and it didn't.* That same morning, she would not have considered herself capable of such a feat. *Charlin will be so proud.*

Thoughts of her mistress brought Mola crashing back to reality. Charlin would never know about her success if she did not hurry and find those healing clovers. *Maybe it's not a fool's mission. Maybe my dream meant something. Maybe I really can make my Herald strong again.*

Grinning, Mola balled up the ruined clothes and shoved them into the pack. She would have rather burned them; but, without their corroborating filth and stench, she doubted anyone would believe her. With a lot of effort, she had managed to clean equally disgusting stains from the effects of her mistress in the past.

Mola looked up. The sun no longer glared down at her, partially blocked by the rocky peaks. The way had grown steeper, stonier; and she could see the crags not far above her, the ones from her dream. If she squinted, she believed she could even see greenery dotted with bits of pink. Using the makeshift spear as a walking stick, tossing the pack back over her shoulder, Mola started up the more sharply rising slope.

Mola had only taken a few steps when she noticed a dark figure towering above her on the path ahead. For a moment, she mistook it for an enormous man in a fur coat. Then, it opened its mouth in a growling roar, and she realized she faced a large and angry-looking bear.

Mola went completely still, afraid to move. A scream bubbled up in her throat, but she forced herself to swallow it. *Loud noises infuriate bears.* She could not remember where she had heard that, but it did not seem worth challenging. Unable to move, she dredged up other lore: *Playing dead doesn't work, bears can climb trees, they won't bother you if you don't bother them, bears can't run downhill.*

That last bit of advice seemed useful in a way the others did not. Spinning on her heels, Mola broke into a terrified run, back the way she had come.

Behind her, Mola heard the creature roar again, then the slam and rattle of heavy paws behind her. *It can't run. It can't run downhill.* The advice cycled through her head in a desperate chant. Yet, to her ears, the bear was moving. And swiftly. She dared a look behind her. Not only was the bear running downhill, but it was clearly gaining on her. In a moment, it would have her.

The scream Mola had suppressed tumbled out, unbidden. Another followed. And another. Not knowing what else to do, she ducked her head and came to an abrupt stop.

The bear launched itself, landing where Mola would have been if she had still been running. Thrown off-balance, the bear lost its footing, stumbled, slid partially down the hill, then tumbled a few steps further. Mola tensed to run back up, cursing whoever had assured her that bears could not run downhill. If she survived this, she would do whatever it took to counteract that myth. And punch that person in the lying face.

Before Mola could take a step, the bear gathered its paws back under it. Running now, Mola realized, only made her a target. Gathering her courage, she jabbed the makeshift spear toward the animal.

The bear reared back up. As the spear rushed toward it, it slammed a massive forepaw against the pole. The branch shattered. The biggest pieces flew in opposite directions, rattling down toward the mountain's base. Bits of wood showered Mola.

"Demons!" Disarmed, Mola stood, rooted in panic, as the bear ambled toward her. She could read murder in its dark eyes, smell the fetid odor of its breath, see the teeth and claws that would maul her from existence.

:Move!: The voice in Mola's head was not her own, but it mobilized her just the same. Shrugging the pack from her shoulder, she grasped it by the strap and swung it at the bear.

The pack slammed the beast in the face.

Roaring, the bear caught the pack in its teeth. Its nose twitched. The pack crashed to the ground, and the deadly claws ripped into it instead of Mola.

Move! This time, Mola chastised herself. Her supplies would not distract it long. Whirling, she tore back up the mountainside, desperately seeking the rockiest cliffs. Grass turned to stone beneath her feet, and she staggered up onto a crag.

Not as far away as she had hoped, the bear ripped through the remains of her pack, then raised its head. Nostrils twitching, head swiveling, it finally found her and loped effortlessly toward her.

Mola leapt from her perch to a higher crag, then another. She hunkered down, gaze never leaving the animal, hands mindlessly raking stones and small boulders into a pile around her.

Shuffling directly beneath Mola, the bear rose on its hind legs to stare at her.

Heart pounding, Mola found herself now more angry than frightened. *How dare it want to kill me. I'm no helpless rabbit to be eaten on a whim.* Grabbing a large stone, she hurled it at the bear.

The rock hit the bear squarely on the cheek. Enraged, it rose taller, roared louder. Took a menacing step toward her.

Mola threw another rock, and another, pelting it with anything she could get her hands around. "Go away!" she yelled. "Leave me alone, you stupid, smelly beast!"

The pain only infuriated it more. Its roars echoed. Its ears pinned tightly to its head. It roiled the air with maddened swipes of its massive paws.

Struggling with a boulder, Mola drew together all the strength she could muster and, with the help of her higher position, sent the rock crashing into the bear's chest. It hit with a loud thud, driving the creature backward and to its haunches.

That proved enough. The bear whirled and fled, seeking less dangerous prey.

Mola sank to the crag, out of both ammunition and energy. She did not know how long she lay there, but the sky had greatly darkened by the time she opened her eyes, as the sun slipped behind the mountain. Weeds tickled her nose, green and leafy, filled with pink flowers. *Pink flowers.* Mola sat up. *Pink flowers?* She started to laugh. She lay in a patch of five-leafed clovers. *I found them! Thank the gods, I found them.*

Mola seized the clovers by the handful and shoved them into her pockets until they bulged. Only then she rose, and nearly tumbled from the crag. Her legs had gone as shaky as slender twigs in a wind storm. It took her inordinately long to clamber down from the rocky ledge. But, once there, she dropped to the ground and rolled like a child down the grassy mountainside.

My dream was real! I found the clover! None of the pains in Mola's body, nothing she had suffered, could take away the joy of that moment. She still had a slog back through a swamp that might contain another drake. She might not find her mount waiting when she returned, and she would have to drag her weary, painful bones all the way home. Yet, none of that mattered. She had survived a drake and a bear. She would make it home. She would save Charlin and prove that she had some worth, even without the Gifts of the Heralds and Healers.

Mola slammed into something hard and stable that brought her to an abrupt halt. She lay for a moment in utter uncertainty, hoping for a rock, worried for another bear. Dizzily, she focused on the unwavering thing that had blocked her path. Two blurry white pillars stood in front of her.

Pillars? I'm inside. Tears welled in Mola's eyes. *It was all a dream? Just a big, fat, stupid dream?* Disappointment flooded through her, erasing the happiness that nothing else had managed to dispel. Yet, the grass remained green beneath her. The terrible odor of swamp still filled her nostrils. Her pockets protruded. She looked up the long, white pillars to a sweet pink nose and two blue eyes studying her curiously. Mola was still on the mountain, at the feet of a Companion.

"Rexla?" Mola tried, hoping Corry had changed his mind and come to rescue her.

The horse-like creature lowered its head to whuffle into Mola's face.

Though the Companions all resembled one another, with their white coats, silvery hooves, and enormous blue eyes, years of helping in the stable allowed Mola to notice their differences as easily as a mother distinguishes her identical twins. She sat up, waiting for the vertigo to disperse. Now, she recognized the creature in front of her. It was Melahar, Elborik's colt, who had not yet Chosen.

"I'm sorry, Melahar. Forgive me, I was dizzy from rolling. And I just fought a—" Mola crinkled her eyes in confusion. "What are you doing here, Melahar?" She did not expect an answer. Companions could not directly communicate with those not Gifted.

:I've come to Choose.:

"Oh." Mola looked around, trying to find the Herald lucky enough to bond with Elborik's son. She had not seen another human on the cliffs.

:Don't be stupid, Mola. I Choose you.:

:Me? You Choose me?: Only then it occurred to Mola that she had used Mind-hearing, Mindspeech.

:The clover made the Herald stronger!:

Mola pulled a handful from her pocket and looked at the drooping plants. "But I haven't even delivered it yet." The significance of the words penetrated deeper. "Charlin is better? She's better?"

Melahar reached down and gently ate the clover off of Mola's palm: *:No, Mola. I'm afraid Charlin's dead.:*

A boulder hurled at Mola's chest could not have hit her harder. *:But . . . how can that be? You said the clover made the Herald stronger.:*

:And it did, my Herald. It made you stronger.: Melahar nosed through Mola's pocket for more clover. *:Your mind channels were just open enough for me to send you the dreams. It took this journey to fully activate them.:*

Absently, Mola pulled out a huge batch of clover for her Companion and reveled in the soft touch of Melahar's nose against her hand. *My Companion. I have a Companion.* She threw her arms around the delicately arched white neck, spilling the clover to the ground. Joy beyond what she had ever known surged through Mola and, with it, an incredible sense of responsibility. *:Melahar, can you help me find Corry's knife? I need to return it.:*

Melahar whinnied. *:He said not to worry about it.:*

:He said . . . You mean he was . . . in on it?:

:They all were. I had to spread the word. Otherwise, you might have talked one of them into going instead of you.:

Mola flushed scarlet. She had tried to do exactly that.

:Corry would have done it. He's sweet on you, you know.:

The warmth spread from Mola's cheeks to the roots of her hair. Now that she had her own Companion, a relationship with him became a real possibility.

:And then the journey would not have made the right Herald stronger.:

:Me.:

:Yes.:

:I'm a Herald.: To Mola, the words seemed more like random sounds. Such a thing could not be true.

:You will be once you finish your training. I had to take a bit of poetic license.:

:And the clover. Does it really have healing properties?:

A wicked sense of excitement wafted from Melahar. *:It heals my cravings. I love that clover.:* He lowered his head to pick up the bits Mola had dropped. *:Hop on, soon-to-be Herald Mola. I sent your other mount home.:*

Mola did not need a second invitation. She scrambled onto Melahar's back, feeling like the tallest person in the world. "Home, trusty mount!"

Melahar raised his head proudly. *:There's not a bear, nor a swamp drake, that could stop us.:*

The Cheat

by *Richard Lee Byers*

Richard Lee Byers is the author of over thirty fantasy
and horror novels, including *Unclean*, *Undead*, *Unholy*, *The Rage*, *The Rite*, *The Ruin*, and *Dissolution*.
A resident of the Tampa Bay area, the setting for
much of his horror fiction, he spends a good deal of
his leisure time fencing and playing poker. Visit his
Web site at richardleebyers.com.

Falnac was nervous. I could tell by the way he kept
swallowing.

I put my hand on the lad's shoulder. "Use what we
practiced," I said. "Leap into the distance, feint to the
groin, and finish on the outside."

"Yes, Master Selden," he whispered.

"And if the two of you wind up close together, stay
there and stab like a madman. Alsagad's taller than
you. Close quarters will make him awkward."

I could have said more, but a swordsman about to
fight for his life can only retain so much advice. Indeed, given that this was Falnac's first duel, it was an
open question whether he'd remember anything I'd
just told him, or anything from his six years of lessons, either.

When they deemed the light sufficient, the seconds
called the duelists to a patch of ground where there
were no tombstones to trip them up. As they advanced, Dromis caught my eye. He was Alsagad's
fencing master as I was Falnac's, and the protocol of

dueling required that we treat one another with stately courtesy. Instead, the big man with the curling mustachios, pointed beard, and hair all dyed a brassy, unnatural yellow gave me a sneer, as if to assert that my teaching and my student were so inferior to his that Alsagad's victory was assured.

For a heartbeat, it made me want to see Alsagad stretched out dead on the dewy grass, and then I felt ashamed of myself. Like many quarrels, this one had materialized over a trifle, and any decent man would hope to see it settled by, at worst, a trifling wound.

The seconds gave the principals the chance to speak words of reconciliation, and of course, being proud young blades of Mornedealth, they didn't. So Alsagad's second whipped a white kerchief through the air. That was the signal to begin.

The duelists circled one another while waking birds chirped, a cool breeze blew, and dawn stained the river on the far side of the graveyard red. Then Falnac sprang forward.

His blade leaped at Alsagad's crotch in as convincing a feint as I'd ever seen. But the move didn't draw the parry it was meant to elicit. Instead, Alsagad simply cut into Falnac's wrist. My student's blade fell from his hand.

The seconds opened their mouths to shout for a halt, but they were too slow. Alsagad slashed Falnac's neck.

Falnac collapsed with blood spurting from the new and fatal wound. Dromis crowed and shook his fist in the air. "Yes!" he bellowed. "Yes! Yes! Yes!"

"That murdering little whoreson," I said. I reached to refill my cup and knocked the wine bottle over.

Marissa's scarred, long-fingered hand caught it before it could spill. The close-cropped hair framing her heart-shaped face was inky black in the dim candlelight of the tavern. "You're drunk," she said.

"It was murder!" I insisted.

"If no one had called the halt, then Alsagad was within his rights to keep fighting. And he was a boy, too, wasn't he, no doubt as frightened and frantic as Falnac."

"Don't bet on it. All of Dromis' pupils are arrogant and vicious."

"And yours aren't? Mine are, and thank the gods for it. Otherwise, they wouldn't pay good coin to learn to kill."

I shook my head. "There's a difference, and you know it."

"I suppose. By all accounts, Dromis himself is a ruffian, and brutish fencing masters turn out brutish swordsmen. There's no great mystery in it."

"The mystery lies in how they win duel after duel. If you'd seen that feint—"

"Yes, you said it was very pretty."

"Better than pretty. Perfect. Even you would have gone for the parry. But Alsagad didn't."

Marissa sighed. "I admit, I'd love to find out exactly what Dromis teaches that makes his disciples so formidable. Hell, I may *need* to find out to go earning a living. Students have started leaving me to study with him. I imagine it's happened to you, too."

"Now that you mention it." I took another swig of the tart white wine. "And maybe my students are wise to desert me, if I can't prepare them to defend themselves."

Marissa rested her callused fingertips on the back of my hand. "People die in duels for all sorts of reasons, including sheer bad luck. Falnac's death is sad, but it's no reflection on you."

"It is if Alsagad cheated and I didn't catch him. I'm supposed to be an expert on every aspect of dueling, including treachery and sleights."

"Is that what you think? Dromis is helping his pupils cheat?"

"They win and win and win, don't they, even when facing swordsmen with more experience. How else can you account for it?"

Marissa took a drink, then wiped her mouth on her sleeve. "I don't know. It's hard to believe that Dromis' system is really so much better than everybody else's. Maestros may claim to know secret invincible techniques—I've done it myself to drum up trade—but you and I know that's mostly rubbish. There are only so many ways to stick a blade in another man's carcass.

"But if Alsagad did cheat," she continued, "I don't see how he could have managed it except by magic, and I assume you were on guard against that."

"Yes." For a moment, reminded of its presence, I felt the round shape of the talisman beneath my shirt. It should have grown hot if Alsagad were carrying a beneficial enchantment on his person or sword, and cold if anyone had cast a curse on Falnac. "Still, I'm not a wizard. It's possible someone slipped something past me." I suddenly wanted to be sober, and took a deep breath in a futile attempt to become so. "I'm going to find out."

"Stick your nose into Dromis' business, you mean."

"Yes. If he and Alsagad conspired to deny Falnac a fair fight, then they truly are murderers according to city law, and I'll see them hang for it."

"Thus mending our tattered reputations and drawing our strayed students back to us. I like the idea in principle, and you do have a knack for solving puzzles."

Or at least I'd had some luck at it. Enough that, when people sought my services as a hiresword, a trade I still practiced from time to time to supplement the money I earned teaching, it was often as much for the sharpness of my eyes and wits as the keenness of my blade. "Why do you say you like it *in principle*?"

"Because I'm sure Dromis is at least as jealous of

his secrets as any other maestro. And if his methods empower his students to kill yours, then it's possible they would also enable him to do the same to you. So watch your back."

I tracked down Olissimal where I should have expected to find him: in the mansion of Falnac's kin. I had no doubt that, supported by his ivory crutches, he'd hovered over the boy's corpse for a long time, ogling the wounds. Now, gray eyes bright, twisted, stunted leg propped on a leather footstool, he sat in a corner savoring the more rarefied nectar of everyone else's grief.

My mouth and stomach sour from last night's overindulgence, I felt an urge to grab him and drag him out of the room, but of course that wouldn't do. Instead, I paid my respects to Falnac's parents. Who didn't reproach me, unless it was with their eyes.

Afterward, I approached Olissimal with at least a semblance of the courtesy due a scion of one of the Fifty Noble Houses. "Master Selden," he said, the corners of his crooked mouth quirking upward, "I didn't expect to see you here today. Come to collect for the boy's lessons?"

I took a breath. "I came to express my sympathy and talk to you."

"Truly?"

"If you'll favor me with a moment of your time."

"I suppose. It's just that you surprise me. You are, after all, the same fellow who called me a degenerate, forbade me to observe the classes at your academy even when I offered to pay, and threatened to whip me if I ever dared watch one of your pupils fighting a duel."

So I had. Many men who are not themselves warriors are interested in the martial disciplines, and generally that's all right. But it had always been plain to me that Olissimal's fascination rose from an underlying thirst to witness killing and mutilation, and while such passive cruelty was relatively harmless, it repulsed me nonetheless.

But now Dromis and his students concerned me more. "Help me," I said, "and I'll lift the ban. You can watch everything but the private lessons." Those were where I passed along my own "secret" techniques, inadequate as they had begun to seem.

"How generous. What sort of help do you require?"

"Nothing difficult. I'm sure you've watched many of the duels Dromis's students have fought. I want you to describe them."

He laughed, startling the mourners and offending against the solemnity of the occasion. "Trying to figure out what makes Dromis' protégés so deadly? Maybe you should have done that before you sent poor little Falnac out to fight one of them."

Once again, I clamped down on my anger. "Will you do it?"

"Oh, why not? After all, there isn't much I enjoy more than chatting about swordplay."

To give him his due, the descriptions were clear and detailed. He was observant and understood dueling as well as a man born with a useless leg ever could. After he finished, I said, "So it's mostly dodging, stop thrusts, and counterattacks. Aggressive responses to the other man's attempt to score. They seldom take the initiative, give ground, or parry."

"Exactly."

"Damn it!" I said. "Only a truly accomplished swordsman can hope to fight that way and get away with it, and even he, only when facing an inferior opponent."

"Yet Dromis' pupils invariably win. Even the novices typically fell their opponents at the end of the first exchange." He smirked as though enjoying my mystification.

"Their success aside," I asked, "do they look like prodigies?"

"No. They display the same defects of stance, balance, guard, and what have you as other students."

"Then . . ." I groped for a sensible follow-up question. "What about when they brawl in the cockpits and brothels?" Olissimal frequented such places for the same reason he haunted the dueling grounds: he hoped to see men who could walk unaided cut one another to pieces. "Are they similarly successful?"

Olissimal frowned, his pale eyes narrowing. "Now that you mention it, it's a strange thing. Unlike many other young blades, they rarely brawl, even though they're as pugnacious a lot as you'll find in the city. Whenever they give or take offense, they try to steer the dispute in the direction of a formal challenge."

"And what happens when the other fellow insists on drawing on the spot?"

"They don't display their accustomed superiority. Not consistently, at any rate." He cocked his head. "Curious. What do you suppose it means?"

"I don't know yet." I turned and left him to play the vulture.

Clad in the nondescript garments he'd borrowed from a servant, the brim of his hat pulled down to shadow his sharp-nosed face, Tregan Keenspur smiled and looked with interest at the bustling life of the street. I realized he was enjoying walking incognito among the common herd like some eccentric prince in a ballad.

That was just as well since I needed him disguised. Dressed in his normal rich attire with lackeys in attendance, a prominent noble and wizard of House Keenspur couldn't go anywhere and do anything without attracting attention. And I didn't want Dromis to learn I was making a study of him.

"That's the school up ahead," I said. "The dark green building with the rust-colored door and shutters."

Tregan cast about. "I need a place to work. I can't cast spells in the middle of the lane without somebody noticing."

"How about there?" I indicated the narrow, shaded gap between two houses. The space was a stride or two removed from the traffic, yet still afforded a view of the fencing academy.

"That should do," the sorcerer said, so that was where we went.

I kept watch and did my best to shield Tregan's activities from view as he whispered incantations and crooked his fingers into arcane signs. The mystical force accumulating in the air made me feel feverish and sick to my stomach. Then it discharged itself with a soft sound like the pattering of rain.

Tregan put his hand on my shoulder and shifted me aside to get a little closer to Dromis' establishment. The wizard's eyes now glowed with their own inner radiance, but the effect was subtle. No one could have seen it from any distance, not in the daylight, anyway.

He peered for a time, and then said, "The top floor."

"There's something magical there?"

"Yes."

"Is it Dark Magic?" If so, then Dromis' possession of it was a crime in and of itself, and my aristocratic companion was just the man to call him to account for it.

"No. I sense that the enchantment may have served a violent purpose, but it isn't Dark as the law defines the term."

I sighed. "Of course not. When were my problems ever solved as easily as that? What is it, then, exactly?"

"I can't say. Not at such a distance, with at least one wall in the way. I'm sorry, Selden. We Keenspurs owe you a considerable debt, and I fear I haven't done all that much to repay it."

"I wouldn't say that." Not out loud, anyway. "At least I know more than I did before."

"But is our discovery relevant? I still don't see how. Dromis may possess some form of magic, but if there were no mystical energies in play when Alsagad killed Falnac, how can the one thing pertain to the other?"

"That's what I have to find out. Now tell me: when was the last time you had a drink in an utterly sordid and disreputable tavern?"

Tregan grinned. "Not since I was a wild young troublemaker myself."

"Then I'll stand you one before we go back to Keenspur House."

Later, it was my turn to don a disguise. Clad in homespun with dirt beneath my nails, I became a prosperous but unsophisticated farmer from Ruvan, dazzled by his first look at Mornedealth and eager for tales of her notorious fencing academies, duels, and blood feuds. Excited enough to buy wine, spirits, and supper for any knowledgeable local willing to regale me.

As I expected, many of Dromis' students were willing; they were as given to spendthrift habits as the other young rakes of my acquaintance, and thus often out of funds even when their families were wealthy. And once I had them talking and—I hoped—drunk enough to be indiscreet, I steered the conversation to their maestro.

It turned out that before coming to Mornedealth, he'd been a soldier in Brendan, forced to flee after he killed a noble in a duel over a courtesan. Or a slaver in Ceejay, a bandit in Karse, or a zealot who wound up on the losing side in a religious war fought somewhere far to the south. It depended on who was telling the story, or, for all I knew, they could all have been true. It didn't matter. There was nothing in any of them to account for his students' extraordinary string of victories.

Nor was their description of their training any more illuminating. Dromis seemed to teach pretty much the same techniques and principles as his rivals. When a student was about to fight a duel, he worked with him intensively, but the rest of us did that, too. If he used magic to enhance the efficacy of his instruction, his pupils didn't appear to know about it.

In the end, I decided I'd wasted both my money and my time, but I told myself it didn't matter. I'd find a way to unmask Dromis' perfidy eventually.

I didn't realize I was running out of time.

The Silver Trumpet was just downstairs from my own fencing academy, and it served the best trout, perch, and crawfish dishes in Mornedealth. I ate there often, so I don't suppose it was difficult for Dromis to find me there.

I didn't know he'd come in until the room fell silent, and Marissa, my companion at my corner table, turned in the direction of the door. "Damn it!" she snarled.

I looked where she was looking. Sneering, Dromis was stalking toward me with half a dozen of his students and Olissimal following after. The cripple smirked.

I realized I'd made an error consulting him; I'd underestimated his capacity for holding a grudge. I'd hoped that by allowing him into my school, I could win back what passed for his good will, and in fact, he had answered my questions. But then he'd plainly hurried to Dromis to tell him I was making inquiries into his affairs.

"Get up and draw!" Marissa said. I'd explained to her how Dromis' protégés preferred a formal duel to an impromptu fight. Accordingly, she surmised that I'd be better off in the latter, and I suspected the same.

Still, I didn't move.

"Do it!" she urged. "Lords Pivar and Baltes are your friends! They'll keep you out of trouble with the law!"

Possibly they would. But several of my pupils were in the room. If I drew, so would they, so too would Dromis' followers, and the gods only knew who or how many would die in the melee that would follow.

And even if I could prevent such a fracas by commanding my students to keep their seats, I'd labored to teach them that combat was serious business, best avoided whenever possible. If I jumped up and hurled myself at Dromis like a starving wolf, seemingly without provocation, it would make a mockery of all my homilies and admonitions.

So I simply ate another bite of batter-fried perch and waited for the yellow-beard and his companions to reach my table.

Once he arrived, he didn't waste any time. Glowering down at me, he said, "Olissimal tells me you claim I teach my duelists to cheat."

I hadn't, not to the cripple, not in so many words. Olissimal had figured out what I suspected for himself. Still, I saw no reason to deny it. It wouldn't change what was about to happen. "That's right," I said.

Dromis' students glared and muttered.

"Then I say you're a liar." Dromis pulled a daffodil-colored leather gauntlet from his belt and slapped it down on the tabletop. I picked it up and that was that.

"Marissa will act for me," I said.

"And Olissimal for me," Dromis replied.

Olissimal's leer stretched wider. "I wouldn't miss it for the world."

Later on, it occurred to me that perhaps I should be glad Dromis had challenged me. It gave me what I wanted: a chance to avenge Falnac's death.

For after all, I was reasonably confident of my own

prowess. I'd survived three decades of warfare and duels. I'd destroyed a fire elemental and the undead warlock in the vaults under Keenspur House. It was conceivable that I could defeat Dromis, too, no matter what tricks he had in store.

But I didn't really believe it. My instincts warned me I was in desperate trouble, and the only honorable way out was to uncover Dromis' secret.

Of course, not everyone would agree that house-breaking was "honorable," but given the circumstances, I was willing to make allowances.

Skulking in the same dark, narrow space where Tregan had performed his divination, I watched Dromis' school until all the lights went out and for a candlemark thereafter. Then I tied on my mask and, hooded lantern in hand, scurried across the benighted street and around to the back of the building, where there was a secondary entrance.

I didn't know how to pick a lock—I kept meaning to learn—but I did know how to break open a door with a crowbar. I waited until I was certain no one had heard the crunching noise it made, then crept into what proved to be a kitchen.

Shining my light only when absolutely necessary and only for an instant at a time, seeking the way to the top floor, I groped through darkness. In time, I passed bedchambers and heard the snoring buzzing from within, and I'll admit, it crossed my mind that I could settle this whole affair by killing Dromis in his sleep. But that would have made me just as vile as he was, especially considering that, my suspicions notwithstanding, I didn't yet have any proof that he and his pupils were cheats.

I pulled a folding staircase down from a ceiling to reach the garret. Once there, I risked letting my lantern shine continuously. As I played the beam about, it illuminated cobwebs, dusty trunks and crates, and then something more interesting.

It was a block of dark, silver-flecked stone, about the size of a horse's head, sitting on a little table with a chair in front of it. Though I'd traveled far before settling in Mornedealth, I didn't recognize the type of mineral, nor the style of the glyphs carved into it, either. I certainly couldn't hazard a guess as to their meaning.

What I could tell was that the block was broken, some of the sigils marred or defaced. Either the artifact had fallen from a height, or someone had taken a hammer to it. And I could sense the power emanating from it, like a hum so faint that a man didn't quite realize he was hearing it.

Plainly, it was the talisman whose presence Tregan had discerned, and if he were here, playing burglar along with me, perhaps he could have told me what the magic did. In his absence, I'd have to try to discover on my own.

I sat down in the chair and inspected the block at close range. It didn't look appreciably different, nor did it react to my proximity. Warily, like a man testing the edge of a blade, I touched a fingertip to the front of it.

That one light contact was all it took. Suddenly everything vanished, including my sense of my own body. In its place there suddenly rushed a torrent of darkness that tumbled me along like a raging river. Except not exactly. But that's as close as I can come to describing the sensation.

Terrified, I reached out—not with the hands I could no longer feel, but with sheer willpower, I think—for something other than the black rapids. It worked; abruptly, the nature of my experience changed. I could still feel the current sweeping me along, but now I was more like a man floating precariously on the surface than one drowning in the depths.

As a result, I could see. Mornedealth lay far below me, as if I were a hawk floating on the wind, while the sky arched overhead.

But the sky wasn't behaving properly. It flickered from dark to light and back again in an instant, quick as the beat of a hummingbird's wing.

Then the trees dropped their leaves almost as quickly. Snow blanketed the earth, then melted away. Several new houses sprang up, the frames clothing themselves in solid walls like a man pulling up his breeches.

Frightened and befuddled though I was, I had a vague idea what was happening. The dark stone had drawn my spirit from my body. That trick was common enough that even nonmagical folk like me had heard of it. What was unusual was that in the process, it had also yanked me loose from my proper position in time. Now something—perhaps simply the inexorable momentum of time—was whisking me into the future.

I was afraid that if it carried me too far, it would prove impossible to get back. I started swimming against the current, though my struggles had nothing to do with stroking arms or kicking legs. As before, it was a matter of pure resolve.

For a while, I couldn't tell if I was making any headway. Then, for just an instant, I caught a glimpse of the room and moment from which I'd come.

Unfortunately, my body wasn't alone anymore. Dromis was creeping up behind me with a dagger in his hand.

I struggled even harder, if that was possible, and fought the pressure until I was certain the effort had taken too long. If I managed to return to my body at all, it would be to find my life gushing from a slit throat.

But evidently a man's sense of time doesn't count for much when he's already come unstuck from it as it's commonly experienced. For suddenly I had a solid form again, and it seemed unwounded. I sensed Dromis looming just behind me.

I threw myself sideways out of the chair before he could cut me. He came after me, and, sprawled on my back, I kicked at him. I connected with his knee and knocked him staggering off balance.

That gave me time to roll to my feet and draw my sword. The trouble was that when I did, the floor seemed to pitch and I nearly fell down again. My forced jaunt into tomorrow had left me weak and dizzy. I couldn't win a fight with a fellow fencing master in this condition.

I bolted down the folding stairs. Dromis took a moment to unsheathe his own sword, then gave chase.

Given a chance, he'd catch me, too. He wasn't suffering from vertigo, and he was thoroughly familiar with the layout of the lightless house.

I spied a square of lesser darkness: a window on the far side of a doorway. I charged it and crashed through the laths and oiled paper.

I fell two stories and landed hard, but when I tried to stand up again, I could. I hadn't broken anything. Apparently unwilling to trust to fool's luck as I had, Dromis didn't jump after me. I staggered away into the night as fast as I was able.

Luckily, the feebleness and dizziness didn't last long. They were gone by the time Dromis came to call at my school the next morning.

As before, he appeared with several of his students tagging along, serving as bodyguards whether they realized it or not. But he consented to leave them loitering in the main training hall while he and I sat at a table in one of the alcoves along the wall. His disciples would still see it if I attempted any violence, and he likely realized I wouldn't talk honestly about breaking into his house if anyone else was close enough to overhear.

"How's your leg?" I asked him.

"Fine. You didn't kick me that hard." He took a

breath. "I moved the stone. The City Guards can search my academy from top to bottom. They won't find a thing."

I shrugged. "Even if they did, I couldn't prove that the thing can be used to cheat at dueling, let alone that you actually have used it that way. Even though I'm sure of it."

He frowned. "What exactly is it that you think you know?"

"The talisman carries a man's spirit—and his perceptions—into the future. I couldn't control exactly where I went or what I saw. But you can, either because you know the words of command or just because you've practiced. Prior to a duel, you observe exactly how a student's opponent will behave, and precisely what the pupil does to overcome those tactics. Then you drill your fencer in the proper moves, and everything works out just as you foresaw. Magic gives him an unfair advantage even though no enchantments are active on the field of honor.

"The only limitation," I continued, "is that to guarantee victory, you have to seek revelation and provide special instruction for each individual combat. But you've minimized that problem by stressing to your charges that formal duels are always to be preferred over spontaneous bloodshed."

Dromis scowled. "I truly am a fine swordsman, and a fine teacher, too."

"If you say so."

"But since I had an edge, why not use it? How else could I achieve preeminence quickly in a city already famous for its fencing masters? You'd have done the same thing in my place."

I shook my head. "I'd use your stone or any other trick in war, but never in dueling. The code of the duel is an attempt to bring order and restraint to that which would otherwise be chaotic and bestial, and for that reason, decent men value it."

He sneered. "I've always heard that Selden is a strong man, but you think like a weak one."

"Let's not debate moral philosophy. We're not likely to reach an accord. I'm much rather hear how you came by the stone."

"All right, why not, if you're curious. When I was as young as those lads—" he nodded toward his students, "—a new creed arose in my homeland. Given the chance to flourish, it could have changed the world. But corrupt lords and false priests declared our prophet a demon in disguise, and hundreds of idiots believed them. An army marched on us when we were still too few to defend ourselves."

I remembered the stories his pupils told. "Then you really did fight on the losing side in a religious war."

He glared as if my matter-of-fact way of speaking was an insult to the exaltation and tragedy enshrined in his memory. "I survived the final battle, then returned to the temple of the prophet. The unbelievers had defaced the black stone along with everything else, but it was still a holy relic, and something about it called to me. I decided to carry it with me into exile, and when I touched it, it revealed its power to me."

"And you've no doubted cheated your way through life ever since."

"I'm tired of hearing you use that word. It's good to know that after we meet two mornings hence, I won't have to hear it anymore."

"Indeed not. You won't hear anything ever again."

Dromis laughed. "I thought you understood, Selden. You can't win. I've already watched our duel. I already know the tactics you'll employ even if you haven't yet decided on them yourself, and I know how I'll defeat them and cut you down. In a very real sense, you're already lying dead at my feet."

I found Marissa in her armory repairing a leather-and-wire-mesh fencing helmet. As she got caught up in my story, she abandoned her task and left the protective mask to lie in pieces on the cluttered worktable before her.

"I told you we should kill Dromis before the duel," she said. "Luckily, it's not too late."

"Actually, it is," I replied. "He's hiding behind a wall of his students, and he'll stay there until he comes to keep our appointment."

"In that case, go to Lords Baltes and Pivar."

"Without proof?"

"You shouldn't need it. They owe you. They're your friends."

"They're also committed to governing Mornedealth in a less arbitrary manner than their predecessors, and that's a good thing. I won't ask them to set aside their own rules of law just to save my arse."

"Then what? You can't simply refuse to fight, or people will think you a coward. No maestro or hiresword can afford that."

I felt a jab of anger. "Don't worry about that. Despite everything, I *want* to duel. I want to beat Dromis at his own rotten game and pay him back for Falnac's death." I took a breath. "And even if I didn't, the dastard has evidently seen that I show up, so perhaps I don't have a choice. Maybe, somehow, I'd wind up at the designated place and time no matter what."

Marissa made a sour face. "That's so contrary to common sense, it makes my head hurt just to think about it."

"Mine too. So why don't we try thinking like warriors?"

A dank mist blurred the mausoleums and grave markers, and the dawn was just a luminous smear on a wall of gray cloud. The birds hadn't yet begun to sing.

I'd done my best to keep Dromis' prophecy of doom from affecting my morale. But perhaps the dismal morning helped to dampen my spirits, for as we approached one another, I did indeed have the fey sense that my fate was sealed. That all that was about to happen had, in some ultimate sense, happened already.

I couldn't afford to feel like a helpless sleepwalker, so I focused on Dromis' sneer and Olissimal's gloating smirk, stoking my hatred for them both. It wasn't something I would have done ordinarily; I prefer to fight with a cool head. But in this instance, it steadied me.

We took our places, and then Olissimal said, "We, your friends, urge you to seek a peaceful resolution to your dispute." I doubted that anyone in the history of swordplay had ever made that traditional plea with such a transparent lack of sincerity.

"I do not apologize," Dromis said, "and I know for a fact that my opponent won't, either. Isn't that right, Selden?" He grinned at me as though sharing a secret jest.

"Yes," I said.

"I'll always wonder: Could you simply not accept the truth of your situation, or did your notions of honor oblige you to show up even so? Either way, you die a fool."

I looked to Marissa. "Let's get on with it."

"As you wish," she said, backing away to give Dromis and me room to fight. Shifting his crutches, Olissimal likewise hobbled clear.

Marissa then lifted a white cloth and whipped it through the air. Dromis and I started to circle one another.

Fear welled up inside me, and of course, given the life I'd led, it was scarcely the first time. But it was the first time it balked me. For a heartbeat, I couldn't attack because the craven part of me *knew* that whatever technique I attempted, Dromis would offer a perfect—and perfectly lethal—response.

I screamed a battle cry to jolt myself into motion.

I sprang into the distance, feinted to the chest, and cut to the head. Dromis ducked under the stroke and thrust at my torso as he'd surely watched himself do while using the power of the stone.

It was a nasty counterattack, but fortunately, I was ready for it. I deflected it with a heavy beat-parry that weakened his grip on his hilt, then slashed at his face.

Dromis had boasted he was a good swordsman, and it was so. Hc didn't drop his weapon, and he managed to jump back and evade my cut. But his eyes were wide with shock. Whereas I wanted to laugh, because from this moment forward, nothing about our encounter was predestined. Now it was just another sword fight.

Having experienced the turbulent power of the stone, I'd conjectured that, while Dromis had learned to use it, the process wasn't easy for him. For after all, he was a warrior, not a mystic, and, moreover, the artifact was damaged.

And if Dromis had to struggle mightily to swim through the time currents in the same way I had, then it stood to reason that he couldn't navigate to a scene he wanted to witness with any extraordinary precision. He had to flounder about until he happened across it, then fight to hold his position long enough to obtain a serviceable glimpse.

So I'd called in the favor owed me by the players of the Azure Swan Theater. On the previous morning, they, Marissa, and I had thrice staged a mock duel, with actors made up to resemble Dromis, a band of his students, and Olissimal. Each time I attacked with a feint to the chest and a cut to the head, and each time my adversary dispatched me with a stab to the body. His sword was blunt, but still capable of bursting the bladder of pig's blood concealed inside my doublet.

The idea was for Dromis's spirit, adrift in time, to observe one of the fraudulent duels and mistake it for the real one, and I admit, I've hatched schemes that inspired greater confidence. Even if all my unsubstantiated guesses were correct, there was still one chance in four that my foe had watched the actual combat. But now I knew the trick had worked.

We traded attacks, neither scoring as of yet. But as the moments passed, I felt more and more in control of the action, and he had to give ground repeatedly.

I judged that if I could stop him retreating, I could finish him, and there was a marble tomb, crowned with a statue of a dove lighting on the hand of a goddess, several paces behind him. I started the process of backing him up against it.

Then Dromis used the thumb of his off hand to rotate the gold ring on his middle finger, perhaps another keepsake he'd carried away from his cult's desecrated temple. The medallion I wore next to my skin turned icy cold, warning me of hostile magic. Unfortunately, the warning was redundant. I was able to guess that my opponent had cast a curse stored in a talisman from the way the world suddenly went black.

Acting by reflex, I parried, and steel rang as I stopped Dromis' sword. I riposted, and felt my blade cleave flesh and stick there. When Dromis fell, his weight dragged it toward the ground.

My feat was lucky, but not, I think, pure luck. Throughout the duel, I'd studied Dromis' fighting style and learned his favorite attack. Thus, even blind, I was able to defend. And when our blades met, it gave me a sense of his position. That made it possible to land a cut.

Much to my relief, my eyesight returned a moment after Dromis dropped. Blinking away a certain residual cloudiness, I checked to make sure he was dead, then pivoted to find Olissimal. I wanted to witness his dismay at his champion's demise.

But in that regard, I was disappointed. Supported by his crutches, Olissimal stood shivering with his lips parted and his eyes half closed, a picture of perverse delight. He didn't really care who'd died a bloody death, only that someone had.

I suppose no moment is perfect. But, Olissimal's bliss notwithstanding, this one came close, and tasted sweeter still when Marissa strode up to me, a rare smile of genuine admiration on her face. "Nicely done," she said.

"You have no idea," I answered.

"So what happens now? We find the black stone and try to use it to prove Dromis' duelists cheated?"

"No, because they didn't. Not knowingly. They didn't understand Dromis used sorcery to determine how they should fight. They just thought he was a brilliant teacher."

"Then I guess we're done. We can get down to the serious business of using the stone to pick winning horses."

I was reasonably certain she was joking. But since coming to Mornedealth, I'd lost a ridiculous amount of coin wagering in the hippodrome, and I confess that, just for an instant, I was tempted.

A Dream Deferred
by *Kristin M. Schwengel*

Kristin Schwengel's work has appeared in the anthologies *Sword of Ice and Other Tales of Valdemar*, *Legends: Tales from the Eternal Archives*, and *Knight Fantastic*, among others. She and her husband live near Milwaukee, Wisconsin, where she has a full-time job that, as she puts it, "pays the bills" and allows her to pursue other interests part-time, including massage therapy, gourmet cooking, and, of course, writing.

On silent feet, Laeka padded through the darkened house. Her steps wove from one side of the entrance hall to the other, her feet remembering from years of habit where each squeaky board was even when her mind had not yet fully awakened. She held her oldest boots in her hand, and her well-worn clothing barely rustled with her movements. A few hushed words with the guard at the front door, and she was outside, sitting on the front stair to pull on her boots before she stepped into the dew-damp grass.

As always, her first stop of the morning was the private corral, where the mares that were the foundation of her breeding line moved at their choice between the open outdoors and the large loose-box in the stable. Tonight the mares had slept outdoors, and soft whickers greeted her approach. She slipped the latch and walked into the corral, and the mares crowded around her, lipping at her hair and clothing, bumping their heads affectionately against her. Laeka spent a moment with each mare, cupping the wide heads in her hands and whispering to them in the Shin'a'in language that she had learned for them.

These mares were her pride, the culmination of breeding that had started with the few mares sold to her so many years ago by the Clan Liha'irden at the Shin'a'in Horse-fairs. Though she had been young, she had taken the advice of the hawk-faced Clanswoman Tarma shena Tale'sedrin, and Liha'irden had made good on the Clanswoman's promise to her. Each year, they had made sure she had the pick of what they were selling, and even a few that they would never sell to any but her, once they had seen that she valued their horses as highly as they deserved.

False dawn was starting its approach when Laeka left the corral. Taking a deep breath of the crisp autumn air, she turned toward the woods with anticipation. Her step lightened as she walked among the trees, letting the mood of the quiet forest settle into her. Her family would doubtless not approve of these early walks, but then she had never feared the woods as others did. After all, her corner of the Pelagiris was far from the wild and strange places where unknown creatures made their homes. A smile lifted one corner of her mouth, softening the deep creases formed by wind and wear. *At my age*, she thought, *I think I've earned the right to walk where I will*.

A scratching, dragging noise in the brush caught her attention, and she held herself in midstride, turning her head by slow degrees to locate the sound. As she listened, her mind sorted out the pieces of noise. An animal, large and probably injured. Laeka moved forward, keeping her own steps as silent as she could, ignoring the twinge in her right leg as she placed her feet with care.

The dragging steps ceased, and Laeka heard the soft thud of a body falling to the earth, followed by rasping, panting breaths. Shifting her direction to the right, she crept forward until she stood concealed by a great tree on the edge of a clearing. Taking shallow, quiet breaths, she prepared to crane her head behind one of the branches to see what lay in the clearing.

:I am no threat to you. I need your help.: Laeka froze, her eyes darting around her, but she saw nothing.

:Please.: The voice was fainter now, and Laeka realized that she had only heard it inside her head. She peered around the tree into the clearing. The shaggy animal slumped on the bracken, pain-shadowed eyes focused on hers, was larger than any wolf she had ever seen, despite the similar shape of its head. She guessed that it would stand as tall as her waist, if not more.

:Please.: The head sagged down, resting on two great paws. Laeka read the pain and exhaustion in both the voice and the body as it lay, its limbs crumpled beneath it. Though the structure of the body looked more feline than canine, there was no grace or ease in its movements now.

"I did not realize that *kyree* dwelled so close to this edge of the forest," she said, keeping her voice quiet and stepping into the clearing.

:Not so very close,: the *kyree* responded. *:But you were still closer than the nearest Vale.:*

"What brings you to me instead, and in such a state?" She moved over to the wounded creature, kneeling down in the dead leaves beside it.

:My cubs.: Laeka nodded. The voice had somehow *felt* female. *:Bandits found our cave, stole them, and left me for dead. They plan to sell my cubs, to make a handsome profit.:* Despite the *kyree's* exhaustion, her helpless fury rang in her mind-voice.

"They would need to travel far, I think, to find someone fool enough to buy them." Although it would bring great prestige to have a *kyree* for a pet, to do so would surely incur the anger of the Tayledras, who looked on themselves as guardians and protectors of the creatures of the Pelagiris. And the Hawkbrothers were not known for kindness to abusers of those they protected, most especially the sentient races like the *kyree*.

:Not so far as you might think. The Blood Mages are always wandering, seeking power to steal.:

Laeka's hand closed into a fist on her thigh. Yes, there were always those who would seek to take advantage of the weak, innocent, or powerless. Long, long ago, she had dreamed of taking up the sword to battle in defense of the weaker kind. She had still been young when she had learned from the Tale'sedrin Clanswoman what the reality of that life would have been and had realized that she had not the temperament for the task. It seemed that the dream, however, had slumbered on in her heart. "So, what can a half-dead *kyree* and an old horse trainer do against a troop of bandits?"

The *kyree* tilted her head at Laeka, a half-question in her eyes, for her voice had rung with determination.

:I think they mean to take them east.:

"Ruvan. Huh. There might be buyers there who do not fear the Tayledras. How far are they?"

:Not even a day to my cave. After they stole my cubs, they settled for the night only a short distance away. They'll be coming in this direction, I think, but more north.:

Laeka sat back on her heels, turning her head up to the canopy above her while she thought. With her daughter Jeatha gone to the trade fairs in Mornedealth, the stables were as lightly guarded as possible, so more outriders could travel with the string and protect the valuable animals. To take away any more guards, even for a day or two, would mean risking the entire breeding line, should the bandits come further south, and it would be foolish to send anyone but the trained guards. Foolish to send any of her people.

She stood, brushing leaves and fir needles from her

leggings. "I will be back in a little while. I promise you, we will free your younglings."

Laeka trotted back down the path, her mind making plans and as soon discarding them. In the few minutes it took her to reach the stables, she had the essence of her plan clear in her head.

"Who goes?" Meros' voice rang out as she approached, and she sighed in relief. Meros, she thought, she could talk around to her side. They had been friends for a long time, ever since the guard's ornery gray gelding (*not* one of her breeding) had bashed in her right leg. Her knee, never properly healed, throbbed at the memory. With quick words, she explained the situation and outlined her plan.

"You're a fool, Laeka. How in Agnira's name do you expect this to work?"

"Do you have a better idea? We can't just let those cubs be used by a Blood Mage."

"Send the *kyree* to the Tayledras."

"And how long do you think that will take? Why do you think she came to me, traveling ahead of the bandits instead of going in the opposite direction to the Tayledras?"

"Well, shouldn't someone else go instead of you? Or at least take someone with you."

"Who else should go? The *kyree* will recognize me, at least. Who else could be spared? Certainly not any of the guards. Duty roster's thin enough already, with Jeatha gone with the outriders. Unlike the other trainers and horsefolk, I at least have a little bit more than the rudiments of training with the sword. It's not so far-fetched as you think."

Meros looked at her long and hard in the growing light, then finally nodded. "I'll help you gather what you'll need."

The sun was not even fully risen when Laeka returned to the forest, this time mounted on the intelligent coppery mare that was her favorite, the lead lines of another mare and a gelding tied to the pommel of her saddle. She wore a leather jerkin and breeches now, and a sword hung at her side. It was an unfamiliar weight, a reminder of the reality of what she was attempting. When she practiced with the horses that would be sold to fighters, she never actually bore the weapons for very long.

The *kyree* had not moved from the clearing, although she sat half up on her side when Laeka approached. Dismounting, Laeka dug a small jar and a larger, wrapped package from one of her saddlebags and came forward to the *kyree*. In the stronger light, she could see the matted blood in the animal's fur and was glad she had made sure to bring the jar.

"I brought food and some of our strongest healing ointment for you," she said, unwrapping the raw meat and laying it on the ground before opening the jar. "It will only take a few minutes to apply, and you will be much the better for it." While the *kyree* ate, Laeka used swift, gentle strokes to spread the sharp, clean-smelling salve over the barely healed cuts and gashes, kneading it into the muscles where she noticed swelling. Even as she worked, she could see the *kyree* lifting her head, becoming more alert as the pains eased.

"Now, can you stand and walk, even just a few steps?"

:Thank you, yes. The rest has been good.: The *kyree* shifted her legs beneath her, then pushed to her feet, swaying only slightly.

Laeka stood and walked over to the horses, pulling at the lead line on the chestnut gelding to bring him to where the *kyree* stood. He shied at first from the strange scent, then quieted, and Laeka noticed a look of concentration in the *kyree's* eyes.

:It is only to get past their first fear.:

Laeka nodded her understanding of the *kyree's* manipulation of her animals' minds. "Speed is more important." She gestured, and the gelding bent his knees and folded halfway to the ground. With Laeka's guidance, the *kyree* walked over and climbed onto the gelding's lowered back, settling herself on the pad that Meros and Laeka had rigged onto the gelding's saddle. One hand on the *kyree* to steady her, Laeka tugged at the gelding's bridle, and he rose back up.

Remounting her mare, Laeka turned to look into the *kyree's* eyes. "Where?"

:West, and north after a bit. I will recognize the path I took.:

Laeka nodded and tightened her knees. The mare headed out at an easy jog, and the other two horses followed into the deeper forest.

For a long time, they rode in silence through the twisting deer paths, alternating periods of walking with a loping run. It would never match the ground-eating pace of purebred Shin'a'in horses, but she had bred the best of the mares she had acquired from Liha'irden to the strongest stallions she could find to replicate that trait. She noted landmarks as the horses moved deeper into the Pelagiris Forest, marking them in her mind just in case.

Each time the *kyree* Mindspoke to her to change their direction, her Mind-voice seemed stronger, but still tinged with anger and pain. Laeka ate waybread in the saddle, bringing the gelding up next to her mare to place some on the saddlepad for the *kyree*, who gulped it down whole.

Early in the afternoon, they came upon a small clearing where traces of recent occupation remained. New scorch marks blackened a long-disused fire-circle, and the grass was freshly cropped. Laeka dismounted to examine the area more closely, stretching her leg as her knee protested the long candlemarks in the saddle.

:The smell is still fresh.: The *kyree's* nose wrinkled as she sifted the air. *:My cubs were here, and not long since.:*

"Perhaps they stopped for nooning." She walked the perimeter of the clearing, her eyes following the patterns of crushed grass. Bending, she pushed some branches aside and found several clear hoofprints. "They're heading almost due east, now. Definitely going toward Ruvan."

She swung into the saddle on the other mare, a dark gray, absently rubbing her knee as she settled herself and turned the horses east. The *kyree* kept her head up, her nostrils flared in the breeze, seeking the scent of her cubs or the men who had taken them. As the afternoon wore on, traces of both became more frequent, and Laeka kept the pace slow, not wanting to either lose the trail or alert the bandits.

:Stop.: Laeka pulled up the gray and turned to her companion. *:They are very close. I smell smoke, too.:*

"They must be making camp for the night. We will wait until they are settled, then move in. We could not take them all, so we must be sure to act when few of them are able to respond. We need only a few moments to get to the cubs and then flee." The *kyree* bared her teeth in a silent snarl, clearly unwilling to be so cautious, but Laeka held up her hand. "My abilities with the sword will not stand a true test, and you are still injured. Full revenge will gain us nothing, and could lose us much."

She dismounted and flipped the reins of the gray mare over her ears, so they hung down to the ground. The mare stood for a moment, then bent her head and cropped at the rich grass. Leaving her, Laeka moved over to the gelding, gesturing for him to kneel as he had before. This time, the *kyree* required no aid to jump off the saddlepad, only holding up her left foreleg as she landed. Again, Laeka pulled out some meat for the *kyree*, who settled to feed while she tended to the horses. She loosened the saddle girths, reaching underneath the tack to test for swelling or heat, running her hands down each of the horses' legs, checking their hooves. When the horses were as comfortable as she could make them, Laeka retrieved the jar of salve, returning to the *kyree* and reapplying the ointment. The wounds seemed to have improved after the day of travel, not worsened as she would have guessed. Laeka raised her eyebrows but kept her silence. The *kyree* had Healers of their own, after all.

:I will scout their camp,: the *kyree* said. *:Even wounded, I can move more quietly and in smaller places than you. And I will know their thoughts.:* Laeka nodded, and the *kyree* stood, shaking herself and stretching, then trotting into the underbrush with only a little stiffness in her stride.

Dusk was beginning to settle when the *kyree* slipped back into the clearing, sitting on her haunches in the bracken.

:They are confident. Only one guard sits to the south edge, looking toward where they will meet their buyer at the main road tomorrow. There is a tent, where most of them sleep. My cubs are in a woven cage to the east, just on the other side of the fire. One bandit sleeps on each side of the cage.: The *kyree* paused, then bared her teeth in a fiercely lupine grin. *:They are mine.:*

"Their horses?"

:Loosely hobbled in a separate clearing. Unguarded.:

Laeka smiled. "We'll take care of them first."

Laeka went back to her horses, tightening the saddle girths and fastening the stirrups securely up underneath the saddles. She untied the lead lines from the two mares, flipping their reins back and tying them to the pommels so that they would neither constrict the horses' movements nor drag and catch in the brush. She pulled the rigged saddlepad off the gelding's saddle, stowing it in one of the saddlebags that she had filled with meat for the *kyree*, and mounted. She held out her hand, and the two mares followed the gelding into the trees as surely as if she still held lead lines.

She kept the pace slow, letting the horses choose their way carefully, guiding them where the grass was still soft and avoiding brush and deadfall that would give away their approach. The *kyree* moved noiseless through the trees, a shadow in the twilight.

:Over the crest of this hill. The horses are in the clearing on this side.:

Laeka dismounted, ground-tying the gelding with his reins as she had earlier, then slipped into the trees behind the *kyree*, moving toward the bandits' horses with steps as quiet as she could make them. While the *kyree* stayed downwind in the trees, she walked into the clearing, speaking to the horses in the soft whistling words she had learned from the Shin'a'in. A few of the animals chuffed nervously, but she soothed them with gentle hands on their necks. Working quickly, always keeping the bodies of the animals between herself and the camp, she used her boot knife to slit the hobbles. When all the horses were untied, she backed out of the clearing.

Mounting the gelding again, Laeka loosened the sword in its scabbard and looked down at her strange partner.

"Well," she whispered, "we'll never have a better chance, *hai*?" She shook out the reins and gestured to the two mares, then kneed the gelding into a run, over the crest and straight through the center of the bandit camp. With an eerie howl, the *kyree* followed her.

As she passed the lone guard, Laeka lashed out with her sword, catching him on the side of his head and neck. He slumped to the ground, and she tried not to notice the spray of blood that spattered her arm and the side of the horse. Somehow it was very different from the cow's-blood–filled bags she and her trainers used when sword practicing with the horses that, like the gelding, would be sold to fighters.

While she moved through the bandit camp from

south to north, followed by the galloping mares, the *kyree* darted off to the side. Laeka heard a cry of alarm cut off with a gurgle and knew that the *kyree* had dispatched one of the guards by the cubs.

She kept the horses moving through into the darkening trees on the other side of the camp, then turned to the west, repositioning herself for another pass through the bandits' midst. Her angle brought her to the clearing where the thieves' horses had been hobbled, but the startled horses fled at the noise of her charge. She smiled grimly to herself. If there were pursuit, it would be slow. She tightened her knees, and the gelding and mares headed back into the camp.

This time, two of the bandits, who had been sleeping on the ground near the fire, were standing and searching the trees surrounding the camp, swords drawn; but with most of their armor set to the side, she simply ran them down, using the horses' bodies and hooves as weapons. On the other side of the fire, the *kyree* had set her back to the cubs' cage, defending them with all the fury Laeka had heard in her Mind-voice. She could see a body on each side of the cage, but two more of the bandits approached the *kyree*, and she would not be able to account for both of them. Laeka guided the gelding to leap over the fire, pulling up behind one of the men with a swing of her sword at his exposed back. His companion glanced over at him, startled, as he fell, and that moment was all the *kyree* needed.

Laeka dismounted and ran to the cage. The men her horses had run down were struggling to their feet, one leaning over to aid the second. The noise had also roused the sleepers in the tent, and she heard shouts and thrashing inside the canvas. With surprise no longer on her side, she had no desire to test her rudimentary skills against more foes. Grabbing the cage, she hoisted it onto the copper mare's saddle, using the lead line to lash it into place. Pulling herself back into the gelding's saddle, she gestured to the mares. The *kyree* snarled at the men, but when Laeka and the horses moved out of the clearing, she followed.

"Are you able to skirt back, to see if they mount a pursuit?" Laeka tried to pitch her voice so only the *kyree* would hear.

For answer, the *kyree* melted into the underbrush.

Thankful for the near-full moon, Laeka pushed the horses in the darkening forest, putting distance between them, the remaining bandits, and the buyer. Finally, she pulled up in one of the clearings where they had rested late in the afternoon. A small creek ran along one edge, and she led the horses to drink while she cleaned her sword and refilled her waterskins.

:One stays with the injured. They found several of their horses, but we have a good lead,: the *kyree* Mindspoke, coming into the clearing behind her. *:One is a passable tracker, so I took some time to muddle the trail. If we walk in the stream for a while, that should throw him enough that we can get a little rest tonight.:*

Laeka swallowed her sigh, rubbing her knee a little bit before swinging up into the gray mare's saddle. "Then we ride, as long as we have the moon to guide us. The creekbed does not seem too full of stones, so the horses should be safe enough if I let them choose their own pace."

:I will go ahead a bit, to find a place to spend a night.: The *kyree* stepped into the water and started to wade downstream, and Laeka nudged the horses to follow. She allowed the horses to pick their way carefully, to find the best footing, and it wasn't long before the *kyree* had vanished ahead of them. Try though she might, Laeka could hear no sign of pursuit. *Not that I could hear much over our splashing in the stream, anyway,* she thought.

The moon's light was waning when the *kyree* returned, pacing them along the farther bank of the creekbed. *:I have found a shelter. Follow me.:*

The horses were clearly relieved to be out of the creek; the chestnut gelding almost seemed to shake the water from his hooves as he stepped onto the bank. Not too far into the forest, there was a thickening of undergrowth, but the *kyree* led her down a twisting path that avoided the worst thorns. They broke through into a tiny clearing, just large enough for the three horses. One edge was marked by a giant treefall, and the lower half of the tree had rotted away to form a natural half-cave.

Immediately after dismounting, she pulled the cage from the copper mare's saddle, using her knife to work at the knots that held the cage together until the top came off. Silent until now, the cubs spilled out, swarming over their mother with excited yips and Mindspeech so enthusiastic they even broadcast it to Laeka.

Laeka smiled as she stripped the horses' tack, then poured water from her waterskins into the clever folding leather trough she had acquired from the Shin'a'in and held it up to each thirsty muzzle. When they had drunk their fill, she readied them for the night, wiping them down, rubbing salve into cuts and scrapes, lavishly praising them in Shin'a'in while the ebullient cubs' Mindspeech washed over her.

:*Where did you find the lady? Why is it only her? Wasn't she brave? Will we go back to the cave? Will they come after us? Will you make this into a tale, just like the stories of our famous cousin Warrl? Will you tell us everything so we can tell it to everyone?*:

Most of the Mindspeech was in one bright voice, and Laeka looked to identify the speaker in time to see his mother put her paw over his small body, gently pinning him to the ground.

:*Rris, that is enough. Now is not the time.*:

:*There's always time for stories. Please?*:

Still holding the pup down, the *kyree* raised her head and gave Laeka a long-suffering look, one so elementally maternal that the woman had to hide her laughter in the copper mare's shoulder. When she had regained sobriety, she turned back to them.

"We should be ready to ride with the first light of dawn, little one, so you must rest. As must I, and your mother, and the horses." The pup stared up at her with fascination.

:I heard you speaking Shin'a'in. How do you know it? Are you a fighter? How far to your home?:

Laeka resisted the urge to roll her eyes. "I will tell you tomorrow, and I will even tell you how I once *met* your famous cousin Warrl, but I will *only* tell you if you sleep now." If a creature with the face of a wolf could look awed, this one managed. He stared deep into her eyes, as though trying to either read her intent or impose his own, and she folded her arms and stared back at him. *I am a mother with a daughter long grown*, Laeka thought. *You, little one, don't stand a chance.*

Whether the pup heard her thoughts or not, he curled up with his littermates in blessed silence.

Laeka took the saddlepad that the *kyree* had ridden on, unfolding it on the ground to make a sort of bed-roll and lay down, willing herself to wake before dawn. She did not see the measuring gaze that the *kyree* gave her before she, too, lowered her head to rest.

Morning seemed to come mere moments after they had made their camp, and Laeka woke to the first birdcalls before dawn. She stretched experimentally, biting back groans as her every muscle protested the treatment it had received in the last day. It took several moments before she felt sufficiently limber to stand and begin to ready herself to travel again.

She opened the last saddlebag, pulling out the last of the meat that she had packed the day before and placing it before the *kyree* and her cubs. The *kyree* pushed several of the smaller pieces to the little ones before bolting the rest. The cubs, too, ate quickly, and it seemed that the cold predawn light had diminished their spirits, as well.

Laeka could well share their mood. *An adventure is only grand while it is exciting, with swordplay and horses and firelight*, she thought. *After a cold, damp night on the hard ground, it is difficult to be enthusiastic.*

While Laeka tended to the horses, saddling them and rigging the extra pad on the chestnut gelding's saddle, the *kyree* slipped out of the clearing. *:I will see if we are pursued. Travel west, and I will find you. The cubs* will *cooperate with you.:* The little ones ducked their heads a little at that last, especially the garrulous Rris, so Laeka knew that she was not the only one to hear it.

She watched until the *kyree* was out of sight in the underbrush, then finished preparing the horses before turning back to the cubs.

"I do not wish to force you to this," she said to them, "but I think that for speed you must be in the cage."

Rris, however, nodded. *:We thought we would have to. But* you, *we trust.:* They clambered into the cage, and Laeka again secured it tightly to the saddlepad. This time she arranged it with the door-lashing to the top and left it uncovered so the cubs could lift their heads over the edge.

Loosely fastening the lead line of the gelding to the gray mare's saddle, and the gray's line to the copper mare's saddle, she mounted the copper mare, stifling a grunt as she forced her leg to stretch over the horse's back. Settling herself, she shook out the reins.

They had barely found a game trail to the west when the *kyree* came down the path behind them in a leaping gait. A pulled step and shortening of stride on the left side were the only signs that the injuries of the day before were still present. *:The pursuit is* *closer than I thought. I will go back and blur the trail again—at least they do not have dogs to track by scent. I do not think we are too far from your home.:*

Laeka studied the brush around them and did a quick calculation in her head. "A few marks, perhaps a little more at this pace."

:They smell of greed and desperation. They are hungry for the wealth, and maybe fear the anger of their buyer. But I think they would be more afraid to be caught.:

"They will not come too close to signs of settlement. We will move, then." The *kyree* disappeared back into the brush, and Laeka kneed the mare out of her easy fast-walking pace. She urged the horse to take the forest paths as fast as she dared—with their Shin'a'in blood, her horses would be faster and more surefooted than any of the bandits' animals.

For a mark or more, they ran, until Laeka could feel the copper mare's stride beginning to shorten. Her breathing was still even, though, and her coat was not yet completely sweat-darkened. Glancing back, she saw that the less burdened gray and the chestnut gelding were still running smoothly. The next time the *kyree* ghosted along the path beside them, Laeka spoke to her.

"The horses need to rest a bit. How close behind us are they?"

:We have gained ground, but not as much as I would like. A short rest, though, we can spare.:

The game trail had been following a creek, and Laeka slowed the horses at a point before the path split, one fork angling deeper into the forest. She urged them to stand in the shallows to cool their hooves and forelegs, dismounting in the water herself to check their harness and quickly brush at the sweatiest spots with the extra saddlepad. With their Shin'a'in-bred intelligence, she could trust the horses to wait until they had cooled a bit to drink, and not to drink so much as to bloat their stomachs and make themselves sick.

Too soon, Laeka led the horses out of the water and mounted up, this time astride the gray mare. *Well, I've thoroughly ruined these boots*, she thought with a sigh. *By the time we get back, the water will have soaked them beyond repair. Not to mention what cold, wet leather after a night outdoors might do to my health. If all I get is a nasty cold, I'll consider myself lucky.*

Taking the bend of the game trail deeper into the forest, she kept the horses at a slower pace while she studied their surroundings, finding the triple-leaved plants that only grew in the Pelagiris around where she had built her stables. This trail should connect, then, with one that crossed the road to her steading. Even if the bandits tracked them to the road, she thought the pursuit would end once they neared populated areas.

A faint echo of a surprised shout startled her—she guessed it was close to where they had rested. And they had not hidden which fork of the trail they had taken. The path widened, and she bent forward over the mare's neck, urging her into a steady canter, the *kyree* falling behind them. The soft pounding of hooves on grassy sod filled her ears, the mare's mane lashed her face, and a strange exhilaration swelled up within her. So this was what adventuring felt like! The horses behind her, the frightened cubs, the *kyree* mother all vanished from her head, drowned by this wild delight. She wasn't even aware of guiding the mare out of the woods until they were on the road and the sound of the hoofbeats changed. Still entranced by the strange joy, she pushed the mare to a full gallop, thrilling to the rise and fall of each stride and the power of the horse beneath her.

Only when they rounded the last corner and approached the fenced areas and the guardhouse did she ease back in the saddle, bringing the mare down to a canter, a trot, a walk.

The guard on duty hailed them but recognized the horses and Laeka almost in the same breath. The cubs stayed hidden in the cage, and when Laeka glanced back, she saw that the *kyree* appeared a great deal smaller and more doglike. Smothering a smile, she nodded to the guard, ignoring the question in his face.

She took the horses to one of the farther corrals— shamefacedly making use of the block to dismount on the way there and nearly losing her feet anyway. Meros appeared out of nowhere, and she was silently grateful for his aid as they pulled down the cage, placing it in a nearby tack shed before unsaddling the spent horses and brushing them down, their only words soft murmurs of praise to the horses.

When the horses were finally made comfortable, Meros walked to the stable, his arms full of sweat-laden tack while Laeka went back to the shed.

The *kyree* had gathered her family, ready to return to the forest.

"Will you be safe?" Laeka murmured.

:We cannot go to our cave, but I know of another place where we can stay until the little ones are more grown and able to travel longer distances. Foolishly, I had wanted to live away from the Pack, but . . : She tilted her head towards the cubs. *:I believe I shall rejoin them.:*

"Fair travels to you then, and may Agnira watch and bless you and yours."

:And the same to you and yours.: The *kyree* turned and herded her pups ahead of her, crossing the pasture toward the woods. Just before they slipped under the fence and between the trees, she looked back.

:I am Rheena, of the Hyrrrull Pack. I name you Friend to the Pack, for we are in your debt. We shall return to repay our debt.: She turned again and nudged the cubs before her.

:And I still want to hear how you met Cousin Warrl.: The plaintive Mind-voice drifted back from the tree-line, and Laeka laughed aloud as she walked stiffly back toward the house. *A hot bath*, she thought, *as hot as I can stand it. I haven't ridden like that in many years—and there's a reason for that.*

Passing the private corral, Laeka paused while the brood mares pushed against the fence in front of her, their eager noses stretched out for her strokes and gentle scratches. It was good to know that she had helped save the *kyree's* cubs. But it was better to be home again.

The Sword Dancer

by Michael Z. Williamson

Michael Z. Williamson was born in the United Kingdom and raised in Canada and the U.S. A twenty-three-year veteran of the U.S. Army and U.S. Air Force combat engineers, he is married to a reserve Army combat photographer who is also a civilian graphic artist. They have too many cats and two children who have learned how to fight anything, including zombies, from the age of four.

Riga Gundesdati, called Sworddancer, swigged from her bottle and pushed her helmet back on. Tendrils of flaxen hair obscured her eyes until she pushed them under the sweat-soaked leather padding.

All the students were working especially hard. Swordmistress Morle was watching, and some Herald from far Valdemar stood at the Yorl's spot, studying them.

"Fight!" called the judge. Her new opponent, Ruti, looked nervous, so she charged.

"Yaaaaaah!" she shouted, and he hesitated. She swung her wooden practice sword and dropped her wrist, aiming for his thigh. He blocked and leaped, defensive, cautious, and timid. This fight was over, even if he didn't know it.

A twist of her hips and shoulder brought her shield up against his swing. His blow was firm enough but without heart. She blocked it easily. His next strike was better placed, but he hadn't yet realized that her

162

presented stance—sword foot forward instead of shield foot—gave her longer reach.

With his third swing she had his rhythm. She shot her arm forward, pivoted at the hip, swung, snapped her wrist, and laid timber between his shoulder and helmet. A loud *crack* indicated what would be a killing strike in battle, and she cocked her arm for a followup before he realized he'd been hit. He stepped back and bowed out.

She bowed in return and stepped out of the rope-edged vollar. She'd won three of five bouts so far.

Father was waiting, and she smiled. He took her in a huge hug. When young she'd complain about him squashing her, and he'd bellow, "I like squashing you!" He was getting on in years, but he was still tough and muscular.

He stepped back and kept hold of her shoulders.

"I already saw Erki. I'm called for a scout ride. I should be back in a week. Meanwhile, take care of Erki and ask the Swordmistress if you need help."

Whatever was happening was huge. She kept the sob she felt to a sigh and hugged him close, hampered by leather and iron.

"Yes, Father," she said.

"Good luck, girl. I'll watch one bout. Show me your form."

She nodded and hugged him again, then redonned her helmet and got in line.

Ten youths about her age were here today, having finished their letters and numbers. All the children learned to fight, even if they might go from here to pursuits like counting, textiles or motherhood. They were sea- and river-borne tradespeople and often had to fight attackers.

She wrapped up her musing because she was next. At a wave, she entered the vollar. Her opponent was Snorru, two years her elder, just now a man, big and proud, but he sometimes hesitated, worried about his appearance.

"Sworddancer and Strongarm. Honor having been given, *fight!*"

"Go, Riga!" her father shouted, then was silent. Coaching from the rope was not allowed, and he never had. He gave her her own mind, and she loved him for it.

Riga strode straight across the vollar, shield up and sword ready. Snorru swung, and it was accurate and strong. She deflected it, but it staggered her. His follow-up blow cracked on her shield and skinned her helmet.

She recovered, hiding behind her shield as she brought her sword up in front with a snap. The tip slapped Snorru's wrist. His grip slipped and his weapon fell, as she swung up and around, cracked him in the back of the helmet, then his kidneys, then over into his chest. Her joints were trained to impart all their energy in a moment. He staggered down under the rain of blows.

"You could hit harder," he said, rising and breathing hard, "but I grant you style."

"Harder is better only so it breaks armor," she replied. "Undirected force is wasted." She offered a hand to him, and he took it.

She turned to find her father's smile . . . but he was gone. He'd known she'd be occupied with the bout, and he snuck out. She sighed. He was an honest but shrewd merchant, and that was so like him.

"He saw you," her friend Karlinu said from the rope.

"Kari?"

"He left just moments ago. He saw your bout and grinned to split his face. That was great, girl! But you need to keep your tip higher when in guard."

She knew that was a problem with her form, but she pushed Kari aside, hoping for a glimpse of Father.

"He's gone. I'm sorry. And the Swordmistress wants to see you."

She glanced at the youth vollar where Erki was working on his form. He was too eager, brave but incautious. Good with a sword, but his shield tended to drop.

She doffed her helmet, shimmied from her mail and left it in a neat pile near her cloak. Her real sword came with her, slung and ready. No warrior went without a weapon. She held the dressy bronze-tipped scabbard as she jogged. It was chased, with a falconeye jewel and a silver appliqué of a cat, its tail knotted about it. The plain fighting sword within was steel fitted with unadorned bronze around a chatoyant wood grip. She and Erki had fine blades. She tried to be worthy of hers.

Riga entered the Swordmistress's tent at the field edge. She always felt nervous facing her teacher, as if there was something she would be chastised for. Nothing came to mind as an infraction, so she put it aside. Her sweaty gambeson didn't help her nerves.

Not only Swordmistress Morle but also the visiting Herald were within. She bowed first to her Mistress, then to the guest. She faced Lady Morle but turned so she could study the Herald. He was tall, handsome, and very well dressed. His outfit was plain with just a touch of piping, but well fitted and spotless. He looked like something from a royal court.

She'd only heard mentions of Heralds, but they were highly regarded. This one had arrived a few days before, escorting a High Priest. He wasn't one for any of the Kossaki gods, so he'd been made welcome as a guest.

Riga had no idea what had come about. The elders and her father, seemed aware of these Heralds and the priest and were unbothered. Now, though, her father had ridden off, as had most of the men and some of the women, all those trained and able to ride.

"Sworddancer, you must guide a party," the Swordmistress said.

"I am honored," she replied at once. Honored and scared. At sixteen, she was a capable fighter and skilled, but lacked the wiles and polish of her elders. She flushed hotter than she already was, then chilled.

"You hide your nerves well," Morle said with a grin. She continued more seriously. "I don't ask this lightly. A great many people need us."

"I'll do what I can," she agreed. They were asking an adult task.

"Then look at this map."

Morle unrolled the scraped vellum across her table and pointed.

"We're here," Riga indicated. "Little Town is there."

"Yes. And there are refugees down here." Morle indicated the south. "The villages south of Paust Lake are being sacked and destroyed by Miklamar's thugs."

Riga understood. "They're fleeing. We can't support them in our lands, and we must hurry them through in case we need to defend our own borders. We also don't want the attention they'd bring."

"Very perceptive," the Herald spoke at last. "I'm impressed."

"Thank you, my Lord," she replied, meeting his eyes and trying not to be shy, "but I've studied since I was four. A map and supply count tell me all I need to know.

"I will lead youths, I presume?" she asked of Morle. "I can't imagine I'm to lead senior warriors."

"A youth," Morle replied, and Riga gulped. "This is scouting, not fighting. There are thousands of refugees, and we're not a large outpost."

They weren't even truly an outpost, Riga groused. Gangibrog, meaning "Walking Town," was a glorified camp with little besides docks. Nor would the local resources permit it to become much larger. They were a trading waystop. River barges came from the coast; lighters went across Lake Diaska to rivers inland. Her family had traded widely; then Father retired here to raise them after their mother died.

"May I take my brother?" she asked. "He's strong and sharp when he listens."

"And you're loud and bossy when he doesn't," Morle chuckled. "Why him?"

"Because if he has to go with someone, he'll feel safer with me, and he'll make me feel better if not safer."

"Ordinarily not. But you're right. I've allowed each party five coins in supplies. Any others must come from your own hus. I wish I had better news."

"I'll manage. Who'll watch our hus?"

"Someone will, I promise. I know you have no mother or sister, Riga. Hurry to Arwen and leave as soon as you can. She has your directions."

"Yes, Mistress." She bowed to both and left.

It was exciting and scary. Guiding wasn't like war. However, two youths going into hostile territory made her guts twist. She might be trained as a warrior, but everyone understood that women guarded the hus and family. They were defenders, not campaigners, except in emergencies.

Erki was waiting, his gear a jumbled heap as usual.

"Erki, neaten that up and move your helm before someone steps in it!" she commanded. Not only that, but it would rust if left on the damp ground.

"I forgot!" he said. "Did you see me beat Sammi?" He grabbed his stuff quickly.

"No, but good. He's a stone larger than you. Did Father see you?"

"Yes, he's off on a ride."

"We're going, too, by ourselves. You have to do as I say."

"I'll try! Where are we going?" He almost jumped in glee. The boy never held still.

"We're guiding refugees and I'm not sure yet. You'll do more than try, too. This is real."

"I'll pack Trausti, then," he said.

"Excellent idea. Keep a list."

"Yes, Riga." He took off at a sprint. He'd do that well, she knew. He was bright if impetuous, very much "boy."

She headed for the river and bounded down the floating dock to check on their current workers. Most of them were off riding, too, with boys and old men shifting cargo from a barge to a lighter. The whole town was responding, and fast.

At their hus, she decided the fire was low enough to ignore, then fastened the place down for a trip or storm. Window shutters, back door, hang everything on hooks or shelves away from walls and floor, valuables into a chest in a stone hole under a bench. Then pack light. Blessi was a small horse and wouldn't take more than Riga's weight in cargo. Eir would manage more, since Erki was smaller. Trausti would have only supplies.

Erki could pack well, sometimes too well. She caught him stuffing extra clothes into the pack saddle.

"Good idea, but too much weight," she said. "One change is all. We'll have to hope to air out."

"I already checked and oiled their hooves," he said.

"Good," she agreed. "I'll be back. Get finished, please."

She hurried down the planked timber street to Arwen's warehouse. "Auntie" was good to all of them. She usually found a way to sneak some treats to the children.

"Auntie Arwen, I'm here for supplies," she said as she walked through the open door. The plank-built store was nothing but shelves, neat stacks and crates inside. Traders weren't impressed by pretty presentations.

"Good morning, Riga. You, too? All our fighters are called, even youth. It worries me."

"I need some supplies. Is there spare?"

"Not much. The Corl came first, then others. It seems all who will be left are children, the old, some craftspeople. Even the smiths and tanners have their armor and bows." She pointed at her own panoply. Her blades and armor were well-worn and patinaed with decades of use. Her age had slowed her, but she was still capable. Riga had beaten her once. Arwen had then spanked her buttocks with the flat, to keep her modest.

"That's why I'm called, then," Riga decided. It wasn't flattering to be needed rather than wanted. "I've packed us down to ten stone of essentials, with water."

"Do you have your stuffed bear?" Arwen asked with a faint smile.

Riga blushed, because she did. Mother had made it for her long ago. She said nothing.

"Oh, child, take the toy. It weighs little, and if it offers comfort, it hurts nothing. You can't take a cat or dog."

"I'd like to take signal birds."

"So would everyone. I have two left, both young and not the best."

"They'll fit right in, then," Riga said in self-deprecating humor.

"You plan better than half the men in camp, girl. A dozen I saw without gloves. 'Just a couple of days,' they said. Aye, and it'll be cool those days, and colder at night."

"I'll need extra travel rations, in case of delay. We won't have time for hunting."

"That I have. Thrice-baked biscuits, hard cheese, honeyed nuts, and smoked meat. It'll bind up your guts, but you won't be hungry. Or rather, you'll have to be to eat it." Arwen dragged two prepared bundles over.

"I'm told I'm too picky about my food, anyway. This might help my reputation."

"Only so long as you don't come back half-starved," she chuckled.

"That would be my brother." Erki was finicky beyond belief. Meat and bread were all he would eat, given the chance.

"Ah, I'll talk to him before you leave. I'll fix that."

"Do you have any shooting stars?" she asked.

"One per party. Your colors are purple and green, yes?" She turned and mixed powders and stalk, tamped the end, and sealed it with wax. "Though it'll only help if there's someone nearby."

Shortly, Trausti had a camp pack with food, the birds and shooting star, three large water jugs, the sundries. Their riding horses were trimmed to move fast. If it came to that, poor Trausti was in trouble.

Riga wore her sword high on her side; a brace of javelins and a spear rode up behind her with her bowcase and a capped quiver of arrows. She wore a large knife at her belt, a small one in her boot. A broad round shield, iron bossed, covered the pack over Blessi's rump; the edges of her mail and bedding peeked out, with her helm mounted atop.

Her fighting clothes were masculine, a thigh-length tunic and trews. The heavy cloth was a luxuriant, comfortable weave that would stop the whipping wind. Her family might have money, but they didn't waste it, so the clothes were repaired and patched, multiply over knees and elbows. Her boots were calf high and well worn, hard enough for riding, soft enough for walking or fighting. She hoped the dull fabric made her look a bit worn and experienced.

Erki only looked like a boy. He carried a sword with bone and wood fittings, the scabbard carved with beasts and tipped in bronze. He had no spear, just a bow, and only the one knife. His garb, like hers, was fine but well worn. Eir was a pony at best, but Erki handled him surely.

An hour later they were riding, leading Trausti behind them at a fast walk. They each had a pannier of oats to supplement forage. The horses weren't the massive chargers of warrior lords, but sturdy beasts used to skirmish and short rations, not to mention shipboard travel.

Riga kept glancing at her map. It wouldn't make things move faster, but it was a nervous habit. She'd never gotten lost, though, so she didn't plan to change.

"There's Acabarrin," Erki said, peering over. "Why do the refugees have to leave?"

She sighed. She wasn't sure of the politics herself, certainly not enough to explain them to another child. She hated the subject, but her father was the town teacher. He insisted relations between countries and groups were the key to trade, war, even happiness. She thought he exaggerated on the latter.

"You've heard of Miklamar. He wants their land."

"Why doesn't he just trade? Ships come from the Black Kingdoms, all over the seas. Why waste money on a long campaign?"

She sighed. The boy was right, and wiser than some adults.

"He doesn't think that way," she said. "No, I don't know why," she added, before he could ask. "He wants everything."

"The way I used to take all the biscuits and make you come and get them? Because I was afraid of running out?"

"That could be," she agreed. It very well could be. "That would make him as mature as a five-year-old." With some of the more gruesome stories she'd heard, that also made sense. It wasn't comfortable to think of adults being so immature.

They stopped talking except to coax the horses through puddles in the terrain, still ice-skinned from the chill night. Anyone without gloves and hood was going to regret it. It was cool and getting colder. Brisk gusts of wind punctuated the air.

On the way back they'd not take this route, she decided. She'd mark it in ink later. Improving the map was the duty of every Kossaki. She marked larger copses of trees, deep gullies, bare rocky tops, and stream courses that were landmarks.

They stopped at dusk, wanting enough time to pitch a proper camp on a slight rise with a nearby copse as a windbreak and for fuel. She easily found what she needed in this rolling terrain.

"Erki, trample grass."

The boy was enthusiastic about the task, stomping and jumping. As he did so, she made a quick sweep around the copse and hill. Nothing and no one in sight. It was as if they were the only people in the world.

Erki had the grass flat. With a tarp, a spear, a rope and three pegs, they had shelter in minutes. A few moments' digging with a trowel shaped sleeping hollows; then Erki threw his smaller tarp and the blankets within. Riga grabbed hobbles so the horses could graze without straying. The plowpoint shelter opened downwind, and she dug a firepit before grabbing food.

"Beef and honey-nuts, Erki," she said, holding a bag aloft.

She was amused to see the boy tumble grinning toward her with an armful of fuel, dropping and recovering it as he came, just as if he had too many biscuits. They had been born fair-skinned Northerners, though they were tanned now from the plains, and Erki had sky-blue eyes and straw hair that would have the girls lining up to be courted, especially with that grin. They grew taller and more robust than the plains natives, too.

It was close to freezing by the time she backed into the tent and rolled under the blankets with her fleece and linen bear. She snuggled up tight to Erki, who was cuddly but getting bony as he sprouted up. He put out a lot of heat. He also kicked and tossed even when asleep. The fire burned its small sticks and moss quickly, offering little heat. She took a long time to fall asleep, starting at every howl, flutter, and gust of wind. They were safe, she told herself. She'd made a sweep, and the horses would alert them to trouble, not to mention kick a wolf.

She woke stiff and groggy in the chill silver-gray dawn. Actually, it was the fourth or fifth time she woke, due to Erki's incessant twitching and kicking and stealing of covers. Kari would have been a better choice to camp with, but she was on another route.

Riga chewed her tooth bristle as she struck the tent with its feathery fungus of frost. Oh, she ached. At home, she had a four-poster bed, like any town-bred girl of means. She could sleep on the ground when she had to, but even bundled warm was not enough when cold fog rolled past. She'd been fine until she stood; then her spine and neck protested.

There was nothing to do but ride. They chewed hard biscuits, hard cheese and dried meat, all cold. She longed for an apple.

Half the morning, then rest, lunch and unsaddle, resaddle and ride half the afternoon, then rest. Blessi was doing great for such a long trip. The two signal birds in their cages on Trausti's back were not so calm. They twittered. She sent one aloft in midafternoon. "Circle and see," she told it.

It landed a few minutes later and cocked its head south. They rode that way.

Dinner was also a saddle meal. They should be getting close, she thought. They were in from the coast, and she thought she could catch occasional glimpses of the Acabarrin border hills south of here.

"I see them," Erki said.

She squinted and saw movement in the dusk ahead of them and west, a small caravan seen from the side. The wagons were not plainsworthy, only meant for use in farmland. The rough, rolling ground would disable them soon. Some people walked alongside. The horses and mules were old but healthy. One wagon was drawn by oxen. Chickens, children, and caged rabbits filled out the swaying loads.

"Good job," she said. "Look sharp and we'll ride up."

She called softly, not wanting to echo through the night. "Ho!" They heard and faced her, but she was far too close for them to have done anything against a threat. A few of them might know enough fighting to hold off brigands, with enough numbers. None of them were warriors.

She trotted to the front, watching them watch her. No one gave any indication of status, so she chose the driver of the lead wagon.

She spoke in Acabarr. "I am Riga Gundesdati called Sworddancer, Scout Archer of Gangibrog of the Kossaki. This is my brother Erki. We will escort you to Little Town."

"We'll meet your war party there?" Clearly, he didn't know where he was on the map.

"No, that's your destination, out of Acabarrin and past our lands," she said firmly. His wife looked relieved under her shawl.

He said, "But we're pursued! And you are two youths." He eyed Erki with disdain, and her with an admiring stare, but probably not for her martial bearing.

"Many are pursued, and we're not a large town. You needn't worry. Two Kossaki are more than enough for a caravan of thirty." Riga smiled in false pride. She didn't believe her own tale. She was sure she could fight most adult men, certainly peasant levies. However, some of the pursuing forces were professionals.

"We're at least headed in the right direction," a man commented from the second wagon. "I am Walten, the smith."

"Greetings," she said. "Yes, near enough the right direction. It's time to stop, though."

"We should travel through the night to make distance," the first driver said.

"You should stop now before losing a wheel or a horse in the holes and dips hereabouts."

"That's wise, Jarek," Walten said. Jarek clearly wanted to argue, but acceded.

The drivers stopped their wagons, and she dismounted.

"You'll need three pickets," she said, taking charge. "Front, aft, and steerboard. We'll take port."

"Yes, I've traveled before," Jarek said.

She bit her lip. While she might have come across a bit presumptuously, she was the local guide and warrior. His presentation and gear marked him as a trained village militiaman, no more.

Still, he was doing the right thing. She let them maneuver and get sorted, then chose a slight hummock to camp on.

Remembering that Erki had been nodding in the saddle, she ordered him into the tent to sleep. She'd need him alert tomorrow. She inspected their pickets herself and forced herself to say nothing. They weren't worth much. She'd sleep with her sword and with her bow strung. She warned against fire. There was little to use as fuel unless they wanted to burn animal dung, which was not only unsavory but would stink for miles.

This night was worse than the last, with squalling babies. They might be uncomfortable, but they made more noise than a seasick Kossaki whelp. Clearly, they were not a traveling people. Riga awoke about dawn, still groggy but unable to sleep, and crawled out. Her cloak had been over them as another blanket. Now it was a tangled heap next to Erki. She grabbed it, wrapped it around herself, and looked around. She'd dislodged her bear, which was outside. She blushed and stuffed it into a sack.

The caravan was readying to move. They had no trouble fleeing and seemed adequate in their care and preparations, but, gods, they made a racket and left a trail a noseblind hound could follow.

She understood their fear, but they were already mounted and inching forward, as if they planned to leave their guides. She prodded her brother with her toe and said, "Erki, strike quick." She walked briskly to the front wagon.

"I didn't get your name last night, driver," she said to the gruff man.

"Jarek," he said.

"I'm impressed at your speed in striking camp," she said. "We'll make good time today."

"Guide us west, then," he said. He still didn't look at her.

"West is Rissim and Kossaki territory. I'm to take you to Little Town on Lake Diaska."

"It's too far," he said.

"Our territory is too close and can't support many people. My orders are to take you to Little Town," she repeated. He was frustrated and scared, but he had only vague notions of where he was going. "We go north, slightly east."

"The lake is north-northwest," he said. Blast the man for having to argue every point.

"Which takes you through hummocks that'll tear off a wheel. I won't even take a horse through there."

"I'm sure when you have as much experience as I do, you'll be able to."

Riga boiled and had to pause before replying.

"Have you more experience with this steppe?" she asked.

He ignored her and reined forward, toward the west. The trailing drivers shouted to their teams to follow.

She sprinted back to Blessi and mounted fast. "Erki,

mount now!" A squeeze of her heels, a quick gallop, and she was in front.

"Have you?" she asked again.

Jarek snorted and turned away.

If he wanted to rouse her ire, he was going at it the right way.

She slid over her saddle, stood off-stirrup, and stepped over to his seat. He looked up surprised just in time to catch her slap full across his face. His wife gasped.

Riga realized her mistake. She'd hit him either too hard, or not nearly hard enough. He shoved her in the middle and she bounded off. Almost catching her stirrup and bridle, she wound up on the ground, wincing at a twisted ankle and gritting her teeth as she remounted. This was not a good way to lead.

She looked at her brother and saw him fingering his hilt, a dark look on his face.

"Erki," she commanded, and pointed. He nodded at once and trotted forward to block the route, trying to look mean and only looking like a boy playing. She sighed. Jarek attempted to steer around, and she interposed with his draft mules. They all bound up in a knot and stopped.

She fought down anger. If it were reversed—Erki the teen—he'd probably be accepted, and she a cute mascot. As it was, he was seen as a mere boy, not a warrior in training, and she as a flighty girl. She was angry with herself over the bear, also.

"Girl, I will spank you if you don't move," Jarek growled. His eyes hinted he'd enjoy it, too.

Well, that put it in terms she understood as a fighter. She looked him over. Wiry. About her height. Shorter legs.

She swung to the ground. "You're welcome to try."

His first move was to detour again. He thought better of it, apparently realized he had to take the challenge or look foolish. Growing red in the face and tight-jawed, he stepped down from his seat. He shrugged off his wife's restraining hand.

He'd look foolish spanking her, too. Either way, he'd lost, but Riga had not yet won.

This could be dangerous several ways, she realized, not the least of which was he might spank or beat her. She'd certainly lose face and status from that and from losing her charges. Erki would probably let the story of any spanking slip. Accidentally, of course, but it would still shame her.

Luckily, Jarek was so contemptuous he didn't even consider she might actually know how to fight. He grabbed her wrist and pulled to bend her over his knee. She locked his elbow with a methodical yank, caught his wrist in her own hand as she broke the hold, then kicked his calf until he was on his knees. He grunted as he went down. He struggled until she pressed on his elbow. It would take but a moment to follow through and stand on his neck, but she decided to hold back.

"I ask that you trust me," she said, loud enough to keep it public and diplomatic. "I know these plains, and they're not just empty fields. I'll speed you through and keep eye out for threats, animal or man."

Walten said in loud reply, "I call to follow her. We'd look silly stuck in a bog." Riga wondered why he wasn't in charge. He was much more mature and thoughtful. Politics.

Jarek was clearly incensed, embarrassed, and offended, but he seemed to grasp that he was outmaneuvered. He nodded and clambered silently up to his wagon.

"So lead us," he said, grinning. He thought to be clever and leave the entire problem in Riga's lap.

Perfect.

She smiled, mounted, and led the way. She pointed north and slightly east.

Then she had to rush to help Erki gather their camping gear and Trausti. It detracted from her warrior presentation.

She didn't try to talk to Jarek, and cautioned Erki with hand signs to keep quiet. She couldn't have them sounding like children, and nothing was going to warm this man up until she accomplished something.

Of course, when one needed everything to go right, it would invariably go wrong. Shortly, a party became visible ahead. They were on tall horses with no wagons. A patrol.

She'd gain nothing by withholding the information, and it was unlikely they'd suddenly turn east and clear the way.

"Party ahead," she said clearly and simply.

"I wonder if it's too late to turn west," Jarek said loudly. "Men, arm up!"

"Wait!" she called. "I will go and treat with them. Erki, take this," she said, handing him the map satchel.

She galloped ahead, both to avoid the tension of two armed parties meeting and to get away from Jarek's scared but derisive laughter.

She slowed to a canter once she had space. She watched the soldiers to see how they reacted. They faced her and kept moving at a walk. That was encouraging so far. She matched that pace. No need to rush to meet death.

Gulping and sweating, she remembered her position. She was the warrior. Her duty was to protect these people. With that in mind, she sat tall in the saddle and approached, doing her best to look casually proud and secure in her status. They weren't in livery, but that meant nothing. Her own people didn't wear set colors.

She brushed her bow with her fingertips. She might have to draw, shoot, and drop it before reverting to steel. She wished for one of the short, laminated bows of the plains people. Hers was a longbow of two horns with a center grip, stronger but awkward from horseback. She was a foot warrior, not a plains rider. She wished she had time to don her mail.

Her opposite number was a bearlike man she knew she could never beat in any fight. She might cripple him, but even that was a long roll of the dice. Once inside bow range she had nothing but projection and attitude. Still, his bearded face and shaven head were visible because he was unhelmed. That was a helpful sign. His three compatriots followed his lead.

"I am Riga of the Kossaki," she said simply. No rankings here. They'd just sound silly. "I am guide and escort for these refugees." She wondered which languages they spoke.

"Balyat of the Toughs," the man said in broken Danik. "What is your destination?" She could comprehend.

"I won't discuss that," she replied. "It is north, as you see, and away from here. That's enough for you." Had she delivered that properly? She wanted to sound firm but not arrogant.

"If you go that way, we won't call you hostile," he said. "But we don't speak for our employer."

"Good to know we might only be killed for money, not for care, mercenary," she said. Four of them. She might take the smallest down before she died, if she was quick. She held the shiver to a bare twitch.

"Keep moving," Balyat advised. "We report tonight."

"Fair enough," she said, and meant it. With luck and speed, a few hours would have them safe. If not, at least they would suffer a quick, clean death from professional warriors, not the nauseating horrors of the Empire's troops.

"I hope not to meet again, Kossaki," Balyat said and turned his mount.

As she turned, she smiled slightly to herself. A renowned troop of mercenaries seemed to accept her as warrior, even though inferior.

Civilians were harder to persuade, though. They always wanted to tell you how to conduct a fight, while not fighting themselves.

The look on Jarek's face as she returned was interesting. It wasn't one of trust, but it might have a glimmer of respect.

"Who were they?" he asked.

"Oh, just some mercenaries," she smiled. "I told them who I was, and they agreed to let us pass." It wouldn't have worked with most of the hired thugs on the peninsula, nor fealted troops. She wouldn't share that, though.

Erki looked ready to burst out with something that would wreck it. "Erki, take the rear for a bit, and keep watch," she said to interrupt him. He nodded and trotted back.

She turned further north and kept them driving until full dark. Jarek argued to keep going, but his own wife spoke up, and others. They were so exhausted the walkers staggered, and the riders could barely stand.

It wasn't any warmer that night, though the ground was flatter and the grass thick enough to offer some padding. They didn't dare risk fire. They were a few miles from where the mercenaries had patrolled. Fire could mean the difference between being passed by a few hundred yards away or being seen from miles.

Wake, and move. This distance had taken Erki and her under two days. It was taking three for the caravan, and that was at a speed that strained human endurance.

Toward afternoon, they saw movement to the west, paralleling them. It took most of an hour to discern it was a larger caravan with outriders. Then a messenger bird swooped in, lit on Erki's shoulder, to his delight and nervousness, and twittered, "Helloooo from Karlinooo." It stretched out a claw with a tiny note bound to it.

It was a rough map with a list of family groups. Riga read them off loudly. "Fenk the Smith, Nardin the Banwriht . . . boneworker? It's your language in our letters. Rager the Fitter." She hadn't talked much to the caravan members, but they muttered and exclaimed in relief that some of their friends and acquaintances were accounted for.

The other caravan was huge. It must be a dozen families, perhaps an entire village. One of the half dozen escorts shouted and broke off. Riga gave a warbling shriek, and reined back.

"Kari!"

"Riga!" Her friend galloped up, and they hugged from horseback, sweaty and dusty and warm to the touch.

"Gentles, this is my friend Karlinu the Quick, Scout Spear."

Jarek just grunted. Walten nodded, smiled, and said, "Hello." The others offered greetings.

Karlinu said, "Herald Bellan wants a tally. He's here, and another Herald is in Gangibrog."

Riga gestured with her head and moved a bit forward. Kari nodded and paced her.

Once out of earshot, Riga said, "I've barely heard of these Heralds before. Why are they so influential? Our entire town has stopped working." She didn't want to be presumptuous, but she had a vested interested as part owner of her father's dock and transfer business. Their safety was also her concern, with all this attention.

"Talk later," Kari said. "Tally?"

"Twenty-seven. And how is your mother the Swordmistress?" She changed subjects, since she wasn't going to get an answer.

"Frazzled and harried and snapping as if we're at

drill, even for mundane matters. It's not just us. Knutsford is about, and the Ugri. The Morit as well."

"The Morit. I wonder if Brandur . . ." She stopped talking and blushed.

Karlinu laughed. "I expect your suitor will be there. But is it wise to be with a man you can easily best with sword?"

"I don't care. I like him, and he's not much poorer than we."

"I must report. Hold on." Kari reached into her horse's pack and drew out a bird cage. It took her moments to inscribe a note and whisper another message while she attached the parchment to the bird's leg sheath. "Fly home, fly home!" she said and tossed the bird skyward.

"Fly hoooome!" it agreed, circling and heading west.

Within the hour, the Herald came up personally. He wore riding clothes that were also white. His mount was a white stallion with vivid blue eyes. Riga hadn't seen it closely before. Looking at it now, it seemed to stare at her and delve into her thoughts.

"You seem to be doing well, Riga," he greeted.

She increased her pace and gave him a bare twitch of a rein finger. With a slow nod he moved to pace her. She waited until they had distance to speak.

"They treat me as a girl," she said, "except when things go bad. Every problem is mine. Either my advice is bad, or I'm naïve . . ."

"They are villagers of a farming culture," Bellan said. "You are a woman of a trading culture that grew from warriors. I knew this would be a problem, which is why I hurried to gather you all. You've done well, no matter how it feels."

"Now they'll just feel you've taken over," she groused. She wasn't sure why she was sharing so much with this stranger. He exuded trustworthiness, though.

"Of course," he nodded. "But more importantly,

they will be safe for now, and your people won't be burdened with noncombatant refugees as you prepare. I can't fight for you, but I can clear the field for you."

Riga didn't like the sound of that. It made sense that Miklamar was heading their way, but still . . .

"Wouldn't it make sense for your people to join us and fight here, before it reaches your lands?" she asked.

He laughed. "Oh, Riga, Valdemar is weeks away by road, even as fast as my Companion can travel." He patted the horse's flank. "I'll do what I can to help, but Miklamar is no threat to my nation. Our rulers are busy with things close to home. Nothing as important as an empire-building butcher, but far more immediate. It's one of the tragedies of the world. Your people must deal with this as best you can. Still, I'm glad we were in the area and can offer some help."

He paused for a moment, as if listening to the air, or his horse. Riga took the time to consider his words. No, she didn't think her remote town, nor even their small nation, were important worldwide. She'd hoped for more, though.

"There is a war band ahead," Bellan said.

"Is it the mercenaries?" she asked, half in hope, half in dread.

"They're on foot, crossing us, probably from the coast road. We can outride them, but the refugees can't." Their wagons managed a walking pace at best in this terrain. The children and elders wouldn't be able to keep up on foot.

"Not the Toughs I met, then."

"Behind them may be more. We can't detour that way. We also can't wait. We'll have to go through, then ride fast and through the night." He seemed to shift back to the present. "Please come with me. We need to plan this."

"Yes, certainly," she agreed. She turned and called, "Erki! Take point."

Riga nodded to the others as she approached. No one here saw her as only a girl. Most had felt her blows. Kari, Snorru, Rabal and his uncle Lar, three other men and two women, and the Grogansen boys.

A dozen Kossaki, half youths and women, and the Herald. The army ahead was hopefully less than eight times that size, but might be the van of a far larger force.

"What would you do, Sworddancer?" Lar asked. She realized things were being hashed out and she'd missed some of the talk.

She breathed deeply and stared at nothing. A prayer cleared her mind and she thought.

"I'd shoot arrows from distance and continue until closing. We should dismount close to cause surprise and hopefully break their ranks with fear of the horses."

"Not bad. We need wranglers. Nor do we want a long fight with infantry. We must hurt them and re-treat fast, then look prepared to repeat it. Those levies won't have the heart for a long fight against professionals, without the mercenaries."

"We're to look like professionals?"

"Worse," Kari grinned. "We're *girls*."

Girls with twelve years of training in horse, sword, bow, map, languages and business, Riga thought, and grinned back. No Kossaki would underestimate a youth. They were fighters, traders, and travelers from the time they could walk.

She said, "Erki should wrangle and recover bows and glean points, but he'll complain I'm being protective." Of course, she was, but it made sense for him as youngest to hold back. He could also ride fastest if need be, to carry a message.

"I'll tell him," Bellan said.

"Also, we should fire off a shooting star."

"What good will that do?" Snorru asked. Our nearest element is hours away."

"They don't know that. Act as if we expect over-whelming backup, and hit them hard. As Lar says, they won't stomach a long fight."

"And best we scare them now," Bellan said. "Soon enough Miklamar will want your port, also, if he's not stopped."

"It might alert another patrol, too," Rabal said.

"It might. What do you think of that against its advantages?"

"Yes, it's risky," Lar said. "But the mercenaries have reported by now. That's probably why this force is crossing bare steppe toward the caravan."

"Yes," Riga agreed.

"Do it."

Riga and Bellan rode back to the caravan, now combined with the others.

"We'll be fighting, then cutting across fast and continuing," Bellan told them.

"We will arm up, then," Walten said, looking old but sounding firm.

"No, you should move fast and protect your families if it comes to that."

Jarek nodded, and Riga steamed. He didn't question Bellan. Had she given the same advice, she knew he'd have argued.

Bellan said, "Northwest, and fast. There are towns. Stop only for feed and water, and be sure they know the threat. From Little Town, head north to the rivers."

"Start that way now," Riga said. "We'll catch up and guide you later."

Then she turned, not wanting to know what they thought, and trying not to care. She saw a blue and yellow shooting star scream up: Snorru's colors. It crackled and burst, visible for miles. She grabbed for her mail, and shimmied in. Then she helped Erki with his quilted staghide. It was loose on his frame, but it wouldn't be for long. Handsome boy, she sighed. She worried more for him than herself.

One in seven, she thought. Wound or kill one in seven, and all but the most dedicated force would retreat. There were seventy-two troops, eight across and nine deep, with two mounted officers. They had bills and spears mostly, with shields, and leather armor. They were not elite, but they were definitely professional, even if levied.

They needed to wound about one each, if they didn't lose too many themselves, though desperation gave them determination.

The troops looked nervous as they approached. The small Kossaki force approaching with weapons drawn was either insane or expected backup beyond the hundred militiamen in the caravan. The shooting star suggested backup. Where was it, though? Riga watched them cast glances about and ripple their neat formation.

Bellan quietly said, "First line, dismount, shoot on my order. Second line, prepare to charge." He wore gorgeous mail with iron joints, and a polished helm.

She swung from the saddle, drew an arrow, and stood next to Blessi.

"Shoot. Charge."

She nocked, drew, loosed, and shot again. She had three arrows in the air before he called, "Hold!"

Their timing and discipline were good. The other half of their force and Bellan had galloped ahead and were dismounting right in the faces of the enemy, hurling javelins as they did so.

The troops moved their shields in response. Only a couple shouted from wounds. A score of arrows and a half-dozen javelins used for that. It was amazing how expensive battle was.

Riga dropped her bow and sprinted forward, unslinging her shield and drawing steel. She saw Erki gathering reins and backing, cajoling the horses. They were holding up well in the fight, and he was earnest in his task. She saw all that live steel, and her knees went weak. Sparring with blunt steel in the vollar was nothing like ugly strangers who wanted you dead. Her helmet was loose, but there was no time to adjust it.

The enemy spread out for envelopment and slaughter, and Bellan pointed to the left. She moved over that way, between Kari and Snorru. Lar tossed a javelin right past her, to break their line into clumps. One flinched as it caught on his shield and made the mistake of reaching over to unstick it. She reached him, snapped out her sword and took a chunk from his arm. He staggered back howling and got in the way of his mates.

The troops had numbers and were trained to follow orders. They had discipline but not the years of precision and skill she'd learned. She deflected a raised pole and got in close to thrust at anything exposed. The three nearest all turned to face her and started jabbing. It turned into a deadly dance.

This was how she'd earned her name. Father had always taught her that if you were blocking, you should also be attacking, if attacking, also moving. One foot should be aground for balance, one shifting, and both arms fighting. The shield boss could also bash, its binding smash, its broadness conceal your movement from your opponent. The sword could threaten as well as strike. Silence and noise were each intimidating. Moving targets were harder to hit. She'd inflicted no lethal blows yet, but her opponents, four so far, were cut and bleeding. A gimp arm took a warrior out of the fight and was easy to score. If they wanted to stick them out, she'd cut them. She was smaller, lithe, agile, and used to fighting one to one as well as en masse.

"One, back!" Bellan called, and Kari and Snorru turned and whipped away. She gulped and tingled in fear. Knowing it was planned didn't make it easier to be left in front, face to face with angry strangers. They pushed forward, seeing the Kossaki retreat and believing they had won.

"Two, back!" Bellan shouted.

She turned and ran, keeping low so javelins could fly over her. Then she saw Erki off to the side. He'd dismounted to recover a bow, and one stray fighter was closing on him.

Her first thought was that it made no sense. The man was chasing a target of little value. She wondered if his plan was to take a hostage, or chase the horses off, but he was waving his polecleaver vigorously.

Then raw pain and nausea flooded through her mind. *He was going to kill her little brother.*

Tactics said she should stick with the element and her orders or she'd make the disparity of numbers worse. Tactics be damned. *"Erki, your left!"* she shouted to alert him, and dodged past Bellan's mount. Erki turned and grabbed for his weapons.

"Go, Riga!" Bellan said, acknowledging her, but she didn't care. The first swing of that long weapon tore and splintered Erki's shield to the boss. He stumbled back and raised his sword to block. The cleaver fell, met the sword in a dull clang. He dropped his weapon and howled, face contorted in agony, but he hadn't been opened up yet.

Then the soldier realized he was being flanked and turned. He had no time to swing, so he thrust. Riga caught the tip straight into the tough leather and wood of her shield, twisted into it. He made the mistake of trying to hold on to the haft, and wound up sideways to her.

Her first swing hit too hard. She felt the blade bite and stick in his thigh, and had to fight it loose as he fell, kicking and screaming. Real battle was tremendously noisier and dirtier than the vollar, she thought as she followed up with a thrust to his torso.

She retained enough presence of mind to make a sweep around herself. Some officer had drawn the force back into a bristling defensive formation. Kossaki javelins chunked into shields but rarely found a mark, and one of the Grogansens had recovered his bow. She was safe for the present.

For a moment she thought Erki had lost an arm. He shrieked and squirmed and was painted with blood. A fresh bout of nausea started, and she grabbed for a bandage from her belt. It was only his thumb, though, or part of it. The blade had not been sharp and had mangled it. He might retain some use.

She dropped her sword in front of her, slapped his helmet to draw his attention back to the world and shouted, "Use this!" as she thrust a bandage at him. He gasped in surprise and nodded, before she reached under his hips and heaved him back across his saddle and the added pain of moving set him screaming again. She bent, grabbed her sword, made another sweep, then grabbed his blade and Snorru's bow. It was heavier than hers, but she'd draw it if she had to. She said, "Off hand!" and flipped Erki's sword up to him as he tumbled upright. Then she turned back to the fight, clutching at her quiver. Her hands were sticky.

Her first arrow wobbled. The bow needed heavier arrows than hers, but the range wasn't great. She wondered where the brilliant flash of flame came from, then realized four shooting stars had been fired horizontally. Half the front rank clutched at their eyes and dropped their guard, during which Snorru, Lar, and the Grogansens charged in and speared any handy flesh, then jammed the points into shields and left them as they dove and rolled away. Those troops had to drop their shields, and she shot an arrow straight into the revealed mass. Two javelins followed.

She put her third arrow into the officer riding down on them. It was a lucky shot. She'd been aiming for the torso and caught him in the throat, right under the helmet. No one could see luck, though, only a hit.

He tumbled from his horse, and the fight was over, the foot troops retreating in ragged order, glancing back but with no heart to fight. They carried and dragged their wounded. Only two dead yet, four lame and being carried, perhaps twenty wounded, but infection would take others, unless their leaders were the type to waste healing magic on arrow fodder. She suspected not.

Still, the caravan would have to move faster, even if it meant losing a wagon and any contents that couldn't be shared in a hurry. Where those troops came from there would be others. There wasn't time to properly loot, only to grab pouches, weapons, and the occasional helmet, and to recover a few bows and javelins.

Snorru, mounted, led Erki by his left hand. The boy looked faint from pain and shock. They reached the caravan, and Snorru helped Erki down as Riga jumped from her saddle.

Bellan caught up, grabbed Erki, inspected his hand in a moment, and shoved him down on the gate of a wagon.

"Let's do this fast. Riga, can you hold him? And Kari."

"I can," she said, voice cracking and tears blinding her. She grabbed his arm, pinned it down, and leaned her weight on it. Kari did the same on the left, as Erki panicked and started thrashing. Only his feet could move, drumming and kicking on the wagon deck. She closed her eyes and wished she could close her ears and nose. Snorru ran up and shoved a leather rein between his teeth for him to bite on. Riga heard his cries, and under them, the sound and smell of battlefield surgery. His screams hit a crescendo as Bellan said, "That's it. Only one joint. You'll still be able to work and fight. Drink this." He handed over a leather bottle as he turned to help bandage Lar's arm. There were several moderate wounds.

Erki was too dazed to handle the bottle, and Riga helped him drink. He guzzled five times, and she pulled the bottle back. He needed help with the pain, but not enough to get sick. Then she took three burning swallows herself. Kari did, too, then Snorru. They swapped looks that combined compassion, fear, horror, and the bond that came only with shared battle.

After easing Erki into his saddle so he could rest, they rode another five miles before Bellan called a halt, well after dark. Everyone slept on wagons or under them, ready to fly if another troop came. Walten offered his wagon to the Kossaki youth, and slept underneath.

Erki cried and cried. He'd quiet down, drift fitfully to sobbing sleep, then some tortured nerve would jolt him awake to writhe and scream again. The herbs were supposed to lessen the pain and prevent infection, but hand injuries were among the most painful.

Riga cried, holding him tight in the damp cold amid dust and tools, comforting him. They were children, not warriors. They shouldn't have to fight, certainly not Erki. He was barely lettered and just big enough to ride. She cursed Miklamar and his troops, the mercenaries, Jarek and his helpless bumtwits, the Swordmistress, Bellan. Couldn't they fight their own battle and leave her out of it? She clutched her bear, not caring if anyone saw.

She realized part of her distress was fear of losing Erki, had the blow been better aimed. Or her father. Or herself. A warrior was willing to risk such things, but she wasn't sure she was.

It was only a thumb! People lost worse in grindstones, forges, even looms. Bjark had lost two joints of fingers just last year. It could have been worse.

But this was Erki, and it had been in war. That made it different.

And it could have been worse.

* * *

In the morning, pressups and sword drill did nothing to loosen the knot in her shoulder or the ache on the side of her head. Erki looked groggy from shock and fatigue, but he'd stopped crying. He let nothing near his hand, though.

It took all day, but by dusk Lake Diaska was visible, the sun glittering off its windblown waves. Gangibrog was at the south point, Little Town, now part of the Kingdom of Crane, to the north. They pushed on, saddlesore and stiff, but with a huge burden lifted.

They stopped, late and exhausted to staggers. The refugees rolled up in blankets where they sat or sprawled and made snide but quiet comments about the Kossaki setting camp. Riga finished pitching the shelter quickly, despite working alone, disregarding their snickers. Tonight would be cold. They'd learn as they traveled north.

Erki looked unhappy, able only to hold a javelin while she drove spikes and dug them in. She shooed him in and crawled in alongside, with an extra blanket against the chill.

In the morning, the elders were locked in conference. They didn't break for long minutes while the mist and dew burned off. Riga secured the gear and handed Erki a bowl of hard cheese and nuts.

"Thank you," he said, staring at his bandaged thumb.

"I'm sorry." If she'd been a moment sooner . . .

"I wonder what it feels like to die?" he asked.

That was the type of question children asked parents. She wasn't ready for it yet. And she knew what it felt like to kill.

Bellan finally came over with a wave for attention.

"We'll have to split up. You'll take Erki home, with the other youths. Now that they're one group, we'll take them north. The Morit will meet us."

Riga choked a little and took a deep breath. She'd

spent all night nerving up to continue, and now she was being replaced, just a girl again. She did want to go home, badly. She also wanted to finish the job. She'd completely forgotten that she and Brandur might meet, and that chance was also gone.

"I understand," was all she could say.

"You're named well, Sworddancer," he said with a reassuring smile. "Morle was right to select you."

Riding back wasn't bad, with Kari and the Grogansens for company. Even Snorru, who'd always been a bit self-absorbed, treated Erki almost like his own brother. They made good time toward the road and saw lake barges towed by sail tugs. They passed occasional traffic at a run.

Once in town, she could see things returning to normal. The hus was open, too. Father was home!

They galloped alongside the planked road, heedless of the splattering muck, and she dismounted as he came out the door.

"Riga!" he shouted, grinning and arms wide. She charged up and leaped at him.

A moment later she said, "You're squashing me."

"I like squashing you," he said, very softly. She started crying.

The fire was going, and he'd made a large pot of stew. It was so like being home, and so like being a girl again. She ate and warmed herself, peeling off layers. Meanwhile, Father looked at Erki's thumb.

"Arwen has fresh herbs, not like the dried ones for the field. And it's not much of a wound. You'll get used to it and be able to work just fine. Remember this?" He showed one of his own injuries, a smashed fingertip.

Riga moved away, not wanting to see it again. She hung her clothes, mounted her mail and helm on their stand, and set about cleaning her sword.

Before she took over the ledgers, she might have

to be a warrior. She'd trained for it all her life, but she'd never thought to actually use it, beyond a tavern brawl or a mob of thieves at quayside, the occasional bandits or brigands. It was a cold thought.

Meanwhile, she was home with her family, a soft bed, her toys and crafts, and a chance to be a girl again, for the little time she could.

Broken Bones
by *Stephanie D. Shaver*

Stephanie Shaver lives in St. Louis, Missouri, with her cats and her computers. When she isn't working, cooking, wrestling with her lawn, or writing, she's out in the woods climbing something or frantically checking for ticks. Her day job involves creating online games for Simutronics, where she acts as a lead designer and creative know-it-all for the fantasy-based MMORPG *Hero's Journey*. You can find out more about her at her website, www.sdshaver.com.

"So. There I was—"

"A likely story."

The Bard paused, inky nib poised over parchment. She hadn't even written two words. "Do you want this report or not?"

She could *hear* the smirk in the Herald's voice. "Can't you just skip to the good part?"

"They're all good parts!"

"Oh, fine then. You may continue."

"*You*," she said, stabbing her quill at the air, eyes still fixed on the parchment, "could test a Companion's patience."

"And often do."

Lelia resisted the urge to roll her eyes. She took a big gulp of ale, then a deep breath, and squared her shoulders.

"So," she said, scribbling once more. "There I was.

Halfway to the middle of north nowhere, freezing my delicate Bardly bits off."

Lelia's teeth would not stop chattering. She had tried clenching them to make it stop, but that only made her feel like her teeth were going to crack from the strain.

I don't remember the north being this cold when I was younger, she thought as she trudged forward. Midmorning had started out warm, the snow melting a little, but by afternoon the temperature had plummeted, freezing what had thawed. Irregular gusts howled out of Sorrows to the north. Sunset threatened, casting hues of apricot and blush across the road.

"Sweet Kernos," she muttered into her scarf, "I'm too young and precious to die." Every breath she took tasted of greasy wool and the cold egg and onion pie she'd eaten for breakfast.

"I'm sure your overall adorableness is an important deciding factor for Lord Death," a sweet voice said.

Lelia glanced in the direction of the speaker, and felt only a distant and winter-numbed surprise at seeing her best friend from the Collegium walking beside her, dressed out in the lightest summer Scarlets.

"Oh, hey, Maresa," Lelia said. "Out for a stroll?"

Maresa snorted.

"I know. You're not really here." Lelia returned to focusing on trudging through the snow.

"Ah, but maybe *I* am?"

The voice had changed, and when Lelia looked again, it was her brother Lyle—more appropriately dressed in leather Whites—forging down the road with her.

"Really doubtful," she replied to her figment, "but nice try. Still, I know you wouldn't go anywhere without your horse."

Her twin smiled at her, that heartbreaking, guileless smile that made her want to beat him over the head with a gittern and tell him to *be more careful, dammit*. He was safely out of gittern range, however, riding the Exile's Road on the tail end of his first circuit with his mentor, Herald Wil.

"Oh, I could really be here," Lyle said. "You've read enough stories. You know that strange things regularly transpire between twins." The vision blurred, and he became a shade taller, his features sharper and his gray eyes less trusting. The Whites stayed the same. In his place was—

Lelia stopped, her narrative stalled.

"What?" the Herald asked.

"I am debating whether this bit is relevant," she replied. "I was definitely hallucinating. My brother. Maresa . . ."

You. She toyed with the pendant around her neck.

"Too much time alone," he said sagely.

"That, and I was half-starved, I couldn't feel my extremities, and I'd been walking for candlemarks in the wind. My head had all sorts of reasons for dipping me into a vat of crazy."

Her hand trembled with the name it was still poised to write—then she set the paper aside and reached for a clean sheet.

"Might be relevant," she muttered to herself. "Might not. I'll know later."

She picked up the story a little further down the road.

"Lelia, you need a warmer jacket, and you should eat more." The hallucination had kindly returned to being her brother, his lips curved in a beatific smile. "You can't suffer for your work if you're dead."

"You think about yourself!" she growled back. "I'm not the one hoofing it around Evendim Sector under the tutelage of the Herald most likely to smother a burning orphanage with his own body!"

"Hickory," Lyle replied.

"What?" she said, whipping her head in his direction—but no, he really *wasn't* there. There may have been twins born with bonds strong enough to let their minds touch across massive distances, but Lyle and Lelia's was not one of them.

This may all be delirium, but at least it's a sensible *delirium,* she thought. The hallucination was right—it killed her to spend money on anything, but if she didn't acquire a better jacket, it would just flat out kill her.

She shut her eyes against the glowing white snow and breathed in deeply.

A whiff of woodsmoke—hickory—caught her olfactory attention. Too real to be another waking dream. Squinting northward, she was pretty sure she could see a smudge of smoke against the horizon.

Village. Fire. Inn? Hopefully. Someone to make me clothes? Maybe. Her mouth watered. *Food.*

It took another half-candlemark for the promise of a village to resolve into something other than woodsmoke and hope. It was not unlike many in this region: slate-roofed, large enough to sport a palisade, and with a central building in the square that was most certainly an inn.

She'd have wept for joy, if not for the fact that she was pretty sure her tears would have frozen on her cheeks.

"That's how you wound up in Langenfield," the Herald said.

"I was aiming for Waymeet."

Stony silence.

She sighed. "I *know*. I missed by a few miles."

A polite cough.

"Okay, I missed by *a lot*." She took a long draught of ale. "Doesn't matter. The ultimate goal is to get to Sorrows."

"About that. *Why?*"

She shrugged. "One of my teachers at the Collegium always drilled into me to *live* Valdemar. *Go* to the battle sites, the weird forests, smell the smoke in the resin down at Burning Pines. I wanted to do that."

She turned her mug. It was only one side of the jewel of truth. Just enough to convince an inquisitive Herald.

"And, as always, I wanted a song," she added, flashing another facet.

"Oh?"

"Found it, even." She grimaced. "I just didn't know it when I first met her."

Lelia staggered into the inn, and the middle of an argument.

"You ain't listening!" a tall, powerfully built young man was saying to a petite blonde woman with greasy hair, tunic, and trews. He wasn't quite yelling, but it was clear he was building up to that point. "There're no bones on my hearth and none in my scrap pile!"

The girl flushed. "You were cooking a ham just last night—"

"I said I ain't got any, and even if I did, I don't know that I'd sell 'em to you! What part of that don't you conjugate?"

"The p-part where y-you're lying," the blonde said in tones that could have frozen spirits of wine, even with her frustrated stammering. "And the w-word is c-c-*cogitate*, you country o-oaf!"

She spun and stormed toward the door, her warpath bent on bisecting Lelia—until she actually saw the Bard and stopped dead.

"Can I help you?" the young man said.

"A Bard?" whispered the blonde.

"That's me!" Lelia said cheerfully, mustering what she hoped was a disarming grin and not a grim, half-frozen rictus. "Does your innmaster have room for one? I don't have much money—"

"Bright Havens!" the man said, rushing over to relieve her of her pack. She kept his big, clumsy hands away from her gittern—no one handled Bloom but her—but gladly gave him the rest.

"If you're playing, you're staying!" he went on, and from what she gathered, he *was* the innmaster—just an awfully young one. "Hellfires, even if you're not playing, you can still stay—how fares the Queen? The last we heard, there was a hunting accident!"

That's the official story, yes, Lelia thought as she recounted what she knew—officially—to the innmaster, even as she edged toward a stool by the fire. The savory aroma of fennel sausage and sage nearly swept the strength from her knees.

Lelia sat, taking the opportunity to smile at the openly staring blonde. "And you are?"

The blonde's nostrils flared. She turned and walked out.

Well, Lelia thought. *Nice, friendly locals.*

"Ah, I'm sorry, m'lady Bard," the Innmaster said, hurrying over to a keg and taking a mug off a shelf. "That's Herda and she's . . ." He shook his head. "Different. You'd do best to just ignore her."

I would, but the argument you two were having actually sounded interesting. "Village madwoman?"

"Something like that." The young man grinned, bringing her a brimming cup. "I'm Olli, and I'm the innmaster you're looking for—you mind ale?"

Lelia raised her brows. "Good sir, you could serve me trough-water and I'd ask for more!"

He chuckled. "My brew's not *that* bad! Now, you get warm here, m'lady Bard. I'm going to go get the word out that you're in town!" He swept a heavy woolen cape down from a wooden peg by the door and hurried out into the dusk before she'd taken so much as a sip.

Lelia appraised the inn silently as she drank. Shabby but clean. It looked like it would hold a fair amount, though nothing like the alehouses in Haven, where more sensible Bards like Maresa made their names.

But it had seemed a grand adventure at first when Lelia decided to do as the Masters did: see, experience, integrate. A chance to find a song and change her scenery, to pursue a different kind of romantic notion—the kind that didn't end in wine cups and broken hearts.

But blisters were not romantic. Fumbling around with numb fingers for dry firewood was not romantic. Eating snow to stave off hunger—downright *prosaic*.

"Should have been a Herald," she muttered, turning her face toward the fire. "Should have saved a few brats from drowning and made one of them blue-eyed horsies Choose me. Then I'd have a convenient mount *and* I could melt brains with the Truth Spell." She grinned, drowsing away into a happy fantasy where she could get any story anytime she needed it.

The inn filled with alarming speed. Lelia picked out farmers, housewives, and a few artisans, taking time to move through them and share brief exchanges, getting a feel for what jokes and performances would work with these folk. Her chats revealed that the village wasn't big enough for a permanent Healer or even a priest, but it saw enough trade that not everyone made their living from the earth.

Herda's "welcome" was no indication of her fellow villagers—everyone Lelia met seemed genuinely grateful to see her. Bards and skilled gleemen didn't travel these roads often, and she and they knew it. She threw herself wholly into her performance, giving them her boisterous best. There was dancing and foot stomping. The wooden shutters shook, and the rafters rained dust.

Six pints, two sets, and three encores later she finally flopped over on the hearthstones, convincing the room that, yes, it was really over this time. Sleepy locals filed out, leaving her alone with the innmaster's enormous cats, already drawing up plans to colonize her head and belly.

"Time to go, Herda," she heard Olli say.

"I w-wanted to talk to the B-bard," the familiar voice of the stammering Herda responded.

"Oh, *now* you want to talk?" Olli replied with flat stubbornness. "Come by tomorrow morning and *talk* then."

"But it's three miles from here to my home—"

"Herda." Another voice, one worn with age. "Come along, dear. The Bard's tired."

Lelia heard the heavy door thud shut and the bar drop across it, accompanied by Olli's grunt. Lelia continued emulating a hearth-puddle.

"A fine set tonight, Bard," the innmaster said cheerfully. She could hear the scrape of the benches across the rush-strewn wooden floor as he put the room to rights again.

She raised her sore and throbbing right hand in a gesture of agreement and thanks.

"How long are you in town for?" he asked.

"Only as long as it takes me to acquire fresh provisions." She liked phrasing it that way. It made it sound like she'd headed north with all the proper gear from the get-go.

"It's been a long while since we had a Bard visit," Olli said. "We've seen hard times."

She raised her head a little. "Oh?"

"Snow fever. Last year. We're only really recovering from it now."

"I'm sorry." She understood now why the innmaster was such a young man.

"Life on the Border. We're just glad to have you. Bards remind us that there are other lights, other fires burning in the long nights." He doffed an imaginary hat. "Sleep well, Bard. We'll see you well fed in t'morning."

"Thanks, Olli," she replied. When she was sure the

innmaster was abed, Lelia dragged herself up and sifted through the coins that had landed in her boot. She'd earned enough to commission a coat, as well as set some aside for what she liked to think of as the "stormy day" fund, or possibly the "buy an old pony" fund. She was not quite yet at "buy an Ashkevron destrier," but hope sprang eternal.

She tucked the coins into various places on her persons before curling up on the stones. A cat landed on her side and oozed over her narrow hips. *Hope you like sleeping on bones, furfoot.*

Lelia herself didn't care for sleeping on mortared stones, but they were warm, and she was exhausted. She fell asleep to the crackle of the fire and the droning purr of the hearthcats.

"Wine cups and broken hearts?" the Herald asked as Lelia reached for her drink to wet her throat.

"Did I say that?" Lelia asked, alarm in her voice. She scanned the sheaf of papers and grimaced. "Hellfires, I did." She made a clucking noise. "Sorry, song lyric I've been working on. Crept right in, didn't it? I mean, that was just plain *gratuitous*. And *really* not relevant." She realized she was babbling and shut her mouth.

"How were things worse when you were wandering around Forst Reach?" the Herald asked, clearly confused. "It's not nearly as cold; there are far more inns and alehouses to sing at. I'd think you'd be happy there. Granted, it was *annoying* sometimes to find you in the villages on our circuit. Lyle in particular always worried about you."

"I wasn't happy," she said, forcing a smile. "But after what happened the night of my first performance here—" she indicated with a sweep of her hand the otherwise empty common room of the Langenfield Inn "—I too thought that I'd been better off sticking to the Exile's Road."

*   *   *

The outhouse door clapped shut behind Lelia, and she started the short, slippery walk across cobble-stones icy from the evening's thaw-and-freeze. The sky was free of clouds, the luminous moon gazing down from her heaven.

Warm fire, Lelia thought muzzily. *Blankets. And then breakfast.* Her mouth watered. *Bright Lady, let there be* bacon.

Something cracked behind her—a fallen branch, or a tree splintering under the chill of winter. She glanced back reflexively but could see nothing. She took an-other step without looking, and suddenly there was no ground, just her body tumbling head over appetite.

She threw her arm out, but she knew instinctively that the angle was off. She landed seconds before it seemed she should have, every dram of breath driven out of her. The snap of the little bones in her left hand was not unlike the crackle of the fire-devoured logs in the inn's hearth. The pain that followed was certainly fiery, a white-hot shock that whipped up a frenzy of realizations, starting with *something is not right,* followed by *is it broken?* and finally *oh, gods, no.*

She screamed, as much in despair as agony.

"The worst part," Lelia said to the Herald, "was that it could have been so easily avoided."

"But it kept you here."

"Yes."

"That turned out to be a good thing in the end, right?"

She frowned, not wanting to answer. "Olli heard my screams. He found me in the snow—"

Lelia flatly refused to cry. She sat in the inn with clenched teeth as Olli hovered and a gray-haired woman poked at her hand.

"Broken," the woman said. Her worn voice seemed

familiar. Her disheveled hair bespoke an unexpected rousing from bed.

"Oh?" Lelia replied in a tight voice.

"Mm-hm." The woman raised her eyes. "Healing Temple is a week away."

"Is that so?" Lelia replied, feeling alternately faint and nauseated.

"In good weather."

"Ah."

"Healer just left here, in fact."

"Mmhm."

"Won't be due back for another month or more."

Lelia pressed her eyes shut. "I see."

"You—"

"Stop." Lelia raised her good hand. "Just a moment." She took a deep, steadying breath. "Okay." She opened her eyes. "Can you set it?"

The old woman nodded.

"I mean, really, truly, *can you do this?* Not—I did it once with a goat and well, Havens, I *think* I got it right because the goat sure never complained, tee hee." The old woman's brow lifted, but Lelia drove on regardless. "Really, honestly, truly, can you set this right?"

The old woman pursed her lips, then nodded again.

"You are certain?"

A third nod.

"Okay." Lelia thrust out her good hand. "Hi. I'm Lelia, what's your name?"

The old woman took her hand and shook. "Artel."

"Right." Lelia looked her makeshift Healer square in the eye and held the faded blue gaze as firmly as she gripped her hand. "Artel, I believe you." She released the crone's weathered grip. "Now set my hand."

"I am not too proud to admit that I passed out," Lelia said, not looking up from her growing pile of papers.

"Of course."

"But I did so with immense heroism."

"Naturally."

"Some of the greatest heroes I know have passed out *at least* once."

"Carry on, O Brave One."

Lelia woke up on a pallet between a row of barrels and canvas sacks of grain.

"Hellfires, Lyle," she said to the air. "What now?"

"Fall three times, stand up four?" She could even hear her brother's warm, friendly voice saying it. She wished she could also imagine him helping her up, but no such luck. The best she could do was a mental image of him kneeling by her side, smiling encouragingly.

She sat, then stood, her arm pressed tightly to her chest to keep from inadvertently using it. She suspected that she was in a storage room at the inn, and confirmed her deduction as she passed through a hallway leading to the common room.

"Ah, there she is!" Olli leaned on his broom amidst a heap of rushes. "Gave us quite a fright, little sparrow." In a gentler tone, he asked, "How d'ya fare?"

"My hand's broken," Lelia replied blankly.

He winced and made no reply.

She looked behind her at the hallway she'd emerged from. She thought about slogging through the snow to the Healing Temple. She thought about trying to build a fire with one hand, or what would happen if she fell again, or unwrapping food, assuming she even had food to unwrap.

She thought about bandits and could not contain a shiver.

She gathered her wits, turning to regard the innmaster. "How much would it cost me to stay here and convalesce?"

Olli rubbed his chin. "Your voice still works, yeah?"

"Clearly."

"So then, you can still sing." His wildly unkempt brows rose. "And maybe help a little with the picking up?"

"So long as the picking up in question only requires one hand."

He grinned. "Mugs and plates, bread and bowls. Shouldn't be too hard."

"Olli, I am forever in your debt."

He snorted. "I'll be in your debt, before it's over. A Bard—even a broken one—is going to make me money."

"Well, when you put it that way—how much are you going to pay me?"

His eyes twinkled. "How does a room in the back sound?"

She made a show of thinking about it. "Sounds glorious."

"Sounds like a deal."

"That, too."

"Being a Bard without an instrument," Lelia said, setting the quill down and flexing her fingers, "really makes you rethink your repertoire."

The Herald said nothing.

"I did a lot of duets, changing my voice for the different roles." She cocked her head. "Conversations with myself seem to be a specialty, now that I think about it."

He chuckled.

"I decided not to look at it as a restriction so much as a chance to explore other avenues. I used to have to play an instrument to really get my Bardic Gift going."

"Now?"

"Just talking a certain way lets me use it."

"Interesting."

"Attendance slacked off after the first three nights, but Olli said it was still more business than usual."

She eyed the pages of writing she'd already done. "Herda came nearly every night."

"But never said anything?"

She shook her head. "She lurked. I got the feeling she *wanted* to talk, and a few times I initiated, but she'd always scurry off. At first I was relieved—she was weird, you know—but after a while, I got curious." She felt her mouth stretch in a grim smile. "You know that I met the Ashkevron Bard?"

"Really? Or did you just imagine it?"

"No, I really, truly did." She traced one of the knife marks in the table. "At an inn in Forst Reach. After he assured me there was no chance in hell I was going to inherit his position—" The Herald coughed delicately, and Lelia grinned. "—he gave me some useful advice. He told me any idiot could write a song about a hero. It takes real skill to dig the stories out of the commonfolk. They all have stories, he said; you just need to ask the right questions and then frame the answers."

"So . . . ?"

"I started asking questions."

"She can talk to wolves, and chickens squawk in terror when she walks by!"

"I hear there's a colddrake in her stable. She drinks its blood, and that's why she doesn't need a coat in the cold!"

"Her family died from fever, but she keeps their bodies under the floorboards, so now her house is haunted, and they eat those bones she keeps stealing!"

Lelia propped her head up in her good hand, regarding the three scamps with some amusement. She'd made friends with the children of the village, and Jarsi, Bowder, and Aric were three of her best informants. They'd do anything for a song—literally.

Questions about Herda, unfortunately, had yielded nothing but childish speculation.

From what Lelia had gleaned, Herda really *was* the village madwoman. She lived out in the woods, in a cabin once shared by her family until they'd perished of snow fever. She foraged for a living: mushrooms, medicinal roots, rare minerals, exotic barks, and so on. She also had a thing for creatures of all sorts, especially abandoned ones: wounded rodents, broken-winged birds. She loved—or perhaps the proper word was *related* to—animals more than people. There were even rumors of wolf cubs that had been tended to by the wild-eyed Herda.

That, Lelia suspected, was why she'd been pestering Olli for bones. Whatever menagerie she tended, she had to feed them.

No one shunned Herda, per se, but no one invited her over for tea and jam tarts, either. The kindest emotion Lelia had seen directed at the girl was pity. She was considered impoverished, even by local standards. No one sat next to her when she watched Lelia's performances.

"Wolves and monsters and ghosts, eh?" Lelia arched a brow at the boys. "And you're all three reliable eyewitnesses, I take it?"

"My cousin saw the colddrake!" said Aric. "She, uh, ran before it could eat her."

"I saw the ghosts!" said Jarsi.

"So you're saying you *did* see them?" Lelia asked.

"Yeah." Jarsi squirmed. "Kind of. It was dark. I saw *something*! I ran before it could suck out my eyeballs." He looked nervously at his two friends, both clearly skeptical. "What? That's what ghosts *do*!"

"Wolves," Bowder, the eldest boy, muttered. "I'm telling you, she *talks* to *wolves*. You ask her! She won't deny it! She just . . ."

"Grins," Aric whispered.

"Right." Lelia smiled and sat back. "Well, if you can *prove* any of this . . ." She palmed a coin into her good hand, walking it up and down her knuckles. "We'll talk, eh?"

Olli wandered in when the boys were gone, his mouth tugging to one side. "You seem keen on finding out more about our dear, touched Herda."

"I admit a bit of a fascination."

"I've heard it all before." He nodded with a rueful smile toward the door the boys had left through. "Her story was sad once. Now it's just a curiosity for the children to make up wild tales about and the elders to discuss at night." He met her gaze directly. "You ask me, there's a part of her heart that went to the Havens when the fever caught her."

"Hm." Lelia pursed her lips. "What if it's true? The wolves, the colddrake, the ghosts—any of them. But not true to us, just to her." She raised her brows, contemplating her own dance with delirium on the road to Langenfield. "It doesn't need to be real. She just needs to believe it is."

He rubbed his chin thoughtfully. "That'd be a powerful delusion."

"Just a theory." She stood, arching her back in a brief stretch. "I suppose it's time for me to set the tables. How many you think we'll get tonight?"

"Who can say? Last time I saw this much business we had a gleeman claiming to be from Haighlei."

Lelia scoured her memory but could not place the word. "Never heard of it."

"Neither had we. Havens know how he wound up here, but he assured us he was from there, and after seeing his trick we half-believed him. A little snake he would coax out of a jar by playing music." Olli mimed playing a flute. "Strangest thing. The snake would sway back and forth, just like a dancer . . . people came from miles to see it."

"Herda, too?"

Olli laughed. "You never give up, do you? Oh, yes.

Herda was fascinated, just like all of us. He had a side business selling versions of the little egg-flute he played." He grinned. "Took some doing convincing the littles that they weren't magical, and snakes don't just answer when you blow a few notes."

Later, as Lelia set out pots of honey, she thought about the Haighlei gleeman. *A Bardic Gift of a different color?* Her hands itched for a flute. She might even be able to play it one-handed. *First snake I see, I'll have to try.*

Lelia filled her mug herself and reclaimed her seat. Outside, the sun was a candlemark past dawn. She could hear the distant *clop clop clop* as Olli chopped the wood for the day. The Herald said nothing.

"In retrospect," Lelia said after a long drink, "it was very foolish of me, sending the children to pry."

"You didn't know better."

"True, but . . ." She shook her head. "I like to think I would pick up on something—not right."

"What makes you so special?"

She tapped her chest. "I'm a Bard, remember?"

"Bard or not, we all make regrets. And mistakes."

"Yeah. The scamps never got me anything useful anyway." She sipped ale.

"How are you not even a little tipsy?" he asked, a note of criticism in his query.

"Heyla." She tapped the rim of her cup, grinning. "*Still* a Bard."

"Whoever set this did an excellent job," the Healer—introduced as Kerithwyn—said as she poked and prodded Lelia's hand. "There's little for me to do, really."

Artel puffed up with pride. "Excellent job," she echoed.

Lelia felt a smile glide over her lips. The old woman had checked on her hand daily for three weeks, suggesting poultices and brews. Lelia was confidant that she owed her a whole book of songs immortalizing her care.

Kerithwyn sat back and regarded Lelia. "It may be stiff and weak, but it'll be back to its old callused self with use. No reason you can't have a long and illustrious career."

"Provided the snow doesn't kill me," Lelia said.

Kerithwyn nodded. "There is that." She looked up at Artel. "You said something about Sandor's wife carrying twins?"

The two bustled out of the inn, leaving Lelia to flex her fingers experimentally. Her eyes went to the gray cloak hanging by the front door, sewn from local fibers. It wasn't red, but it was warm, and that mattered far more to her at the moment.

Evening came on the wings of a howling wind. The patrons who did wander in were notably subdued, shaking off snow and ice as they took their places. Lelia marked when Herda entered, waiting for her to settle and order her thinned ale from Olli.

Lelia approached her cautiously, as if confronting an easily frightened beast.

"Hey," she said.

Herda looked up at her. "Wh-what?"

"Nothing." She set a plate with a fat joint of meat in front of Herda. The girl's eyes lit up, her tongue flicking like a snake's. "I just wanted to talk." Lelia indicated the plate. "For you. From me."

Herda's eyes darted up at Lelia and then back at the meat—and the marrow bone sticking out of it. "T-talk?"

Lelia sat down beside Herda, but with her back to the table so that her elbows rested on it and her hands dangled off the edge. "Sure. About anything."

Herda carved off a sliver of meat and nibbled. One of the hearthcats wandered by, and she gave it an absent scratch. Lelia waited patiently.

At last, Herda leaned over, eyes downcast. "Can I trust you?" she asked softly. Her stutter had vanished.

Finally, Lelia thought. "Of course."

"I—" Herda's voice lowered further "—have a magical flute."

Lelia closed her eyes briefly. The urge to scream was powerful.

"Really?" she asked, focusing on Herda once more. "What does it do?"

"Magic." Her gaze flashed briefly upward. "Amazing magic." She leaned close to Lelia. "But dangerous."

"How so?" Lelia asked.

"Can't explain. Only show. Do you want to see?"

Not really. Lelia wondered if she would be arrested for punching the Ashkevron Bard next time she saw him. She supposed that would not be the wisest of career moves.

Herda touched her arm, the first time Lelia thought she'd ever seen her touch anyone. "I'll show you," she said, with grave intent. "You of all people should understand." She glared past Lelia, at the unsuspecting villagers. "You're not ignorant."

Completely insane, Lelia thought, but she smiled. "All right."

"Come to my cabin. Just you!" Herda hissed, squeezing Lelia's arm so tightly she was sure it would leave a bruise.

"Just me," Lelia replied solemnly.

Herda let go, snatching up the joint of meat and wrapping it in her cloak. "Good." She smiled. "Tomorrow morning, Bard. Three miles to the north. I'll be waiting."

When Herda was gone, Lelia went and found Olli.

"Performance starting soon?" he asked, looking hopeful.

"Real soon," she said. "But first—how good are you at following someone without being seen?"

* * *

"So you aren't completely stupid." The Herald sounded relieved.

"Coming from a guy whose sense of self-preservation is comparable to that of a turnip's, I choose to find your accusation amusing rather than a grave assault on my character."

"Come now. What did turnips ever do to you?"

She smiled grimly. "As Herda requested, I got to her house a little after dawn."

Herda walked them through a forest of naked raival and hickory trees, stopping when they came to a cottage situated in a wide clearing. A modest stable stood across from it, the double doors shut and barred. Herda said nothing as she led Lelia to her home.

The door glided open on well-oiled hinges. Lelia had expected something fetid and disheveled, but instead she found a tidy domicile, every corner swept, every jar labeled and ordered in place. Colorful curtains decorated the windows, and herbs hung from the rafters.

As nice as the day her family left it, Lelia thought.

Herda plucked an egg-shaped clay flute from the room's only table and held it out.

"May I?" Lelia asked politely.

Herda solemnly passed the instrument to the Bard. Lelia turned it over, the glazed ceramic cool in her palm. A simple whistle, the sort any child could learn on with time and determination.

She brought it to her lips, but Herda's hand shot out.

"No!" she shrieked. Lelia pulled the flute away instantly. Herda snatched it from her. "It's magic. You need to be careful with magic!"

"Oh. Sorry." Lelia's heart pounded. Herda's panic was beginning to infect her.

Herda glared at her as she went to the door. "Stay here. I'll call you when it's safe."

When what's safe? Lelia thought, but the door shut, leaving her alone.

Outside, she heard the sound of a thud and the creak of wood coming from the vicinity of the stable. Herda's voice crooning, and then the soft whistle of the flute. A simple tune, five notes over and over, a hypnotic pattern of high-low-high-high-low.

Lelia went over to one of the windows, but the shutters were in place and doing their duty of keeping the light and cold out. She couldn't see through the cracks. She eyed the door.

She was reaching for the handle when she heard Olli boom out and Herda scream.

"Monster!" he yelled.

"No!" Herda's cry ended in a strangled shriek.

Lelia stood with her hand over the handle, listening. Nothing followed the outburst. The silence was as disconcerting as the brief shouts that had preceded it.

Lelia cracked the door and peered out.

The stable doors were flung wide. Sunlight showed a floor strewn with splintered bones and hay. Something stood half in and half out of the stable.

It was not unlike the moment when her hand broke. Despite the evidence before her, Lelia was convinced this couldn't *really* be happening. But the snake's body and stubby legs, the amethyst eyes, the glittering silver scales—it could only *be* one thing.

The colddrake had its gaze fixed on Olli, who stood halfway between the house and the stable, trapped in the beast's hypnotic stare. His wood-ax was raised over his head, his arms beginning to tremble from the strain.

"No!" Herda sobbed. "No, stop it." She flung her arms around the monster's neck—it was easily the size of a small pony. "You can't! Be good, Snowglass, be good!"

It craned its neck around and looked at her. She gazed back, her eyes shining with tears. A fragile smile lit her face and, without a sign of hesitation, she reached out to stroke its cheek.

The colddrake bent forward and clamped its jaws around her arm.

No! Lelia thought, jerking forward as Herda screamed. The monster wrenched its head back, ripping her arm from the socket, the clay egg-flute going with it. The colddrake turned its gaze back toward Olli, Herda's arm slowly disappearing down its gullet as it advanced on the helpless innmaster.

What can I do? What can I do? Panic and fear made Lelia's stomach churn. The colddrake stood between her and the flute. She looked for weapons, but saw none. There was nothing—

Oh.

Lelia took a deep breath and threw the door wide.

"Hey!" she yelled, bursting into the yard. "Over here, you bastard!"

The colddrake's head turning toward her, its tongue tasting the air. She kept her eyes fixed above the beast, and yet even so she felt a wave of *something* pound against her, compelling her to *look*.

Instead, Lelia sang.

Her Gift reached out as she sang the same five notes, over and over. The colddrake stopped advancing even as Olli staggered forward and Herda made mewling noises on the floor of the stable, crawling through the blood toward her pet.

The colddrake lowered, bowing to Lelia's song. The amethyst eyes closed as the monster settled its head on the snow as if it were a pillow.

Olli raised the wood-ax. The beast never made a sound, but Herda keened like a wounded beast.

"When we set out from the inn, I remember telling him he was silly for bringing that ax along," Lelia mused.

"Sometimes silly is good."

"Don't I know it." She finished off her ale. "We staunched Herda's bleeding and carried her back to Langenfield. Kerithwyn and Artel took her from there." Lelia frowned down at the page, setting her quill aside. "Herda will always hate me."

"Good time to leave town."

"She's not a bad person."

"She was raising a colddrake."

"She thought she could make it good." Lelia shook her head. "She loved it, even when she realized that she loved something that could never be. She wanted to believe she could make it work." Her throat knotted up, her vision blurring.

The Herald's voice softened. "Do you still refer to Herda?"

Lelia sat in silence, and then smiled. "Oh, that's a pretty sentiment, isn't it?" She looked square into the face of her pain. "But that's what I *want* to hear." Her throat tightened. "You'll never say that, Wil."

She spoke it because it was true.

And because he wasn't really there.

"The world hates a heartbroken Bard," she said, the same thing the Ashkevron Bard had told her when he advised her to go south, go north, go anywhere that would take her away from what she couldn't have.

"You can't vie with a Herald's first love," he'd said. "The Kingdom needs him. You can't compete with that."

"Kingdom's got far more acreage than me," Lelia had replied miserably. It was meant to be a joke. It didn't feel like it.

The comfort of a stranger's ear had been too tempting, and she'd spent so many months of her journeyman days doggedly trying to cross paths with Herald Wil. She'd ended up telling the Ashkevron Bard all about her little obsession with her brother's instructor. On Companion-back he and Lyle always outpaced her, but the Heralds often were mired in the local politics, giving her time to be at the next village when they got there.

The elder Bard had shaken his head. "You need to find a song. Find *something*." He had patted her arm gently. "It'll kill you at first, but you'll be better for it."

Lelia thought, *I found my song, and it nearly did kill me. Or Herda, at least. I've found something else, though. Between a Bard with a broken heart and a girl who tamed a colddrake, I know which one folk want to hear about.*

She took a deep breath and seized the quill again. "So, Wil, what *would* you ask?"

The Herald who was not really there replied without hesitation. "How'd a colddrake get this far south?"

Lelia nodded, filling the last page of the report. "A-a-and—was it just this colddrake, or can Herda's trick be reproduced? Is anyone mad enough to try?"

The front door of the inn opened, and Olli walked in with an armful of wood. "Talking to someone?" he asked.

Lelia looked up at him and smiled. "Just me." She plucked a page out of the collection and tossed it in the fire. "Making sure I answer the right questions. It's a little game I play."

"You talk to yourself?"

"All the time. Here." She rolled up the notes and handed them to the innmaster. "Give this to whatever Herald shows up. Tell 'em that it's an official Bardic record of the events. I signed it and everything."

"Great." Olli took the scroll, and then watched as she hoisted her pack. "I—we'll miss you."

"I know." She hugged him tightly. "I am forever in your debt, Drakeslayer."

He blushed. "Take care, m'lady Bard."

"Will do, innmaster." She winked and strolled out, heading north.

*   *   *

Artel found Olli sitting by the fire and poking the coals.

"Your sparrow has flown, I take it?" she asked.

He nodded.

Artel looked about the gloomy common room. "Time to get things ready for the evening, eh?"

He replaced the poker in the stand. "I almost had myself convinced she'd stay."

She smacked his shoulder. "She's a Bard, you besotted fool! You keep someone like that here, and everything good about her dies. Her first love will always be the road."

Olli grimaced. "Where I can't follow."

Artel rolled her eyes and threw her hands in the air. "Bright Lady, lad, get yourself on top of a woman already, and forget the one that never paid notice to you!"

She stormed out. The innmaster roused not much later, rolling his stiff shoulders. He built up the fire and then went to pulling out tables and benches, placing plates and bowls of honey.

The fire burned merrily all the long night.

Live On
by *Tanya Huff*

Tanya Huff lives and writes in rural Canada with her partner Fiona Patton and five, no six, no seven . . . and a lot of cats as well as an elderly chihuahua who mostly ignores her. The recent adaptation of the five Vicki Nelson books to television (*Blood Ties*) finally allowed her to use her degree in radio and television arts some twenty-five years after the fact. Her twenty-fourth and most recent novel, *Valor's Trial*, came out from DAW in hardcover in June 2008, and she is currently working on *The Enchantment Emporium*, a stand-alone contemporary fantasy. In her spare time she practices the guitar and tries to avoid some of the trickier versions of a Gm7.

"Are you the young man who wrote that report about Appleby?"

Heralds didn't tend to grow old. Even in times of peace, they lived lives that lowered the odds of them dying in bed to slightly less than negligible. It seemed that the elderly Herald who'd appeared at Jors' side was the exception to prove the rule. His shoulders were hunched forward, his eyes were red rimmed and moist, he stood with his weight supported on a polished cane, and above the scarf he wore in spite of the heat of a sunny, late spring day, age had pleated his face into a hundred wrinkles.

"Are you deaf, boy? I said, are you the young man

who wrote that report about Appleby! Are you Herald Jors?"

Age had roughened his voice but not lessened his volume.

People were beginning to gather, and Jors could see a trio of Companions heading in across the field to see what all the noise was about. "I am. I'm Jors."

"Who taught you to write reports? Never mind. You leave too much out. That report about Appleby? All apples."

"That's pretty much all there is in Appleby."

"What? There's no people? No dogs? No cats? No buildings? No apple trees for pity's sake?"

"Of course there are and . . ."

"Of course there are," the elderly Herald snorted. "Why didn't you mention them, then, eh? You mentioned the apples, why not the apple trees?"

Jors smiled and spread his hands. "They didn't do much."

The rheumy eyes narrowed. "Don't get smart with me, boy. I've had my Whites longer than your father's been alive, maybe even your father's father, and there has been a distinct disintegration, no, dispersing, no, *erosion* of writing ability over the last few years." He shook a swollen finger at Jors—or perhaps he merely pointed and it shook on its own, it was hard to tell. "Reports used to say things. Give details. Tell stories. They used to bring Valdemar to life. Now it's all apples!"

Since he seemed to be waiting for Jors to respond, the younger man ventured a reasonably sincere "I'm sorry."

"Don't be sorry. Do it right the next time. Honestly," he muttered, turning and making his way toward the stables. "What are they teaching them when they're in their Grays?"

Jors watched him go, watched him correcting a lat-

eral drift every six steps or so, and wondered if he
should have offered his arm.

"I see you've met Herald Tamis."

He turned to see Erica, one of his yearmates, leaning on the fence, one arm stretched out over the top
rail so she could scratch up under Raya, her Companion's mane. "He doesn't like the way I write reports."

"As near as I can tell, he doesn't like the way anyone writes reports." She put a quaver into her voice.
"It's all business now, I tell you. No stories." Then
her expression changed. "Raya says we shouldn't
mock him."

"I wasn't."

She smacked his shoulder with her free hand. "You
would have."

"Who is he?" Jors asked, climbing up onto the top
rail so he could pay a similar attention to his own
Companion. Who seemed to be sulking.

:I was not sulking,: Gervis protested, pushing against
Jors' leg almost hard enough to knock him off the
fence. *:You were ignoring me.:*

:I wasn't.:

:I had an itch.:

Jors rolled his eyes as he pushed a hand up under
the silken mane and began to scratch. *:Better?:*

:Yes.:

"Tamis is a historian," Erica told him. "He has
rooms behind the library—I think they used to be
storerooms until he took them over. He's working on
the history of the Heralds."

"Why have I never met him?"

"Because you're never here."

Gervis snorted. *:She's right.:*

*:I don't like cities. Circuits have to be ridden. I might
as well ride them.:*

:We.:

:We,: he repeated apologetically. And then some-

thing occurred to him. "Don't histories usually get written after the fact?"

Erica shrugged. "It's an ongoing history."

"Let's hope."

Tamis had reached the stables and dealt with the heavy door by pounding on it with his cane until someone opened it from the inside. Obviously someone who'd opened the door for Tamis before as he danced back so the next blow missed him.

"How old is his Companion then?"

:She's not young,: Gervis answered diplomatically.

His room still smelled slightly musty, as if no one had been in it for months. Since he *hadn't* been in it for months, Jors wasn't terribly surprised. Crossing to the window, he pried it open and brushed the two dead flies on the sill outside, allowing the living fly to leave under its own power.

On the top floor of the Herald's Wing, his room had a wounderful view of the Companion's Field but was so small—a little smaller, in fact, than the rooms housing the Grays—that no one had wanted it until he'd chosen it. Since he'd probably spent less than two months in it over the five years he'd had his Whites, Jors had no problem with the size. He didn't see much point in claiming space he never used.

A trio of gleaming white figures galloped across the field, kicking up their heels and playing what looked like the Companion version of tag. Even at a distance, he could see all three of them looked distinctly coltish.

:Gervis?:

:What is it?: The young stallion sounded a bit petulant.

:I was just checking to see if you were all right.:

:I'm in the Companion's Field, surrounded by Companions, on a beautiful day. Why wouldn't I be all right?:

:I just . . . :

:Don't like being stuck in the city,: Gervis finished

his sentence. *:If it helps, don't think of it as being stuck in the city, think of it as being stuck at the Collegium.:*

:I'm not sure I see the difference.:

:Did I mention I had carrots?:

:No, you didn't.:

:And that Raya is here?:

:And you'd like me to leave you alone?:

:Yes.:

Jors grinned. Gervis and the mare enjoyed each other's company whenever they crossed paths. *:You know where I am if you need me.:*

:Companion's Field, beautiful day, Raya . . .:

:Yeah, yeah, I get it. You're not likely to need me.: Still grinning, he let their connection fade down to the gentle touch that was always with him and drew in a deep breath. Probably his imagination that he could taste the population of Haven on the breeze, and there was no way he could hear the noise those same people had to be making on the other side of the walls.

His new Whites came in time for him to attend a spring garden party at the palace.

:I can't believe this is what I'm reduced to,: he muttered, delaying the inevitable by lingering at the Companion's Field for as long as possible.

:Things are quiet. Quiet is good. And you will not be the only Herald there,: Gervis reminded him. *:Perhaps you should try enjoying yourself.:*

"Most of the stains will come out." Lips pursed, the laundress turned his vest around in her hands." How on earth did you manage to make such a mess?"

Jors sighed. "My Companion suggested I enjoy myself. That seemed to involve Lord Randall's eldest daughter, a full glass of wine, two rosebushes, and a dessert tray."

Her brows rose nearly to her hairline. "That was you?"

"You heard about it?"

"Oh, sweet boy, everyone's heard about it." She patted his shoulder with a plump hand. "They'll be telling the story in the kitchens for years."

"Herald Jors?" The boy grinned up at him, seemingly oblivious to the bruise swelling his left eye shut. "The Dean wants to see you."

"Thank you . . . ?"

"Petrin."

"What happened to your eye, Petrin?"

"Weapons training." He grinned. "I forgot to block."

Impossible not to grin back. "Now you know why you're supposed to."

"That's what the Weaponsmaster said. Me and Serrin, that's my Companion, Serrin, we can't wait to get out on the road."

Jors rubbed at the marks of thorns on the back of his right hand. "Yeah. I know how you feel."

"I've got escort duty available, heading south to Hartsvale, a small village up in the hills east of Crescent Lake. Interested?"

"Havens, yes!" Jors felt his cheeks heat up as Dean Carlech raised both brows at his vehemence. "Sorry. Things are just . . . *I'm* just better out on the road."

"I suspect the palace gardeners would agree with you. Herald Tamis' great-niece is to be married, and he wants to attend. Verati, his Companion, is also elderly and we don't want them traveling that distance on their own, so your job will be to get them there and back." He looked down at the papers spread over his desk, one corner of his mouth twitching within the shadow of his beard in an obvious attempt not to laugh. "Enjoy yourself at the wedding. Try not to demolish any topiary."

"It was an accident."

"Hellfire, lad!" The laugh escaped. "No one thinks you did it on purpose."

"So, you're the one who'll be *escorting* us south." Eyes narrowed, arms folded, Tamis raked a scathing gaze over Jors. "I'm not thrilled with the idea of a babysitter, just so you know. Verati and I have traveled from one end of this country to the other in our time, and we don't need a Herald barely out of his Grays assigned to keep an eye on us."

"I've been riding Circuit or Courier for more than five years."

"Of course you have. I've had rashes longer. Verati and I, we'd be fine on our own, I've told Carlech that. Not that he listens, the young pup. Well, as long as you're here," he said, waving a hand toward the pack on his bed, "you might as well put those young muscles to use and carry that down to the yard for me."

"Is this it, then?" Jors asked as he lifted the pack. He appreciated the older Herald's ability to travel light. He never carried more than the bare necessities himself.

"Don't be absurd, no silly, no *ridiculous*, boy. There's three more already down there." Fingers white around the carved head of his cane, Tamis wobbled out into the hall. "We're not riding Circuit, we're going to a wedding."

Verati was the closest Jors had ever seen to a stout Companion.

:*I wouldn't think that quite so loudly, Heartbrother.*:
Jors shot a near panicked glance at Gervis, standing saddled and waiting in the yard. :*She can't hear me, can she?*:

:*Of course not, but your face gives your thoughts away.*:
Tamis lifted his forehead from where it had been resting against the creamy white forehead of his Com-

panion and shuffled aside, steadying himself on the bridle. "Herald Jors, this is my lady, Verati."

Jors bowed.

Verati inclined her head carefully so as not to topple her Herald.

:She says that was remarkably graceful considering your inclination to dive into rosebushes.:

:Why does everyone keep harping on that!:

:Because things are so quiet there's not much else happening. And speaking of harping, one of the younger Bards has composed a rondeau. It's quite good, although I'm not sure befores *is actually a word.:*

It took forever to get out of Haven as Tamis seemed to know everyone they passed.

"Move too fast and miss the point of travel," Tamis snorted when Jors mentioned it. "Everyone has a story. And you're thinking, 'Why should I care about everyone's story? What adventures could a cobbler, no a butcher, no a *whore* have that would be worth telling?' That's the trouble with the young. They think there's only one story and they're the hero in it."

"I don't . . ."

"You'd be surprised," Tamis continued, interrupting Jors's protest. "Surprised, I tell you, if you took the time to listen. Back in my day, we listened or we got what-for. I remember Shorna, one of my yearmates; she'd never ridden before she was Chosen, and one day, during a class, she went right off over her Companion's head, and Herald Dorian, she was the instructor, she said, 'Well, at least it's a nice day.' Shorna was so mad Dorian would say it was a nice day after she landed on the grass like that." He nodded so vigorously, he began to topple, and Verati had to sidestep to keep him in the saddle. "It *was* a nice day though," he added thoughtfully. "They're all dead now, you know, except for me. It's no fun getting old, boy. Although . . ." he gave a wet cough that Jors

realized, after a moment, was meant to be a chuckle."
. . . it beats the alternative."

:Speaking of old; how long can he stay mounted?:
Jors wondered as Tamis greeted a water seller with a
question about her father.

:Verati won't let him fall.:

*:Not what I meant. Riding, even riding a Companion,
can't be easy on old joints, and I'd like to at least be
out of the city before we have to stop for the day.:*

In the end, Willow, the younger of their two mules,
got them moving, objecting to the crowd at the Hay-
market with a well-placed kick. Jors made a mental
note to thank her with a carrot at the first opportunity.

The South Trade Road offered a wide selection of
inns between Haven and Kettlesmith, and, for a while,
Jors was afraid they'd be staying in all of them. What
had seemed like a ridiculously generous amount of
travel time up in the Dean's office now made more
sense.

Tamis was an early riser but only because he
napped for an hour or two after they stopped at midday and went to bed while the chickens were foraging
for one last meal in the inn yards. Jors spent his evenings grooming both Companions. Verati had a disconcerting way of falling asleep the moment he put
brush to withers, but then Verati had a disconcerting
way of falling asleep whenever they stopped, her head
falling forward until her breath blew two tiny, identical
divots out of the dusty ground.

They let Verati set the pace, and Tamis either
talked about Heralds long dead . . .

*:And Shorna was so mad Dorian would say it was
a nice day after she landed on the grass like that.:* Jors'
silent chorus followed the inflections of the older Herald's voice exactly.

:Does he not remember he told this story?: Gervis
wondered.

:I don't think so.:

:He called me Arrin this morning.:

:At least Arrin was a stallion. He called me Janis.:

. . . or slumped back against the high cantle and dozed in the saddle. Dozing, Jors discovered, did not cut into actual naptime.

When they reached Dog Inn and the turn east to Herald's Hill, Tamis decided to join Jors in the common room for their evening meal.

"Are you sure? Your digestion wasn't too happy after lunch."

"Stop fussing, boy. My digestion is none of your business, no responsibility, no *concern*."

Given how early they were eating—Tamis' digestion also had strong ideas about eating too late—even the presence of two Heralds couldn't fill the room. There were four equally elderly locals playing Horses and Hounds at a table on the other side of the small fire and tucked into a corner, a merchant waiting with no good grace for the smith to repair a cracked axle on his wagon.

"That's apple wood." Tamis sniffed appreciatively as he settled. "Can't beat the way it smells as it burns. Why didn't you mention *that* in your Appleby report?"

"I never noticed it."

"Of course you didn't. What are you doing?"

He'd been pulling the crusts off the thick slices of brown bread. Unless there was stew or soup to dip them into, previous meals had taught him Tamis couldn't handle crusts. Waving one of the slices, he tried to explain. "I'm uh . . ."

Tamis snatched it out of his hand. "Stop fussing."

"So, Heralds." The innkeeper settled at their table expectantly. "What news?"

"It's quiet," Jors told her. "The borders are peaceful, trade is good, and even the weather has been fine."

"He writes his reports the same way," Tamis sighed. "Accurate but not exactly memorable." He took a long swallow of ale— *"Only ale worth drinking should be dark enough to see your reflection in."* —coughed a bit, then smiled at the innkeeper broadly enough to show he still had most of his teeth. "You want a story, I'm afraid you're stuck with me."

:Oh, no.:

:What is it, Chosen?:

:Tamis is about to tell a story. I bet you a royal it's either Shorna or Terrik up the tree.:

It was neither.

". . . and although he may have defeated the first rosebush, the second, I fear, was the victor. Everyone has a story, boy," he added. "You can thank me for not mentioning your name." He likely thought the laughter would cover the comment. Which it would have had Tamis' voice not been at his usual compensating-for-being-mostly-deaf volume.

On the other hand, Jors reflected philosophically, even the merchant with the cracked axle seemed to have cheered up.

". . . and Shorna was so mad Dorian would say it was a nice day after she landed on the grass like that." Tamis gave his wet cough chuckle and tossed a stick into the fire. "I remember it like it was yesterday."

:Gervis . . .:

:Verati does not see that there is a problem.:

:But . . .:

:She says age is not a problem. It just is.:

Jors glanced over at the elderly mare, providing a warm support behind Tamis's back and wondered if, all things considered, she was the best judge. *:What do you think?:*

He felt Gervis's mental sigh. *:I think I'm tired of hearing that story.:*

"I wanted to be a Bard, you know," Tamis said

suddenly. "Good thing my lady arrived when she did or all that wanting would have broken my heart."

"Your family didn't want you to be a Bard?" Jors asked after it became obvious Tamis wasn't going to continue.

The old man started and peered across the fire at him. "What do you know about it, boy?"

"You said wanting to be a Bard would have broken your heart."

"I did? Well, it would have. Couldn't carry a tune if my life depended on it. I never forget a story though, and there's so many stories that are forgotten. You wouldn't believe the stories I found going through the old reports, stories about Heralds long dead who lived lives that should be remembered. Not because they made the great heroic gestures—those, they get put to music to inspire a bunch more damned fool heroics—but because they did what needed to be done. Those are the stories that should live on. But if you write a report that holds just the facts and has none of you in it, well, that's you gone, isn't it?" Tamis snorted. "Heralds don't die in bed, now do they?"

"Well, you're not dead yet."

Verati opened one sapphire eye.

:*She doesn't think you're funny,*: Gervis translated helpfully.

At Herald's Hill, Tamis stirred three spoonfuls of honey into his breakfast tea and told a full common room the story of the merchant they'd met at Dog Inn. Later, while loading the mules, Jors saw a carter in the inn yard checking his axles.

:*Oh, look, the moral of the story.*:

:*Chosen, that's . . .*: The pause continued long enough that Jors turned to look. Gervis tossed his head, looking a little sheepish. :*Okay, it's actually pretty funny.*:

At Crescent Lake, Tamis told the story of a farmer

he'd met back when he'd been riding Circuit and the girl he'd spent twelve years wooing.

:*He remembers every detail about that but he can't remember my name?*:

:*Or that he told us about Shorna falling off her horse?*:

:*What does Verati talk about while we're walking?*: Jors wondered, setting the pack on Willow's pad.

:*How the roads were straighter and carrots were sweeter when she was young.*:

:*And I bet mules were better behaved,*: Jors muttered, dodging a flailing hoof.

On their own, even with a mule, Jors figured he and Gervis could have made Crescent Lake to Hartsvale in one long day. Tamis and Verati didn't do long days.

When it started to rain about mid-afternoon. Jors pulled an oilskin cloak out of Tamis' bag, tucked it around him, and gave some serious thought to riding all night. He wanted to get Tamis out of the damp as soon as possible.

:*Do you think Verati could do it?*:

:*I think she would try for her Herald's sake, but she is also very old. We've been traveling for some time, and she is more tired than she will admit to.*:

:*All right, then, I'll build a lean-to.*: He repeated his plans out loud as he dismounted.

"You're fussing." Tamis's protest would have held more heat had he not begun to cough.

"Gervis hates getting wet." Which had the added benefit of being the truth. His Companion had a cat's opinion of water.

"You're handy with an axe."

"My family are foresters."

"My family are foresters," Tamis repeated, rubbing a gleaming drop of mucus off the end of his nose. "What kind of a story is that?"

"A very short one," Jors grunted as he drove the first of the stakes into the ground.

* * *

No children ran out to greet them as they entered the north end of the village late the next day.

Gervis lifted his head. *:I smell smoke.:*

:So do I.:

Verati stopped so suddenly Willow trotted up her lead rope and smacked into a gleaming white haunch. Tamis, wrapped in every piece of dry clothing he had remaining, looking more like a pile of white laundry than a person, pulled his cane from the saddle ties. "Something's wrong."

Then a dog started barking and, between one heartbeat and the next, men and women spilled out of the houses, children watching wide-eyed from windows and doors.

"Heralds! Thank the Lady you've come, we've had . . ." The heavyset woman out in front rocked to a halt and frowned. "Uncle Tamis?"

"Who were you expect . . ." The querulous question turned into coughing, his cane tumbling to the ground as he clutched at the saddle horn with both hands.

"What happened here?" Jors snapped, pitching his voice to carry over the coughing and the babble of voices it provoked.

"Quiet!" The heavyset woman turned just far enough to see that she was obeyed, then locked her attention on Jors. "Raiders," she growled. "They hit around noon, when most were out in the fields and no one much here to stand up to them. Eight or nine of them rode in and tossed a torch onto Kervin's roof. Same group as has been hitting the farms—ride in and set a fire, grab a lamb here or a chicken there, and ride out thinking no one can touch them. But Bardi— that's Merilyn and Conner's youngest girl . . ."

A man and a woman, neither of them young, pushed forward through the crowd and stared up at him with grieving eyes.

". . . well, she's a dab shot, and she put an arrow

into three of them. Knocked one out of the saddle, hit one in the meaty part of the thigh, and the third up in the shoulder. Well, they didn't like that, did they? And the one on the ground, I'm guessing he was a brother or something close to him they called their leader because when they saw he was down, and folk were starting to run in, they grabbed her." Thick fingers closed around a handful of air. "Grabbed her and rode off."

So much for peaceful and quiet. Jors cursed himself for thinking it ever had to end. "The raider Bardi shot, do the others think he's dead?"

"No, he was thrashing and yelling."

"So they've probably taken her to trade. Her for him."

"Then why not do it? Then and there?"

"You said she injured two of them? It's hard to drive a bargain when you're in danger of bleeding to death. They've ridden just far enough to tend their wounds, and they'll be back." He glanced west, at the sun sitting fat and orange just above the horizon. "Tomorrow."

"So we wait?" A voice from the back of the crowd.

"No!" Tamis answered before Jors could.

"No," Jors agreed, cutting him off. There was no need for more detail than that. And everyone knew it. Twisting around, he untied the lead line and began tossing unnecessary gear to the ground. "Which way?"

"East. We tried to follow, but they're on hill ponies, tough and fast, and we lost the trail in the rock. Nearly lost two of our own as well." Her voice grew defensive. No one wanted the Herald to think they'd given up too soon. "The hills are treacherous if you don't know them. They do."

"We can handle the hills." He checked that his quiver was full. "I'll find them."

"We'll find them," Tamis protested, struggling to free himself from his wrappings, Verati shifting her weight to keep him from falling. "When I was a boy, I all but lived in those hills. I know their stories!"

:*Chosen . . .*:

:*I know.*:

But fate intervened before Jors had to speak as another coughing fit nearly pitched the old Herald out of the saddle. Would have pitched him out of the saddle had the heavyset woman not moved close enough to support his weight.

"Take care of him," Jors told her. He swept his gaze over the gathered villagers, who needed hope as much as anything. "I'll mark the trail for those who follow."

Then Gervis spun on one rear hoof and headed east.

Easy enough, even as the daylight faded, to see where a group of mounted men left the track, following a deer trail into the trees.

:*What are you going to do when we catch up?*: Gervis asked, barely slowing.

:*Depends on what we find.*:

:*If that woman is right, there's at least eight of them.*:

:*But two of them are wounded.*: Bending low in the saddle, he tried not to think of what the others might be doing.

:*Verati isn't happy.*:

:*We were sent with them to keep them safe. Safe does not include tracking armed raiders through hill country at night. I know her heart is willing, but . . . .*: Underbrush pulled at his boots. Gervis was larger than the horses they followed and was breaking a path a blind man could see. :*We'll bring them a story with a happy ending. That'll have to do.*:

When they emerged into one of the long ridges of rock that ribbed through the hills, the sky was a deep sapphire blue, and long, dark shadows hid the trail. Jors dismounted and found a scar where a hoof had scraped lichen off rock. :*Southeast:*

He nearly missed the point where they left the rock to go east again, but Gervis caught the scent of fresh blood, and a spattering not yet entirely dry showed the way.

:I smell smoke.:

:They must have lit a fire. They've made camp, then, and we're close.:

The camp, when they found it, looked almost familiar. Jors checked his mental maps. Unless they'd traveled a lot farther from the village than he thought, they were still some distance from the border, but there was no mistaking the pattern of fire and picket line and the way the weapons had been set, butts to the ground, points crossed.

:They're army, or ex-army. Hardorn lancers.: Bow in hand, he moved closer carefully. *:I'm betting some bright officer came up with a way to use their troublemakers to their advantage. It's why they took the girl. Why they'll want their man back so badly. I bet their first order was not to get caught.:*

:I don't see the girl.:

:Neither do I. We have to get closer.:

He lifted a foot and set it down again as a rough voice growled, "I may miss you in this light, but I'll not miss the big white horse. You keep him calm and you do what I say, and you might just survive this."

:Gervis?:

:Crossbow bolt up in under my jaw. Point touching skin.:

Companions were fast and moved in ways a man seeing a horse wouldn't expect. But were they faster than a finger tightening around a crossbow trigger? Jors couldn't risk that.

:How did he move in so close?:

:I don't think he moved in, I think we stopped right beside him.:

Not so much *ex*-army that they didn't have a man on watch.

*   *   *

"Let me kill him, Adric."

"He's a Herald, you idiot." Torso bare but for streaks of blood and a field dressing on his shoulder, Adric scowled down at Jors, who struggled up onto his knees. With Gervis' life in the balance, he'd walked into the camp and been slammed to the ground with the butt of a lance. The point of that lance was now centered in his chest. "Kill one and they all come down on you."

"Then we tie him and leave him here," the first man grunted. "Take the horse with us, probably get a pretty penny for it."

:Chosen!:

:I'm okay.: More or less. *:You?:*

:He hasn't moved the bow away.:

They might not understand what a Companion was, but they'd dealt with Valdemar enough to know Jors wouldn't provoke the shot.

"We're not," Aldric growled, "going anywhere without Lorne."

"And that's why we have the girl."

Eyes adjusted to the firelight, Jors could see her now, sitting on the ground with her knees drawn up, gaze locked on his face. Fifteen maybe, no older, on that cusp between girl and woman. She looked frightened but determined. A boy, not much older, stood behind her, arms crossed, and a man with his breeches cut away and a bloody dressing on his thigh—the man who'd spoken—reclined beside her.

"Not the only reason, mind you," he added reaching over and lightly smacking her cheek.

Bardi jerked away from his touch, provoking a shove from the boy behind her, but as near as Jors could tell, it hadn't yet progressed beyond touching and threat. They'd got there in time and had provided, if nothing else, a distraction. Now, they just had to get away.

He'd seen six of the eight men—Adric, obviously their leader, the one who spoke first, the one with the lance, two by Bardi, the one with the crossbow on Gervis. The other two had to be behind him, but the point of the lance kept him from turning to make sure.

"You know, I've heard stories about Heralds. This one . . . "A boot impacted with his thigh without much force, making the point that Jors was there to be kicked. ". . . isn't much."

Seven.

"He tracked us over rock in the dark," Adric snorted. "What more do you want?"

"He got caught."

"Yeah, well, you can't sneak for shit wearing all that white. Get the rope, Herin, and tie him. We'll leave him here when we move out," Adric added as the kicking man moved toward the piles of gear, "but we'll kill the horse. Drive it off a cliff. Everyone knows who the damned things belong to, and we don't need that kind of trouble."

"If you don't need trouble . . ." Jors forced himself to look in control regardless of position or lances or crossbows. ". . . then you should pack up and go now. You don't think I came out here alone, do you?" He added as Adric's brows pulled in. "You don't think Valdemar is going to ignore Hardorn violating the border, do you?"

"I'll give him violating," the man with the thigh injury snarled, reaching for Bardi.

"Leave her be!" Adric snapped. "I want to hear this. Go on."

Jors met his gaze and held it. "We were already on our way out to deal with you. When you took the girl, you just hastened the inevitable. Lorne is in custody, all you can do now is run for the border." He was giving them an out. If they thought they were cornered . . .

"All I see is you," Adric told him.

"I was out front, tracking. I've marked the trail for the Heralds following behind me."

He could hear men shifting position nervously, but he kept his eyes on Adric's face. He thought for a moment he'd done it; then Adric shook his head.

"I think you're telling me a story."

"He isn't!" Bardi tried to stand but the wounded raider dragged her back to the ground. "We sent for the Heralds after you burned down Kirin's barn!"

:Smart girl.:

:We will free her, Chosen.:

Adric stared at her for a long moment. "How many?"

"Heralds?" She rolled her eyes. "How should I know? I was with you when they arrived!"

:Brave girl.:

:We will *free her.:*

"Two lies," Adric growled, "do not make a story true." He turned, firelight painting orange streaks on his torso. "Herin, the rope!"

"Got it." Herin straightened, coil of rope on one shoulder, started back and paused, head cocked toward the surrounding woods. "There's something out there!"

"Animal."

"Something big."

"Big animal," Adric scoffed. "Now get your thumb out of your ass and get that rope over . . ."

The sound of a large animal moving through thick brush was unmistakable.

:No one could have followed that quickly from the village.:

:Verati says Tamis says to be ready.:

:What?: That was all the protest he had time for as Verati charged out from between the trees, screaming a challenge as she galloped through the camp. Gone was the stout old lady who fell asleep being brushed,

replaced by a gleaming white dervish ridden by a rider in white whirling a sword above his head.

A man screamed on the side of the camp, going down under her hooves.

Eight.

Diving forward under the lance, Jors took the man who held it to the ground as Gervis answered Verati's challenge. A crossbow bolt slammed into packed dirt. The distinctive crunch of shattering bone was nearly drowned out by another scream.

Verati charged back out of the trees, closer to the fire, sending the raider with the wounded thigh rolling away from her hooves. Bardi seemed to be dealing with the boy. Jors got his hands on the lance, drove the butt hard into the lancer's stomach, and twisted just in time to block a blow from behind. Gervis reared. Herin dropped the rope and ran.

"Call them off!"

Jors looked down to see a lance point driven into his stomach, the edge sharp enough to cut through his leathers. Pain caught up a second later as blood began to dribble out of the tear. "Call them off," Adric repeated. "Or I'll gut you."

"It's too late," Jors told him. On the other side of the fire, the boy threw himself up onto a horse and rode out into the darkness. Adric was now the last man standing. "You've lost."

"No."

"It's over."

"No!" His eyes were wild. His chest heaved. Blood seeped through the bandage on his shoulder. "Not possible! We were riding against farmers! Shepherds! Stupid villagers!" He spun on one heel, shifted his grip, drew back his arm, and hurled the lance directly at Bardi, silhouetted in front of the fire, snarling, "Her fault."

* * *

Bardi and the lance in flight. Then a white blur.

The lance took Verati in the throat. Blood sprayed. She slammed to her knees, Tamis flying over her head.

Jors took Adric down, quickly, efficiently, not even thinking of what he was doing. Gervis was already there when he slid to his knees by Verati's side. The blood had already begun to puddle, it was pouring so fast from the wound.

:You cannot save her, Heartbrother.:

:Maybe not her, but Tamis . . .:

The old man lay crumpled, reaching back weakly for his Companion. He still wore his scarf wrapped around his throat, and instead of a sword, his cane lay broken by his side. Jors had seen dying men before, and he knew he saw one now. He moved him, carefully, until he could touch Verati's face. She sighed her last breath against his fingers.

Tamis smiled. "Every story," he said, his voice barely louder than the breeze in the surrounding trees, "has to end."

He moved a finger just enough to wrap a line of silver white mane around it. "Stop fussing," he murmured. Then he closed his eyes. And never opened them again.

"My fault?"

Jors looked up to see Bardi standing on the other side of Verati's body, the firelight glinting on the tears running down her cheeks.

"My fault?" she repeated.

"No." He tried to put all the reassurance he could into his voice. "Not your fault."

"I just . . . I just couldn't let them ride in and ride away. I just needed to do something. I just needed . . ."

She needed her story to start.

One of the raiders was dead, skull caved in by Gervis' hoof; the rest they tied with their own ropes, trussed up by their own fire waiting for justice. Only the boy had gotten away, and Jors found himself hoping he made it safely to the border, that he carried the story home of how Valdemar's borders were defended—farmers, shepherds, villagers not there for the plundering.

Bardi helped him take off Verati's saddle, then watched as he tucked Tamis up against her side. "What do we do now?" she asked, wiping her nose on her sleeve.

"We wait until help comes," Jors told her, moving to build up the fire. The villagers might not have followed him, but he knew, knew without a doubt, that they'd followed Tamis. One thing to let a young man in Herald's Whites save the day and another thing entirely to let an old man do it. While they waited, he'd tell her a story. Practice the story he'd write in his report.

It wouldn't be a big, heroic story, the kind that got put to music to inspire more heroics although, in the end, he supposed, it would be that kind of story too.

"He wanted to be a Bard, but he couldn't sing. He liked his tea sweet and his beer dark and the smell of apple wood smoke, and he had a friend named Shorna . . ."

Passage at Arms
by *Rosemary Edghill*

In addition to her work with Mercedes Lackey, Rosemary Edghill has collaborated with authors such as the late Marion Zimmer Bradley and the late SF Grand Master Andre Norton. She has worked as an SF editor for a major New York publisher, as a freelance book designer, and as a professional book reviewer. Her hobbies include sleep, research for forthcoming projects, and her Cavalier King Charles Spaniels. Her website can be found at http://www.sff.net/people/eluki.

Aellele Calot's family were smallholders, with a farm in the Sweetgrass Valley, north of the Terilee River and east of the Trade Road. The land there was all farming country, settled and serene (too far north to ever have to worry about Karsite raiders, too far south and east to fear bandits). She was a middle child (two older brothers and one older sister, two younger sisters born a year apart—and a caboose set of brothers) and middling in every way: middling height, middling brown hair, middling eyes neither gray nor blue. She could spin a little, weave a little, play the gittern and the drum, make cider and churn butter, and she had always expected that when she grew up, she would either marry and run a farm somewhere in the Sweetgrass, stay here on hers and help her Ma and Da, or move to one of the nearby towns and become an independent guildswoman.

Or so she'd thought until the day that Tases came walking into her father's dairy and said that she was Chosen.

Aellele had asked him if he was really sure he'd come for her (because there were seven kids besides her tumbling around the farm, not to mention apprentices and hired hands), as Heralds weren't people you saw every day (Aellele was twelve, and she'd only seen a Herald up close in person twice). But the Heralds and everybody else right down to the head of the local Grange made sure that everybody knew what their duties and privileges were when a Companion on Search came calling. And he said (inside her mind, where she heard the words just as clearly as if he'd said them out loud) that he *was* sure, and that his name was Tases, and that it was her he'd come for, not any of her sisters or her brothers, but that she certainly had time to eat her dinner and have her Ma pack her a bag and say goodbye to everyone before she came away with him.

And she looked into his eyes, and they were bluer than jay-feathers or clear Harvest-tide skies, and she could feel something about *him* and something about *her* locking up together hand in hand. Aellele knew that it wouldn't matter anymore whether the day was warm or cold; she'd always feel warm.

And that was how Aellele went off to Haven to become a Herald.

Only . . . it wasn't *absolutely certain* that she'd become a Herald, because being Chosen was really only the beginning. There were lessons—years of lessons. Some of them were simple, things she didn't need so much but others did (reading and writing); and some were things she had a little bit of but now needed more of (math and history—not just Valdemar's, but of every land that surrounded her—Karse and Hardorn and Rethwellen and Iftel); and others were things she didn't know anything about at all (swordplay and diplomacy and legal codes and precedent). All meant to shape her and prepare her for the day when she and Tases would ride out on their first Circuit, accompanied by a senior Herald and Companion, of course, who would make the final judgment as to whether the two of them were ready to set off on their own.

Privately, Aellele was sure that day would never come.

She loved Tases (how could anyone *not* love Tases?) and she loved Haven and she loved the Heralds' Collegium and she even loved some of her fellow students, because some of them were nobles (who knew it was their duty and honor to serve in this wonderful special way), and some of them were the sons and daughters of soldiers (who had been brought up to service in a different way), and some of them were from farming families just like hers (so it was almost like having her own family with her), and some of them were the children of tradesmen (who had led lives so different from hers that hearing about them was like hearing a Harvest Festival wondertale), and the ones she didn't love, she liked.

And she was pretty good in her classes (except for combat and self-defense, and it was early days yet, and the older students said that *nobody* satisfied either Master Alberich or themselves in the first moonturns of classes).

But.

Heralds (she heard this morning noon and night, more from the senior students than from the instructors, and she already knew—in the back of her mind—that the reason she wasn't hearing it from them was because they *didn't want to scare any of the First Years to death)* had to not only be perfect and *right* all the time, but they had to be *nice*, too. And being *nice* meant not being petty or small-minded or cruel or deliberately handing down a false judgment or a less-than-the-best-judgment just because they could get away with it, or shirking their duty, or . . .

The fact that Aellele knew that if she ever did such an awful thing she'd disappoint Tases horribly just made it all worse. And it didn't matter how many times he told her she *wouldn't* do something like that, that she was years away from ever even getting the *chance* to do something like that, well . . . Aellele knew herself. Hadn't she thrown a handful of feed at the head of the old rooster who'd pecked at her instead of scattering it properly—and more than once? And switched the salt for the sugar in the canister (making sure to leave a layer of sugar on top so the switch wouldn't be noticed) when she'd known Saraceth was going to be baking something special for that boy she was courting? She'd said hurtful things—true things and flat lies both—more times than she could count, and gotten into fights, and stolen things (and lied about it), and when she came to reckon up all the bad things she'd done, it was a complete mystery to her why she was here at the Collegium at all.

Tases kept saying there was time enough—years— to get it all right, but it wasn't the part about being *right* that had her worried. She figured he could help her out with that. It was the part about being *nice*. She didn't think there was anybody under the sun— not even a Companion—who could help her with that. And the real trouble was, all of her new friends didn't think that would be a problem—at least not once they'd finished their training. And none of them seemed to have any doubts that they *would* finish their training, and their Circuits, and become Heralds, either. She *knew* that.

That was the real joke.

Because every Herald had a Gift, some kind of Talent that set them apart. It wasn't the whole reason they were Chosen, but it was part of it. Farsight, Foresight, Fetching, Mindhearing and Mindspeech, Mage-sight, and the almost unknown Firestarting . . . these were all Gifts with which young Herald-Trainees might show up at the Collegium to have fostered and nurtured. Some with the barest whisper, some with Gifts so strong they'd been a burden to them until their Companions arrived.

And hers was Empathy.

Not strong and probably never would be (Tases said she was lucky at that, because strong Empaths spent their time puking their guts out or learning to Shield, or both). But strong enough for her to be able to put herself into somebody else's shoes whether she wanted to be or not. To know just how they were feeling, and if it wasn't quite as good as setting a Truthspell, she could at least tell (most of the time) whether somebody thought they were telling the truth. At least if she was close enough or they cared enough. And the more she learned about her particular Gift, the more Aellele had to figure: if knowing what somebody was feeling wasn't enough to make her a nice person, then she suspected there wasn't any power anywhere in all of Velgarth that *could* make her into a nice person.

That was depressing. Because being a Herald was *important.* And Heralds didn't just maybe short the next farm on the egg count because the neighbor boy had thrown a rock at them last sennight or not bother to take the spoiled apples out of the bushel because they were too tired and didn't care if the basket was half-rotten by the time it reached market. And she would *pack right up and go home this minute* except for the fact that she couldn't take Tases with her and she couldn't leave him behind; and there wasn't anybody here she could talk to about it because they'd all say "time enough to worry about that later," and Aellele knew damned well that all "later" meant was the chance to make really big mistakes instead of mid-dling little ones, and nobody (even Tases) would tell

her what they did with Heralds who just didn't work
out. It was probably something so horrible that there
weren't even *stories*. (Except that even when she was
trying to work herself up into a good scaredy-fit, Aellele knew that was silly. They probably just found
work for them here in Haven where they couldn't
make a mess of things and just didn't tell anybody
why.)

And four moonturns ago it hadn't occurred to her
to wish for being a Herald any more than it had occurred to her to wish for being a butterfly or a
gryphon or a traveling Bard, but now that she got up
every morning and put on Trainee's Grays, the thing
she wanted most in the world was to change out of
them when the time came for Herald's Whites and be
able to ride her Circuit and have the people come up
to her just like she'd seen them come up to other
Heralds and know she could always be calm and fair
and *nice*. And she was starting to think: "Well,
maybe . . ."

And then one day everything went wrong at once.

She had morning kitchen duty, and normally she
enjoyed it, even if it meant getting up earlier than
usual, but she'd been up late the night before studying,
and she overslept. And Helorin (who was in charge
of the floor) had to bang on her door and wake her
up, and she'd already been late when she'd been hurrying to dress and wash, and her brush had caught on
a tangle in her hair, and she'd flung it across the room
in exasperation, and it hit the wall and broke her
lamp, and then there was oil all over her course assignment and the rest of her half-done sennight's work,
and all over the floor, and when she looked, her brush
was broken as well. By the time Aellele had cleaned
everything up, she was too late for kitchen duty at all,
and Tavis had to take her place, which meant she had
to take Tavis' task for the day, and Tavis had Linens,

and Mistress Housekeeper was never pleased by anything (to the point that there was a brisk trade in
desserts among the Trainees to avoid working under
her).

She was scolded in the kitchens for not showing up
for her work shift, and again in her morning's class
because her paper was unfit to turn in; she had to
spend most of lunch recopying it (and she'd been told
it would still be marked down for lateness), and weapons practice was after her stint with Mistress Housekeeper, and by then she was so out of temper that
she threw her practice weapon across the floor when
she missed an easy counter and had to spend the rest
of the class running laps.

And all she could think of the whole time was that
a Herald, a *real* Herald—someone who knew that lives
might depend on whether she could keep her temper
and keep her head—wouldn't have thrown the
damned hairbrush in the first place. Wouldn't have
thrown her sword across the floor. Wouldn't, wouldn't,
wouldn't.

She didn't want sympathy, and she didn't want advice. (She didn't deserve the sympathy, and the only
advice she was getting was "it's going to be fine," and
she knew perfectly well that *it wasn't going to be.*) So
after dinner she took her pen case and her (new) lantern and a sheaf of fresh paper and the rest of her
ruined coursework (which she fortunately had time to
copy before she needed to turn it in tomorrow) to find
a good place to hide.

Back home it would have been up in the hayloft.
The Collegium didn't exactly have a hayloft (well, it
did, but it was the loft over the Companions' stable,
and that wasn't anything like a haybarn, and it wasn't
very private, either), and any place the Trainees were
allowed to be in their free time was fairly public. They
could go to the Common Room, or the Library, or
down to the stable, or out to the paddock, or to their

own rooms, and there were people in all of those but
her room, and anybody might poke a head into her
room at any moment to see if she was there, what she
was doing, how she was feeling. And she thought she
might *hit* the next person she saw.

So since she couldn't do anything else right today,
Aellele figured she'd add trespassing to her list of sins,
transgressions, and general *total failures* and go break
in to one of the classrooms. It wasn't exactly breaking
in—since they weren't locked—but she knew perfectly
well that Trainees weren't supposed to be in them outside of class hours. She blocked Tases out of her mind
as well as she could (which wasn't very, but she didn't
think she could bear his sympathy right now, and he
was good about giving her privacy) and went off to find
the one that was farthest from . . . anywhere.

Her penmanship had always been good (one of the
reasons that getting lectured this morning on a paper
too messy to turn in had hurt so much), and one of
the joys of coming to the Collegium had been having
as much fresh paper to use and almost as much time to
write as she wanted. Recopying the pages was actually
soothing (an essay on the history of the evolution of
the Karsite religion, another one on the system of
tithes and land taxes in the Jaysong Hills), and once
she was done, she could crumple up the oil-spotted
pages and toss them into the nearest stove. Then
there'd be nothing left to show what had happened
today. Oh, except for the fact that she'd broken the
hairbrush Saraceth had given her as a *special present*
when she'd left home just because she couldn't hold
onto her temper any better than if she were a two-
year-old child.

She looked up in surprise when the door opened,
but the man coming in wasn't anybody she recognized.

It was a long-standing joke around the Collegium
that Kailyon had been here so long that they should

just give him Whites and have done. Kailyon didn't mind the teasing. He was never going to wear Whites—no Herald he—but you didn't need to wear Herald White (nor Healer Green, nor Bard Scarler, nor even Mage Yellow) to serve. And he was proud of the work that he did here, for it was vital.

For every Herald (and Healer and Bard and Mage) and Trainee at the Collegium there were dozens of servants whose only task was to make it possible for those others to concentrate on their work. Some of the tasks were common to the four Schools and invisible (like the laundry), and some were specific to just one (like the small army of grooms who cared for the Companions when their Heralds could not, and in many cases, taught young Trainees who had never seen a horse—much less a Companion—what to do to keep their new friends comfortable), and some were similar in each of the schools but were managed separately (Bard or Mage or Healer or Herald, one must eat, but it was far more efficient to have separate kitchens and staffs for each). It was both an honor and a privilege to be in service at the Collegium, and it was a point of friendly dispute between the Collegium's servants and the Crown's servants (one that would never truly be settled) as to which staff held the more honored post. Certainly service to the Crown of Valdemar called for uttermost loyalty and uttermost discretion, but such qualities were required of those who served in the Collegium as well—from the lowliest laundress to the lofty and rarefied Collegium Seneschal, who was in charge of all of who served within the walls of the Collegium.

Such as Kailyon.

Kailyon had come to Haven as a child barely five years of age, gaunt and big-eyed and carried across a Herald's saddle, brought to Haven along with news of sickness and a failed well. His earliest memories were of blue leather and silver bells, and of the world as it

looked from the height of a Companion's saddle, and
the years after that were happy ones spent growing
up in the household of one of the Collegium's grooms.
It was no surprise to anyone that he would seek to
serve among those who had loved him and cared for
him. And so he had, through King Sendar's reign and
into Queen Selenay's, and if he was fortunate, he
would continue to serve for many years yet.

Like most of the servants at the Collegium, Kailyon
was an invisible presence to the Trainees. Some of
them had grown up in houses filled with servants. Others had *been* servants, or been destined to be servants,
before they had come here. It didn't matter, since
once they donned their Grays, all were equal within
these walls. Though many of his fellow servants often
grumbled—and loudly—about how completely they
were ignored by the students ("They treat us as if
we were furniture!" was a complaint he often heard),
Kailyon never thought so. The business of turning a
citizen of Valdemar into a Herald was a demanding
task, and it left the young students little time to focus
on anything else, and if they did not (for the most
part) precisely *notice* the servants who made sure that
their lives were comfortable and well organized, neither did any of them—from highest-born noble to orphan child of the streets—ever *abuse* the Collegium
servants. That would be grounds for correction swift
and stern, from teachers, senior students, and their
Companions alike.

As for a greater recognition, well, over the years,
some of those who had begun simply as anonymous
bodies in Trainee Gray ricocheting in-and-out of Kailyon's orbit (for if he and his fellow servants were
anonymous to them, well, the young Trainees were
just as anonymous to the Collegium servants, really)
had gone on to become friends, and Kailyon had followed the news of their lives as they exchanged Trainee's Grays for Herald's Whites, had greeted them with

pleasure when they sought him out upon their returns to Haven—for the Collegium was home to the Heralds as well as school for the Trainees—and on a few sad occasions had heard it whispered that someone's Companion had returned—alone—to seek rest and healing within the Grove, and hearing the name of the Companion, knew that he had lost a friend.

In his youth (decades gone now) Kailyon had fetched and carried heavy loads, rebuilt toppled walls, and dealt with every matter that a strong back and a strong arm could serve. If those feats were beyond his grasp now, he was not *quite* useless (as he had told Master Seneschal not two years past), nor was he ready for his pipe and his pension and his mug of beer in one of the rest houses that the Collegium kept for those of its servants who had no families to go to. Not yet. Dust fell as surely as rain, and boots left scuff marks, and woodwork needed polishing, and that was work a man could do and be proud of the doing. If it was not so fine and grand as serving as a groom in the Companion's stables, nor a thing where the absence of his labor would be noted instantly (as it would did he toil in kitchen or the pantry), it was still honest, necessary work, and Kailyon had lived and worked among Heralds long enough to know that there was no need to be noticed or praised or thanked for doing what needed to be done.

It wasn't arduous work by any means. A wing of classrooms to keep clean, and the Library as well, and while the Library was a full night's task that couldn't fairly be started until after the students were out of it, old bones kept late hours, and Kailyon did not mind laboring through the long, quiet hours when others were abed. Truth be told, he liked the solitude, the time to spend with his own thoughts. Each new Trainee who came to the Heralds' Collegium was both a puzzle for the present and a promise to the future. Some of them were children barely older than Kailyon had been when he had come, some of them were verging on adulthood. All uncertain, in one way or another, about what the future might hold and what their place in it would be. Over the years, he'd seen so many of them—from skittish, wide-eyed arrivals to equally skittish, young Heralds departing on their first Circuits—and they all had one thing in common: the fierce determination to be *worthy* of the trust being placed in them.

As soon as he opened the door to the next room on his cleaning schedule this night, he saw the glow of the lantern at the back of the room (heard the faint mortified squeak and the rustle of papers, too) and knew he wasn't alone. No point to asking, "Who's there?" as if he were a panicky grandmam hearing imaginary housebreakers in the night. If nothing else, the Companions would stop someone who shouldn't be here before they even got onto the grounds, and though these days, the younger servants entertained themselves by scaring themselves sick with tales about what the Mages *might* do if one had a mind to, what Kailyon was pretty sure of was that what the Mages *did* do was make the Collegium safer. So he merely took his large lantern off the cart and hung it up on the hook by the door and opened its doors.

If it were merely a regular lantern, holding a candle or burning oil, it would hardly be enough to light his work. But it held, instead, a spell of Mage-light, and so when it was opened, it cast a glow bright enough for him to work by. Certainly it cast enough light for him to see who was here that oughtn't be.

It was just as he'd figured. Sharp-boned and big-eyed, and here long enough to have Grays that had been made for her, but not long enough to have gotten herself to the point where she wouldn't stare round-eyed at a lantern full of Mage-light.

There was silence for the space of several heartbeats while the child stared at him as if he were seventy

Karsite demons in one skin. She knew full well she oughtn't be here, and up to no more mischief than seeking out a quiet place to study, if that inkwell and pile of papers was any indication.

"It will be a nice change to have company," Kailyon said mildly, and set to his work as if she weren't there.

"I didn't think anyone would be in here," she said after a little while, and Kailyon grunted. "Place doesn't clean itself, you know."

"No, I . . . I guess I never thought about it," the girl said, sounding surprised and just a little put out. "We keep our rooms clean, and we do some of the clean-up in the Refectory and the Salle, and I never thought about the classrooms. My name is Aellele. My family has a farm near Sweetgrass Creek—oh, I know you won't ever have heard of it . . ."

"But you're a long way from home, and you've been away from home for a long time, and you're wondering if you'll ever get to go back home again," Kailyon said. Aellele looked at him in surprise, and he smiled. "The Sweetgrass Valley is north of here, isn't it?"

She began to tell him about the farm—he'd heard many such tales over the years, from many homesick young Trainees—and broke off in the middle of her tale to offer to help him in his chores. Kailyon saw no reason to object—it stood to reason that a farm girl knew a little something about dusting and cleaning— and soon Aellele had her own dust rag and was working along beside him.

Kailyon had never been one to chatter, but he had the knack of listening without making it seem to the one who spoke that it was any great burden for him to do so. And in truth it was not, for Kailyon had not only spent his entire life in Haven but had spent most of it within the grounds of the Collegium itself. If the wider world was to come to him at all, it must come through the stories and voices of those who spoke with him. And so he listened willingly to Aellele as

she told of the life that she'd left and the life that
she'd found, and if what she had to say was almost
entirely composed of things he had heard many times
before, well, it was new to her, and he gave her the
respect of offering her words his full attention. Besides, there was one thing here that he did not yet
know, and that was the reason she had chosen to
transgress the Collegium's rules to the extent of placing herself where he had found her, for if the majority
of the Trainees were anonymous to the servants, the
scapegraces and troublemakers were not, and Kailyon
knew already that Aellele was not one of these.

When they finished that classroom, they went on to
the next, and went on working side by side. Aellele's
flow of words slowed, then stopped. "Master Kailyon,
you have been here a very long time," she said, after
a long silence. "Do you know . . . what happens to
someone—if they're Chosen and just can't learn to be
a proper Herald?"

The last words came out in a rush, and it was such
an utterly foolish question that if long years hadn't
granted him wisdom (or at least prudence), Kailyon
would have laughed out loud. If the child had given
the question half a minute's thought, she would realize
that what she was asking wasn't a question about
Herald-trainees, but about *Companions*. Who chose
those who wore Trainee Grey in the first place but
the Companions? And how could anyone imagine that
the Companions could ever Choose someone who
couldn't learn to become a proper Herald of Valdemar? (Although—Kailyon did grant—it might take
years and tears to do the job up right, it was also
true that the Companions never chose someone who
couldn't be turned out as a Herald . . . eventually.)

But Aellele was far too young (and much too worried) to think things out logically, and to the young,
their small sins often loomed as large and black as
any villainy out of myth.

"Well," he said, affecting to consider, "I suppose that would depend on why it was they couldn't be a Herald."

And now the truth of the matter came tumbling out—a litany of childish wrongdoing and temper fits (he'd done as much—and worse—at her age, but he hadn't been looking toward an awful and glorious future as a Herald). And of course Aellele had the manners to try to keep her fretting to herself, and of course her Companion knew about it, and of course he (and everyone else who saw her worrying, and people *would* have seen it because the teachers and the older students and everyone whose business it was to care for the young Herald-trainees were neither fools nor brutes) would have told her not to worry, that there would be time later to worry, if worrying needed to be done. And she would have paid as little attention to all their well-meant advice as the weather paid to Mistress Laundress when she wanted to dry linens and it wanted to rain.

"—and a Herald has to be *nice* all the time—when they're riding Circuit—and I can't be—I know I can't—not if I live to be a thousand years old—and *oh!* what will happen then? I don't know!"

"Hm," Kailyon said. He sat down on a bench—as talking was more work than thinking—and gestured for her to sit beside him. "Well. Here's how I see it. And of course you needn't pay any heed to me. I'm not one of your instructors. Not a Herald neither. Just an old man who polishes wood and mops floors. But I've seen a good few Heralds come and go."

Aellele seated herself beside him and composed herself to listen, her face grave and solemn.

"Of course you mustn't do something to shame the Crown or your Companion while you wear the Whites. Everyone will tell you that. They'll be telling you that for some years yet. And some Heralds ride Circuit and some don't, you know. Every Herald goes to work they're best suited to. Still, you aren't wrong. If you put on the Whites, there'll come a time when you're asked to give a judgment. I don't brag to say I've known a Herald or two in my time, though, and not one of them has ever worried one tick about being *nice*, and every single one of them has worried about being *right*."

Aellele regarded him with doubtful hope. "Everyone else seems to think that all we have to do is study everything in our books and—and—and—learn to ride and use a sword and a bow!"

"Maybe yes, maybe no," Kailyon said. "Maybe they've got as many doubts as you do. Maybe they *do* think it's just that easy—now. Those as think they know everything already are always the hardest to teach. They've got the most to learn, and it's hard as hard to make them let go of what they think they know. You, now, you already know you've got a hard road to ride. So you'll work just as hard as you need to in order to get yourself to the end of it. I'm no farmer, but a friend once told me there wasn't any point to planning the harvest at plowing time."

To Kailyon's pleasure, Aellele actually giggled, then stopped and regarded him solemnly. "A lot can happen between planting and harvest," she agreed.

Kailyon nodded, as much to himself as to her. He thought she had the look of someone who might be ready to hear what everyone had been telling her now, instead of just listening to it. "And now, I've a bit more dust to make away with, and it's more than time for you to be in your bed, young Aellele."

Aellele stood, and regarded him hesitantly. "You . . . You wouldn't mind if—if I came back and talked to you again some time, would you?"

"Just as you please," Kailyon said, pushing himself to his feet with a faint grunt of effort. "And now, off with you."

He watched as the young Trainee gathered her pen-

case and papers and lantern from his cart and went
skipping off in the direction of her dorm. So very
young! But he knew that to him it would seem like
sennights instead of years before he saw her riding
out in Herald's Whites. "Better too much doubt than
too much confidence," Kailyon quoted to himself. It
was a proverb Aellele would not hear from her instructors for some time yet, and by the time she did,
Kailyon suspected she would already have learned the
lesson herself.

Aellele scurried back toward her room. For the first
time since she'd been certain that she *had* it, her Gift
was actually more of a comfort than an annoyance
(and a rebuke, shaming her because even knowing
how people felt couldn't make her be nice to them).
Because she'd been able to tell that Kailyon hadn't
been saying all those things he'd said just to make her
feel better, or because he had to, or even just to make
her *go away*, but because he thought they were true
and were worth saying.

She didn't know what hour it was, though she
suspected—from the emptiness of the corridors—that
curfew bell had already rung, and if she were seen,
she would round off a day of disaster with demerits
for being out after curfew. And while yesterday the
thought would have devastated her, today it did not.
If it happened, well, it happened. "A lot can happen
between planting and harvest." Tomorrow she would
try to do better.

Tomorrow, and every day after that.

Heart, Home, and Hearth

by Sarah A. Hoyt and Kate Paulk

Sarah A. Hoyt was born in Portugal, a mishap she hastened to correct as soon as she came of age. She lives in Colorado with her husband, her two sons and a varying horde of cats. She has published a Shakespearean fantasy trilogy with Berkley/Ace, Three Musketeers mystery novels, as well as any number of short stories in magazines ranging from *Isaac Asimov's Science Fiction Magazine* to *Dreams of Decadence*. Forthcoming novels include *Darkship Thieves* and more Three Musketeers mystery novels.

Kate Paulk pretends to be a mild-mannered software quality analyst by day and allows her true evil author nature through for the short time between finishing with the day job and falling over. She lives in semi-rural Pennsylvania with her husband, two bossy cats, and her imagination. The last is the hardest to live with. Her latest short story sale, "Night Shifted," is in DAW's anthology *Better Off Undead*.

The air had a sharp bite, and Ree could smell snow even deep in the narrow earthen burrow, under the roots of a great oak tree, where he and Jem had taken refuge.

Winter is coming, Ree thought. *There's no escaping it.* He felt Jem shake with coughing in his sleep and snuggled closer, trying to keep the younger boy warm. Summer had been all right for living wild and putting more and more ground between themselves and Jacona—and the Emperor's soldiers.

Even though Jem was all human and didn't have the sharper senses of the rat and cat that had merged with Ree during the Change-circle last winter, he'd got wicked good with a slingshot. With Ree's animal instincts to lead the hunt, they'd rarely missed a meal. But the last few weeks, it had gotten so cold, and it seemed like all animals were either hibernating or had gone south for the winter. He could see Jem's bones through his skin. Hells, he could see them through the rags that passed for his clothes. Jem was cold all the time, and the last three days he'd been coughing all the time and wheezing when they walked too fast.

Ree remembered being cold, back before the Change-circle, when he'd acquired thick brown fur, now growing a winter undercoat. He remembered how everything hurt until you couldn't think, and you thought you'd never be warm. Jem had never been as sturdy as Ree had been, even as a human. Smaller and thinner, not eating enough, he couldn't fight off this illness.

Ree sighed and wished he knew what to do. They'd kept to the forest-covered highlands and avoided the valleys where villages and farms clustered. Avoiding humans, like Jem. Because Ree wasn't a human like Jem. He was a hobgoblin, part animal, to be killed on sight. He extended his hand in front of his eyes, in the almost total darkness of the burrow, and looked dispassionately at fur and claws.

If not for that, they could go to a farm and get food and clothes. And if Jem were a hobgoblin, like him, they could live here in the highlands and do okay. There were other hobgoblins here, and they seemed to survive well enough. Of course, most of them were older and looked meaner than Ree. And most of them would probably eat a sick human. Ree wouldn't.

He put his arm over Jem and felt him stir. Jem's

human, pink hand, covered his. He coughed and asked, "Is it time to get up?"

Ree sighed. If they went on like this, he didn't think Jem would survive the winter. Ree would, but . . . he wouldn't be him. He'd end up strung up on the walls of some city, a bad hobgoblin who'd killed people and maybe eaten them. Someone who no longer remembered he'd started out human. "We're going to have to go to a farm," he said. "We've got to steal you some clothes and decent boots. And food, too."

"What?" Jem said, and half turned around, his blue eyes wide in shock. "Why? They'll kill you." His voice sounded like he was on the verge of tears, and Ree thought it showed how sick he was, how low his defenses were to cry so easily.

"Nah," he said, trying to make his voice sound casual and hiding his fear. "We haven't seen any soldiers for weeks. I bet we're so far from anywhere that now that the magic's gone, no one even comes here. They've probably never heard of hobgoblins." Ree didn't think that was likely. "The wild ones never go near towns. People might notice clothes and stuff disappearing, but they'll just think it's thieves. And no one's going to brave the forest to find thieves."

"Why do we have to?" Jem coughed, but he tried to make it silent, so Ree could only tell he was coughing from the shaking of his body and the sound like distant, muffled explosions. "We're doing okay, Ree, really. We hunt and . . . and stuff. We don't need to go near people. Everyone knows hobgoblins. Everyone has edicts. They'll kill you."

"Hush now," Ree said, enveloping him in his arms and rocking him slightly. "Hush now. They won't. I can hear better than them. I'll keep clear."

Jem shook against his shoulder, and Ree knew he must go, and he must be successful. If he died it wouldn't matter—Jem would be able to go back to the world of men. But Ree couldn't go on without

Jem. They had escaped Jacona together, and Jem had saved Ree's life, killing the giant snake thing that would have devoured him. More important than that, Jem, by caring what happened to Ree, by needing him and treating him as if he were fully human, had saved Ree's human heart.

Ree's body might survive, but not his heart.

Jem said, "Something's wrong." He was almost impossible to understand, he was shaking so hard. They stood atop a hillock sparsely grown with thin pines.

Ree turned to look where Jem pointed. A narrow valley cut deep into the forest. Fences had fallen, and Ree could hear animals making what sounded to him like distressed noises. He could see three cows, one of them with horns, a horse, and possibly a goat. Squawking sounds like chickens suggested the farm had some, somewhere he couldn't see.

"Maybe it's been abandoned?" Ree didn't really believe his own suggestion, but it was an excuse to try raiding the place. Jem had resisted it all the way here, and even now his lips were set in that straight line that was often the only indication of his steely resolve under his compliant exterior. Jem shook his head and didn't try to speak.

"Come on. I can hide if I have to." Ree didn't like the way Jem's breathing sounded and would have picked the younger boy up and carried him, if he thought Jem would allow it. At least this valley was isolated even from the other farms and villages. No one outside the farm would see them.

Jem leaned on him as they picked through cold mud and patches of burrs that caught in Ree's fur and hurt his bare feet. Jem gasped the first time he stood on one of the burr patches; then he started coughing and couldn't stop.

If that wasn't enough, as soon as the cows saw them, they started bawling and hurried over to them, com-

plaining as loudly as they could. Being sandwiched
between the bodies of animals big enough to squash
him wasn't how Ree wanted to die. He held tight to
Jem, his heart pounding in his chest while his nose
twitched with the smell of *food*. They were too big.
He had to stand on his toes to see over their backs.
He tried to breathe slowly, to pretend he wasn't
scared. That was one thing he'd learned—you *never*
let anything know you were frightened.

If he fooled the cows, they were dumber than the
ugly hobgoblin he and Jem had found in the hills. But
the animals didn't do anything to stop them going to
the farmhouse, and they didn't try to hurt him or Jem.
Ree almost cried when he saw the door. Jem was still
coughing when Ree hauled the door open and pushed
him inside. He slammed the door closed and put his
back against it, panting. The cows were complaining
outside, loud enough to wake the . . .

Ree swallowed. The too-familiar reek of waste and
sickness fouled the room. He blinked, and the shape
on the floor a few paces ahead resolved into an old
man whose face twisted into a grimace of pain but
who still found strength to glare. But he wasn't dead.
And that was good. Or perhaps bad, as the grimace
of pain became a concentrated look of something
like hatred.

The rough wooden door at his back was the only
thing that kept Ree's knees from buckling. He swallowed again. Jem bent over, still coughing, his whole
body shaken by those wracking coughs.

Jem. I have to look after Jem. He darted forward, his
toe-claws clicking on the wooden floor and catching in
a woven rug near where the old man lay. Catching
the younger boy's shoulders, he helped him to sit near
a hearth large enough to stand in. Someone, presumably the old man, had piled wood in the center and
topped the wood with a collection of twigs and fluffy
stuff Ree didn't recognize.

Ree looked at the old man. He vaguely remembered his mother telling him how old people always expected you to be polite. "Sir?" His voice trembled. "If you could tell me . . . Is there a fire starter around here? My friend is sick. He needs warmth."

The old man's blue eyes softened. The hatred—Ree wondered if it had been hatred or fear—abated. "There on your right side, on the mantel," he said in a raspy voice, as if he were holding back pain.

It took Ree several tries and some colorful curses to get enough of a spark from the flint to light the fire. First the fluffy stuff caught and burned in the blink of an eye, but by then the twigs were burning and the bigger logs were starting to catch.

Ree breathed in slowly, almost a hiss. An echoing hiss came from the fireplace, followed by a gray cat twice the size of any cats he had ever seen in Jacona. The animal sniffed, meowed. "Sorry," Ree found himself saying. "I didn't see you in there."

The cat made a sound that could have been a complaint, then walked up to the old man's face and rubbed its forehead against his cheek, meowing. Ree stared in amazement. Crazy animals inside and out. All he wanted was food and warm clothes for Jem.

But the old man wasn't screaming or anything, and he clearly needed help, too. "Sir," he said again, hesitating. "You . . . are hurt?"

"Caught my feet in the hearthrug three days ago," he said. "I ain't been able to get up since, and the livestock to look to, and the snow coming down, and no way to light the fire."

Ree hesitated. It went through his mind like lightning that the old man couldn't even get up to light the fire. That meant he couldn't chase them away or hurt them, or denounce them. He couldn't defend clothes or food, and Ree could look after Jem and they could leave.

He looked at the old man, but the man was studying Jem, with an intent, concentrated frown. Not as if he disapproved of Jem, but more as if he were trying to add something together. And perhaps trying not to show his own pain. By the flickering light of the fire, it hit Ree that boy and man had the same profile. The man's face was just aged and weathered and seemed to have frozen in that expression Jem only got when he was riding high on stubborn.

Jem looked back at the man, his eyes wide and guileless. "We'll help," he said, softly. "Won't we Ree? We'll stay till you're back on your feet."

What could Ree say to that? They could leave, could take clothes and food, enough to survive the winter, but in Jem's eyes he'd never be the same. And perhaps not in his own eyes either, if he knew he'd left an old man to die. Much less an old man who looked like Jem. He'd killed a man once, but that was different.

So he crossed his arms and tried to look strong. "Of course. But first you need some warmth. He needs a blanket, sir. He's got something that makes him cough. Cold too long and not enough food."

The old man looked from Jem to Ree. "I lost two boys to consumption," he said, and shrugged. "No healers for miles." He pointed. "There's beds with quilts in that there room. It was my boys' room."

Ree found a cold, empty-smelling bedroom with quilts piled high on two large beds. It looked like a metal stove had been added, probably to replace the magic ones that Ree remembered being sold at marketplaces. The hole in the wall where the stove chimney let out had been plastered over, but it looked crude and rough beside the faded paint on the rest of the walls.

Ree peeled two quilts off the bed and carried them back into the middle room. Now that his heart had stopped trying to leap out of his chest, and with fire-light warm and buttery in the room, it looked almost cozy.

Jem huddled by the fire, with his ragged clothes and bones showing under his skin, wasn't so good. Ree dropped one quilt around the younger boy's shoulders; then he laid the other one over the old man. "Sir? You need food, too." He was asking the old man's permission to feed him as much as stating fact.

The old man sighed. "There's stew in there." He pointed into the hearth, where a pot of something hung on an hinge. "It's been so cold, it's probably still good. You can swing it over the fire and it will be bubbling nicely in no time. My wife's recipe." He cast a look at Jem. "He needs to eat. But you and I have something to do, before we eat."

"We do?" Ree swung the pot over the fire. His stomach growled when he smelled it. He and Jem had tried to roast things over camp fires, but they hadn't had real cooked food in . . . much too long.

The man gave a cackle like a whiplash, and Ree wondered if it was just the pain making him mean. How could he look so much like Jem and act like he hated the entire world?

"This is a working farm," he said. "Ain't no one been working at it for days. The cattle will be starved, and the cows'll need milking."

Ree had a vague memory of going to a fair with his mother once, and a pretty lady who milked a cow and for a coin poured some milk in people's cups for drinking. Ree's mother had bought him some milk, and it was the best thing he'd ever tasted. But he was hungry now and stew would do. "Why do we need to milk them? We have stew."

The old man looked at him, disbelieving, as if he thought that Ree was addled. Then he made a croaking sound that alarmed Ree until he realized it was laughter, or at least the laughter of someone who must be dying of thirst. "The cows need the milk out, boy, or they get infected teats, and eventually they die. You ain't going to set there and eat while the animals starve."

Ree remembered the gigantic creatures outside. Sitting here eating while they starved seemed like a good idea, but something warned him he shouldn't say so. "I'm not?"

"No, you're not," the old man said, and continued studying Ree with an evaluating look that implied that, as far as his sums were concerned, Ree came up short. "I don't suppose you know one end of a cow from the other?"

Ree shook his head, unable to speak. To make things worse, Jem had wandered away, still wrapped in the quilt, and now there was a creaking sound from the kitchen.

"Don't you worry none. It's the water pump. I guess he was thirsty," the old man said, and rasped in a slightly louder tone, "I could use a cup of water meself."

When Jem came back into the room carrying a water cup, the old man was giving Ree very odd instructions. They started with: "You get yourself out there and around the side of the house. The lean-to has . . . a lot of stuff. There's a wheelbarrow there. Bring it in."

Ree left the old man sipping water and went to the lean-to—trying to ignore the desperate animals that surrounded him—and got the wheelbarrow, a sturdy thing with a big wheel, back into the room.

The old man was talking to Jem in almost confidential tones. "Brothers, are you?" Ree heard him say, as he pushed the door open.

"Uh, no. We're . . . friends," Jem said, and that clear skin of his betrayed a raging flush.

Ree's stomach tightened, but the old man only said, "Ah. My brother—" Then he saw Ree and said, "Ah, you got the wheelbarrow. Good."

Thus started the strangest few hours of Ree's life. Outside it was snowing hard, but the old man, wrapped in the quilt, sitting as comfortably in the wheelbarrow as the combined efforts of the three of them could make him, only said, "You might as well get snow on your fur now as later. It's going to get much worse before it gets better this winter."

"Go to the barn there," he said. "That's where their food is." He gestured at the animals who surrounded them as soon as they were outside. Although he ignored the cows and the goat, he patted the horse's head with his gnarled fingers, and his eyes looked almost wistful.

Ree pushed the wheelbarrow to the barn, where he opened a door that ran on some sort of track and required much less effort than he expected. Then he pushed the old man in.

Like a king on a throne, the man barked out despotic orders.

"Pump water for them now, then hit them on the nose if they drink too much."

Ree pumped water from the biggest water pump he'd ever seen, which poured clear, cool liquid onto a trough. "Now, hit them on the nose. A cow will drink till it bursts, boy."

So Ree hit them on the nose, all of them, even the maybe-goat, It tried to bump him back, causing the old man to unleash his cackle once more. But the respite didn't hold. "Now up that ladder. Can those paws of yours climb ladders?"

Ree, whose arms already felt like they would fall off their sockets from pumping the water, could only nod. "Good. Up the ladder. There's sacks of feed up there. Pour about half of one of them into the hopper."

This was easier said than done. The sacks weighed enough for Ree wonder if the animals ate lead, but what poured into the hopper seemed to be some sort of grain.

"Now get your arse down here and milk the cows."

Ree, sweat pouring down his body, under his fur, came down the ladder on legs that felt like they'd fall out under him. He'd walked for whole days and not been this tired. No wonder the farmers he'd seen in town were both muscular and cranky.

"The milking stool's there," the old man said, pointing with a finger that looked like the end of a branch, all brown and gnarled. "Milk the cows into that there pail. The cows, you fool, not the bull." This as Ree tried to sit next to a cow who, on second look, displayed a rather prominent pair of balls.

"I guess he wouldn't like it if I tried to milk him," Ree said, weakly.

"I bet he wouldn't. That's right, sit there where Spotty can't kick you. No, what are you doing? You don't squeeze the udders like that." The old man showed Ree the motion. It was simple, and yet harder work than it looked. His fingers ached by the time he was no longer getting any milk out of the teats. He retreated from the stall, shaking his hands to try to loosen his fingers. And people thought doing this was romantic and good?

He walked up to the second cow and almost cringed as the old man's voice cracked out like a whip, "No, wait up."

What had he done wrong now? Was this another type of cow that couldn't be milked? He looked wearily at the old man.

"My hands ain't broken. Just wheel me up to where I can reach the teats."

Ree wondered if it was meant kindly, but he couldn't tell with that gruff voice. Perhaps the man just thought he'd done it wrong, which he was sure he had. But then the almost-for-sure goat came bumping against his knee and the old man said in what was unmistakable amusement, "You milk Jesse. She never liked me. Was my boy's pet." Then in a more serious tone, "Goat milk is good for sickly young ones. We'll warm up some for your *friend*, shall we?"

Ree didn't like the emphasis on *friend*, but the old man looked as calm or as irascible as ever, and he seemed to want Jem to get better.

But before they took the milk in, they had to feed the chickens. This wasn't such hard work, but Ree couldn't understand how small creatures covered in feathers, creatures who couldn't even figure out how to fly, could be so scary. They crowded around him like mobs when noblemen handed out food to the poor.

While they ate, the old man—Ree had parked him next to the nests—picked out more than a dozen eggs. "These will be good too," he said.

When they got to the house, Jem had food laid out on earthenware bowls and the smell filled the air. Ree thought he was too tired to eat until he had his first mouthful. The old man watched them eat, his eyes intent, then said, "You two." His voice still rasped, but less than before. "What're you doing here?"

Jem almost dropped his milk, but Ree answered with only the slightest quiver in his voice. "We needed food and warmth, and we thought this place might be abandoned."

"Ha!" The old man's laughter was as harsh as his voice. "Ain't abandoned while I'm here." He turned his head to meet Ree's eyes. "You're one of them hobgoblins, ain't you?"

Ree sighed. As if what wild magic had made of him wasn't obvious. "Yeah. So what?"

"You got guts." More of that rasping laughter. "There's bad critters come out of the forest, and some

of 'em look near as human as you. You're lucky you
never got a pitchfork in your belly."

"That's why we stayed in the forest." Ree looked
at Jem. The younger boy was so frail-looking, so thin.
"But Jem needed warmth." He nodded to the old
man. "And it looks to me like you could use a bit of
help." His chest tightened at his daring.

The man matched his stare. "Yeah, I could. You're
a good worker, boy. Twice as good as many bigger
men."

It was said in such a gruff voice that Ree needed a
while to absorb the compliment. Not just that he'd
said he was good, but that he'd called him "boy" and
compared him to men. That he wasn't thinking Ree
was an animal.

It didn't mean he wouldn't change his mind and
denounce him when he got better.

For now, it was enough. Ree ducked his head and
minded his manners. "Thank you, sir."

"And you," the old man said, leveling a finger at
Jem. "Hurry up and get well so you can lend a hand
around here." Ree bridled, seeing the little tremor
that shook Jem, and would have said something, only
before he could, the old man added, "That's your job,
right now. Getting better."

Later the old man—Garrad, he said his name was—
had Ree wheel him into the other bedroom, behind
the hearth. It was bigger, with a bigger bed. They
arranged the man on the bed and covered him with
quilts, set a candle on the bedside table.

As the boys turned to go, he said, "That, on the
wall. That's my wife and boys."

On the wall was a painting done on a board, like
the ones done by traveling painters before the magic
disappeared. "We used to be better off," he said.

The painting showed a blond woman and three little

boys, maybe between ten and three. They all bore a startling resemblance to Jem.

"The oldest one, the Imperial army took him. Year my wife died. The other two were dead already. Of the coughing consumption. Buried out back." He looked at Jem, his eyes dreamy in the firelight. "Where do you come from, boy?"

"Jacona, sir," Jem said.

"And do you know your father?"

Jem shook his head, and the man sighed. "Ah, well," he said. "Sometimes we have to trust the gods."

"I think he thinks I'm his grandson," Jem said later, as they snuggled under the deep quilts in the big bed in the room Ree had first entered.

Ree shrugged. "I think he thinks you could be."

"I feel sorry for him," Jem said, solemnly. "He doesn't have anyone."

"People would say we don't have anyone, either."

Jem gurgled a little laughter. "We have each other, silly."

Ree nodded and cuddled closer. Perhaps it was a good thing Garrad liked Jem. That way even if he denounced Ree, Jem would be safe. That was really all that mattered.

The next morning, Garrad woke Ree up by calling his name, before the sun had got up enough in the sky to cast more than a mild glow. "You have to get the hay in," he told him. "Before it's all wet and rots. And we ought to chop up some more wood, in case we're snowed in. I don't like the look of those clouds."

By the middle of the day, when Ree could no longer feel his arms, they'd gone in to a lunch that Jem had prepared. Bread and butter with milk and eggs. "Found out how to make bread in an old notebook," Jem said.

"My wife's book. She was a great cook, your Gr—"

He cut it off abruptly and turned it into a cough, but Ree heard it and felt reassured that Jem would be looked after. He had to remember that when he felt like flinging off in the middle of work, whenever Garrad called him a fool or an idiot.

The old man started another complaint. "Ain't been this helpless since I got the white fever years back." His face twisted. "I suppose that damn cat's been piling up food for me." The cat purred as if recognizing its name and rubbed against Garrad's legs.

To disguise his embarrassment, Ree extended a clawed finger toward the animal. It sniffed, then made an inquiring mew. "Yeah, I'm part cat these days." Ree scratched behind the cat's ears and smiled a little when the animal leaned into his tentative gesture. He nodded to the old man. "By the back door. Rats, mice, birds, and at least one rabbit." He shrugged. "It's a good thing it's been cold."

Garrad grunted. "Sounds about right. Damn cat thinks he's got to hunt for me as well as himself." He studied Ree before he added. "Looks like he likes you. Normally he'd scratch anyone as ain't family."

Ree wondered if he meant his family or the cat's family. It seemed Garrad didn't care for the affection of any creature he didn't feel attached to. At least he liked Jem.

Garrad was right about the snow, which started coming down shortly after, carried on a harsh wind. Over the next few days Ree had to do everything needed to get the place ready for a hard winter, from getting the hay in, to chopping wood, to repairing the henhouse roof—all with the old man barking orders from a wheelbarrow.

Two weeks later, he was barking orders standing up and leaning on a stick, while that damn cat wended his way around his and Ree's ankles. Jem wasn't coughing as much, and his bones weren't so obvious beneath the skin. He'd picked up on feeding the chickens and making bread every morning, too.

When Garrad tried to scold him for this, it set off a staring match between two identical sets of blue eyes, and Jem had won.

Jem and the horse were the only things the old man seemed to care for. He had not a good word for the people of the nearby town, and when Jem had said—after Garrad had spent half an hour telling Ree exactly what he'd done wrong when repairing the roof—that they could leave and he'd call the people of the town to look after Garrad, he'd started off a tirade. "Them? They never bothered even when I buried my wife. They let my son be taken off without trying to stop the Imperials. I'd rot in all the hells before asking *them* for help."

Sometimes, amid the orders and complaints, Garrad talked of how his farm had been much more prosperous, how the forest had once been a hunting reserve for the Emperor himself, but no one took care of it or even tried to keep it safe any more. There'd been talk in Three Rivers that bandits claimed whole duchies for themselves and the Empire did nothing to stop them. Hobgoblins came out of the woods and killed people and livestock until they were killed, Garrad told him. He'd lost half his cattle to hobgoblins before he got a pitchfork in one's guts and sent its companions running for safer prey. When Ree shivered at that story, the old man gave his rusty laugh. "You got lucky, boy. Really lucky."

Ree couldn't disagree, when he was warm and fed and had a safe bed for the first time in years, perhaps ever. His mother hadn't lived so well, and the work was better than many of the things he'd done to survive. If the best he could hope for from Garrad was tolerance because of Jem, well, he could live with that. And he would, as long as he had it. Even though it

made Ree sick to think about killing humans, he
didn't regret killing that one, no matter that he'd been
too terrified to know what he was doing. The big bastard would have killed Jem, and Jem had brought back
the little bit of human Ree still had.

During a break between snowstorms, two weeks
later, Ree was using a pitchfork to shove hay down
from the loft to where it could be spread in the animal
stalls when he heard the horse scream. He raced out
of the barn, fork in hand. A creature that might once
have been a bear stood over Garrad, and the horse
reared and danced back from it. The thing's white fur
made it almost invisible against the snow.

Before he could think, Ree found himself sprinting
toward the thing. The fork left his hand, flew through
the air.

He heard Garrad scream, "No, Ree, no."

The three tines made a solid sound when they hit
the creature and buried themselves deep in its chest.
The horse fled, leaping the fence without slowing.

Ree caught the handle of the pitchfork and shoved
with all his strength. Scarlet blood sprayed the white
fur, and the beast swung paws as big as Ree's head.
Step by step, Ree forced it back, away from Garrad,
until it shuddered and collapsed.

"Garrad?" Ree kept half an eye on the creature as
he edged towards where the old farmer lay.

"Brownie." Garrad sounded tired, not his normal
half-growl. "I raised that horse from a foal." He spoke
between gasps, and his face had an unhealthy gray
look. "Her dam was my boy's horse. She's all I've got
left of him."

"Get inside and rest." Ree didn't have to think
about that. "I'll go after the horse."

"Not on your own." Jem must have come from the
house. "Not with things like that out there."

Ree shook his head as they helped Garrad regain his footing. "Someone needs to look after Garrad, and you're better at that than I am."

Jem's mouth tightened, and his eyes got that hard, determined look Ree hardly ever saw. He said nothing.

Rather than waste time, Ree slipped away while the younger boy was getting Garrad into his chair in the main room. If it started to snow again, he might never be able to follow the horse's tracks.

He found the horse easily enough—the mare hadn't run far. She stood by a stand of half-frozen grass, nipping the few green blades free. Ree smelled nothing worse than horse. The animal let him get close before she lifted her head and snorted into his chest. Ree sighed and caught a handful of mane. He should have brought rope for a halter. "Come on, girl."

Ree kept talking softly as he walked her back through the dim, snow-covered forest.

The snow in front of him erupted. The horse shrieked and tried to rear, almost wrenching Ree's arm out of its socket. He struggled to free his fingers while the mound of shaggy white fur unfolded arms and claws that could gut him without effort.

How did I miss it when I came this way before? Ree twisted from a clumsy slash, his head ringing and his arm and shoulder burning. The horse backed away, bringing Ree with it. Between the animal's retreat and the white-furred beast's attacks, Ree couldn't untangle his hand from the horse's mane. He struggled to avoid the creature's claws—he couldn't use his own.

The creature howled. It lurched a step toward Ree and the horse, spun away. A sharp crack made it howl and lurch again. Ree pushed himself and the horse to the side as the creature lost its balance and fell toward them. He heard his shirt tear, smelled blood.

By the time he'd got the horse standing still, his arm ached and he was shivering, but the creature lay on the snow with a pitchfork buried in its back. The

handle quivered, but Jem stood steadily, reproach in
his eyes. "You shouldn't have left without me."

Ree swallowed. He couldn't talk.

"Oh, never mind." Jem shook his head. "Let's get
back. I'll bring ugly here—" He indicated the dead
creature. "Fur like that should be worth something."

Ree wrinkled his nose as he stirred the furs in the
barrel. The ammonia reek of the tanning mix made
his eyes water and burned his nose. His shoulder still
ached, a dull pain that flared every time he shoved
the wooden paddle against bulky fur.

He blamed Garrad's sense of humor. "You killed
'em, boys, you can fix 'em."

The sound of arguing echoed from the nearest road.
Ree looked up. It looked like a group of men approaching. He stepped away from the barrel to where
he could breathe cleanly.

Humans, none too clean. "Garrad, Jem! Company!"
Ree returned to the tanning as soon as he'd called.
He'd best not be too obvious.

Jem supported the old man—whom he'd taken to
calling Granddad—as he hobbled out into the field,
his other hand clutching the walking stick Ree had
carved him.

The visitors reached the far fence at about the same
time as Jem and Garrad did. Ree's stomach tightened,
but Garrad seemed unconcerned by the pitchforks and
hoes his visitors brandished. "So what brings you folks
up from the Rivers?"

"Monsters came out the forest and killed two of
Kederic's best pigs." The speaker was younger than
Garrad, with dark hair graying at the temples. "We
chased 'em off, but they came up this way."

Garrad snorted. "It took you all of a week to follow
'em? You're a bigger coward than your da was, Meren
Anders son, and that's saying something."

The leader paled, and then flushed, then cast about,

clearly wanting to say something. "So where did these strangers you've got come from?" He looked straight at Ree.

Ree let the paddle fall and stalked over to where Garrad and Jem stood. "I'm not human enough for you?" His voice shook with a fury that surprised him. "You can see clear up this valley from town, I'm told. Three cold days without smoke and not one of you *humans* thought to see if anything was wrong? Not even for valuable livestock? Without us there'd be nothing alive here." He spat the words out as though they tasted bad. "No need to worry about those creatures, either." He turned his back on the men—a deliberate act of contempt that made the skin between his shoulders crawl—and stomped back to the barrel, where he used the paddle to heave one of the half-tanned furs out.

The white fur glittered in the cold light, sun catching on every drop of water. Ree let it drop back in with a splash.

Garrad spoke before anyone else could. "They're not strangers. They're my grandsons," he growled. "My boy sent 'em to me. Being with the army, he couldn't come himself, but he made sure I'd have someone who didn't need to be nagged into seeing I was well. Who wouldn't ignore others as needed help."

The lead townsman gaped. "You . . . They never came through town."

" 'Course not." Garrad sniffed. "What with bandits and all, much too risky." He raised his walking stick and poked the leader's stomach with it. "So you can get yourself back to your Amelie and stop bothering me with your nonsense."

If there was any more conversation, Ree didn't hear it. His eyes stung. His grandsons, he'd said. Not just Jem, but Ree. Jem looked like the family. Jem might be a gift of the gods. But Ree didn't even look human. Ree wasn't anyone's gift.

After a while, he heard Garrad's limping gait approach. "Them furs should be fine a while without turning. Come on in and get something to eat." Garrad paused a moment, then added, "Son."

Ree swallowed. He had to blink several times before he dared turn to look at the old man. Jem's smile made it harder. "Thanks." He swallowed again. "Granddad."

Haven's Own
by Fiona Patton

Fiona Patton lives in rural Ontario, Canada, with her partner Tanya Huff, an ancient chihuahua, and a menagerie of cats. She has five heroic fantasy novels out with DAW Books: *The Stone Prince*, *The Painter Knight*, *The Granite Shield*, and *The Golden Sword* in the Branion Series and *The Silver Lake*, the first book in the Warriors of Estavia series. *The Golden Tower*, the second book in that series, is due out in September of this year. She has published thirty-odd short stories, most with Tekno.Books and DAW. She is currently working on the third book in the Warriors of Estavia series tentatively titled *The Shining City*.

There was no hint of smoke on the morning breeze. Standing in the window of the tiny back bedchamber he shared with three of his brothers, Hektor Dann of the Haven City Watch took a tentative breath of the crisp autumn air before staring out past the rows of tenements and shops to the blackened area at the far end of the street. A fire had swept through the crowded iron market a month ago, destroying many of the tents and stalls and killing half a dozen people, including Hektor's own father, Sergeant Egan Dann. No one had known how the fire'd started but there were always rumors.

Reluctantly, his gaze turned to the roofs of Candler's Row to the east. Iron Street and Candler's Row had been at odds for years, with street fighting and vandalism breaking out every few months, but nothing like this had ever happened before. Angry mutterings of retaliation from the street's more vocal hotheads had kept the watchhouse on full alert. Something was going to blow; everyone knew it. It was only a question of when.

As if on cue, a pounding on the door interrupted his thoughts.

"Move it, Hektor, or we'll be late." His oldest brother's voice, the familiar impatient temper masking a more recent hint of barely controlled anger beneath it.

"I am movin', Aiden."

"Then move faster. The Captain wants us at the watchhouse early in case things get out of hand."

"I know."

"Then know faster."

Aiden's footsteps stomped down the hall and, with one last glance out the window, Hektor followed.

Avoiding the tottering charge of his three-year-old nephew, Egan, he made his way through the flat's narrow hallway to the front room, accepting a cup of tea and a piece of bread and honey from his sister-in-law, Aiden's wife, Sulia. Then, crossing to the main window, he bent down and kissed his mother on the top of the head.

Setting her embroidery to one side, she rose to straighten the collar of his blue and gray watchman's uniform.

"Don't forget today's sweets day," she reminded him, tucking a pennybit into his hand.

"I won't."

"Did Jakon and Raik remember to leave their money on the dresser before they went on shift last night?"

Hektor nodded. "I've got theirs an' Aiden's," he

answered, then frowned as Sulia handed him three pennybits, one each for her, Egan, and their youngest, Leila, who was just six months old.

"We've got plenty, Suli," he offered. "You don't have to put any in now."

"Never you mind what I put in now," she said sharply. "And don't you let Aiden bully you into givin' these back to me either. He paid the whole of the rent yesterday."

"He did."

As one, they glanced at the empty chair at the head of the kitchen table without speaking.

"You knew he would, Hektor," Sulia said gently. "He's the oldest. It's his duty."

"I didn't know he would," Hektor grumbled. Short-tempered and wild, Aiden had never been easy to get along with. Marriage and children had done little to change him, and since their father's death, he'd been even more unpredictable. Aiden was also going to blow; it was also only a question of when. But hopefully it wouldn't happen in front of the family.

Now, smoothing his own expression, Hektor turned and held his hand out to his only sister, Kasiath, sitting with their grandfather beside the small coal stove, blonde head and gray head bent over a bird tucked in a wooden box. She handed him a full penny with a serious expression that belied her thirteen years.

"Peachwing's ailin'," she said in answer to his questioning expression. "The herbalist is makin' up a packet of medicines for her and one for Granther. Can you pick 'em up after your shift? We'd have asked Jakon and Raik, but they're guardin' the iron market rebuild first thing this mornin'," she added quietly.

He nodded. "What's wrong with her?" he asked, peering down at the bird.

"She misses her clutch. We moved 'em to the trainin' coop yesterday."

Beside her, their grandfather snorted. "I've told ye

a thousan' times, girl, birds don't miss their littles when they leave. It's mites."

Kasiath just patted him on the arm. "Course they miss 'em, Granther," she said. "They just don't show it the same way people do. But she's also got mites," she agreed. "She's s'posed to be lead messenger bird for the watchhouse next week," she added, returning her attention to Hektor. "But she can't 'less we get the mites cleared up."

Hektor jiggled the money in his hand. "Can't you pay the herbalist in eggs?" he asked. "Not from your messenger birds," he added swiftly when both sister and grandfather gave him a dark look. "But your pigeons've gotta have few to spare?"

"Oh, aye, if you wants to go without your breakfast tomorrow," his grandfather snapped.

"There are a few extra," Kasiath allowed in a mollifying tone, "but we didn't think you wanted to keep 'em at the watchhouse over your shift."

"We didn't think they'd still be there, is what she meant," their grandfather snorted. "T'was different in my day. You could leave a fortune on the front step, and no one'd look twice at it. Nowadays, with your Da gone, there's no order up there. Them greedy ba . . ." He broke off at Kasiath's reproachful look, hunkering down in his shawl with a barely audible mutter.

"I'll get 'em," Hektor promised, then turned with an attempt at a stern expression to his youngest brother, eleven-year-old Padreic.

The boy studiously kept his eyes on the pig's bladder ball he was mending until Hektor coughed pointedly. "That's all right, Hek," he said without looking up. "I don't need any sweets this month."

"Don't need?"

Padreic shrugged, then glanced up with a rueful expression. "I don't have a pennybit," he admitted.

"You got paid last week," Hektor reminded him. "And I saw you put money on the mantle."

The boy just shrugged again, and Hektor sighed. "You gave it away, didn't you?" he asked.

"To Rosie."

With a shake of his head, Hektor reached into his pouch for another pennybit, then stopped as Aiden's hand came down heavily on his arm.

"Rosie earns her own money," he said shortly.

Both younger brothers nodded in resentful obedience, but when Aiden turned his back, Hektor quietly added a pennybit anyway.

"Who're we to stand in the way of true love," he whispered, smiling as the comment caused Padreic to redden. "Are you sweepin' up at the watchhouse today, Paddy?" he asked loudly to cover up the movement.

" 'Course I am," the boy declared at once. "Today's postin' day."

"I thought you were doin' deliveries for the bakery this mornin'," their mother said with a frown.

"Traded with Ollie so as I could be at the watchhouse."

"The captain may not post today," Hektor warned him, casting a quick look for Aiden, but their elder brother was now deep in conversation with their grandfather and was at least pretending not to hear them.

"He'll post," Padreic insisted. "Aiden'll make sergeant an' I'll come on as watchhouse runner, you'll see."

Hektor frowned down at him. "Maybe. But all the same, keep quiet about it till then, all right?"

"But Hek . . ."

"No buts. Now hurry up or we'll be late."

Padreic obediently set the ball to one side and stood.

"Tell your brothers to be careful today," their mother called after them as Aiden joined them at the door. "I don't hold with double shifts, whatever the pay might be, and I don't want 'em so tired that they slip up."

"We'll tell 'em."

"And you be careful, too. Things might get out of hand out there."

"We know."

"Then know safer."

The three Dann boys took the tenement stairs two at a time, emerging into the bright sunlight a moment later. The Iron Street watchhouse was ten long blocks away, and they walked quickly, nodding to their neighbors as they went. The Danns had lived on Iron Street for as long as there'd been a street and had served at the Iron Street watchhouse for as long as there'd been a watchhouse. Ordinarily the street would be bustling with people at this time of the morning, all talking and trading, arguing and calling out their own greetings, but the fire had cast a pall of nervous suspicion over the entire neighborhood. All eyes tracked their progress and Hektor did his best to ignore the growing sense of unrest until a burly figure stepped in front of them. Beside him, he felt his older brother stiffen.

"Mornin', Linton," Hektor said casually.

"Mornin', Watchmen." The large, beefy mastersmith cocked his head to one side.

"You an' your brother gonna be guardin' the iron market rebuild today, Corporal?" he asked Aiden pointedly.

Aiden's expression hardened. "That'll be up to the captain," he answered in a neutral tone.

The smith spat a gob of spittle onto the cobblestones. "Yeah, well, the captain's not from around here, is he? He's only been on the job a few months. Hope he's got enough sense to do what's expected of 'im. I hear it's postin' day an' all."

"Maybe."

"Figure he'll name you sergeant now that your Da's gone?"

Aiden gave a noncommittal shrug, but Hektor saw a muscle in his jaw begin to jump. "Hard to say," he answered stiffly.

" 'Course he will," Padreic replied, then yelped as Aiden clipped his ear.

"I only ask 'cause the whole street wants to know," the smith continued, ignoring Aiden's warning expression. "The fire hurt a lot of families here. We wanna know there'll be justice done on account of most folk think it was a Candler's Row crew what set the fire in the first place."

"The Guard investigated an' said it was an accident," Hektor said at once.

"An' rumor-mongerin' ain't 'elpin' any," Aiden added darkly.

"It ain't rumor-mongerin', it's belief. An' a belief shared by half the Iron Street Watch if they was to own up to it," the smith snarled in reply, jabbing a finger at him. "Your own Da suspected a Candler's Row crew of sowin' nails into the ground around the market last year what gave Charlie Woar the gangrene an' lost him his leg. An' as I remember, Aiden Dann, you wasn't too high an' mighty back then to go up there an' settle the score with your fists."

"That was then, Linton," Aiden growled. "Times have changed."

"Not by that much, they ain't."

"Then they'd better start. Anyone headin' over to Candler's Row is gonna get their heads busted by the Watch, you hear?" Aiden glared around the street, daring anyone to gainsay him.

"Your Da woulda seen to it by now," the smith pointed out. "Course your Da woulda made captain afore the inquiry caused some fool incomer to be brought in," he added. "That's when all this trouble started."

Aiden's face darkened dangerously. "Get out of our way, Linton," he grated.

The smith's eyes narrowed, but he stepped aside as Aiden pushed past him. When the other two made to follow, he caught Hektor by the arm. "No one blames Aiden for your Da not gettin' that promotion," he hissed, "nor for the fire neither, but it's up to you lot to do somethin' about it; not the Guard, you, the Danns. Don't forget where you live, boy."

Hektor shook him off. "We live in Haven, Linton," he snarled. "Don't you forget that." But his expression mirrored the smith's as he followed Aiden up the street.

The Iron Street watchhouse was crowded with watchmen, both on duty and off, when they arrived. Gesturing Padreic toward a broom, Aiden stalked past them, but Hektor paused, glancing at the captain's closed door with a frown. "Has he posted yet?"

As one, the gathered shook their heads.

"It outta be Aiden," one of the older men said quietly. "Course, it's anyone's guess what the captain'll do, bein' . . . you know, from outside and all, but it outta be Aiden."

Hektor nodded, then turned as Jakon and Raik pushed their way through the crowd toward him.

"How're the streets last night?" he asked in a quiet voice.

"Tense," Jakon answered. "People are huddlin' in the taverns, just sitting there an' talkin'."

"An' everyone falls quiet when we go by," Raik added.

"Everyone always falls quiet when we go by," Hektor reminded them. "We're the Watch."

"Not like this," Raik argued. "It's like everyone's

watchin' us, waitin' to see what we're gonna do about the fire."

"Waitin' to see what Aiden'll do mostly," Jakon amended.

"Aiden's not gonna do anythin'," Hektor said firmly. "It was an accident."

"Nobody's believes that, Hek. Hell, even I don't believe it."

"And maybe Aiden should do somethin' about it, anyway," Raik added. "I mean, we can't just sit back and let this sort of thing happen again. We have to protect the street."

"It was an accident," Hektor repeated.

Neither brother looked convinced.

"Think the captain'll post today?" Raik asked, changing the subject.

Hektor just shrugged.

"Think he'll make Aiden sergeant after the inquiry an' all?"

Hektor sighed. "I dunno, Raik," he said.

"Anything you do know, Hek?"

"Yeah. I know Ma said to be careful."

Both brothers gave an equal snort. "We will."

With it clear that the captain was not going to post that morning, most of the watchmen disappeared swiftly. Hektor was on his way out the door with his patrol mate, Kiel Wright, when the captain stuck his head out his office door. Signaling Kiel to wait, he gestured Hektor inside.

Captain Travin Torell was an older man with a more refined air than most of the Iron Street watchmen. Originally from Breakneedle Street—one wall and an entire world away—he'd served as that watchhouse's lieutenant before been being promoted to Iron Street's captaincy last year after the inquiry into the events surrounding Charlie Woar's injury. Hektor had done his best to avoid the tension between first his father and then his older brother, and the new captain. Now he closed the door, waiting to see what he wanted with as neutral an expression as possible.

"You've been with the Watch for some time now, haven't you?" the captain said at once.

Hektor nodded cautiously. "Came on as a full watchman five years ago, sir," he allowed. "I was a runner before that."

"And before that a sweeper like your brother Padreic," the captain added. "Like every Dann on the street, or so I've been told. A family tradition, yes?"

"Yes, sir."

"Yes." Staring out at the watchhouse yard beyond his window, the captain tucked his hands behind his back. "The Danns have been an integral part of the Watch since time immemorial," he said almost to himself. "And I'm sure that, in the past, their methods served the city well enough, but times have changed, and so must all our methods."

He turned. "The veterans speak highly of you. They say that you have an even temper and a decent grasp of the law. You should go far."

Hektor's eyes narrowed cautiously. "Thank you, sir."

"And the Watch needs men with even tempers in these uncertain times," the captain continued. "Men who can lead by the proper example. This trouble between Iron Street and Candler's Row, for example; I doubt whether anyone even remembers how it began. But I will tell you this, Watchman, it's going to stop." He jabbed a finger in Hektor's direction. "I won't tolerate acts of retaliation, not by the populace and most certainly not by the Watch. Do I make myself clear?"

"Yes, sir."

"Yes, well, on that note, I'd like to offer you the rank of sergeant. What do you think about that?"

Hektor blinked. "Are you postin' my name, sir?"

The captain frowned impatiently. "No, I'm not, not yet." He ran a hand through his hair. "I know what the Watch expects, what the entire street expects for that matter," he said peevishly. "but I'm not running a popularity contest, and I don't believe seniority should have the final say in something this important. Aiden's a hothead. Last year's events proved that."

"Beggin' your pardon, sir," Hektor said, a spark of anger causing him to scowl. "But nothin' of last year was proven at all."

"Yes, I'm fully aware of the inquiry's report, Watchman," the captain answered stiffly. "And why it read as it did. But there's no honor in covering up unlawful behavior.

"Now I understand that this might put you in an awkward position," he continued before Hektor could voice another protest. "But I expect you to do what's right by Haven and not just what's comfortable for your family. I want your answer by the end of the dayshift."

Hektor snapped to a sarcastic attention. "Sir."

"And I will be posting your younger brother Padreic's name for watchhouse runner," the captain continued before Hektor could turn for the door. "He seems a diligent and hard-working lad who merits the position. I trust he'll do his best to bring honor to the Watch."

"Thank you, sir."

"I am not out to get the Danns, Watchman, whatever the rank and file may think."

"No, sir."

"Yes, well, that will be all."

"Sir."

Hektor left the captain's office with all eyes upon him. Shifting his expression to one similar to Aiden's, he glared at them until they all found something else to do, then signaled curtly to Kiel and headed out the door. But it didn't matter. The rumor mill had already begun to turn; the speculations would be all over the street by noon.

He fretted over what the captain had said—and what Aiden would say—for the rest of the day. Around him, the street seemed to be holding its breath, as if waiting for an approaching storm to break above the city. As his brothers had noted, the people fell silent as he and Kiel approached, then huddled together, talking quietly after they'd passed. As the afternoon sun touched the tops of the western roof-tops, the two watchmen turned their steps back toward Iron Street with visible relief and walked right into a smash and grab.

Two youths were squeezing past an elderly man in a heavy muffling cloak, arms overladen with packages. Just as they came alongside him, one of the youths seemed to stumble, falling against the old man, while the other threw out a hand with an exclamation of alarm to steady him. As one of the smaller packages disappeared into the first youth's open shirt, Kiel gave a shout. The youth immediately took off running, and Hektor leaped after him.

The youth pelted down the street, but Hektor was one of the fastest runners in the Watch, and he gained on him quickly. Usually more than happy to partake in the hue and cry, the people made room for them, shouting encouragement. One single dive was all it took, and Hektor brought the youth down hard, knocking the breath out of him as they hit the cobblestones.

The crowd cheered. For a moment Hektor smiled; then as someone shouted "Iron Street!" his expression dropped to a frown once again.

By the time he returned, dragging the youth by the collar, Kiel had taken his accomplice into custody, and Aiden had arrived on the scene, trying to placate the old man, who was upbraiding him in an accent that showed plainly that he was not from the Iron Street area. A crowd of people had already begun to gather in response to the sound of indignant scolding.

"I am not inebriated, Corporal," the old man now snapped, weaving slightly.

"No, sir, of course not, sir," Aiden answered with exaggerated politeness, casting a jaundiced eye across the crowd as this statement provoked an murmur of laughter.

"And I do not require a Healer," the old man continued. "I'm right as rain."

"Yes, sir." Aiden eyed the blood trickling down from an abrasion just visible above the old man's hairline. "Pardon the liberty, sir, but rain isn't always right."

The old man drew himself up to glare at him through a pair of rheumy blue eyes. "And when isn't it right, pray tell?" he demanded.

"When there's too much of it, sir." Aiden offered him his handkerchief with a neutral expression, and the old man took it in grumbling acceptance, pressing it against his forehead with an involuntary hiss of pain.

"At least let one of us see you home, sir," Aiden offered. "The night comes on fast this time of year, and you'll want to be indoors afore the sun goes down."

His unspoken words hung between them, but the old man cast him a shrewd glance. "You mean you want me off your streets and safely home before the end of your shift, Corporal," he accused.

"As you say, sir." Aiden gestured at Hektor. "Watchman, see the gentleman home," he ordered, piling the old man's parcels into his younger brother's arms until he could barely see over them.

As the crowd began to laugh, Hektor sighed. "Yes, Corporal."

*　　*　　*

Leaning heavily on his shoulder, the old man directed them toward an area much more affluent than the ones Hektor was used to. It was slow going, but eventually they fetched up before a sturdy, well-maintained house with a small front garden planted with flowers. The old man fished a key from his voluminous cloak and, opening the door, gestured Hektor inside.

"Just set the parcels on the table there by the largest of the cages."

Hektor did as directed, then stared about in undisguised awe. The front room was huge, more than twice the size of his own, and was crowded with large, ornate birdcages housing tiny yellow and brown birds that filled the room with music. Floor-to-ceiling bookcases marched along every wall, with complex bits of wood and metal and strange objects he couldn't possibly identify competing with books, scrolls, and maps on every surface. A number of open doors hinted at more overstuffed rooms beyond.

The old man threw his cloak in the general direction of a chair stacked high with books. "A lifetime's collection," he said in response to Hektor's expression. "I'm a bit of a pack rat, I'm afraid. Comes with the territory. I'm an Artificer . . . was an Artificer . . . am a retired Artificer. The sight goes with age," he added, poking a finger dangerously close to one eye. "Couldn't see a drawing now to save myself. But life goes on, doesn't it?"

"Uh, yes, sir?"

The old man gave an amused snort. "You're polite to say so," he acknowledged. "Of course, I don't expect you to understand that just yet, do I? No, later, when you're older. That's the thing about wisdom, it comes with age. Or at least it should. Now . . ." He began rummaging in a huge golden oak desk piled with a similar number of strange items and papers. "You must let me give you something for your trouble."

Hektor drew himself up. "No, thank you, sir."

The old man chuckled. "Too proud to accept money like a porter, Watchman?"

Hektor blushed. He made to shake his head, but something in the old man's friendly tone made him shrug instead. "S'pose I am, sir," he admitted.

"An honest answer. No money, then, but, now where is it, where is it, ah yes, this might do, I think." He plucked a small metal disc from a pile of similar objects. "Perhaps a bit premature, but I believe in the power of optimism. All Artificers do, or they wouldn't attempt half the projects they take on." He held it out. "You must accept it. It's just a trifle after all, and it will keep me from insisting."

Hektor took it reluctantly, stuffing it into his pouch without looking at it.

"And now tea is in order, I should think," the old man continued.

Hektor shook his head. "I really can't, sir," he said, inching towards the door. "An' pardon the liberty, but you outta get a Healer to look at that cut on your forehead."

"What?" The old man dabbed at his head with a grimace. "Oh, yes, I shall, of course. And it just so happens that I have a Healer friend coming to take an early supper with me. I'm sure he'll see to it then, but in the meantime, you must stay for a cup of tea."

As Hektor opened his mouth to make a second protest, the old man waved a dismissive hand at him. "I insist. Besides," he added with a mischievous smile. "I might suffer a terrible collapse as a result of my injury. You might say that it's your duty to remain until my friend arrives. Sit." Pointing at a chair covered in scrolls, he bustled into the kitchen, and with a sigh, Hektor did as he was told.

The room was stuffy and warm, the tea expensive and strong. A plate of fancy cakes sat on a silver tray by the teapot, and Hektor allowed himself to be prodded into eating several. The old man was interesting company, telling a short tale or two of his own life and inviting his guest to do the same. The sun had passed the window, casting the room into darkness before Hektor remembered his errands with a guilty start. He glanced surreptitiously at the door, but the old man caught the movement at once.

"Do you need to get away so soon?" he asked. "Surely your shift is over by now?"

"I need to report back to the watchhouse, sir," Hektor answered, rising. "And I have errands to run before I go home."

"Errands?"

"The sweetshop and the herbalist. One of my grandfather's birds is ailing."

"Well, I'm sure my friend will be along any moment. Just finish off that final cake, won't you, or it will go stale. Now, you were telling me about this business of the iron market fire."

With reluctance, Hektor sat back down again.

It was at least another half candlemark before they heard someone at the door. The old man called out a greeting, and Hektor rose at once as a heavyset man in the dark green cloak of the College of Healers entered the room. He came forward quickly to take the old man's hand.

"I only just learned of your accident or I would have come much sooner, Daedrus," he apologized in a gruff tone. "You should have sent for me."

"Nonsense, Markus. I'm right as rain. You had lectures and rounds. Besides, I had my young rescuer here to keep watch over me. May I present Hektor Dann of the City Watch? One of Haven's finest."

Hektor started, and Daedrus began to chuckle. "Well of course I know who you are, boy. Do you think I'm just some lonely old man who lets anyone into his home? The Danns may not be known within the second gate, but they're well known beyond it. And I do most of my shopping beyond it.

"We were just discussing the iron market fire, Markus," he continued as the Healer began to examine the wound on his forehead.

"Oh?"

"Yes. A bad business, that. Young Hektor lost his father, you know, who was trying to bring people out. It's caused a lot of bad feelings in the neighborhood."

"Has it? Please stop moving your head, Daedrus."

"Indeed. There's even some fear that the citizens of Iron Street may take matters into their own hands if the issue isn't resolved to their satisfaction. Or so I've heard in the marketplace."

"Really?"

"Oh, yes. I suppose we should reconsider our supper at the White Lily if the streets are this unsettled."

"Quite right." The Healer straightened. "Well, your head needs to be properly cleaned and possibly stitched before we can even think about supper, and I'm sure the young watchman would like to get home for his own."

Hektor moved immediately toward the door.

"You will come and see me again, won't you?" the old man called after him. "I quite enjoyed our conversation, and I'm eager to learn the outcome of this latest drama."

Making a mumbled promise, Hektor almost ran for the door.

It was full dark by the time he reached the watchhouse. The captain had long since left, and it was with some relief that he made tracks for the herbalist's. Grumbling all the while, the woman stuffed two small packets into his hand, accepted his money, then shoved him unceremoniously out the door. He just managed to catch the smell of meat pies wafting from the back before the door was shut firmly behind him. With a sigh, he headed for the sweetshop.

It was closed, and no amount of pounding on the door could elicit a response. Glaring at the tightly locked shutters, Hektor turning toward home, imagining what his family would say.

The scene that greeted him was not what he expected. Kasiath met him at the door, her face beaming.

"Oh, Hektor, they're wonderful. Such sweets. Come and see."

He allowed himself to be dragged into the kitchen, where the family were all crowded about the table. An open package of untouched sweets, each one nestled in its own little piece of wax paper, sat in the center. Beside it, a small card held a single letter *D*. Egan hovered impatiently behind his father, a deeply aggrieved expression on his face as Aiden gave his younger brother a suspicious frown.

Hektor shrugged weakly, filling in the events of his evening as quickly as possible. "He must have known the shop would be closed," he hazarded.

"And how did he know you would be going there?" his brother demanded.

"I told him. He wanted to talk, and you know how old men are, Aiden. I couldn't get away."

Both his brother and their grandfather snorted at that.

"We don't take charity," Aiden growled.

"It wasn't charity," Hektor retorted angrily. "I didn't know he would send 'em, but it was a nice thought from a lonely old man." Grabbing one of the sweets, he stuffed it into his mouth with a defiant expression.

Egan sent up a loud wail, and all eyes turned to Aiden, who finally threw up his hands.

"Fine, have 'em." As the family pounced on the box, he scowled. "I'm goin' out."

Hektor turned, noting that his brother was still in his watchman's uniform.

"Where?" he demanded.

"The iron market."

"The captain set you on guard duty tonight?"

"No. What's it to you?"

The family exchanged a worried look as Hektor gave a studied shrug.

"Nothin', 'cept I'm comin' with you."

"I don't need you."

"I don't care."

The two brothers glared at each other; then Aiden threw up his hands again. "Do what you want."

Jakon and Raik looked up. "Should we?" Jakon began, and Hektor shook his head.

"You'll want to get some supper before your shift," he answered. "We'll be all right." He glanced over at Sulia. "I promise."

The two brothers walked along the darkened street in uncomfortable silence until they reached the stretch of fallow field where the iron market was being rebuilt. Aiden nodded at the two watchmen on duty by the ruined gates, then made for the far eastern end. Leaning against a newly built stall, he pulled out his pipe, clearly settling in.

Hektor cocked his head. "Why are we here, Aiden?" he asked. "There are guards."

Filling the bowl of his pipe, Aiden just shrugged. "You're here 'cause you don't trust me not to start somethin'. I'm here to make sure no one else does."

"The Candler's Row folk?"

"Nope, our folk."

"Then shouldn't we be hoverin' around the closes that lead to Candler's Row?"

Aiden shook his head. "They'll meet here at the iron market."

"How do you know that?"

" 'Cause this here's where we always met."

As his brother stuck a twig into the nearby lamp, Hektor stared into the darkness. "Got called into the captain's office today," he ventured.

Aiden just grunted in reply.

"He figures no one even remembers how the trouble 'tween us started."

Aiden touched the twig to his pipe, drawing in a deep breath. "What would he know about it?" he said, once the pipe caught.

"Does anyone remember?"

"I doubt it. It was long afore Granther's day. But it don't really matter how it started; it's here now, and we've gotta deal with it now."

"Yeah, but how?"

Aiden blew a long trail of smoke into the air. "I got no idea," he admitted. He glanced sideways at his younger brother. "So, what else did you and the captain talk about?"

Hektor started. "Nothin' much else really," he said a bit too quickly.

"Bollocks. He offered you the sergeancy."

"I didn't tell him yes or nothin'."

"Then you're an idiot."

Hektor started. "What? But everyone knows it outta be you."

Aiden gave a bark of derisive laughter. "Why? 'Cause I'm the oldest?"

"No, 'cause . . . well, 'cause you're . . . All right, yeah, 'cause you're the oldest. It's your turn."

"Bollocks." Aiden stared out at the pale half moon. "I knew he'd never name me sergeant, Hek," he said quietly. "Not after the inquiry an' all."

"Nothing was proven," Hektor declared loyally, and Aiden chopped a hand down to silence him.

"Nothing needs to be proven. Everyone thinks they know what happened. They think I went to Candler's Row that night to even the score for Charlie Woar."

He took a deep draw on his pipe. "And I shoulda," he said more to himself than to Hektor. "Charlie and I are friends. It should have been me that went that night, not Da."

"Da? But I thought . . . everyone thinks . . ."

"That he followed me? That he pulled me off a man on Candler's Row? That the man almost died an' Da an' the Iron Street Watch covered the whole thing up 'cause I'm a Dann?"

"Well, yeah."

Aiden stared out past the gates, his expression unreadable. "Sometimes you get boxed in by what people think," he said. "So boxed in you can't hardly breathe. It starts makin' your choices for you. I wanted to do justice by Charlie, but not like that. I wanted to find the folk that sowed those nails and bring 'em in, but the street wanted revenge, an' they wanted it fast or they'd get it themselves. Da knew that. That's why he went. But he wasn't thinkin' straight neither. He was drunk an' angry, an' he jumped the first man he saw on Candler's Row. If I hadn't followed him, he mighta killed 'im."

"So you covered it up an' took the blame? Why?"

"Made more sense. Da was a respected member of the Watch, an' I've been the family troublemaker since I was a little. Like I said, you get boxed in."

"You coulda told folk the truth."

"No one wanted to hear it, Hek. Just like now." Aiden turned a suddenly intense look on his brother's face. "You figure the fire was an accident?"

"The Guard said it was."

"But do you figure it was?"

Hektor stared out at the blackened field. "I dunno. I guess not, probably," he admitted.

"An' if you figure not, what do you expect the street to figure? They figure it was set deliberate. An' they want the score settled, an' they want it settled by me, 'cause that's what I do for 'em."

"But the Candler's Row folk ain't stupid," Hektor protested. "They gotta know it too, an' they've gotta be waitin' for you to make your move."

"Right. But the longer I don't, the more likely it is that Linton or someone else is gonna. Or worse," he added, "someone from Candler's Row's gonna figure the best way to belay our strike is to make their own."

"So what do we do?"

Aiden shrugged. "Folk expected Da to lead with his fists. They expect me to do the same. But they don't expect you to, an' that's a good thing. It leaves you free to make your own choices. Maybe you can sort somethin' out. You're smart."

"The captain said I had an even temper," Hektor noted sarcastically.

"That's just compared to mine. You're a compromise, Hek. The captain don't want any Dann promoted, but the Watch and the street does. He didn't just post your name though, did he?"

"No, he asked me if I would take it first."

" 'Cause he don't wanna to look like a fool if you say no. He wants things to look smooth, even if they ain't."

Hektor rubbed his face. "It's all too complicated," he complained.

"Then make it simple. Do what's right by the family. Take the promotion. We need the money."

"But what do we do about Iron Street and Candler's Row? Do we ask a Herald to mediate or somethin'?"

Aiden snorted. "Mediate with who? They're all shopkeepers and tradesmen by day. The Guard said it was an accident. That shoulda been the end of it, but it wasn't, 'cause they're all vigilantes by night. The Heralds can mediate all they like, but it won't change folk, 'cause they don't wanna be changed."

"Then we have to make 'em change," Hektor argued. "An we gotta start by provin' the fire was an accident."

"How?"

Hektor straightened. "By askin' someone who knows about this kinda thing," he said. "Someone they respect. We ask an Artificer."

"And this is where the fire started?"

Standing in the charred ruins of the market's one permanent forge, Daedrus turned an expectant look on Hektor.

"Yes, sir. There's been a lot of rebuild around the perimeter, but not here in the middle. No one's wanted to go near it as yet, I 'spect. The Fair Master died inside."

"I see, yes, very interesting, very interesting indeed."

The retired Artificer had been puttering about the iron market for over an hour, muttering to himself and drawing an ever-growing crowd of onlookers beyond the gates. "I think I should like to bring in a few of my colleagues as consultants if you don't mind," he said. "If you could send someone to the Compass Rose Tavern and have them bring back, oh . . ." he waved a hand absently. ". . . whoever happens to be there."

"Yes, sir. Paddy?" Hektor jumped as Padreic appeared at his elbow immediately. "You know where the Compass Rose is?" When the boy nodded vigorously, he gestured. "Off you go then on your first assignment." As his brother took off at a dead run, Hektor turned back to the old man. "Was there anything else, sir?"

Tugging at the plaster bandage on his forehead, Daedrus nodded. "Well, it would help me to come to a more accurate conclusion if I could consult with someone knowledgeable in the circumstances under which this area would be made use of. Do you know of anyone like that?"

"Sir?"

"A smith, Watchman, who is familiar with the forge."

"Oh." Scanning the crowd, Hektor spotted a familiar face. "Yes sir, I do."

It only took Linton a moment to understand what Daedrus required. Tipping his cap back, he scratched his head thoughtfully. "This be the market forge," he explained. "The Fair Master's in charge of it, though he don't usually work it hisself. We all work it through the fair to cast a horseshoe or make somethin' small as a customer might want."

"And the Fair Master sets the forge schedule?" Daedrus asked. "He sees to it that every smith who needs it gets a chance to make use of it?"

"Every local smith," Linton corrected. "Only Haven smiths can use the market forge. That's tradition. If a smith from outside wanted somethin', he'd have to ask one of us for it." He snorted. "An' good luck to 'im.

"My cousin Bri was Fair Master for years," he continued. "Did a good job he did, too, keepin' everything movin' along smoothly. There weren't never too much waitin'." He frowned. "Come to think of it, with him gone, I reckon I'm Fair Master now."

Daedrus nodded. "And so he, your cousin Bri, would know everyone who made use of the forge. As you will next year?"

"Yep."

"So it would be very unusual to have a stranger lurking about unescorted?"

Linton snorted. "Wouldn't happen at all. We keep an eye out; we all do."

"I see. Ah, here come my colleagues."

Daedrus turned as more than two dozen Artificers and students descended on the iron market. He'd set Hektor and Aiden to checker off the entire field with a ball of twine pulled from his voluminous cloak, and now he sent each of his consultants off to an individual square to take measurements and make notes. As the Artificers spread out, he returned his attention to Linton.

By late afternoon the Artificers had finished their investigation and were now clustered about the ruined forge, comparing their findings. Several other smiths had been drawn into the conversation, and, as the sun sent long fingers of shadow across the field, Hektor could hear their voices rising and falling as they argued over the events leading up to the fire. But one thing they all agreed on was that no one except a local smith was ever allowed near the market forge. After a particularly heated piece of debate, he heard Linton's voice rise above the rest.

" 'Course any fool can see it started by accident, right here. Sparks is what done it, sparks an' wind. It's happened before more'n two decades back; Bri told me hisself. Nearly sent the whole fair up that time."

Shaking his head, Hektor turned to find Captain Torell standing beside him. He started.

"Sir."

"It seems the street is close to its verdict," the captain said dryly.

"Yes, sir." Hektor shrugged. "Folk here don't take too kindly to bein' told what's what." He glanced over to where Linton was now jabbing another smith in the chest to emphasize his point. "They'd rather do the tellin'."

"So I see. And I imagine the people of Candler's Row are much the same."

"I 'spect so, sir."

"Do you have a plan that will take the wind out of their sails as well?"

"Sir?"

"Never mind, one crisis at a time." The captain now turned as Daedrus called out to them.

"An accident," the old man said once they'd joined the crowd of smiths and Artificers. "Tragic, very tragic, but avoidable in the future, I think. Yes, very much so. We have some ideas for the rebuild that will prove quite advantageous."

Turning, he pulled a small metal disc from the depths of his cloak. "Does anyone have a . . . oh, thank you." He accepted one of the dozen small hammers that were immediately held out to him and, reaching up, affixed the disc to the forge with two tiny nails.

"Artificer's seal," he said in answer to Hektor's questioning expression. "Usually we place them after the building is complete, but as this project was in fact an investigation, not a construction, I think it's neither unreasonable nor premature to place it now, hm?"

A murmur of assent from the Artificers made him smile. "Good. Now, Fair Master Linton, do come by some time this week, won't you? I'm eager to get started on our plans. Do you have my address?"

Linton chuckled. "I do, sir. I cast your nails."

"Do you really? Well, they're very fine work. What, hm?" He turned as the captain now cleared his throat.

"It's growing dark, Daedrus. Time to lock up the field."

"What? Oh yes, of course." The old man waved at the gathered smiths and Artificers who began to leave the iron market still deep in conversation. "And will the young watchman be escorting me home again?" he asked with a twinkle in his eye.

The captain nodded formally. "Sergeant Dann will be only too happy to oblige you, after which he's to report back to the watchhouse. Sergeant?"

Hektor looked up from the small metal disc he'd

pulled from his pouch with a confused expression. "Sir?"

"Escort the Artificer home."

"Yes, sir."

"You'll be at the White Lily tomorrow night, Daedrus?" the Captain asked.

The old man beamed. "I wouldn't miss it, Travin."

"Very good. Carry on, Sergeant."

"Sir."

Hektor glanced back at the metal disc in his hand, staring at the colorful Artificer's seal embossed over Haven's coat of arms, then up as Daedrus began to chuckle.

"Not so premature, as it happens," the old man said with a smile. "Now, if you will be so kind." He gestured towards the gates. "I have drawings to begin, and my eyes aren't what they used to be."

"Of course, sir." Tucking the disc back into his pouch, Sergeant Hektor Dann of the Haven City Watch escorted Artificer Daedrus from the iron market.

Widdershins

by Judith Tarr

Judith Tarr is the author of a number of historical and fantasy novels and stories. Her most recent novels include *Pride of Kings* and *Tides of Darkness*, as well as the Epona Sequence: *Lady of Horses*, *White Mare's Daughter*, and *Daughter of Lir*. She was a World Fantasy Award nominee for *Lord of the Two Lands*. She lives near Tucson, Arizona, where she breeds and trains Lipizzan horses.

Egil was as ordinary as a Herald could be. He was no hero or villain or Herald-Mage. In the Collegium he was solidly in the middle of every class. When he rode out on his internship, he did well enough, but nothing that he did was especially memorable.

Other people had dreams of greatness. Egil dreamed of peace and quiet, and time to read or write or simply sit and think.

Egil's Companion was named Cynara. Like Egil, she professed no grand ambitions. She did love to dance when she had the chance, and Egil was happy to indulge her. It was the one thing at which he was truly distinguished, and as he said, it was mostly a matter of not getting in Cynara's way.

Once Egil was past his internship, he was happy not to travel any longer. He settled in at the Collegium, teaching logic and history to the recruits and taking on whatever other tasks seemed most in need of doing. If there was anything that no one else had the time or inclination to do, Egil did it. He never complained, and he always got it done.

That, like dancing with his Companion, was a talent he had, but neither he nor anyone else thought overly much of it. "Not everyone can be a hero," he liked to say. "Someone has to keep everything in order while the heroes are off saving the world."

When the Mage Storms began, this was truer than usual. While the world tried to shake itself to pieces, Egil and Cynara helped to hold the Collegium together. It was thanks in part to them that after the Storms ended, there was still a Collegium in Valdemar and a place for Heralds and Companions to enjoy a well-deserved rest.

Now the world was safe, more or less, and for a while, Egil was content to disappear into his office and classroom. Most mornings as soon as it was light he went with Cynara to one of the riding arenas and danced. Sometimes people came to watch, but mostly the two of them had the oval of raked sand to themselves. It was their private time, a sort of meditation for them both.

One morning after an especially satisfying dance, Egil came back to his office to find a summons from the Queen.

He had met her, of course. All the Heralds had. She was one of them, after all.

He doubted she remembered him, and he had no particular desire to be remembered. The summons made no sense to him, unless he had done something wrong without knowing it; more likely this was a mistake and she had meant to summon someone else. The Herald Elgin, maybe. Or the Trainee who shared Egil's own name.

Yes, that was probably it. He dressed carefully in any case, though he decided against formal Whites; if this had been a ceremonial occasion, the summons would have said so. It was more an invitation, really, bidding Herald Egil attend the Queen in her office. He had sent more than a few of those himself to students in need of discipline or extra tutoring.

Neat, clean, and as ready as he could be, he presented himself at the door to the Queen's office.

Queen Selenay felt like a Companion. At a distance, she was naturally more Herald than courtier, but face to face across a desk piled high with books and papers, she was not so much a Herald as something . . . stronger.

The realization put Egil more at ease than he had been since he received the invitation. Companions invited awe, but in a way that Egil understood.

Whatever important matters of state the Queen had been contending with before he came, she fixed her full attention on him while he was there. She studied him for some time in silence that he made no attempt to break.

Eventually she folded her hands and leaned forward. Egil managed not quite to feel as if he had been called into the schoolmaster's office for a rebuke. She seemed interested, even intrigued, but neither angry nor disappointed.

"Your family breeds horses, I'm told," she said.

That was not what Egil had expected. He could only think to bob his head like an idiot and answer, "Yes. Yes, madam."

She smiled. It did not comfort Egil at all. "All's well there, I understand, and your sisters report that this year's foal crop is the best they've seen in years."

Egil gave up trying to hide his confusion. "What is it, madam? Has Zara had her baby? Was one of the others Chosen? Though I would know about that. Wouldn't I?"

"You would," the Queen said. "I'm sorry; I don't mean to torment you. I need a Herald with knowledge of both horses and riding."

"All Heralds can ride," Egil said. "Some are extraordinarily good at it."

"I am told," said the Queen, "that none is as good as you."

Egil flushed. "I would hardly say that. I have some talent and a fair amount of training, but there are others who—"

"Not your particular kind of training," the Queen said.

"I don't understand," Egil said.

"It's little more than a rumor," she said, "some odd stories and the occasional magical anomaly off the South Trade Road toward the Goldgrass Valley. What's strange is that they seem to revolve around a riding academy."

Egil's brows rose. "A school of riding? In the middle of nowhere?"

"Not exactly nowhere," the Queen said with the hint of a smile. "It's horse country all around there, and certain elements of the court have taken a fancy to it: they've been buying land and building summer houses and stocking them with the finest in fashionable horseflesh."

"And of course," said Egil, "they'll need trainers for the horses and instructors for their offspring, and if those should gather in one convenient place, so much the better."

"Exactly," said the Queen. "Your family has done much the same, I'm told, and done extremely well, training horse trainers and sending them where they're needed."

"You don't think they're involved with—"

"Probably not," she said, "but now I'm sure you understand why I would like you to ride along the South Trade Road and see what there is to see."

Egil did understand, but as sharp as his curiosity had grown, his love of the quiet life was stronger. There was also one inescapable fact. "Madam, I

haven't been in the field since I was an intern. Whatever skills I had in that direction are long since
rusted shut."

The Queen smiled in a way that told him she had
heard every word, but not one had changed her mind.
"It's an easy distance, with inns at every reasonable
stop, and the weather at this time of year is usually
lovely. If it does happen that you have to camp for a
night, you'll have company who can do whatever is
needed to make you comfortable. I'm sending an intern with you. She has some knowledge of horses as
well and some interest in the art of riding. It should
be a pleasant journey."

There was not much Egil could say to that. The
Queen had thought of everything, as she should. She
was the Queen.

Egil had successfully avoided official notice for
much longer than he had any right to. He was a Herald, and Heralds, as everyone knew, were the Arrows
of the Queen. They flew wherever she sent them.

Egil heaved a deep sigh. "As you wish," he said.

When Egil came out into the yard at first light,
packed and ready to ride, and saw the intern he would
be expected to advise and serve as an example for,
his sigh was even deeper. Herald Bronwen had been
Chosen at ten years old—younger than anyone in
memory—but that had come as no surprise: she was
Ashkevron, as Vanyel had been, and her family had
been producing Heralds in remarkable numbers since
the first Companion came into the world. Now at sixteen she had received her Whites and her first assignment, and it was clear she was as dismayed to see Egil
as he was to see her.

Egil had no objection to Trainees who wanted to
make something of themselves. He had helped more
than a few to excel in the classes he taught. Some
were arrogant; some had too much faith in their own

talents and not enough consideration for anyone else's. But he had always seen through the façade to the nervous child beneath.

Bronwen seemed to have no façade. The arrogance, as far as he had ever been able to see, went straight through to the core. She was born to greatness, she was destined for it, and she would achieve it. She had no doubts of that whatsoever. Any instructor in the Collegium who did not give her the highest marks for as little effort as she could be bothered to spare was clearly both benighted and deluded.

Egil had ranked her as she deserved. She had not thought so. Clearly, from her expression, she never had changed her mind.

He thought she might turn on her heel and stalk back into the Collegium. If she had, he would have done nothing to stop her. That made him a coward and a disgrace to his Whites, but if he acknowledged the truth, he was both already.

The one thing a Herald could not do was hide what he was. That was the reason for the Whites. No one and nothing could miss a Herald in the performance of his duty.

Egil had done his best to try. Now he had no choice but to ride out, for the first time in fourteen years. And he had to do it with the one student in fourteen years for whom he felt something close to animosity.

:*For your sins,*: his Companion said.

Cynara's eyes were a very deep blue, the color of some horse foals' before they turned honest equine brown. In most lights, in fact, they did look brown, so that people had been known to mistake her for an unusually pretty gray horse. Cynara, like Egil, liked to escape notice.

"You're not blaming me for this," he said.

:*Not at all,*: she said. He could detect no irony in the words, but he eyed her warily even so, before he gathered the reins and set his foot in the stirrup and swung lightly onto her back.

Bronwen was already mounted. Her Companion could not have been more visibly what he was: he was taller than any riding horse should rightly be, and his eyes were the color of the summer sky, a clear bright blue that no horse had ever had. He was as showy as his rider, with her long legs and her long braid of wheat-gold hair and her eyes as blue as her Companion's.

They were every village child's dream of the Herald and her Companion, and they knew it. Rohanan was as full of his own importance as Bronwen, until he ventured too close to Cynara. She put him in his place with a snap of teeth and a well-placed kick.

Egil was determined to be the mature and disciplined Herald that he had been trained to be. To that end, he resolved to remain neutral toward his intern unless or until she did something to incite judgment. So far she had not said a word. Her expression said a great deal, none of it in his favor, but he could choose to ignore that.

The weather was as beautiful as the Queen had promised. The gardens of the city were in full and fragrant bloom, but even sweeter was the scent of wild roses along the roadside as they rode southward. Traffic was light at this hour, and what there was gave way before the Heralds, bowing their heads and often smiling.

Egil would gladly have put a stop to that. Bronwen accepted it as her due.

Her Companion recovered quickly from Cynara's strict discipline. While Cynara kept a steady and sensible pace, Rohanan crackled with restless energy, cantering ahead and then back, dancing in circles, sprinting off across the fields, leaping fences for the joy of it, snorting and blowing and tossing his mane.

Bronwen was an exceptionally good rider. Whatever her Companion did, she never moved. That took talent as well as skill.

That evening in the inn to which Cynara's unhurried pace had brought them, while Rohanan snored in his stall and the locals dozed over their beer, Egil ordered dinner in the common room. Bronwen would have had a tray sent up to her room; she was in no way pleased when he instructed that her dinner be served with his.

"I thought you didn't like to be noticed," she said: the first words she had spoken to him since she stalked out of his class in formal logic three years ago.

"Some things are expected of us," Egil said. He had his back to the wall, and the table he had chosen sat in the corner with the best view of both the outer and inner doors.

His training was coming back: how to carry himself, how to speak and act in front of strangers, where to sit and what to watch out for. It was a refuge of sorts, a set of ingrained habits that he could fall back on with no need to stop or think.

Bronwen sat across the table from him, frowning. Her back was to the room. Anyone or anything could creep up behind her and sink a knife in her back.

Egil pointed that out, gently. She made no move to change her position.

"There's no threat here," she said. "Everyone's either in awe of us or so happy to see us he can hardly speak."

"Not every threat will announce itself with a scream before it leaps," Egil said.

She sniffed audibly. "This place is safe," she said.

"You're sure of that? Are you a Mage, then?"

Her eyes blazed on him. "No," she said through clenched teeth. "I have eyes in my head. It's as simple as that."

Her vehemence told him a great deal about this girl

who seemed so sure of her own destiny. Of course an Ashkevron of her character and talents would expect to be a Mage as well as a Herald. It must be a great disappointment not only to her but to her family that she had not inherited that particular combination of Gifts. "Come around and sit where you know you should sit," he said mildly.

Their dinner came while he waited, and he began to eat, relieving her of the burden of his stare. After a moment in which he managed to take a bite of roast lamb, chew and swallow it, she dropped into the chair beside him, with her back against the corner's other wall. He said nothing, only slid her dinner toward her and held up the cider jug in mute inquiry.

"No," she snapped. Then, even more crossly, "Yes. Damn it, yes."

He gave her time to cool her resentment and start thinking again, and also to eat as much of her soup and bread as it seemed she was going to, before he said, "We'll be riding for another three days if the weather holds, but I think it's time now to explain where we're going and why."

"I know that," she said. "There's odd magic coming out of a town called Shepherd's Ford. It's in the middle of Osgard Valley, where a good number of equestrian-minded nobles have their summer estates. We're to go, investigate, and pretend we're interested in the riding school in Shepherd's Ford, while we find and eradicate the Mage or Mages who have been disturbing the balance of powers in the region."

Egil finished savoring the last bite of his roast lamb—it had been excellent; he would be sure to compliment the cook—and sat back, as relaxed as Bronwen patently was not. She sat stiffly upright, like a student who had finished a recitation but not yet received the teacher's response.

"Well," Egil said. "It seems you're much more fully

informed than I am. I only know that we're to investigate the riding school. There are Mages, too, you say?"

Her skin was very fair, and a blush showed on it like a flag. "There must be," she said. "What else can it be?"

"Now that is a very good question," said Egil. "Can it be something other than Mages?"

"Do you know what I hated about your classes?" she said. "You never would give a straight answer. Everything was questions in answer to questions and 'Do you think . . . ?' and 'What else can it be?' Did you even know what the answers were?"

"Not everything has an easy answer," Egil said. "This may be one that does, but we can't know that until we've seen it for ourselves."

She pushed her half-eaten bowl of soup away so hard it splashed on the table, barely missing her sleeve. "See? That's what I hate. I need answers. Not more stupid questions."

"The only stupid question is—"

"—the one that isn't asked." She glared at the puddle of soup in front of her. "Do you hate me as much as I hate you?"

She really was young, Egil thought. That kept him from letting her hear the first answer that came to mind. The second might not please her, either, but it was honest enough. "I don't hate you. There's a reason why we've been sent on this mission. We're expected to work together and learn from each other. There's nothing that says we also have to like one another."

To his surprise, she did not fling herself away from the table and run off to her room in a temper as she would have done when she was his student. Apparently she had grown up a little, though she was still very much a child.

It was the child who muttered, "Good, because I

can't stand you." But the older Bronwen, the one who had earned her Whites, added grudgingly, "We can work together. Rohanan says we have to—he's in complete terror of Cynara."

:*True*,: Cynara said from her vantage point in Egil's mind. The smile had curved his lips before he thought to stop it. Again to his surprise, he saw a similar one on Bronwen's. Her Companion must have said much the same.

They did not have to like each other. But they could share a moment of mutual amusement, Herald to Herald.

That was the last such moment they shared between the inn and the valley. Three days of riding in beautiful weather stretched to five as they turned off the South Trade Road and ran headlong into a siege of summer storms. Wind and lightning and torrential rains turned the roads and tracks to mire and made riding a misery, but Egil was oddly reluctant to find an inn or a farmhouse and wait it out. The worse the weather was, the more restless he became.

That, Bronwen declared early and often, was ridiculous. This was perfectly ordinary, early summer weather, a bit ill-timed but in no way unusual.

Egil could hardly disagree. Every Herald knew by now what hostile Magecraft looked like, and this had none of the signs. And yet there was that itch in the region of his tailbone, which nothing but riding onward could scratch.

Cynara had no objections to offer. She said nothing at all of praise or complaint. When the rain soaked her white coat until the black skin showed through, or the little stream she had begun to cross swelled suddenly into a chest-deep torrent, or the smooth road ahead turned out to be a sucking quagmire, she lowered her head and set her ears and slogged silently on.

So did Rohanan. Bronwen was by no means silent,

but she did not turn back, either. She had the stubbornness that a Herald needed, the devotion to duty
that could take her to the borders of death if need be.

Egil had not thought he was that devoted. For years
it had been his secret shame. But in the wind and the
rain and the occasional and increasingly rare moments
of sun, he found he had no desire to turn back. The
Queen needed him. Therefore, he would do as he
was ordered.

By the sixth day, Egil had begun to wonder how
many weeks it would take them to reach Shepherd's
Ford. The town must be flooded, if the weather there
was anything like what it was here. Every stream they
met was brimming over the banks, and while no brid-
ges were out as yet, water was lapping over the highest
of them.

They had had to camp in the rain the night before,
and it seemed they would have to do it again tonight.
The only inn along this stretch of road stood on the
banks of a river, and its lower floors were flooded out.
The best the innkeeper could do was direct them
toward the nearest high ground and wish them luck.

The days were long at this time of year, and Egil
could see clear sky ahead. Cynara was not averse to
going on, though he was less sure of Bronwen. When
they sloshed past the hill, on which a fair-sized village
of tents had sprung up, she seemed hardly to notice.

He frowned. Was the girl ill?

:Rohanan says no,: Cynara replied, though he had
not meant the question for her.

Egil trusted Cynara implicitly. Even so, he had the
same strange feeling just then as he had about the
weather. Something was odd and growing odder the
farther he rode.

The promise of brightness floated ahead, always at
the same distance. The rain slackened, but the clouds
above the Heralds were as thick as ever. Thunder
grumbled inside them.

Egil's thought brought Cynara to a halt. Rohanan went on a few strides but then stopped as well, turning his weary head and drooping, dripping ears to stare at them.

"We're riding in circles," Egil said.

"We're not." Bronwen's retort was pure reflex. But then she twisted in the saddle, staring as her Companion did, in a kind of baffled anger. "What do you mean? The road is as straight as it's supposed to be. We haven't repeated any turns."

"We haven't," he agreed, which only baffled her the more. "Oddities, the Queen said. Strange things surrounding a certain valley to the south. We push on through storms that refuse to stop, moving slower and slower, and now we're at a standstill. We seem to be moving, the land seems to be changing, but the horizon never shifts."

"That's what it does," she said. "It's the horizon. It's always in front of us. We can't ever reach it."

"We can't," he said, "but what's under the horizon ought to change. And it's not."

Comprehension dawned in her face. "It's like one of your classes. Question after question, and the answer's never any nearer."

"It's never any farther, either. The answer is always right in front of you. You just have to understand how to see it."

"Well, how do we see this?" she demanded.

"We stop asking the same question over and over," he said.

She did not understand, but her Companion did. His head came up; he snorted. His tail lashed like an angry cat's. Even Bronwen's unshakable seat rocked visibly as he launched himself upward toward the line of light that had tantalized them for so long.

Cynara gave her Herald more warning. It was the highest jump she had ever tried. The mud sucked at her; the rain and wind tried to beat her back. She shook them off with as much impatience as he had ever seen in her.

The storm rose like a wall, crested, and sank away. Egil braced for the landing—even a Companion might come down hard after such a leap.

She landed like a feather in a wash of clear golden light. Egil stared at the green field around them, the clear sky overhead, and the sun riding low over a line of deep blue hills. There was no sign of the storm.

None at all. Heralds and Companions were dry, warm, and unvexed by muddy feet.

"Now that was odd," Bronwen said. "It must have been magic."

"Or something like it," he half-agreed. "This must be the Osgard Valley, which means that Shepherd's Ford must be—"

:There.: Cynara's head was up and her ears were pricked. The field rolled down from where she stood toward the setting sun, and a cluster of walls and roofs lay not too far ahead, with the glimmer of a river running through it.

The river was running high and quick, as it should in the spring, but it was well shy of flood stage. Wherever the rains had been, they had not caused trouble here.

The town was a clean and pleasant place. It was full of gardens, all in bloom, and there were two inns, both of which looked well and tidily run. Egil might yet find himself lodging at one or the other, but the tickle in the tailbone that had brought him here was urging him to look at the riding school before he went anywhere else.

It had been market day in the town, and a few booths were still up, selling spring lettuces and bright ribbons and an array of saddles so fine that even in his current state Egil would have stopped to admire them, if Bronwen had not pushed on past.

The last thing he needed was to lose his intern just

before they reached their destination. She was drawing all the attention, as usual; people saluted or called greetings, and a few edged a little too close, trying to touch her Companion.

Cynara could have tolerated that, but Rohanan was young and a stallion and it was spring, and within a furlong he was ready to jump out of his skin. Bronwen did not look too comfortable, either.

Cynara established herself beside and a little behind the younger Companion, presenting her broad and well-muscled hindquarters to the next hand that tried to take liberties. Egil smiled down at the white-faced man who had felt a hoof pass within a hand's breadth of his skull, nodded amiably, and rode on.

The word spread as quickly as he had hoped. *Look, but don't touch.*

In some towns, that would not have been enough. This was a town of horsemen. People got the message. They even seemed not to resent it.

The riding school stood on the western edge of the town, surrounded by a patchwork of fields. Egil glimpsed horses grazing on the new spring grass as he rode past neatly kept fences toward the tall wooden gate. It was handsomely carved with scenes of horses at work and play, and riders winding in skeins through a chain of oval arenas.

He had little time to study the carvings. The gate swung open before he had a chance to pound or shout, showing a sandy yard within and a short and wiry man in well-worn riding leathers, whose face broke out in a broad and astonished grin. "Egil! Cousin! What in the world are you doing here?"

"I might ask the same of you," Egil said.

His cousin Godric's grin grew even wider. "I just came here a month ago. I'm in charge of training the young horses—they have so many, and such quality, you can hardly imagine."

"I'll be eager to see," Egil said.

"Oh, you've heard of us?" Godric seemed delighted. He extended his welcome to the younger Herald and both Companions, calling stablehands out to look after the latter and herding the Heralds into what must, in its time, have been a baronial manor.

It still kept the grandeur of its carvings and stonework, and the floor had been paved with mosaics. But the furniture had been made more for comfort than for looks, there were warmly woven rugs over the cold paving, and the once enormous rooms were broken up into clusters of apartments. The smell of leather and horses permeated the place in a way that Egil found quite pleasant.

The grand hall was now half library and half dining commons. Godric led the Heralds into a hubbub of voices, the clatter of crockery and cutlery and a mouth-watering promise of dinner.

The sight of two strangers in Whites stopped the conversation cold. There must have been fifty people in the commons, men and women of various ages and sizes and shapes, but they all had a familiar look, one that Egil had learned to recognize when he was small. They were all horsemen.

They saw it in the Heralds, too; their eyes warmed, and their faces relaxed. There was no head table; people seemed to sit in groups by age and apparent experience, but Egil judged that was more a natural human impulse than a school rule.

The table to which Godric urged him was one of those in the middle. Most of the people at it were young, around the age of senior Trainees, but several were older. One, a woman of middle years, as weathered and wiry as Godric, stood and held out her hand.

"Welcome to Osgard Manor," she said. "It's a great honor to see you here."

"I believe the honor is mine," Egil said.

He was not merely being polite. She was older than

he remembered, but then he was not a wide-eyed boy any longer, either. She still had the perfectly erect carriage and the exquisite balance even on foot that had made her one of the great masters of the horse-man's art.

"Madame Larissa," he said, bowing over her hand. "Now I understand why the world has gathered here to learn the art of riding."

She accepted his homage graciously, as a queen should, but then she said, "Honor for honor, sir. It's a small world we inhabit here, and you're the first of the Queen's own to grace us with your presence. Dine with us, please, and afterwards, if it's not terribly presumptuous, might I be introduced to your Companions?"

The hunger in her eyes startled Egil. It was not that he had never seen such a thing before. Even as diffi-cult and dangerous as the Herald's life could be, few in Valdemar failed to dream that they, too, might be Chosen.

Another gift had chosen Larissa, one that Egil felt was at least as great: to dance with horses in ways that even Heralds might hardly dream of. Yet like any village girl, she yearned after the white beings that had, in their wisdom, taken the shape of horses for the defense of Valdemar.

It was a peculiar sensation to find himself envied by someone whom he had been in awe of since before he was Chosen. She served him with her own hands, picked out the best cuts of the roast and the last of the fresh bread, and sent a boy to the garden for a bowlful of spring greens and tiny carrots. She would have stuffed both Heralds as full as festival geese if she had not been so manifestly eager to meet the Companions.

Rohanan and Cynara were royally housed by true horsemen's standards, in adjacent paddocks with three-sided shelters. There was fresh water in a stream that ran through the paddocks, and fresh green grass to eat, and a manger of oats and barley if they were inclined to indulge themselves.

No horseman would be so crass as to hang over the fence, but a remarkable number of people had found chores to do in the near vicinity. Egil doubted that any of the paddocks or the nearby barns had been as clean as they were that evening, or that the horses in them had been groomed so thoroughly since the last public exhibition.

Rohanan was taking advantage of his celebrity to dance and snort and arch his beautiful white neck. Cynara, never one to shout for attention, grazed peacefully in the waning light.

Larissa spared the stallion an appreciative glance, but it was the mare on whom she focused. "Now there is beauty by any measure," she said. "No nonsense about her at all, is there?"

"None," said Egil, not caring if Larissa heard the fondness in his voice. "Cynara, come and meet someone remarkable."

His Companion cocked an ear, finished the mouthful of grass she had been in the midst of eating, and raised her head. After a moment she deigned to approach the gate.

Egil opened it and bowed Larissa through. She moved with such quiet and deep calm that Egil felt it in himself, and in Cynara, too.

:Interesting,: Cynara said.

"May I?" Larissa asked her.

She bent her head. Larissa laid a light hand on her neck, stroking it in a kind of dizzy wonder.

"Haven't you ever met a Companion before?" Bronwen asked from behind them. Her voice seemed to Egil to be both loud and abrupt.

"Oh, yes," Larissa said with no sign of offense, "but never in my own stable, as my honored guest."

"Really?" said Bronwen.

Damn the girl, what had got into her? Before she could finish throwing down the gauntlet, Egil said in his smoothest tone, "One tends to forget how few of us there are, or how many places see us seldom if at all."

"Now that is true," Godric said. "Come, young Herald, tell me: I noticed your saddle is unusually well made. It's a Stefan, isn't it?"

Godric always had had a gift for defusing the tempers of the young. Bronwen nodded, still scowling, but effectively distracted. "Yes, it was one of the last that he made before he retired. They say his daughter is an even better saddler than he was, but I haven't seen enough yet to be sure."

"I've seen some of her work," Godric said, herding her effortlessly and tactfully away toward the barn that was nearest. "It's very good, and some is rather radical. Have you seen her new girthing system? I'm not entirely convinced, but . . ."

Egil looked from the two retreating backs to Larissa, whose smile made him smile in return. "Is he really only training the young horses?" Egil asked.

"Young riders, too, of course," Larissa said. "He's good. We're lucky to have him."

Cynara lowered her head and went back to grazing. Egil leaned against her shoulder, suddenly and completely comfortable.

It said a great deal for Larissa that she watched him without an excess of envy. Yearning, yes, and maybe a little sadness. "What is it like?" she asked. "Do you ride as you would a horse? Or is there something else—something more?"

Cynara's tail swished at flies; her jaws worked rhythmically, cropping and chewing. She was amused, he could feel it, but there was compassion, too.

"It's different when the creature you ride can understand the words you speak or think," Egil said, "but not as different as you might imagine. Mostly, when I ride, it's a dance: two bodies moving together through constantly shifting space. That's the same with a Companion as with a horse. The harmony—I've seen you ride; it's not so different."

"But Companions don't need training," she said.

"Do horses, really?" Egil asked. "A horse knows how to be a horse. What he has to learn is how to do it while carrying a rider. Companions are much the same. Except of course, with them, there's no illusion of submission."

"That's true of the great horses, too," Larissa said. "Those that are born for the dance, they know. They will share their joy in it, but they never precisely submit."

Egil nodded. She understood perfectly, as he had known she would.

"I don't trust that woman," Bronwen said.

She had dogged his heels to the room he had been given. It happened to be next to hers, but she showed no interest in either privacy or sleep. Everyone else in the school had gone to bed: morning came early, and there was a long day of work and study ahead of them all.

Egil would have been happy to shut and bar the door and get some peace and quiet himself, but she was his intern. He had an obligation to instruct her. "Madame Larissa is one of the greatest living masters of the equestrian art," he said. "There is nothing suspicious or untrustworthy about her."

"Are you sure?" Bronwen demanded, dropping down onto the bed and tucking up her feet.

That did not bode well for an early night. *Patience*, Egil willed himself. "What should I not be sure about?"

She hissed at his maddening insistence on answering a question with a question, but for once she consented to play the game. "Something is odd here. The weather we had to ride through, the way we got out of it—that's not normal. And now we're here, and it's as normal as anything can possibly be. It doesn't fit."

"It does if this place has nothing to do with the strangeness," Egil said. "It's a genuine school, and these really are horsemen. Very good ones, from what I've seen so far."

"Just because they're good with horses doesn't mean they're good people," she said.

"True," he said, "but it's hard to be this good at it and be wicked Mages, too. Evil taints a soul; we'd sense it, most likely, and our Companions certainly would. Cynara isn't alarmed at all. What does Rohanan say?"

Bronwen tossed her head. "That doesn't necessarily mean anything."

"So? I thought you were going to look for evil Mages in the town?"

"I'll do that," she said stoutly, "and look for them here, too. So should you, if you can spare time from drooling at that woman's feet. What was she, your first love?"

"Yes," he said, and that took her quite nicely aback. "She was the first person I ever saw ride who made me understand that riding is truly an art, and worth studying for itself. Thanks in large part to her, I'll study it for as long as I'm alive and able to balance myself in a saddle."

"Oh," said Bronwen in a gratifyingly small voice. "That kind of love. Believe it or not, I can understand it. I had one of those, too, when I was too young to know better."

"It's a good thing," he said, "to have an example to follow."

"It depends on the example," she said, springing to her feet. "For me, it was you."

She left him with that. It was a nicely dramatic exit, he had to admit, though it did not embarrass him nearly as much as she might have hoped.

*   *   *

Egil woke in the dark. He knew at once where he was and why, and somewhat of the when. The air had the taste and the texture it always had just before dawn.

Struck by the desire to breathe it fresh from the source, he left the bed, went to the window, unlatched it, and swung it open. Cool, soft air bathed his face, sweet with the scents of grass and flowers. He drank it in blissful gulps.

The stars were bright overhead, with neither cloud nor moon to dim them. He found the pole star and marked the shapes of constellations rising in the east that, later in the summer, would stand high overhead.

The sky rippled suddenly, as if he had cast a stone into a pool. He staggered, clutching the window frame. When his eyes opened again, it was as if he stood underwater. Wave after wave ran outward from the center of the sky.

:Cynara!: he cried inside his head. :Cynara, for the love of gods! What is happening?:

:Strangeness.: Her reply was as serene as ever. As if she had power to quell whatever had turned the sky to water, the eerie ripples slowed and eventually stopped. The stars were still again. The wind blew soft, bringing the first of the morning light.

No one mentioned what had happened, and Egil decided to keep it to himself. They all must have slept through it.

He entertained the brief thought—he almost called it hope—that he had imagined it. But the shock was still in him. Well after the sun came up, he caught himself looking upward, as if the sky would turn strange again and this time would swallow the world.

Nothing that he saw that morning was anything but sane and earthly. The horses were as fine as Godric had promised, and the riding and training were very good indeed. He was privileged to meet Madame Larissa's new stallion, who showed great promise, and to see her ride him with even more skill and grace than Egil remembered.

No one asked anything of the Heralds—they would not dream of it—but Godric and Larissa between them inveigled Egil into riding Cynara in one of the arenas. Cynara was glad to dance again; she had missed it on the journey.

So had Egil. Riding across country was a fine and useful thing, and pleasant enough apart from rain and mud and wind. But this was the thing he lived for, this art, this dance of horse and rider.

At first he was stiff and self-conscious, but Cynara's rather too obvious air of indulging his frailty brought him to order. He forgot who was watching and let himself enter into the place where his heart truly was.

The world was different there. Words dropped away. Thoughts, hopes, fears were dim and distant things. The dance was all there was. Two bodies so very different and yet so clearly meant to dance together, joined in balance and harmony. The air was a living thing around them, enfolding each movement, shaping and transforming it.

For an instant, at the heart of it, he understood . . . something. Some very important thing about what the sky had done and why, and who had caused it.

The instant slipped away. The dance unraveled. Cynara stood in the center of the arena, washed in applause and cheers.

Egil needed to go back. He had to try to see. The answer was there.

But Cynara had had enough. People were offering other mounts—horses trained with exquisite skill and artistry. Part of Egil wanted to grasp at them all, but the part that shared its soul with Cynara said, *Wait.*

Egil did not want to wait. But he trusted no one else as he trusted Cynara, and for today, she was done.

What riding he did after that was marvelous in itself, but he never went back to the place where the answers were. He never even came close.

The Queen's sources had been right. Whatever was happening here, it had something to do with the school. Whether it was dangerous—he hoped not, but he was afraid that it might be worse than that. Very much worse.

Heralds' training instructed him to share his thoughts with his intern, but he was not entirely sure what they were yet. She was already suspicious, and that was a good thing. No need to swell that suspicion until he had something solid to tell her.

That night he went to bed early and woke even earlier than before, but this time nothing happened. The stars stayed in their places, except for a handful that fell in a shower of silent silver rain. Meteors were a wonder in their own right, but nothing out of the ordinary.

The next few days were among the most pleasant he could remember. To be among horsemen all day, every day, sharing what he knew and learning so much more, was his personal dream of heaven.

Bronwen did not share his obsession with the art of riding. Once she had won the awe of all the students with her bright hair and her splendid mount, she grew quickly bored. By the second morning, she demanded leave to explore the valley.

Egil granted it. Cynara would make sure Rohanan stayed in contact, and there were always students willing, not to mention eager, to play escort. At the very least, she would keep herself occupied—and if she did find anything, Rohanan had orders to report it instantly.

Cynara would enforce those orders. Meanwhile, Egil was free to indulge himself. He was aware always, of course, that he had a mission, and that everything he did should aim toward that end.

After a handful of days, Egil began to wonder what had happened to the moon. It should have been new when they arrived in Osgard, but that was days ago. And yet every night was the dark of the moon. No thin sliver of new moon appeared to wax night by night toward the full.

No one else seemed to notice. He detected no signs of a spell; everyone was normal, and the horses were unperturbed. Yet the sky at night was crowded with stars, and the moon never rose at all.

The following morning, Egil was up hours earlier than usual. By full light he had Cynara saddled and ready to ride.

The arena in which he usually rode was already occupied. That was a minor inconvenience: there were other arenas, and most of those were empty. But he paused to watch, because there were eight riders—a quadrille—and one of them was Larissa on a fine black stallion.

Cynara was happy enough to have her reins looped up and be turned loose to graze for a few moments more before she went to work. As Egil watched, Godric paused beside him, halter in hand, on his way to fetch the first training candidate of the day.

"This is the new quadrille," Godric said in Egil's ear. "They'll perform it in public at midsummer, when the local gentry come to see what we're up to this year. That's when the new students arrive, and the young horses, too. It's a great event all around."

Egil nodded. Others had mentioned that as well. It was still the better part of a month away, and while he was loving this interlude, he was practical enough to acknowledge that by then he should be back in the Collegium.

All the more reason to absorb what he could, while

he could. The quadrille was a courtly dance of riders
and horses, usually set to music, though there was no
musician here to set the rhythm. Larissa and seven of
her best young riders on matched blacks transcribed
a series of intertwining figures, moving in a smooth
skein that Egil knew from experience was anything
but easy to achieve.

His admiration gave way to a peculiar uneasiness.
It was rather like the sensation that had brought him
to Osgard, and rather like a voice singing just percepti-
bly off key. It was a lovely, an ingenious quadrille,
beautifully ridden, and there was something deeply
wrong with it.

:Do you feel it, too?: he asked Cynara.

She had already lifted her head to watch the dance.
Her nostrils flared; she shuddered, a ripple of the skin
over her whole body. The sight of it made Egil's own
skin crawl.

:Tell them to stop,: she said.

He had never felt what he sensed in her just then.
She was calm—she fought for that. Just how hard, he
could see in the rigidity of her neck and the perfect
stillness of her posture.

:They have to stop,: she said.

Egil's fingers were numb as he fumbled with her
reins. When he touched her, sparks leaped. He flung
himself into the saddle with nothing of his usual grace.

She barely waited for him to settle before she
reared up on her hindlegs and screamed.

No horse, even dying in agony, had ever made such
a sound. Even the wind stopped, appalled. The quadrille staggered to a halt; riders clapped hands over
ears, and horses bucked and plunged.

With that one enormous eruption of fear and rage
and sorrow, the tension had gone out of Cynara. She
pawed the sand, ears flat, snapping teeth in the startled face of Larissa's stallion.

Larissa was incapable of being truly angry at a Companion, but she was visibly out of temper. "That had a purpose, I hope," she said.

Egil scraped his wits together and put them in some sort of order. "Those figures," he said. "Where did you learn them?"

"They're my own," she said without either anger or defensiveness.

He shook his head. He did not mean to be tactless, but Cynara's scream still was echoing inside his skull. "Something inspired you. Didn't it?"

"Well," she said, "yes. There's an old book in the library, full of patterns like these."

"Show me," said Egil.

"These are spells."

Egil had known as soon as he saw the quadrille. The book from the high shelf in the library, with its ancient and battered cover and its crumbling pages, had done nothing to change his mind. The drawing on the page confirmed it.

He did not recognize the language in which the book was written, except that it was old. How old, he was almost afraid to guess. On each page was a pattern, deceptively pretty, like something a lady would embroider on a coverlet.

Any coverlet embroidered with these would be weapon enough to start another Mage War. Egil forced his eyes to slide past them and not sink into them, trapped within their curves and corners. Each one was a maze to bind a spirit, along with any powers that spirit had.

"Why did you choose this one?" he asked, not quite pointing at the page Larissa had marked for him.

She shrugged. "It seemed the most ridable," she said. "It has a flow to it that suits a horse's gaits perfectly."

Egil looked for signs of deception, but her eyes were clear. She might be an accomplished liar; that was always possible. He could not bring himself to think so. Horses were the most honest of creatures; anyone who trained them truly well could no more lie than a horse could.

There was a difference between lying and self-delusion. "Did you know these were spells?" he asked her.

"Not at first," she said, "but after a while I began to wonder. There's a pattern to them; they flow from one to the next. They're protective spells, I think. Wards. They bring safety to whoever works them."

"Did someone tell you that?"

"No," she said. "It's a feeling I get when I look at them. They make me feel safe."

That was not the effect they had on Egil at all. This was far outside any sphere of competence he might lay claim to. It needed a Herald-Mage, and he was as mere and ordinary as a Herald could be.

"I have to send word to the Queen," he said. "In the meantime, I'm afraid I have to ask that you choreograph another quadrille for your festival—and not one inspired by this book."

Larissa frowned. She was not angry, or else she was trying hard not to be, but he could tell she was confused. "Why, sir? Is there a law against it?"

"You don't know what you've done, do you?" As soon as Egil said that, he regretted it. She was his elder; she was by far his superior in the art of horsemanship.

He stiffened his spine. He was the Queen's Herald, and Selenay had sent him on this mission. Now that he was here, he had begun to realize just how serious this problem was.

Larissa obviously did not. "I haven't been working spells," she said. "I've been riding patterns, that's all. As training exercises, they're quite ingenious."

"They're more than training exercises," Egil said.

"Have you by any chance been wondering what happened to the moon?"

She stared at him. "The moon? What does that have to do with—"

"I've been here for eight days," he said. "I haven't seen the moon once. That comes on top of other anomalies—the Queen gave me a fairly lengthy list. You've been riding these patterns since last autumn, am I right?"

"Yes," she said, "but—"

"The weather has been exceptionally mild here, yes? Has it rained since autumn?"

"Rained and snowed both," she said, "in appropriate amounts. We haven't been suffering."

"Have you not?" said Egil. Gingerly he picked up the book, not touching it with his skin, but wrapping it in a napkin borrowed from the kitchen. "The Queen will want to see this."

"Of course," she said.

She was not alarmed. That could be simple confidence, or it could be something else. Everyone here was just a little too much at ease.

Protected, he thought. Wrapped like the book in folds of soft and smothering magic.

Bronwen brought the next piece of the puzzle, one that he had begun to expect, but it was no easier to hear. She found him in Cynara's paddock. It was the one place in Osgard where no one would dare to disturb him.

Bronwen had no such compunction. "I think we're cut off," she said. "Every road I try that looks as if it should lead out of the valley just circles around and brings me back in. The people I talk to don't seem to understand when I ask what's happening. 'Why, nothing,' they say. 'Why do you ask?' Have they all lost their minds?"

"Not exactly," Egil said. "They're under a spell. You didn't happen to find a Mage, did you?"

"Not a one," said Bronwen. "I did talk to the village midwife, who has rather more of the Healer's Gift than she'll admit to, but all she could say was that everyone is very, very safe. 'All but the moon,' she said. 'It must have said something indiscreet.' I have no idea what she meant by that."

"I'm afraid I do," Egil said. He was not feeling it yet. He could not afford to, because then he would break and run screaming. *:Cynara, is it true? Is the rest of the world gone?:*

:It's still there,: she answered. Her white calm washed over him. The gibbering fear had retreated; he could think clearly, or near enough. *:We're just not attached to it any more. I can sense the other Companions, but they're distant. They've never seen anything like this.:*

:What, none of them? Not even one of the Grove-Born?:

:None,: she said.

He looked into Bronwen's face. She had been speaking to her Companion, too: her eyes were wide. "What do we do?" she asked.

The question fell on Egil's shoulders with the weight of the lost world. She was not pretending superiority now or falling back on arrogance, either. He was the Herald whom the Queen had sent to instruct her. She needed that instruction.

The one sensible thought he had had, to pack up and take the book back to the Queen and let her deal with it, was no longer a possibility. There was no Mage to undo the magic. No one here had the power or the will to try. The spell protected them from their own defiance.

"But why not us?" Egil asked.

:Because of us,: Cynara answered.

Of course, Egil thought. Heralds were protected by a power greater than earthly magic. The spell recognized that and let them be.

It was a clever construct, but not quite clever enough. It could not seem to distinguish between protecting its charges and subtly but surely destroying them.

Osgard was a prosperous valley, rich in crops and livestock; it might survive for a long time. But in the end it would die of its own isolation.

The people were feeling it already, sinking into passive acceptance of the strangeness around them. From what Egil knew of magic, that meant that the spell was feeding on them, absorbing them into itself.

"We're not Mages," he said. "We're barely full Heralds. We're an intern and a fool who has been avoiding his duty since he came back from his first mission."

"And two Companions," Bronwen said with remarkably little temper. He pulled her around, glaring into her eyes, but the spell had not sunk its claws in her.

Yet.

She reversed his grip, caught hold and shook him. "Stop it! Stop thrashing. The Queen sent you here. She must have known what she was doing."

Egil had serious doubts of that. Selenay had asked for a horseman, not a hero.

What could a horseman do to stop this?

There was one thing . . .

As soon as he thought of it, he knew it was insane. But what else was there?

"Listen," he said. "Fetch Larissa and Godric. Tell them to choose five of the best riders in the school, and saddle the best horses they have. Then run and saddle Rohanan."

He braced for rebellion. Bronwen's brows drew together, but she let him go, turned, and ran.

He had to trust that she was doing as he told her. Cynara had jumped the fence and was cantering toward the barn and the tack room.

She was ready. Egil was not, but there was no time for that. He groomed her carefully, saddled and bridled her, and led her back out into the deceptively cheerful sunlight.

Of course it was cheerful. It was safe. Everything here was safe.

Egil felt it pulling at him even through the Companion's presence. If he just let go, relaxed, let the magic do its work, he would never have to worry again. The spell would do it for him.

Tempting, he thought as he mounted. There were other riders coming toward him: Larissa on an older stallion than she had ridden before, Godric on an elegant bay, and the rest behind, mounted as well as those two, if not better.

Egil sagged briefly on Cynara's neck, limp with relief. Even through the spell, a Herald's word could bind these loyal subjects of the Queen. He only had to hope that it would keep binding them once he set his plan in motion.

Where was Bronwen? He could do this with the riders he had, maybe. But a second Companion would make all the difference.

He could not afford to wait. The day was passing quickly. The brighter, clearer, more harmless it seemed, the more urgently it struck him. He had to stop this now.

"Follow my lead," he said to the riders.

"What are we doing?" one of the younger ones asked.

"Your new quadrille!" Bronwen sang out from behind. "Go on, follow. This will be brilliant."

Hardly that, reflected Egil, but her words did their work. The spell's complaisance quelled the one who still had the wit to question. The rest followed without a word.

He could not remember the exact steps and turns of Larissa's pattern. What he did remember was how it had run: widdershins, against the sun, twisting this part of the earth free of the rest and wrapping it in the spell's protections.

The patterns he rode were familiar exercises from his morning schooling, stretching and suppling, then moving into the gaits and figures of this art that he loved more than anything in the world except Cynara. He was careful to ride the patterns sunwise, to unwind the spell turn by turn.

It was not a living creature. No Mage alive had cast it. But it had a sort of will, an awareness that was part of its substance. It was designed to know when it was threatened.

The sun dimmed. Clouds gathered overhead—the first Egil had seen since he came to Osgard. A cold wind lifted Cynara's mane, lashing it against his hands and arms.

The hoofbeats behind and around him were steady. The riders were focused on him and on the white being he rode.

Bronwen and Rohanan anchored them. The young Herald and her Companion were more focused than he had ever seen them. They had what Egil had: the fire in the gut, the passion that turned sport into art.

They needed every bit of it. When the sky began to pulse and the earth to heave, it took all of each rider's skill to keep the horses on their feet. Egil dared not look up. He could feel the vortex forming overhead.

If its charges must endanger themselves by resisting the spell, the spell would keep them safe—by swallowing them. Egil had no thoughts left and no plan, except to keep riding. His valiant Cynara kept her balance when level ground turned vertical, when the wind howled, when sand blasted her, drawing blood from the thin skin around her nose and eyes.

His own eyes were narrowed to slits. He could no longer hear the riders around him, if any remained. The wind had deafened him.

Step by step and pace by pace, forward, turn, collect, pirouette, forward again. He was drowning in sand. The wind eroded his soul. All he was, all he had, was the movement in his body and the horselike body on which he rode, and the bond between them that would hold until they died.

He was going to die. That thought was very clear. He was not afraid at all. He had a task to perform and a duty to fulfill. He was a Herald; he was doing what a Herald was born to do.

Finally, after all these years.

He looked up into absolute nothingness. Most of Osgard had spiraled down into it, bright green grass and bright yellow sunlight and blandly smiling people and all. Somewhere on the other side of the void was the world from which the spell had sundered them.

:Cynara,: he said, faint and clear in the silence of his mind. *:Can you find the rest of the Companions? Can you ask them to guide us home?:*

:I can do better,: she said, serene as always. *:Remember the Grove in spring: the green leaves, the sunlight dappling the ground beneath them, the Companions dancing on the grass.:*

He saw it as she spoke it. The Companions' dance matched the steps and turns of his own: sunwise and clockwise, righting the tilt of the world and drawing the errant part of it back into its place. Where the vortex had been was the temple in the heart of the Grove, and the sun contained within its walls, dazzling his eyes with living gold.

The sun was setting over the arena. The wind blew soft, with a touch of chill, but that was the spring evening and not the grip of magic.

The spell was gone. Osgard was safe on its own

merits. Egil had reason to hope that the storms outside the valley had abated and the world settled into its normal track, free of meddling magic.

Cynara snorted wetly and shook herself from head to tail. Egil laughed, and as he looked up, he saw Bronwen laughing with him. And that was the third time they shared an emotion other than mutual dislike.

It would not be the last. The thought did not dismay him more than a little. They could work together. They were Heralds. Whatever their personal differences, they were born to live and work and fight side by side, like arrows in a quiver, or riders in a quadrille.

They saluted each other across the darkening arena, while the stars came out one by one, and the moon shone down.

MERCEDES LACKEY

The Collegium Chronicles

Foundation

The first new Valdemar novel in five years!

In this chronicle of the early history of Valdemar,
a thirteen-year-old orphan named Magpie
escapes a life of slavery in the gem mines when
he is chosen by one of the magical Companions
of Valdemar to be trained as a Herald. Thrust
into the center of a legend in the making,
Magpie discovers talents he never knew he
had... and witnesses the founding of the great
Heralds' Collegium.

978-0-7564-0524-3

To Order Call: 1-800-788-6262
www.dawbooks.com